WATCHING YOU FALL

Kirsty A. Wilmott

BEAR PRESS

Kirsty A. Wilmott has asserted her moral right
to be identified as the author of this work

ISBN: 978-1-999-710217
A CIP record for this book is available
from the British Library

For Bear Press
Editor: Bridget Scrannage
Art Director: Sarah Joy
Cover Image: The Lizard - Alice Jackman

Author Acknowledgements
*Thank you, Mike, for keeping my feet firmly on the
ground and for keeping me going through the
difficult moments.*

Technical information about this book
is available at www.bearpress.uk/isbn

Set in 11/15pt PT Serif

4v14

For Jutta,
with heartfelt gratitude

Chapter 1

The dog breathed over Simeon's shoulder, leaving a thin wire of drool across his sleeve. She was a calm dog, which Simeon liked, though he wouldn't stroke her. Such a gesture gave people permission to touch him without an invitation.

The dog ambled away. Simeon continued to stare over the flat-blue sea.

"Are you alright?" The voice floated across the tumps of grass, a tinny spray of words spattering the back of his head.

He wanted to stay motionless but was afraid the woman would come closer. So he pulled the hood down further over his face and lifted a hand. It was barely a wave, but he hoped it would be enough to ward her off.

"Right then, just so long as you're ok..."

He supposed she'd gone, had carried on walking her dog, and he was glad she hadn't insisted on checking. People did like to do that.

He stood up and moved back to the edge. This time a little closer.

"Come away, now Dolly," Fiona called, using her polite voice, high-pitched and firm. She was a little embarrassed at disturbing someone who patently wanted to be left alone but he had been so very close to the edge. She began picking her way southwards towards the point. The path was slick with mud and it made walking difficult. It didn't help that she kept looking back, even after he was out of sight. The path dipped down into a narrow gully. In the spring it would be filled with gorse tingeing the air yellow, but now the bushes were bare and prickly, scratching at her trousers.

She usually turned inland at this point, following the stream back up to the village. Today she would carry on a little, not admitting to herself that it was all about the hunched figure at the top of the cliff. The sight of him had left her feeling empty, almost sick to the pit of her stomach, and she wondered if she ought to have persisted, ought to have gone over to him except that might have forced him to step out, into the air...

Dolly turned onto their normal path, but she must have realised things weren't quite as usual for she plonked herself down to wait.

"You are a clever dog," Fiona whispered. Dolly's head tipped to one side as if trying to catch the words as they gusted past. She was getting on – ten years old – and was a little deaf and often ran out of steam. Fiona hoped the climb up the next bit wouldn't be too much for her. However, in the end it was Fiona who had to stop every few paces to catch her breath. At the top she felt quite dizzy, had to look out at the view, wheezing a little. She'd just come past the hotel so she wouldn't be able to see the man any more. Anyway he was probably sitting down again, out of the wind. He might even have started back to the road or she supposed he might have jumped. That made her chest feel tight and achy.

Fiona let her breathing settle and then made her way to the edge of the promontory. She often came here in the summer, to watch the nesting birds wheeling, squabbling, and screaming. Now it was empty, apart from a couple of gannets far out at sea. Dolly came too, keeping close, looking up at Fiona with her filmy eyes. A couple of feet from the drop there was a hairy fringe of grass bending and twisting away into nothing and suddenly Fiona was afraid that where she stood was just roots and top soil. She pictured the cliff beneath her – worn and hollow – a thin veneer that might easily dip, tumbling her onto the rocks below. The thought made her lungs shrink so that it was hard to breathe again and the skin around her neck became clammy. She spun round, grabbing Dolly to pull her away. She felt peculiar. Dolly tried to twist from her grasp as Fiona collapsed slowly to the ground.

***

She woke to fizzing lights and clattering trays. She was lying flat, so her hip ached. She rolled onto her side to ease the familiar pain.

"Hello, luv."

"Derek."

"How are you feeling? I've rung for the nurse."

Nurse? She couldn't focus.

"My glasses?"

She tried to drag herself to a sitting position but there were tubes and wires, lots of them, and they wouldn't stretch.

"What happened? How long?"

He reached over as if he were going to put her glasses on for her. She tried to snatch them away, but her hands moved too slowly. He put the glasses down.

"They think you've had some form of seizure, possibly a stroke. I phoned and phoned and couldn't get an answer."

She felt the irritation swell because he would insist on telling his part of the story.

"In the end I came home early. You must have been gone hours. So I rang the police and they said they'd look out for you. A couple of constables walked the path. They found you just past the hotel." He sounded proud, as if he had been there, as if he himself had carried her back to the road and the waiting ambulance.

"Is Dolly alright?"

"She'll be fine."

The penny dropped.

"Will I be fine?"

"I don't know," he replied, turning to stare out of the window.

***

Anna shivered and rewound the scarf around her neck. Years ago Peter had bought it for her because it was long and bright pink. He'd said it was so she would never lose it or leave it

7

anywhere by mistake and though it was made from something exotic like alpaca it wasn't warm enough to stop the chill of the pew seeping through. She pulled a couple of kneelers off their hooks, popped one behind her back and one under her bum. That was better, though now she was sitting too high and her feet didn't quite touch the floor. For a moment she wondered how many she could sit on before toppling over. She shrugged away that thought, taming the smile that was beginning to stretch her cheeks and tried once more to pray.

The nave was wide and squat, the pillars narrow. Some of the guide books even used the word elegant. The ends of the pews were carved with bakers and traders from back when the parish contained people with money. Of course most of them had been smugglers who'd bought their place in heaven by helping dress the church in its varnished finery, carvings that highlighted their generosity and suitability to be considered upstanding members of the community. Their legacy was now splitting, pitted with woodworm, and was going to cost a fortune to fix. It made it hard to pray when all she could see was the money she'd have to raise. She probably ought to tell God what she thought of the worm-riddled building he had placed in her care but it didn't feel as though he was particularly interested. The windows were currently the biggest headache, because the kids from the village came out on dark nights to throw stones at the metal grills. It seemed the sweet tinkle of glass egged them on to greater precision or smaller stones. They didn't know or care how much it cost to get each little diamond pane replaced; didn't know that because the glass was ancient, the lead soft, and the draught biting, it cost the earth to set their idleness right. She closed her eyes.

"Honestly God, why is it so hard?"

A breath of air plastered her trousers to her calves. She peered round and sighed. Simeon.

"Hello. Do you want to talk or to be left alone?"

With Simeon it was best to ask. She hoped and hoped he would say that he wanted to be left alone for inside her head she was crying, "Not today. Not today!"

"I tried again this morning," he replied, casually, staring at the floor.

"Oh, Simeon." She slid off her kneeler as frustration burned up her throat, easily masking her embarrassment at being caught perched on the wobbly insulation. Standing felt more grown up and when it came to Simeon someone had to at least try.

"Simeon, do you have any idea how difficult it is, listening to you speak like that?" Her voice caught as if she were about to cry, she knew it would have no effect. And it didn't. He continued to stare down at her feet, had probably already noticed that her shoes needed polishing. That was half his problem she thought. He never looked at you so would never know the toll his words were taking. "How can you not cherish your life? You are fit and comfortably well off." She didn't actually know if this was true. "We live in a beautiful part of the world. For goodness sake people come here on holiday."

Of course she didn't say what was really playing on her mind. The thing that kept her sleepless at night – that one day she would say the wrong thing and when next she heard his name it would be because he was dead, that it had been her words that had sent him flying into the air.

Simeon tipped his head to one side. She could see that he hadn't shaved for a while. When the stubble started to itch he would get out his razor.

"It's your job to listen," he said. "And I'm not dead yet because I cannot believe that falling that far will guarantee it."

She wanted to reply, "Then go and buy some pills." Only what if he hadn't thought of that already?

Simeon tugged his fringe out of his eyes.

"You could do with a haircut," she said, trying to smile,

trying to calm down.

"Yes, I'll get one when I'm next in Helston."

So why get a haircut if you were going to kill yourself? She absolutely hated the sense of powerlessness he filled her with, the sense of unsympathetic illogicality.

"I don't want to talk any more. I'm going home," he said, and walked out of the door. Anna watched him. She wouldn't be able to settle now. Trying to pray in church was a nonsense. You could pray anywhere and at the vicarage there was an electric fire. She locked up and put the key back under its rock.

Outside, rain was hanging in the air. It dampened sound and softened edges, chilled fingers, and left everything slippery. There was a woman shuffling down the path towards her. Anna thought she'd seen her about the village with a black dog, but when she got close she couldn't be sure. The woman's face seemed to have collapsed and her cheeks were slashed pink as if she'd been drinking. She didn't look at all well.

"Hello," Anna said.

The woman jumped. She hadn't seen Anna, had been concentrating on each lift and tap of the walker.

"Is the church closed?" the woman asked, her voice breathy and thin.

"Yes."

"Oh, I thought I could sit down and catch my breath."

"I could open it back up again." It was unconvincing, even to Anna.

"Not on my account, I'll be fine."

Anna knew she should walk back to the church with her, should ask her about herself, but Simeon had disconcerted her and she didn't want to go back inside, didn't want to think about him sitting there calmly telling her he wanted to die.

As she turned away she whispered oh so quietly under her

breath, *and it's not a bloody bus shelter.* The woman looked up. Surely, she couldn't have heard her. Anna headed home, getting hot in her coat – a bargain, but not one that had stood the test of time. Sitting in front of the fire she picked up her novel instead of her Bible. A niggle of anger, a slither of defiance. She ought to have picked up her Bible because she hadn't been loving or generous or seized the opportunity to reach out to the woman in her obvious need.

After a few minutes she got up to make tea and found a packet of unopened biscuits bought specially for the Parochial Church Council meeting. What a big name, she thought. Even PCC sounded grander than it was. The meeting wasn't for a few days which gave her plenty of time to pop to the shop for more. After five of them she began to think about what she'd done, how she'd handled the situation. The woman had looked frail. Maybe she should have done something. What if she was still shuffling up the lane in the chilly darkness? Anna switched off the oven, pulled on her coat, hunted for her church keys until she remembered that she'd left them in the car parked out back. She wasn't going to trail across the unmown grass to get them even though she didn't like using the key under the stone. Groping around in the dark trying to find it made her feel as if the church didn't belong to her, that it was someone else's responsibility.

Her scarf was hanging on its hook. She wound it around her neck, stuffed her gloves in her pocket. She couldn't find her torch and thought she'd probably left that in the car too, which was a pain as there was only the one streetlamp in the lane, high up near the school, so that the church sat in its own pool of darkness.

Obviously she was only going back to make sure the woman had gone home. It was nothing to do with her churlish mutterings, said so quietly she was sure the woman couldn't have heard them. But she had looked up and the words were there, on a continuous loop, round and round in Anna's head,

11

It's not a bloody bus shelter! As she plodded resentfully down the last few yards of lane, into the darkest stretch where the trees meshed above her, the rooks began to squawk and fidget over her head. She peered up into the dripping darkness but could see nothing.

***

Anna had to admit to a certain amount of relief that the woman had gone. In the dark the stones felt slimy and she was sure the grass rustled with damp biting things. It took ages to find the key.

Anna stood just inside the door hoping her eyes would grow accustomed to the dark. They didn't and there was a fluttery sensation at the bottom of her stomach because the shadows wouldn't stay still, the dark shapes refused to resolve into things she could recognise. In the end she had to feel her way across to the switch at the bottom of the tower. Why couldn't it have been fitted nearer the door? She waited for the lights to brighten, building up from their dim efficiency to something short of adequate, gradually hardening the shadow lines between the pews. Then she wandered up and down the aisles. Checking! For what? She felt foolish. She should have stayed in the warm and eaten her pizza but she ought to give it another go. It would be the right thing to do. She began to walk around the nave praying, hoping that the movement would stop her shivering with cold, only before long she found herself simply walking. Past the brass eagle, past the six fluted pillars, past the plaque to some ancient vicar whom the parishioners had especially loved. No thoughts, not even about bus shelters, just round and round and round.

She hadn't heard God for years. That was the truth of it. She had her very own glass ceiling, especially here in church, in her church, where all her words bounced off the rafters and fell back discarded onto the ancient stones. She knew that on some level she was being unreasonable, but she also thought that's exactly what God was being, so why not? Shouldn't it be easier in this ancient praying space? Where people had sought him for hundreds of years?

"So why can't I hear you?" she called out loud. Her voice echoing off the walls, not able to find its way past the heavy wooden roof, not even out through the holes in the windows.

Not long afterwards she locked up, went back to her mismatched kitchen, her noisy electric oven and a soggy pizza.

***

It was the darkness that Derek noticed as he phoned the police. He had been so absorbed in his work. When had it got so dark? He hoped that the night would add urgency to his call, but they were confused, short-staffed, unhelpful. He kept having to repeat that Fiona was missing, again, that she'd taken her walking frame but not the dog, that he daren't go and look for her because of the front steps. She couldn't get back up them without him. She hadn't taken her car, because she couldn't drive, the stroke. They weren't sure when someone could pop round. He put down the phone and realised he would have to go and look for her by himself.

Dolly's lead was draped over the bottom of the stairs where they always left it. He clipped it onto her collar but she was reluctant to go with him into the cold. Derek had to pull quite hard. Everything felt wrong.

He used his mobile as a torch, but once out of the drive he simply didn't know which way to go. The village was spread around a triangle of roads, with a muddle of houses in the middle. There were a few dwellings, mostly holiday cottages, spaced along the lanes that branched off to the coves and inlets around the point. The houses along his part of the road were all dark. There was only the one stretch of pavement, leading up past the football ground to the centre of the village and the shop. Of course, the shop! That would be a

13

good place to start. It was always open and hopefully they might have seen Fiona.

***

"I've lost my wife," Derek said, laughing.

The women stopped talking, looked uncomfortable. He supposed they didn't really know who he was. He and Fiona had moved in just over a year ago, and he worked in Falmouth most of the week. It was Fiona who had been responsible for all the shopping.

"I live down Cross Common, the bit just past Church Cove Lane, with Fiona and Dolly." He pointed outside to where he'd fastened the dog to a likely looking hook. They all looked, but Dolly wasn't visible in the doorway.

"She's a black lab."

"Oh, Dolly. You mean Fiona. She's not been well. How is she doing?" the older woman asked. She was thin, grey hair cut in a severe bob just above her ear lobes. The other woman was taller, wore a pale purple coat. She had a large round face, and hair scraped back into a ponytail. She blinked at him.

Relief washed over him. Someone knew Fiona, someone admitted to her existence. That felt better. Not that it would help him find her.

"She's not walking so well but was determined to go out. You know what she's like," he tried, hopefully. He knew it was unreasonable but he wanted this woman to acknowledge that that was exactly what Fiona was like. That once Fiona got an idea in her head she wouldn't let it go. The woman obligingly nodded. "Didn't take the dog of course, the lead gets caught in the frame. I thought she might have come here, that she wouldn't be gone long, but she hasn't come home and I'm worried."

"Oh, my," the woman said, coming out from behind the counter. The other woman squashed back against the shelves to let her past and a packet of biscuits fell to the floor. "I'm

14

afraid I haven't seen her since her... did you Terry, on your way in?" she asked, turning to the woman behind her. Terry shook her head.

Derek slumped. He wasn't quite sure what to do next.

"She can't have got far."

Derek looked around him, unsure as to where to go next.

"Why not try the road down to the cove?" the woman suggested, pointing.

"Thank you," he said. Dolly got up and wagged her tail as he unhooked her and began to walk back the way he'd come. He started back across the common, checked that Fiona wasn't waiting for him outside the bungalow before making his way down towards the sea.

The cove was a narrow inlet that on a calm blue day made you stop and gaze to the horizon, but it wasn't popular because it was tiny and even at high tide the sea barely covered a line of flat rocks that ran out into the bay, like the spine of a large dinosaur. The waves split round them, coming in fast and high, sucking at your feet, forcing you to step back, to take care. Worse still the lane leading down to the few boats dragged up there was steep and slippery with nowhere to turn a car.

Ahead it was dark, the sky shut out by the overhanging branches. The wind was funnelling up from the sea, bitter and blustery. Dolly stayed close, didn't pull at all. A stream of rain water had formed in the centre of the road, the high banks either side spilling into narrow ditches. In places there were holes where the tarmac had pulled away, water-filled and ankle-wrenching deep. He soon realised that in Fiona's current state there was no possibility she could have managed to get down so far though she probably thought she ought to have been able to. She was pretty determined when the mood took her. Even the rooks were quiet, clinging to their spindly nests in a desperate attempt to survive the battering. He turned back, passing the gate to the church and its car park, a loose term for what was nothing more than a generous turning space. He imagined most people who went to the services would walk except for the vicar who probably had other churches to go to. Dolly began to pull into the lay-by. Derek hauled her away, wanting to get back up the hill. When she whined, he stopped. He allowed her to drag him through the narrow gateway. In the torchlight hart's-tongue ferns, covering the stones either side, made the walls look hairy. The gravel path was pale and empty.

From where he was standing the solid square porch of the main entrance looked menacing. It made him smile. After all he was peering at a church in wind-swept darkness, skirted by graves, moss covered and rounded with age. Just like a B-rated horror movie. He wasn't going to walk any closer to the dimness trapped within that arched opening, even with a torch, so he was glad when Dolly began to pull onto the grass. She probably wanted a wee. He let the lead run as she disappeared behind a large tomb.

Chapter 2

Anna had rigged up a kettle and brought down teabags, as though somehow tea could lift the coldness of the new day. The forensic people had allowed her back into the church but she hadn't been able to use the main south door. Their tent was spread over the tomb and onto the path, a white screen full of secrets, barring her path. It meant she'd had to trail through the winter grass to the north door. This led into the vestry, a small box tagged onto the dark side of the church, accessed from inside by some very steep steps. She hardly ever went in there as it was bursting with old kneelers, parish records in musty boxes, and the previous hymn books which no one knew what to do with. There was a narrow gap leading between the doors, but it was a bit of a squeeze. The south porch, the usual entrance, was piled high with equipment, silver boxes, and lights on stands. That irritated her. It was as if they thought no one came here, that no one used the place. To be fair the police said they had only turned back Simeon and Terry. Anna guessed there wouldn't be any fresh flowers on Sunday.

She took the tray out. A young PC was standing guard. She was pink cheeked and hunched down, avoiding the wind as it skipped over the headland from the north, whipping across the village and down to the cove where it was flattening the waves and gusting the foam out to sea.

"I expect your feet are like ice," Anna said.

The woman nodded and took the tray, gratefully. Anna had brought a small sugar bowl from home, and then had had to go and buy sugar. She was surprised at how quickly she was running through it.

"They're hoping to move her soon," the PC said.

"Oh, good. Get her some place warm." Anna shook her head at the stupidity of that comment. "No news on who it is? Officially."

The young woman shook her head as she disappeared into the tent.

***

It wasn't long before most of the village knew that it was Fiona Harris, one of the newcomers from a bungalow near the top of the lane.

Her walker had been lying beside her and it had been her husband who had found her, or rather the dog. Poor dog, Anna thought, and then caught herself, poor husband. Why was she feeling sorry for the dog? Why wasn't she doing what she ought to be doing, which was caring for the man? Her stomach swooped away leaving her numb and trembling. She had walked away. She had chosen to take the woman's own words at face value when the truth of the situation was plain to see. She couldn't even stretch above her own guilt to feel for the husband whose world had shrunk from husband to widower in a moment fuelled by her own unkindness.

She wondered when she ought to go and visit. Back in the church she tried to pray but she didn't know anything about Mr Harris. She thought he was probably still in shock but she didn't know what else he might need. Then she tried to pray for the two forensic people only they must have seen it all before so that left the young PC. Anna prayed she wouldn't get too cold or bored which didn't take very long. She decided to make herself a cup of tea and added a little sugar because she thought it might help, felt she needed it. It tasted absolutely revolting. She poured it away behind a cracked and leaning headstone. It was no good, she couldn't settle. She might as well return to the vicarage and ring the archdeacon. Let him know what was going on.

As she walked by, the constable looked up from her radio, "The boss wants to come for a chat, to sort out time lines and such. Where will you be?"

"I'm going home."

The PC looked expectantly.

"The vicarage," Anna said, carefully, fingering her dog collar.

The woman dutifully wrote it down in her notebook.

"There's a gate just round the corner, on the right." The woman wrote that down too. "I don't suppose you know how her husband is? I'd like to go and visit."

The PC frowned. She didn't seem to know what to say to that.

"Don't worry," Anna replied, "I'll ask the boss when he pops in."

Simeon was in the lane, waiting.

"Are you alright?" she asked.

"I want to go and sit in church."

"I know you do. But you can't. Perhaps tomorrow."

As Anna began to walk up to the village he called out, "You were in there though, weren't you?"

"Yes." She turned back. "But they don't want just anyone coming through, disturbing evidence and all that. And I made them tea," she added as if she had to justify herself.

"Why do they need evidence?"

Anna shrugged. She thought it was because Mrs Harris's death wasn't quite as straightforward as it ought to have been. Poor Fiona seemed to have had a bit of a bash on the side of her head and they wanted to be sure she'd done it when she passed out, fainted, died, or whatever had happened. It's what Anna had heard the forensic people say, through the walls of their tent and her cracked windows, but she wasn't going to discuss that with Simeon.

Instead of going straight back to the vicarage, she decided to pop up to the shop. She regretted it once she was halfway along the road. The wind careering across the football pitch was icy, and by the time she reached the main road she felt quite battered. The shop was the single glow of warm light at the village centre. At this time of the day even the pub was

19

shut up and dark. The door jangled the bell and Jean came out from the back wiping her hands.

"Any news, Vicar?"

"No, not really. The tent is still there, and they don't know when they'll be finished."

"It's awful. Fiona was a really nice woman."

"I didn't know her that well. I hardly recognised her shuffling behind that walker."

"Well by all accounts it was a nasty stroke. She was lucky to be upright at all. Terry and I wondered where she was off to." Jean leant forward on the counter. "Her husband, Derek, popped in here looking for her."

"They have a black lab don't they?"

Jean nodded.

Anna did remember seeing Fiona striding about the village, a tall woman with strong features and sandy coloured hair that was greying around the temples. No wonder she hadn't recognised her in the churchyard. The stroke had scraped away her robust exterior to expose a frail, shrunken woman. Anna wish she'd known them better but if they didn't come to church then she might not see them from one month to the next which patently wasn't her fault.

"Harriet's upset. Was in here crying," Jean added, beginning to unpack a large cardboard box. Anna was pleased to see that it was full of the biscuits she particularly liked.

"Harriet from the pub?"

"Yes," Jean replied, frowning at a pile of paper in front of her. She picked up a large fluorescent marker and crossed something off. "They used to walk their dogs together."

"Of course."

Anna hadn't known that Harriet had a dog, wondered what sort. It couldn't be very big as she did long hours at the pub, so it would probably have to have a basket behind the bar and there wasn't that much space. She was such a tiny compact woman.

"Are you all right?" she asked, for Jean was looking worried. Anna wondered if it was the order she was unpacking or Harriet she was concerned about.

"Yes, I'm fine," Jean said, brusquely. "Will you go and see Harriet? She was awfully upset."

So Harriet then.

"Of course."

Of course she'd go and visit the woman. It was what vicars did.

**

Derek noticed the darkness fall today. The dimness had crept in through the window and was lurking in the corners. Dolly was sitting against his leg with her head on his knee. He guessed she must miss Fiona too but he didn't want to think about that so he switched on the lamp and stood up. He probably ought to let her out.

Dolly wandered into the garden. Derek didn't know whether to shut the door or to wait for her. He was standing undecided when the doorbell rang. He left the back door open so that Dolly could come back in when she was ready.

Derek didn't know who the man was. He pulled a card from his jacket pocket. The print was small but Derek could just make out the words 'Detective Inspector'. A policeman then. Derek had refused the liaison officer. He wasn't quite sure what they did.

"Any news?" Derek asked as they walked back to the kitchen. Dolly was waiting inside and wagged her tail gently to the stranger.

"Nice dog."

"Yes, she is. Dolly."

Derek closed the back door and switched on the kettle. But it didn't look that full so he switched it off again and took it to the sink. His hands were trembling. The policeman must have noticed.

"Are you sure there isn't someone we could call?"

"No. Our daughter's up in Leeds with her family."

He wondered now that Fiona was dead whether he ought to say my daughter. How could she be ours when there was only him?

"Have you told her?"

Derek shook his head. He'd lifted the phone a couple of times but hadn't managed to get any further than staring at the handset.

"Would you like me to do it? I'll get someone from Leeds to go round."

Derek looked up in surprise. Is that what policemen did nowadays?

"Have you a number?" the man asked.

Derek nodded. He walked into the hall. Dolly went with him. He brought back the handset and gave it to the man. Alice's number was on speed dial, number one. Fiona used to ring her every week for a chat. Derek wondered if he would have to do that now.

The man disappeared into the front room, closing the door behind him. Derek heard the murmur of his voice but couldn't make out any specific words. He turned to face the window, stretched his legs across the floor and rested his head back against the wall. Dolly once more had her head on his knee, he wondered if she was hungry.

The man returned. Derek wasn't sure how long he'd been gone.

"They'll send someone round in the morning – ask her to come down – better not to start out now."

Derek wondered how this man knew what was best for his family. Did he have a daughter of his own? He looked about forty-something, still had dark hair but there wasn't a wedding ring though that didn't necessarily mean anything nowadays. Derek couldn't remember his name or his rank either. He wondered if it mattered.

22

"Do you feel up to answering some questions?"

"I guess so. Shall I make some tea?"

"I'm alright, but if you'd like some I'll get Sandra to do it."

Derek wondered who Sandra was, and where she was. Was she simply hanging around outside until she was needed? He thought he'd only let one person into the house. The policeman led them through to the lounge. A young woman in uniform was waiting there. Derek was reassured. Uniforms knew what they were doing. The inspector wore a navy sweater and dark grey trousers. He looked ordinary, not a proper policeman at all. He didn't seem in a hurry to ask anything until Sandra came back through carrying a tray. She'd found some biscuits and the sugar. She handed Derek his tea in Fiona's favourite mug. He stared at it for a long time, blinking. The policeman was speaking but Derek only caught the last part of the sentence.

"So if you can go through it with us that would be very helpful."

Derek wondered what he wanted.

"So when did Fiona leave the house?"

Derek took a deep breath, he had to pull himself together.

"Mid afternoon, a while after lunch. I'm not really sure. We had a sandwich together. She said she was going to have a little walk." She'd actually said that if she stayed in the house a minute longer she'd go mad.

"And while she was out you were...?"

"I went into my office and worked. I had lots to catch up on after her stroke."

"What is it that you do, Derek?"

"I'm an architect. Nothing grand. Just extensions and the like. They tend to give me the older clients, the ones that need a bit of gentle handling."

"Right. So where's your office?"

"Falmouth. Oh, you mean here. Upstairs, next to the loo. At the end of the corridor."

"Did you hear her leave?"

Of course he'd heard her leave, he'd had to help her down the steps.

"Yes, then I went back up to work. Later I came down to make a cup of tea. It was getting dark. I was worried. So I phoned you. But you weren't very helpful so I decided to go out and look for her. Thought she might have fallen over again, or got stuck somewhere."

"Where did you go first?"

"The shop."

Derek went back over it in his mind. Minute details pouring through his memory. A particular stone that in the light of his phone had looked like a frog. The colour of the tea towel Jean was drying her hands on, bright blue and green. The ferns on the wall by the gate flattening in the wind, covered by dark spots of whatever it was that grew on ferns through the winter. The man cleared his throat and Derek wondered what else he expected him to say. Then I found my wife lying behind a tomb?

**

Archie sat by the phone. When he'd gone to get his sugar lumps from the shop Mrs Bartlett had told him all about it. It was dreadful. He'd rushed down to the church because after all he was the churchwarden but had been turned back by a very nice police lady. He'd then walked up to the vicarage only Anna wasn't there either. He'd come home with the distinct feeling that he ought to be doing something, he just didn't know what. He hoped the Reverend was alright, this kind of thing could be very upsetting if you hadn't dealt with it before. The poor husband would be in shock. Archie remembered what that was like. Not nice at all.

"Well Moira, what do you think I should do?"

Moira smiled back at him from the photograph sitting on the table just beside his chair, her plump cheeks and crinkly eyes reassuring but unhelpful. He frowned, of course he'd dropped the ball before, and Moira hadn't been able to help him then. He hoped he hadn't dropped it again. He ran his fingers over his book lying heavily beside him but he wouldn't be able to concentrate. He looked at the windows. Really he'd like to get on with them – it was best to keep busy – but he was fairly sure the vicar didn't have his mobile number and he wouldn't hear the landline from up the ladder.

***

Anna had rung the archdeacon. He'd been understanding but not particularly interested. Woman dying in churchyard. It hadn't sounded that dramatic. She hadn't mentioned that she had spoken to Fiona, kept her regrets about the last words the dead woman may have heard carefully tucked away where they couldn't do any harm. She had been relieved to put the phone down. After that she'd gone to her snug, the one she didn't invite anyone into. The vicarage had two large reception rooms filled with saggy sofas, scratched tables, and a couple of old dressers that smelled musty inside. The last vicar had had a family, had had parishioners to dinner and also done a good sermon apparently. They'd used her tiny snug as a store room. Anna preferred it because it warmed up quickly, there was only space for two chairs and it didn't feel as big and empty as the rest of the house.

Today she simply couldn't settle. On her way back to the kitchen she found herself staring into the dining room. A large room looking out onto the back lawn, last mowed in August, bordered by a hedge, untrimmed since she'd first come. The hedge hid her car parked in the drive, which came down off the lane, ran all the way around the front of the house and ended in a ramshackle lean-to at the back. She parked just outside the shelter because she was afraid that one day it would collapse. Over the four years, the hedge had doubled in height and width which meant there was less grass. That was fine by her.

The dull anxiety she often felt began to bubble in her stomach, making her feel as though she had forgotten something important. She turned away, pulling the door shut. The kitchen was dated circa 1960, red Formica with frosted glass. The diocese had allowed her to plumb in a dishwasher and they had managed to find room for her washing machine. Where a large kitchen table had stood there was now a clothes horse, never completely empty, and a much smaller gate-leg table with two mismatched chairs. She had used the washing line once or twice but the winds from the Atlantic were ferocious and salty. You couldn't guarantee the laundry wouldn't end up plastered around the garden. Anna waited for the kettle to boil and wondered if there was enough time to go and visit Fiona's husband before tea.

The interview with the policeman had been difficult. DI Tom Edwards. He had wanted a blow-by-blow account of her encounter with Fiona. Anna had not wanted to recount any part of it, wanted to put that shameful incident away in a box and bury it deep.

"I understand it must be a shock for you but we need to know what happened that night."

Anna had nodded dumbly.

"I was praying in church, but it was cold," here she had smiled weakly. And he had nodded. "I left at about... I'm not sure of the exact time. It was only just gone four, it was dark, and raining. I locked up and then on my way up the path I saw the woman just inside the gate. She was having a rest, on her walker."

"Did you speak?"

"Yes, she asked if the church was open. I said I would open it back up for her but she said not to, not on her account. That she would be fine. She only lived at the top of the lane."

Anna felt his judgement. His eyes blinking very slowly. She looked away.

"And you didn't see anyone else?"

"No, but the vicarage is just next door, it's not far at all. And it was so very dark and wet. I'm sorry."

He'd shrugged the tiniest movement of his shoulders.

"I did go back, about twenty minutes later but I didn't see anybody or anything." Certainly not poor Fiona Harris lying behind the tomb. "I was probably in the church about another ten minutes before locking up." It was closer to five.

"Why did you go back?"

"Because I wanted to check that I hadn't made a mistake." Only she had.

***

Alice was at the supermarket. She was apparently sorting things out so she could leave again. She'd been with Derek for three days, was of course planning to come back for the funeral with Anthony and the children, Sarah and Nick. Derek had felt embarrassed that she'd had to come at all, felt he shouldn't have bothered her. Particularly as Anthony was in the middle of an important deal with some Russians and so Sarah and Nick had had to go and stay with school friends. He understood she needed to be at home, was a little surprised that she wanted him to go back with her. He'd refused, perhaps a bit too quickly, which had made her face pucker rather unpleasantly. He explained that the police didn't want him to leave just now. Which wasn't strictly true. The policeman had only said that he thought there might be one or two more things they'd like to ask him when Derek was feeling up to it. Alice had gone all puckered again at that, and had started asking questions he couldn't answer. He'd been relieved when she said she was heading into Helston to do the shopping. It wasn't that he didn't appreciate all that she was doing. It was just that she didn't fill up enough space, she crept about, made him jump, and kept talking to him about the children as if he were Fiona.

The doorbell rang and Dolly gave a little bark. Her job done, she settled down again in front of the gas fire. Alice had insisted he have it on even though he wasn't cold. She kept muttering about keeping warm because of shock, that she couldn't afford for him to get into a tizz. Not that he was about to, but he felt that if he wanted to get into a tizz over Fiona's death he ought to be allowed.

A young woman stood on the doorstep. She was short, a little broad. Her fair hair blew across plump cheeks, and he noticed pale eyebrows above small dark eyes. She wore a full length waterproof coat and good stout shoes.

"Hello, Mr Harris?"

"Yes, can I help you?"

Her face sort of drooped.

"Well, I wondered if I might be able to help you."

For a moment he wondered if she was selling something then he noticed the white collar peeping from under a bright pink scarf.

"Ah, Vicar, come in."

Did you have a choice with vicars? Was there some unwritten law that said they were allowed into your home whatever your religion, or lack of, he thought.

"Can I make you tea?"

He was still getting the hang of things. Though he often started well, he found that by the time the kettle boiled, his visitor had taken over, had sorted the tray with a packet of biscuits, a bowl of sugar, and extra spoons. He'd eaten so many chocolate digestives, custard creams, and cookies he hadn't felt hungry since he'd found her.

This morning when he had woken he'd not wanted to get up, had lain curled around her pillow. He kept to his side of the bed, pretended she was downstairs making a cup of tea. Then he'd panicked, jumped up quickly, and was suddenly anxious that someone might come to the door before he was dressed. It was silly. He knew he didn't have to answer the bell

28

if he didn't want to, yet he wasn't sure he'd be able to leave someone standing there, waiting.

He led the vicar through to the kitchen. She stood at the sink and looked out over their winter-bare garden, out over the fields to the horizon. You couldn't actually see the sea from the bungalow, even from the bedrooms in the roof. You just knew it was there, that behind the hawthorn there were fields of tumbled wind-blown grass all the way to the cliff edge. He'd wondered a couple of times about getting rid of the hedge but Fiona had said not to because you wouldn't have been able to see much more than a bit of extra grass and a larger expanse of sky.

Suddenly he was desperate to go and stand beyond the garden, to see the full width of the view, to feel the wind careering across the fields, through him, past him, and on across the point. He felt closed in and yet shut out by the densely packed thorns that sheltered them from the worst of the easterlies.

"I think I'm going to take out the hedge. What do you think?"

"Well it would certainly open up the view but you'd get quite a battering when the wind came up from the east."

"It just doesn't seem to make sense to live this close to the sea and pretend it's not there."

"Sometimes it's nice to pretend just that. Sometimes it's so wild you feel it might rip you off your feet and drag you away."

He looked at her in surprise. What an odd thing to say. She had settled down at the table. He sidestepped to the kettle to make the tea, grateful that she hadn't taken over, hadn't treated him as if half his brain was missing even though half of it was.

They drank their tea in the kitchen. He didn't take her through to the lounge like the others. He felt more in charge here. Dolly came and sat beside her and the woman idly scratched her ears. The wind suddenly sheared in across the garden and hit the back of the house like a sledgehammer. It did that sometimes.

"I expect you feel a little like the bungalow."

Derek frowned. He wasn't sure what she was getting at.

"Battered."

That was a good word. That was just how he felt.

"Yes, I suppose I do. I keep expecting to turn round and Fiona will be standing in front of the larder saying, 'You daft thing, you didn't think I was going to leave you? Now what do you fancy for tea?'"

"Lots of people feel like that," she said, nodding.

Derek supposed it must be quite normal for a vicar, death, mourning, and all other related things. Hadn't she taken some old woman's funeral a few weeks back? For a few days there'd been a flush of strange cars parked along the common, then a couple of white vans, followed by the inevitable 'For Sale' sign. The lady in the shop had told Fiona she hoped the family would keep the house on but apparently there were debts and a business that needed an injection of cash. Fiona had told him all about it over dinner one evening but he couldn't remember who the woman was, or anything about her. He'd not been interested. Now he wished he'd asked more questions, taken more of an interest. There had been a real person behind that 'For Sale' board, someone who'd had a long life, perhaps kids, someone just like Fiona.

"Didn't you bury a woman recently? What was her story then?"

She looked surprised at that.

"Mrs Philpott? I'm not sure to be honest. I think she and her husband owned one of the local farms. He might have been on the lifeboats too. Most of the men round here seem to have done a stint at some time or other. I don't know what she did before she got... older. Perhaps nothing. Women back then didn't always."

"No. I suppose not. Fiona didn't."

"Did she ever work?"

"She was an archaeologist when I met her."

"Now that does sound interesting."

"She loved it. Even persuaded me to go on a dig once, but I put my back out and I've never enjoyed camping. After that I suppose we got too busy." He began to pick at the skin around his fingers. "Once we were married she managed to get a job at the local museum. She enjoyed that too."

She had loved that job, but they truly hadn't been able to afford her staying on once Alice arrived. Even part-time the child care had been crippling and they definitely hadn't been able to afford two cars. He had tried hard to make it work but his firm had been struggling, a downturn in the building trade coupled with high interest rates. That's when they'd sold their big house and moved into something more manageable on the edge of Falmouth, nearer the schools and shops.

The front door opened with a crash and Alice shouted, "Dad, come and give me a hand, will you?"

The vicar got up.

"I'd best be going. Thanks for the tea."

She left her mug on the table like a normal visitor and for a minute Derek was overwhelmed with gratitude that she hadn't carried it to the sink and rinsed it out.

"Who was that?" Alice asked.

"The vicar."

"Oh, touting for business already. I'm not sure the police will release the body for a couple of weeks." Derek could hear the hope in her voice.

"I expect we get some kind of say when we'd like to... do... your Mum," he said.

"Perhaps a date that will mean the kids won't have to miss too much school."

She started loading the shopping into the cupboards. He stared at the bags. There were so many. He hoped the woman in the shop hadn't seen her. Fiona was always going on about how they should support the local businesses, said it was greener and that they would be glad of it when they were too old to drive. He'd always complained at how expensive it was.

"Use it or lose it," Fiona used to say. "There are some that live round here that don't even own one car."

Now that was something else he'd have to do, sell Fiona's car. Cancel the insurance, get a refund on the tax. Perhaps he ought to start making a list.

"Cup of tea, Dad?"

"Yes please."

Though of course he'd only just had one.

Chapter 3

Simeon leant on the doorbell. Anna wondered whether to hide. If she slipped off the chair and lay on the floor he wouldn't be able to see her through the window, not that he'd ever peered in before. It wouldn't of course occur to him that she didn't want to see him, might not want to see anyone. Now if it had been the other way round… She sighed because deep down she knew she had no real choice. Fiona had shown her that. She took her time, didn't bother with the porch light. All the things she knew Simeon would notice but wouldn't think concerned him.

"Hello Simeon. What can I do for you?"

"I'd like to come in and talk."

"How long will it take? I'm tired and I need an early night."

Simeon tipped his head to one side, tucked his hair behind his ear while he considered her reply. He always did that when he was thinking.

"If you make a cup of tea perhaps an hour. If you don't then forty-five minutes."

"Come on then, and I'm going to make a cup of tea for me so you can have one or not."

They sat in the large lounge in front of the two-bar electric fire. She'd put on a couple of lamps but nothing else. Simeon didn't like bright lights. She held her mug in both hands if for no other reason than to give her something to do. He had put his untouched beside him on a small table. One left behind from a previous incumbent, so covered in rings it looked like it was patterned.

"So, talk Simeon."

"The woman."

"Fiona, Fiona Harris."

Simeon shook his head. Her name didn't matter.

"How do you think it happened?" he asked.

"I'm not sure."

"Do you think she wanted to die when she went to the churchyard?"

"I don't think so."

"How do you know?" he persisted, frowning. His hands were pressed together, clasped tightly, the finger-tips white with pressure.

"I don't. But from what her husband said she wanted to live, wanted to recover."

"Except people don't tell each other everything, do they?"

"No," Anna replied carefully. Talking to Simeon was like a game of chess and she found it hard, tiring. "Do you tell me everything?"

"Of course not. But you're the only person who's listened to me, since Mum."

Anna stopped breathing.

"That's ridiculous Simeon. I'm sure there have been plenty of people." Even as she said it, she knew it wasn't true. He shook his head.

Anna was a middle child so no one had listened much to her either but Peter had seemed to. She had thought he wanted to, had been interested in her opinions, that he'd understood the emptiness that had driven her calling. An emptiness she'd thought God might have filled by now. She shook her head, a tiny movement. She couldn't go down that route, she had to concentrate.

"So what if the woman wanted to die and needed to be somewhere where no one would interfere?"

"No, Simeon. I think she was just desperate to get out of the house, to build her strength up. I think she walked too far in the cold and wet and I think she fainted or something and bumped her head on the way down."

Simeon's fringe, now almost down to his chin, fell across his cheek. It made shadows gather in the fine lines under his eyes, in the hollows of his face.

"Simeon, everyone dies, can't you wait until it happens...

naturally?" she asked wearily.

"Because I can't see the point of my existence and death is the only mystery I can experience without having to interact with people."

"You're interacting with me."

"That's different. This is your job. Vicars are supposed to listen to their parishioners. I live in your parish. I am your parishioner."

He was, and there weren't that many. About a dozen of them came regularly to church, and there were another few she spoke to in the street or at the shop.

"What about God?" she asked.

"God?"

"He's a mystery we can explore while we live. He gives meaning to our lives."

"You don't believe that," he said.

Anna suddenly wanted to throw something at him and was glad the only thing to hand was a large heavy lamp, too ungainly to get a good swing with. It would also need unplugging, which would definitely spoil the spontaneity.

"But I did once, with all my heart, and I hope to again one day."

"So that's why you continue living?"

"I suppose so. It's just not that simple," Anna replied, watching the chess game tip and spill across the floor.

"It is for me. God does not exist."

"But surely that's the mystery of him. We simply can't be sure."

"I need more than that."

So do I, she thought.

"Look, what if we looked for him together. Made sure."

"Made sure of what?" he replied.

"That God exists." There she'd said it. "At least you could put off jumping until you were sure he wasn't there."

"But it's a false premise," he said, shaking his head. "Why

does he need to exist?"

"Because of this," Anna waved vaguely around the room, "I don't mean the house, I mean the world."

"But I don't care about that. It's too big. I want to have meaning in my own life and I can't find any. I eat because I get hungry. I put clothes on because I have to. I wash them because people get cross if I don't. I cut my hair when it irritates me. I listen to the radio when I want to know what's going on in the world. I..."

"I get the picture, Simeon, but my whole life is based on God being real and interested in my life, your life, the lives of my parishioners."

"I think your whole life is based on a lie," he replied, calmly.

Tears filled her eyes. Simeon was the only person she'd spoken to in any depth over the last couple of months, over the last couple of years, and even he believed her life was pointless.

"Is it time for me to leave?"

"Yes, Simeon, it is." She pulled a crumpled tissue from her pocket. "But will you promise not to go to the cliff until we've talked again? Let me... think about what you've said."

She wanted to say pray but then she thought he might not agree.

"I suppose. But why is it so important to you that people go on living?"

Because I'm right, she wanted to scream.

"Because you're a friend and I would miss you."

Simeon stood up. He started to button his coat, to pull his scarf round his neck.

"So it's not about me at all. It's about you," he said.

***

Derek let the detective inspector in. Sandra the PC wasn't with him this time.

"How are you doing?" the man asked, as Derek took his coat and hung it on the hook while he desperately tried to remember his name.

"I'm alright. Tea?"

"Yes, please."

Derek led the way into the kitchen. It was less chaotic now. He'd found that keeping the house tidy meant there wasn't so much time to think.

"I can do coffee if you'd rather."

"Whatever you're having."

Derek hadn't been going to have anything but he thought he would make coffee. The extra trouble would use up more of the moment.

The coffee turned out to be a little weak but Derek was getting better at it. He was getting better at a lot of things. Not the evenings. They were still terrible yawning gaps that had to be endured and sometimes he dragged poor Dolly round and round the village even though it was dark. Once he'd tried the pub but when the girl behind the bar came to serve him she had begun to cry. She must have been another of Fiona's friends. He couldn't bear that so he'd left, hadn't paid for his untouched pint either. One day he'd have to go in and sort it out.

"More questions?" he asked. "This is not very strong. I can make some more if you'd like?"

"Wet and warm. It'll do," the man said, settling onto the sofa. So not that good then, Derek decided.

"I just wanted to sort out the timeline."

Derek thought they already had.

"What time did Fiona leave?"

"Sometime in the afternoon. After three."

"What time did you begin to worry?" Derek couldn't remember what time he'd said last time.

"It was dark."

"Is Fiona insured?" This was a new question.

"We both are." Something else he'd have to deal with. He hadn't tackled the car yet either.

"How's work?" the policeman continued.

"It's going well. Well, it was going well. My partners are dealing with my clients at the moment, at least until I can get all this... sorted."

"So no problems at work?"

"No. Like I said, I like what I do."

He wasn't sure he had said that before because it wasn't quite true. The partners' meetings were getting more and more awkward. They had begun to complain he wasn't carrying his share of the load and that his clients didn't bring in the money. But his clients had been the bread and butter, the rock on which the practice had been built so they ought to be a little less churlish about them. The sort of people he dealt with didn't want to peer at a tablet, they wanted to unroll a good old fashioned drawing. One they could write on, see the changes to. They didn't want expensive stainless steel and glass, they wanted brick and wood.

"Sir?"

"Derek. Call me Derek."

There was no one else to call him by his name. Not any more and it seemed important.

"So why did you turn in at the church? Had your wife been a churchgoer?"

"Oh, no. Neither of us were. I can't remember why I went in."

"Right."

"Oh, yes I do," Derek said suddenly. "It was the dog. Dolly pulled me in. I thought she wanted a wee."

The DI looked down at the dog lying at their feet. Dolly's muzzle was white and she moved stiffly before she got going but she stared up at Derek at the sound of her name.

"She may be old but there's nothing wrong with her hearing," the policeman said, reaching down to stroke her.

Derek smiled and then frowned. Perhaps there was something going on here that he didn't quite understand.

"So are you saying that my wife did not die of natural causes?"

"We're still waiting the final report but it does look as though it was a blow to her head that killed her."

"Surely she hit it on the tomb as she went down?"

"The position of the body was odd."

Derek blinked and swallowed. Wondered if there were questions he ought to be asking. Wondered if perhaps he should make some more coffee. He wanted to get up and do something but the DI hadn't drunk his first cup. The doorbell rang.

"Can I answer that?"

"Of course."

It was the vicar. She had a packet of biscuits. Large chocolate chunk cookies made by a company he didn't recognise. So from the shop then.

"Come in," Derek found himself saying with relief.

She came in, smiling and nodding. Dolly didn't bother getting up, simply wagged her tail. The woman stopped when she saw the policeman.

"This is the vicar," Derek said. He couldn't remember her name.

"We've met."

"Am I disturbing you? I can come another time."

Derek wasn't sure it was his decision to make.

"No, I'm all done," the policeman replied.

Derek was glad and yet he knew that there were things he ought to have asked. He showed the man to the door. When he came back the vicar was sitting by the fire, Dolly had her head on her knee.

"My name is Anna, by the way," she said, "Anna Maybury."

"I don't seem able to remember anyone's names."

"That was DI Edwards, based at Falmouth. He's

interviewed me too, because you found Fiona down at church," she added helpfully.

Finding Fiona wasn't something he was ever likely to forget. The way she was lying, how the white of her eye had caught the torch beam, the way Dolly had simply sat down, not touching her, and sniffed the air. Had she been lying strangely? Of course she was, because she was lifeless. He'd known she was dead from the look of her. He had checked for a pulse but knew there was nothing he could do.

"Why don't you write us down, and then perhaps you'll feel less uncomfortable, more with it when we come to call?"

Derek nodded. He supposed it was a good idea. After all she had experience of this sort of thing. Only he was hoping the policeman, the DI, whatever his name was, wouldn't need to come back. The man always left him feeling profoundly disconcerted.

"I think he thinks I had something to do with her death."

And, he reminded himself, he had.

"Oh, I don't expect so. They have to ask lots of questions, to make a full report. There will have to be an inquest, so I'm afraid we won't be able to get on with things for a little while yet."

Derek nodded.

"Have you been to see the woman at the pub yet?" he asked. "I popped up to get some milk and Jean, the lady who runs the shop," he added helpfully, in case Anna didn't know her name either, "said that she and Fiona knew each other quite well. Which explains why she burst into tears when I went in for a pint the other day."

"No, but I will. Harriet seems to work a lot of hours and I'm not actually sure where in Mullion she lives. How often did she meet with Fiona?"

"I don't know. I don't think Fiona mentioned her more than once or twice." He couldn't remember her mentioning her at all. "I'm not sure they met on purpose, just walked together if they happened to be going out at the same time I suppose."

The vicar suddenly looked really sad and Derek hoped she wasn't going to cry.

She said, "I didn't even know Harriet had a dog. I only know her name is Harriet because Jean told me so a few days back. The most we've ever done up at the pub is talk about the weather and how many tourists seem to be wandering about."

Derek wasn't sure what was wrong with that.

She continued, "I think people are afraid of the dog collar."

And Derek began to feel cast adrift again, as if he had missed an important turn in the conversation.

"I would think it made things easier," he ventured.

"Yes, to do the job but not to make friends."

"Oh," Derek replied. "Shall we have some tea to go with those biscuits?"

"Yes, that would be nice."

"Or I could make coffee?"

***

Terry waited for Anna to notice her standing just inside the gate. Anna was looking back to wave only Derek had already shut the front door. Terry had seen her arrive and had watched for her leaving. She wanted to find out how Derek was managing.

"Hello, how are you?" Anna called out.

Terry thought for a minute Anna was simply going to head back down to the vicarage. She crossed her arms. That wouldn't do at all.

"I'm quite well, thank you," she said quietly, so that Anna would have to come over and speak. Terry smiled; she could see that Anna was struggling to think of something else to say.

"I'm just off to see Harriet, at Mullion, a bit of visiting."

Terry nodded. What else did she have to do?

"I've just been to see Derek. It's a very difficult time for him." There was another pause. Anna was adept at stating the obvious. "I thought the flowers last week were lovely."

"Jean did those." Anna ought to have known that.

"Ah, so we can look forward to a wonderful display from your fair hand this week."

Terry nodded.

"Well I'd best get on." Before Terry had a chance to say goodbye, Anna was hurrying down the lane to the vicarage. What made it worse was that it was ages before Terry saw her car go by on its way to Mullion. So she wasn't in that much of a hurry. She thought she ought to have told Anna that the flowers weren't what she would have chosen herself. That if the arrangement wasn't as good as Jean's it was because she was having to work with whatever the wholesaler had left over. Anna probably didn't realise how much time and energy each of the displays took. It was the sort of thing she'd take for granted.

***

That evening Anna had a PCC meeting that she ought to have prepared for, only she was pretty sure she could wing it as she usually did. Therefore, she had plenty of time to go and see Harriet. There wasn't anything on the agenda other than what needed mending and the annual question as to whether they could afford to update the boiler in the church hall. Occasionally Archie Wainwright added dwindling numbers to the agenda under 'any other business' but that only ended up as a communal rant on how standards were slipping, how everything was the fault of television, and how people didn't want to work for anything any more. She'd heard it all before and often zoned out until she was asked to say the grace. Then as she was about to leave there would be the inevitable conversation, when one of them would approach her and quietly say what they really thought because they hadn't

42

wanted to upset the others. Anna swore they took it in turns to weigh in and wondered if she ought to introduce an 'any other any other' business.

Harriet lived just back from the sea in a flat above an antique shop that was all closed up for the winter. The shop windows were dingy so that peering in didn't give you any clue as to what was inside. It certainly didn't look the sort of place you'd go in to for a nice browse. Anna walked past it a couple of times before she spotted the small number 2a carved into a post, and pinned under that a faded note which said it was up the steps.

The rail shivered under Anna's hand and the stairs were very slippery. Anna wondered what kind of rent Harriet was paying if the landlord disregarded health and safety with such abandon. She knocked, but because the landing was small and the guard rail felt so flimsy she stood too close to the door, which wasn't a great start as it felt as if she was already invading Harriet's privacy. She hoped Harriet would see the dog collar and understand.

"Vicar."

"Anna, please."

"Have you come to see me?"

Anna nodded. People said such odd things. Who else would she have been visiting in such a tiny space?

"It's not very tidy, I'm having a bit of a lazy day."

Harriet was wearing a pair of tartan pyjamas and fluffy slippers. Her top, long sleeved and a little grubby, had something pink and sparkly on the front.

"Sorry, not very grown up. My niece chose it and it seems churlish not to wear it."

"Well I think they're very nice." Anna's pyjamas were M&S, navy, brushed cotton. They were warm and sensible because her bedroom was large and draughty. She had chosen Men's because she could buy a medium rather than an extra-large in the ladies sizes.

"What can I do for you?"

"I came to see how you are. A couple of people in the village said that you'd taken the death of Fiona rather hard."

Harriet's face crumpled and she sat down abruptly right in the middle of the small two-seater sofa. Her long dark hair fell around her shoulders shielding her expression from Anna. Through the only other door Anna could see a double bed, covered with blankets and throws. It was unmade. The kitchen was a cooker, a sink with a small table under a window that might have looked out over the sea if it wasn't for the municipal loos just next door. Harriet was crying. Anna pulled out the chair from under the table and sat down. There wasn't anywhere else.

"Where do you do your washing?"

It wasn't the question she'd meant to start with but Harriet looked up surprised.

She replied, "At the pub."

"That's kind of Phil."

Harriet frowned. "I put it on at the beginning of my shift, take it out when I put the bar towels in at the end. I bring it home here to dry. The big stuff I leave hanging overnight so long as he doesn't have any B&Bers in."

Her eyes sparkled with tears, were red rimmed, and the box of tissues looked nearly empty. Anna took a deep breath, she had to try being a bit pastoral.

"So how are you?"

"I'm alright until people are kind and then I...'

She dissolved once more, her shoulders hunched up around her ears, her fingers knotted together.

"Would you rather not talk about Fiona?"

"No, I'd like to," she said, looking up, her face all shiny as if she had been out in the rain. "It's just that I miss her."

"What was she like?" Harriet considered a moment, unknotting her fingers.

"She was funny, witty, you know, intelligent. She got me

44

reading again. I'd kind of given up after university." Anna's face must have betrayed her because Harriet continued, "Yes, I know. What am I doing here, working in a pub, living in this mouse-hole and crying over a woman I met while out walking a dog?"

"So how did you end up here?"

Harriet looked down.

"A man?"

"Of course. We met at an exhibition. He paints, very well. His work is quite stunning. He's over in St Ives in a rather nice flat with views of the sea." Harriet waved her hand towards the small, salt encrusted window. "Obviously with proper views of the sea."

"There are so many artists about the place, it's unusual to hear of one who genuinely earns his living from it, who's doing well," Anna replied.

"Well he's certainly doing that. Most of his work goes up to London."

"That's good, isn't it?"

"I guess. Except when he became successful I became surplus to requirements, which sadly was way before I realised I didn't like him any more."

Anna was a little confused.

"So you didn't go home?"

"No, because Phil needed a hand. Ade and I used to go to the pub most nights so we got to know him quite well. I think Phil saw which way the wind was blowing a long time before I did. Anyway he offered me the job so I could pay the rent on the flat when Ade left. I thought I'd stay here just until I got back on my feet." It was a tiny grubby sort of place and Anna could see that you wouldn't want to stay there forever. "I love the sea," Harriet said, a little defiantly. "I come from Birmingham, so even here," and she smiled ruefully, "is heaven compared to what I had to go back to. Mum is happy organising my brother's children so I don't think anyone misses me at all."

Anna knew how that felt.

"I do go home to see them but it doesn't feel like home any more." Harriet seemed to run out of breath. She sighed, "What about you?"

Anna wasn't used to people asking for her story. One sight of the dog collar and they thought they knew all about her. It made her stumble over her words as she tried to get them out as quickly as possible before Harriet lost interest.

"I followed God and I actually left my man behind. He didn't want to share me with anyone quite so big, which is why I ended up here. He's in Bristol with a wife and a child or two."

"Ouch," said Harriet.

"Well I'm doing whatever it is I'm supposed to be doing."

"Visiting me?"

"Yes, visiting you. By the way, where's your dog?"

"What dog?"

"The one you walk."

"Phil's dog, Bowzer. Phil never has time to take him out and I need the exercise, so Fiona used to come by and we'd walk the dogs together. Bowzer is fat, and Dolly old, so they suited each other. He misses her."

"Well I'm sure you could ask Derek to let you take Dolly out, if Bowzer is missing her that much. Derek is a bit lost too at the moment." Had she truly just likened Derek's heartache to Bowzer's?

Harriet bit her lip and stood up. Her face had screwed up at the mention of Derek.

"That man is getting all the sympathy, but she's the one who's dead."

Anna was nonplussed by such an angry response.

"Those left behind need a lot of understanding," she tried.

"Not everyone," Harriet replied firmly. "Tea? I think I have just enough milk."

"Yes please." Anna didn't know what else to say.

Harriet made Earl Grey, not Anna's favourite. Harriet seemed very angry, she crashed the cups about and slammed the kettle down. Anna wasn't sure what would be a good question to get to the bottom of it, so she didn't ask anything.

"The funeral will be in the next few weeks."

"Yes," Harriet said shortly. "I know."

"You'll be going?"

Harriet didn't reply for quite a while. Then she said slowly, "I don't think so."

"Funerals can be helpful, enable you to say goodbye. Tough at the time but better than just letting the grief seep out over the months."

It was good advice, Anna felt sure of that. She had used it many times to help those she'd had to visit after a death. Harriet didn't seem to be listening, she was wrapped up in her own thoughts. Eventually she took a deep breath.

"She was so unhappy and she certainly wouldn't have wanted Derek organising anything for her. He's really not that nice, not a kind man at all. He made Fiona's life... well he was selfish and..." Harriet's cup tumbled to the floor. She looked down at it and began to cry again. Not cry, sob. Anna started to pick up the pieces but Harriet told her sharply to leave them and, stepping carefully over the broken china, disappeared into the bedroom, closing the door firmly behind her.

Anna frowned. It was one of those moments when she felt that people assumed she'd know what to do. She didn't. She waited a few minutes, even had a couple of sips of tea, mopped up as much of the spillage as she could and slipped away. Harriet's tears were too dramatic, too loud for such a confined space.

Chapter 4

There were the eleven regulars including Archie Wainwright. She had just shaken each of their hands and all of them had said, "Nice sermon, something to think about." Well, not all of them had said exactly that, but words to that effect. Which meant that as per usual she had rambled and bored them all witless.

"It's been a difficult few weeks for you. Are you alright?" Mr Wainwright asked, turning away from sorting the hymn books, a little reluctantly, Anna thought.

He wore an overcoat buttoned up to his chin and a pale grey woollen scarf carefully folded across his chest.

"I'm fine Mr Wainwright, thank you for asking."

"Churchwarden and all that."

So it was his duty.

He'd been her churchwarden for four years. There should have been two of them but when Mrs Philpott died Anna hadn't rushed to find a replacement. Mr Wainwright was managing admirably. He had even organised a rota though he was rarely absent. Everything seemed to be running better than when Mrs Philpott was alive.

He continued to stand there, his hands dangling at his side. Anyone else would have put them in their pockets but Mr Wainwright wouldn't dream of doing such a thing.

"Well if there is anything you need please don't hesitate to phone me. You know where I am."

She did know where he lived – a large granite house out of the village on the other side of the headland – but she hadn't ever been there. She hadn't been to many of her parishioners' homes, she had thought that would come with time. Four years was evidently still early days down here amongst the seabirds. A couple of the congregation usually asked how she was getting on, but she always wondered if that was because her predecessor had killed himself and they were worried it might happen again. She wished she knew more about what happened, but no one wanted to talk about it, which was understandable.

Out of the corner of her eye she could see Derek hovering in the porch, and, by the tower room, Terry. She too looked as if she were waiting for a word and Anna knew she ought to say something about the flowers only they weren't that... what could she say? They looked as if they had been arranged in the dark by someone who didn't really care that much about colour. Early daffodils still tightly furled, and a couple of hellebores that were a sludgy purple colour, and already beginning to brown at the edges.

She turned to Derek. He'd started coming to the Sunday service. Anna wondered if he thought it was part of the package. We bury your nearest and dearest and you come to church for a few months, to make it all balance out. He was keen to get things organised now they had finally released Fiona's body and, being a man of detail, he had a lot of questions. It seemed important to him to understand the process and he kept getting bogged down in things that didn't really matter. Things like silver or gold handles on the coffin, or what should Fiona wear to be buried in? It had been six weeks since it had happened. She wondered if it was because he had had to wait so long for some sort of resolution that now he couldn't get his mind round the simple practicalities. His daughter, Alice, was coming down again and that too seemed to disconcert him. Anna hoped Alice might help move things forward.

Mr Wainwright was waiting to lock up though he wouldn't dream of saying so.

"Derek, how about adjourning to the pub? It's downright cold in here and I think they've got a fire."

Derek looked panicky. Patted his pockets.

"On me," Anna said.

"I haven't been in there since just after it happened," he

muttered. "And I didn't pay for the last pint I ordered. Do you remember, the woman behind the bar began to cry and I..."

"Phil will understand and I'm sure Harriet will be fine." She believed the first part of the statement, the second part... well no one could be sure of what Harriet would do, not at the moment. Anna half waved at Mr Wainwright as she steered Derek out. He nodded solemnly in acknowledgement. They crunched down the path in silence, carefully looking away from the tomb which now would always be Fiona's tomb. She wondered if the actual family who had relatives buried there would mind, whether they still lived in the area or like many others had moved away. Once they had turned the corner of the lane Anna turned to Derek and asked, "Have you heard from the DI at all recently?"

He didn't reply until they were out from under the trees, until they had moved onto the road running along the common. There were some boys running around the pitch, warming up for a match, she supposed. The sky seemed higher up here. There was space for life and it was where words, any words, felt a lot more normal.

"No, I haven't. You were right, his visit, his questions were probably routine. They did let me have her back very quickly after the inquest. Though Alice was still threatening to speak to someone about the delay and the ridiculous verdict. She's just like her mother, always ringing and complaining about things."

"Does it work?" Anna asked, who never complained about anything even when she'd been served a cup of cold coffee at the local café. "Did she phone the local coroner?"

They had all been surprised at the open verdict. It suggested something sinister but there wasn't enough evidence to call it murder. Anna shuddered, ridiculous! It must have been an accident. She hoped the DI would come back because then she could ask him what it all meant. There had been a clout to the side of her head. Bits within the wound didn't correspond with the stone of the tomb and though there was blood on one of the corners it was barely a trace, no more.

"No, I don't think it does work," Derek replied. Anna couldn't remember what they were talking about. He continued, "Alice probably just needed to make a fuss. She keeps saying she feels powerless and that she needs to be doing something." He shrugged. "We handle things so differently."

"That's quite normal."

"It was such a shock. One minute we were all going along nicely, the next minute Fiona ups and dies."

Anna thought that Fiona probably wouldn't have described having a stroke as "going along nicely" but there did seem to be a before and after moment. Derek's before had been infinitely better than the after.

Derek said, "Sometimes I'm not sure I want to get out of bed in the mornings. It wasn't like I did anything to deserve it. Not really."

"You sound like Simeon."

"I don't think I know him."

"He's a youngish man, always hiding under his hood. He lives on Green Lane, the last house, the only house down there."

"Is he a surfer? A fisherman? Or does he own a café?"

"I don't know what he does to earn a living. I guess benefits. But he's an interesting young man."

"How so?" Derek asked and then added, "It feels good to be talking about someone else for a change."

Anna didn't know how to reply. Talking about Simeon felt like breaking a confidence. She was sure that was how Simeon would see it. How could she explain to Derek who simply wanted his wife back that here was a man who didn't want to live. Who wanted to explore death for goodness sake!

"I'm sorry Derek, I can't really talk about him."

Derek blinked as if he was about to say something else only he'd forgotten what it was. He looked away.

The pub was nearly empty. Later on as winter morphed into spring it would fill up but on a wet March Sunday, there were a lot of empty tables. Phil was manning the bar. Anna guessed Harriet was out walking the dog.

Derek ordered a whiskey, Anna asked for coffee.

"Go on over to the fire. I'll set a match to it. The place needs brightening up." Phil spoke cheerfully, making her smile. She hadn't been in for a while and it made her wonder if she ought to try to drop by more often.

For ages they sat and watched the flames take hold.

"I've been thinking about opening up one of the chimneys at the vicarage."

"You sound as though you have a lot?"

Anna had a think.

"At least three, but they may be capped or something."

"I could take a look if you like. You can often tell from outside."

"I don't expect I could afford it."

"We've got gas at the bungalow. We thought it would see us into our old age." He sighed. "It's funny, it's not a particularly nice house. Feels a bit used. Not quite where I was expecting to end my days, being an architect and all that."

"What were you hoping for, Derek?"

She regretted the question as soon as she'd asked it because obviously Derek had been hoping to spend his retirement with his wife. Just as I had been hoping to share my life with Peter, she thought. Only Peter hadn't wanted to be a vicar's husband, hadn't understood that her calling was for both of them. He'd gone off and got a job that Anna hadn't even known he'd applied for in Bristol and Bristol was where Frances was, the girlfriend before her. So she wasn't surprised to hear that the two of them had started going about together.

In the end she herself had had to go down there to bring their relationship to a close, which seemed desperately unfair when she really hadn't wanted it to end at all.

Anna thought that a lot of her assumptions had been left behind in Bristol. A neat package that, when unwrapped, was dust and ashes. Because from then on everything had become a struggle; the theology course; what sort of job she ought to try for. She'd gone to Bodmin for her curacy because nowhere else had come up. She'd learned a lot about preaching to three people a week, how to juggle eight churches who didn't know how to change, and how to become friends with people who thought all she needed was biscuits, casseroles, and a young man. She managed the casseroles and biscuits but there were no young men available.

At the end of her three years, dragged out to over four because she didn't know where else to go, she'd ended up here. There'd been no choice, no other offers. No blinding light, no prayerful consideration. The parish had been in interregnum for over two years and the only other applicant was patently looking for somewhere to retire to. She had asked God again and again for some sort of sign, for the peace that she'd felt before, only God remained silent and Peter seemed to have taken everything else when he'd married Frances only six months after their breakup.

She started. Derek had been talking she was sure of it and was now staring into the fire. Oh God, she couldn't even listen to a bereaved parishioner. What sort of vicar was she? And no she didn't want an answer to that question, because she knew she wouldn't like it.

"Another coffee, Vicar?" Phil asked, as Derek waved goodbye. They had managed to plan a little more of the funeral. He'd even written down a list of questions he was going to ask Alice which was better than talking endlessly in circles.

"No thanks. I ought to go home and get on." Phil nodded

as if he believed her. That she did in fact have important things to do. "Where's Harriet today? Out walking Bowzer?"

"Yes, she is," he replied.

"How's she doing?"

"So so. She still seems very down."

"She and Fiona must have been close."

"It seems so," he said. "Are you sure you wouldn't like another drink?"

"Oh, go on then, and a pie. I've only got a bit of wilted lettuce at home."

He smiled kindly this time and Anna stopped talking. She didn't want anyone to know the real state of her fridge.

**

Simeon avoided using the main path up to the church as he still couldn't help seeing her lying awkwardly, the shine of her eyeball, her cheek that odd greeny-grey colour in the light of his mobile. No one should have been able to see her from the path but he hadn't been on the path. Walking past the tomb would make him feel again the dizzying sense of falling backwards, the inability to tear his eyes away from her face, the inability to get enough air in his lungs.

Then came the search for the key, feeling such relief when his fingers closed round it. Sometimes it wasn't where he'd left it. Anna was always moving it back to her stone. His was much more secure, less obvious.

He hadn't seen much of Anna recently, hadn't bumped into her praying or wandering about. He supposed she was out doing her job, being a vicar. He'd seen the widower come and go quite a lot and today, the day of the funeral, they'd blocked the lane with their cars. A lot of the villagers had turned up, and a lot of people he didn't know. Anna had led the coffin in and then had led it out. Simeon had had to wait ages while they lowered it into the ground and then for everyone to go. Now the church didn't feel like it normally did. All those bodies, sitting thigh to thigh, sharing the space, and breathing each other's air made him shudder. He liked it cold, he liked it empty, and he liked to see only his vaporous breath curling in front of his nose.

He sat in his favourite pew. It's what he'd started doing. Felt he ought to give the concept of God a chance, needed to give the concept of God a chance. Anna had been right, it was something he could explore by himself. She had said to try to clear his head of questions. There'd be plenty of time for them if God did turn up, but she hadn't sounded as though she thought he would. Which was typical of Anna. She said things she truly didn't seem to believe, but made Simeon want to believe them anyway. It was definitely something he needed to think about now.

The door opened. It scraped on the stones, squealed like a wounded animal. It made him start even though he knew it was just the door. He peered around the pillar. It was the woman from the pub. Her name was Harriet and she often walked Bowzer, the English bulldog cross that belonged to Phil. She always wore flat trainers, or black pumps with grubby white laces without socks. Once during summer last year she had worn pink flip-flops, her toes had been painted pale blue, and her feet were dusty. He hadn't liked looking at them, he'd had to turn and walk the other way. Now, he slipped along his pew so that he was out of sight, back behind the pillar dedicated to the bakers. She came in and stood a while.

"You see God, nobody knows what to do when they come into your house," he whispered under his breath. "You make yourself too hard to find."

Harriet moved to the front. She sat down and stared at the altar, then slipped to her knees. Simeon glanced up and saw her cheeks were wet which he didn't like because it reminded him of Fiona. He quickly looked away. He wondered if he should leave. Only this was just as much his church as hers. In fact more his than hers and today he hadn't been here that long because of the funeral.

She pulled a pack of tissues from her pocket, he could hear the crinkle of the cellophane, and then she blew her nose. When she turned and noticed him she jumped a little.

"Hello."

He didn't like talking to people he didn't know. He kept his eyes firmly fixed on the pew in front.

"Simeon."

It was a small village.

"Anna told me you might be here," she continued.

Well Anna shouldn't have done that. What he did and didn't do was surely private. He stood up to go. He didn't have to talk to anyone. That had been one of the very first rules he had made a long, long time ago.

"I'm sorry I've disturbed you," Harriet said. "It's just that I wanted to come to the funeral, only I couldn't... so I thought no one would mind if I came after everyone else had gone. And I do feel better now. Anna was right."

Simeon was halfway down the side aisle. He came back until he was standing where he could see her.

"Why do you feel better?" he asked, peering at her feet. She was wearing her pumps.

"I don't know," she said. Simeon turned away disappointed. She wasn't going to help. "I suppose when I came in I felt like there was a heavy weight all across my shoulders. Telling God about Fiona, how much I miss her, has made it feel lighter. It's good to know that he listens, that he's interested. That someone bigger than me knows what's going on."

Simeon shook his head.

"Did you believe that God existed before you came in?"

"Yes, I suppose so. Don't you? Doesn't everyone?"

"I don't. And I don't think everyone else does either. But I wanted to make sure that I gave him a chance, to make my life worth saving."

He shouldn't have said that. He hadn't wanted to. Now she would feel that she owned a small part of him. She might want to interfere.

"If you don't believe he exists what's the point of giving him a chance?" she asked. He wasn't sure whether her question was serious or not, he thought he might have detected laughter. He turned away. He knew his logic was flawed but that was because the whole point of God was flawed. Anna was flawed. Everyone was broken in some way. Simeon zipped up his coat, pulled his hat from his pocket, and jammed it over his ears. He knew what he was going to do. He had to stop hesitating. He wanted to see what was beyond this moment, just like Fiona. Because of Fiona, he should have the courage to jump.

He strode away, only faltering a little as another memory surfaced. He'd hoped that he wouldn't have to deal with it again. He tried to ignore it. Lengthened his stride, clenched his fists tighter. The police had said the boys hadn't meant any real harm, that the drop hadn't been that high. They said it was just lads being lads. Eight of them, older, bigger, shouting, laughing, and flinging him into the harbour where there was a burning-breathless cold, the acrid smell of oil, and feathers and shit clogging his ears and nose. Mouthfuls of shallow water that had made him retch for months afterwards, and made it impossible for him to paddle, even now. It's why hitting the water or the rocks had to kill him instantly. Like the stone hitting Fiona.

***

"Terry, Terry, wait up a minute!" Anna had to shout to get the woman to stop. She walked fast, Anna guessed, because she was so tall. Anna, a head shorter, would have had to run to catch up with her. Terry stopped and turned back. Anna hoped the expression on her face was good, it was difficult to tell as she wasn't one to show her emotions.

Puffing a little she said, "I just wanted to thank you for helping with the flowers at Fiona's funeral. They were lovely." Even Terry couldn't go wrong with a couple of vases of white chrysanthemums and lilies, though Anna had made sure that Jean had ordered them well ahead of time. Jean and Terry took it in turns to do funerals and Jean would have done something a little more competent, larger, on a stand using oasis. It was just unfortunate it had been Terry's turn for one of the few occasions when the church was full. Rows of expectant faces, except they hadn't been expectant, more resigned for after all a funeral was a... funeral.

As Anna got more and more lost in her thoughts Terry frowned and said, "Jean helped too. She came down at the end."

"Oh, that was kind of her." So Jean didn't trust Terry to do a good job either. Anna wondered who'd looked after the shop.

Terry bit her lip and asked, "Was it a... difficult funeral to take?"

Anna didn't know what to say to that. All funerals were difficult.

"Oh, you know." Only of course Terry probably didn't and Anna couldn't think of anything else to add. "Well, I'd best be off, sermons to write and all that jazz."

Terry nodded, Anna thought, somewhat relieved that their conversation was over. She certainly turned away quickly and strode towards the main road. Anna suspected that Terry, like most of her parishioners, could see right through her.

***

Derek sat by the fire while Phil cleared away the mess. They'd put on a nice spread, had got a couple of girls in to help with trays and plates and serviettes. Alice had organised it, seemed to know what was needed. He'd been worried in case it had just been the five of them, was surprised when all ten of his work colleagues had turned up and quite a few people he didn't know. He guessed they were friends of Fiona from around the village. He'd seen Jean from the shop towards the back of the church, had looked out for her because he'd noticed the closed sign on the door as they slid past. It was funny but it was seeing that sign dangling there that had made him feel as if he mattered, not the architect's office standing empty in Falmouth nor Alice's husband's business having a quiet day. A convenience store that had inconveniently closed its doors. He was incredibly grateful.

He'd wanted to walk down. It was such a short way from the house to the church and then back to the pub, but Alice wouldn't hear of it even though it meant they blocked the lane for nearly an hour. He supposed it was her way of coping, satisfying the longing to do things well, to do things right, but it felt silly climbing into the huge shiny car that smelt of air freshener and leather. Where there was nothing personal except a box of tissues peeping out from the glove pocket. It didn't feel like a normal car, for when it moved it parted the air without disturbing anything, a bubble of pain that only touched those inside.

Alice had kept asking Derek what Fiona would have liked. He didn't have a clue. The only thing he could think of was having Dolly at the church. Alice thought that was silly, she didn't think Fiona would have been bothered whether she was there or not but when Anna had come the day before he'd asked her all the same. Alice had snorted in annoyance just like Fiona used to. He didn't care, he found he couldn't bear to be parted from Dolly not even for a minute, needed her silky ears within touching distance. He particularly didn't like the nights knowing that she was far away downstairs but hadn't been able to persuade her to come up out of the kitchen. She was a dog used to doing what she was used to doing and climbing those stairs had always been forbidden.

"Of course she can come," Anna had said. "You'll feel better having her at your side."

So Dolly had been there, much to the delight of his grandchildren – something to hold and stroke and worry about while their parents were being all weird and emotional.

Dolly was still here at the pub: at his feet, probably hoping for some more leftovers. She'd mooched around all afternoon, had only sat down briefly when Bowzer had come out from behind the bar to have a sniff. The kids kept giving the dogs the ends of things, which he knew Fiona wouldn't have approved of. Except today it was alright to ease up a bit, today was a day when rules didn't matter. A day that drew a line in the sand, because now there was no going back.

Phil looked tired. It must have been hard work, there'd been so many people. They'd all gone now, only the regulars were left. Even Alice and Anthony had been persuaded to take the children back to the house, though they were worried about leaving Derek on his own. But he wasn't on his own. Not here at the pub.

"Well, I think that went off really well, Derek, don't you?" Phil said, pouring himself a coffee. Derek nodded. "Would you like another drink?" Derek had been nursing a pint for quite a while. "How about a drop of the hard stuff, on the house of course?"

Derek nodded. For the first time in weeks he didn't feel quite so cold. Or was it that he didn't feel quite so numb? Dolly stood up and came to rest her head on his knee. He finished his whiskey, and nodded to Phil.

"Come on then girl, let's get you out for a walk."

He walked down Church Cove Lane because it was where Fiona used to take Dolly. He didn't want to go home, wasn't quite ready for the finality of that, so he hurried past the bungalow, ablaze with lights. He decided to cut across to the lifeboat station, letting Dolly off the lead once they were over the cattle grid. She bounded across the field. He hadn't seen her so energetic for weeks. When he reached the path, for a minute he couldn't see where she'd got to but she was waiting down the steps by the gate. Once through there she trotted ahead and Derek followed her up onto the promontory. He walked fast until they could see across to Beacon Point. Out on the finger of land was a figure, hood up against the cold, staring out over the sea. Derek began to walk towards the lighthouse allowing the wind to fill his coat and his lungs, allowing the simple task of putting one foot in front of the other to absorb him. Not long after he realised that Dolly wasn't up ahead. He turned around. She was heading over to the person standing on the edge, picking her way across the tufted grass. Then she sat down, right at their feet. Derek was a little embarrassed, had to shout loudly before Dolly even looked up. He got quite close before she reluctantly came back to him. The figure ignored them, didn't wave or look round at all. Derek grabbed Dolly's collar and pulled her to him, snapping on the lead. Half dragging the dog, he walked quickly along the path. He supposed it was someone else that Fiona had known, had probably chatted to and become friends with.

Chapter 5

Anna woke with a start, fighting the usual panicky-fluttery sensations, worried she'd forgotten something important. She lay still, wondering what it was that was scratching away at the edge of her thoughts. She tried to visualise the diary. There wasn't much in it, so she supposed it might be post-funeral nerves. The last few days had been taxing, but even they couldn't mask the general downhill malaise.

It was as if her energy, her compassion was seeping away, bit by bit. Every day there seemed a little less available to her. She had to dig a little deeper and already felt as if she were down to the mucky scrapings at the bottom, which wasn't great for someone whose job description was about caring for people, inside and out. She hauled herself upright, searching for her slippers with the tips of her toes, trying not to let her feet touch the icy-cold wooden floorboards. She pulled her dressing gown over her shoulders and went in search of the kettle. She felt she had managed to quell the feeling of disquiet but still decided to double-check the diary while the water boiled.

There was nothing in particular, though she knew she ought to work on some form of talk for the following Sunday. Sermon was far too big a word for what she normally produced. She had the readings written at the top of the page, to remind her to think on them through the week, though this week with the funeral and everything she hadn't even looked them up yet. Perhaps that was what was bugging her. She ought to visit Harriet again. Anna had scanned the pews for her pale thin face but even taking into account the hiding places behind the pillars she was fairly sure Harriet hadn't been there.

Anna had tried to see her, to talk to her, though to be fair mostly when she was working at the pub. It was so much easier to pop in there hoping to get a quiet moment. Only when Anna was just about to ask an important question Harriet was always called away to the other end of the bar, and not for the first time did Anna wonder if she and Fiona had been more than friends. It was quite possible and why not? Anna wondered if Derek suspected. Perhaps that was what was gnawing away at her, that Derek was not telling the whole truth about what had happened that night. She drank her tea standing at the sink, staring down through the trees to the church. She should make a real effort to visit Harriet and she pretended to herself she hadn't done so before because she'd been waiting for the right moment and not because she didn't want to face that tiny flat, oozing intensity and self-indulgence.

The doorbell rang. She glanced at the kitchen clock. It was only just gone seven. Not another death she hoped.

Simeon.

"It's only just gone seven. This is too early."

"What if God doesn't turn up himself? What if he sends people instead?"

Anna blinked, then pulled her dressing gown tighter.

"Well yes, of course that's often how he speaks to us. Uses what's to hand as it were."

"You never told me that."

Why would she have? She didn't want him to come in, she wanted to get dressed, she wanted to make toast and read her Bible. She wanted to wander down to the church and perhaps have a go at saying Morning Prayer to the walls.

"I think God may not want me to jump."

Now she simply stared.

"Come in Simeon. Go and make yourself some tea and I'll get dressed."

As she climbed the stairs she knew he'd notice that her slippers needed replacing, that they were coming unstitched at the back and were so grubby you couldn't tell they'd once been a pretty pale blue. She had to trust that despite how she was feeling God wouldn't allow her to screw up too badly. How inadequate did you have to feel before you stopped trying altogether?

She put on wrinkled jeans from the day before, wiped a flannel over her face, and brushed her hair behind her ears. When she walked into the kitchen he was sitting at the kitchen table.

"Didn't you want a cup of tea?"

"No, I would like coffee."

"Well, you could have made coffee."

"You said to make tea."

"Sorry Simeon. I forget sometimes how straightforward you are."

"I don't know what that means," he replied. "May we talk now?"

Anna filled the kettle. The button sparked. Sometimes it didn't turn off any more.

"So how did God speak to you?" Smiling, she turned and said, "The assumption being that you now think he does at least exist."

Simeon shook his head, like he'd got a fly in his ear. Anna tried not to feel irritated. Everything had to be on his terms. It was very difficult to be patient when any aspect of life that didn't touch him was treated as an irrelevance. How could such a man find God? How could he understand grace and mercy? She clenched her fists. They were such big words for so early in the day and like bubbles they grew and grew, then burst as if the tired dark space in her head simply couldn't sustain them.

"Through Harriet. Harriet and Dolly. Harriet came to church yesterday."

And Dolly is a dog, Anna thought nonplussed.

"What did she say?" She hoped he'd understand that she was talking about Harriet and not Dolly.

"She said that she felt better after she'd told God how

much she missed Fiona. She said a weight had been lifted off her shoulders."

"Good. That sounds very positive." Anna was pleased for Harriet, for encountering God where he ought to have been. In her church.

"Yes, but God knew that wouldn't be enough for me."

Anna nodded, didn't dare say anything because she was afraid that whatever she said would spoil what God was doing here, assuming he was doing something.

"Harriet said she thought she had probably believed in him before she came into church. So I discounted it. Then and there I decided to jump, because it was all nonsense. It was pointless waiting for a non-existent God to speak, crazy and illogical." The words were tumbling out. It surprised Anna as Simeon usually spoke slowly, measuring each syllable, each breath. He continued, "If he doesn't exist, I'm just another creature and I don't matter, except to you. You listen. Even I can see that you hope I'll get it one day and I'm not normally that good at seeing things like that. Seeing things that other people are thinking," he added just in case she hadn't understood.

Anna thought perhaps it wasn't that she hoped he would get it but that she hoped he could be bothered. Only it was too easy to read Simeon like that, too lazy to treat him as you would anyone else.

"So if I matter to you, then I matter and I'm not just another creature, therefore I have some sort of significance. So God could be God. But the important point is that he sent the dog just as I was about to jump. Do you see? She came and sat by me exactly as she did that day.

"That day I was ready to do it too but then that woman, Fiona, came along with her dog. It spoiled everything. I couldn't jump in front of her and by the time she had gone nothing felt right any more. She even asked me if I was alright. It was my moment and she made it hers." Anna leaned away from the anger that suddenly flared with his words.

He glanced up, actually looked at her for a micro-second before his eyes slid away and down again. "This time when the dog came and sat down beside me it was to remind me of how close I had come before and to show me it's not just random. To show me it's not just you who cares. If it's not random, then there is a God."

Anna was very confused and wondered if she'd missed a sentence somewhere. Simeon had certainly made a pretty massive jump, only then she realised that was the point, Simeon hadn't jumped.

"So tell me again what happened?" she asked, trying to sound serious and kind.

"I went out onto the path. I knew it was low tide, that I would hit the rocks before I hit the sea. If that happened I would die instantly. There was even an offshore wind so I would be blown back to the base of the cliff." Anna found the details unnecessary but knew it was pointless saying so. "Only as I was about to jump, and I was going to jump this time, Dolly came over.

"She came across and sat by me. As if God were using her to get my attention to say that I mattered to him. Then I thought that if I died like Fiona you at least would be sad," and he glanced up at her again for the briefest moment. Pale hazel eyes that desperately wanted something from her. "That you would remember me," he continued, "even if I hadn't ever understood what you'd been trying to say. Do you see, Anna?"

Anna pushed away the mug and laid her head on her arms. All the emotion and intensity of Harriet's small flat seemed to have followed her back to her own kitchen.

She whispered, "It's too much responsibility."

"What?" Simeon asked.

Anna lifted her head and looked at him. "That's a lot to put on one person. Because I care about you, God exists?"

"I haven't put anything on anyone. It's on God. It's not just you, he used Dolly and Harriet and..."

Only to Anna it didn't feel like that. She had just had a snapshot of the true nature of her heart and it wasn't very nice. She was battling resentment, deep and jagged at Simeon's expectations of her. He thought she cared about him only she'd just realised she didn't care at all. For when he'd said that this time he was going to jump, she'd felt relief. She didn't want him here in her kitchen demanding things of her at seven in the morning. She didn't want to have to weigh every word she ever spoke to him or to anyone else for that matter. She was fairly sure she wasn't that important. She wanted him to get it over and done with, to jump and to leave her alone.

"I'm sorry Simeon, this is just too..." The word that sprang to mind was 'big' but she said instead, "too early for me. Do you mind leaving? We can meet another time when I've woken up a bit."

That was wise, the right thing to do. She needed time to think and she couldn't do that while he was patently waiting for her to understand.

"I do mind leaving, and I would very much like to talk some more but I will do what you ask." He got up. He hadn't touched the coffee she'd made him.

Anna closed the front door behind him and stepped back to sit on the stairs. He had not jumped because he thought she genuinely cared. He cared that she cared. Of course he did, because no one had ever loved him before, except his mother. Only the truth was Anna didn't give two hoots for any of them. Whiny Harriet, lost Derek, Phil, Jean, awkward Terry, even Alice, the daughter from hell, who probably wasn't, if you just took the trouble to get to know her. Now in this big, cold house, sitting on these threadbare stairs, she wasn't even sure she believed in God even though somehow he had made the connection with Simeon of all people. This wasn't how her life was meant to be. She should have been working in a busy parish, surrounded by families and young couples. Instead she was living in a place that was dying. Full of people who were just like her, too afraid to do anything, too afraid to change and who couldn't hear God speak no matter how hard they tried. Apart from Simeon of course. But right this minute he didn't seem to count.

Anna wondered what she should do. Was there anything she could do? Anything that didn't involve Peter hearing that she had quit her calling, that he had been right all along? She could disappear, get a proper job, move to Plymouth or Falmouth, and find a nice little flat with decent central heating. She thought of Dolly. Perhaps get a dog. Everyone round here had a dog except Mr Wainwright. He didn't have pets, he had pots of geraniums. The thought made her mouth stretch just a little.

***

Anna needed milk. She'd used the last of it up in Simeon's coffee but the shop wasn't where she had decided to go, she'd get the milk on the way back. She pulled on her coat, her over-large, familiar, no longer weather-proof coat, and trudged up the lane. As she walked along Cross Common Road Derek drove past. He stopped a little further on, and wound down the window.

"Hello Vicar," he said, and it sounded like the first time he'd used his voice that day though she'd thought Alice was still around.

"Hello Derek, how are you?" She had to ask; it was all part of the job description.

"Alice went early this morning, there was something Anthony had to do, but she says she'll pop back again soon, so I thought I'd take Fiona's car for a spin, make sure it's alright before I sell it." His voice was flat and functional. There was no choking back the tears because it had been Fiona's car.

"Didn't I hear on the grapevine that you thought you

might give it to Harriet?" The grapevine being Jean in the shop. Anna had thought it was a kind idea, a sensible one, particularly as Derek didn't seem to need the money and Harriet was reliant on the bus.

"I tried to. Thought that was what Fiona would have wanted. I certainly don't need the thing."

"What happened?" Because at the mention of Harriet his face had screwed up, as if he were chewing something disgusting.

"She was quite rude. Told me I didn't know what Fiona wanted, and then refused to serve me. Phil had to send her into the back to get a grip."

"Oh," Anna said. It did seem more than a little self-indulgent and definitely unkind. "Well I suppose she was very fond of Fiona. Grief can make people do funny things."

Why was she defending Harriet? No matter how wonderful or shoddy the marriage had been, Derek would now have to question what he believed about it and where was he going to get answers? Derek stared down at the steering wheel.

"Well I'm off for a meeting with Mr Wainwright," she said.

"I won't hold you up then."

He drove off, heading up to the main road.

It had been quiet, almost still on her side of the headland but you could never tell what it would be like once you got over the top. She pulled her hat out of her pocket, scattering tissues across the path, and walked down past the pub to Archie's lane, high banked and topped with flattened dead bracken. The wind was careering straight up from the sea and made her eyes smart.

His house was square, a little top heavy, as if it had already sunk into the headland with the weight of the granite blocks. Beyond was nothing more than a muddy path leading onto the cliff path. The garden was like everyone else's, winter-plain, though here and there she could see bulbs pushing through the grass. When she looked closely there were hundreds of them. It was the only way to beat the rabbits. No garden was ever truly rabbit-proof, so most people had to make do with shrubs, pots, or sheer numbers. She rang the bell. The door was newly stained and not a single window peeled nor pane of glass was left dull with salt. It wouldn't be his style to let anything look shoddy. He opened the door and blinked. Anna swallowed. He could have tried a little harder to look less surprised.

"Vicar. Is everything alright? The church, is there a problem?"

What did she expect, she'd never been to visit before. But then neither had she been invited.

"No, there's nothing wrong. I just thought I'd pop by and see how you are." Oh and by the way, she said in her head, I think I'm going mad. "You've seemed a little less than yourself of late."

"I'd hoped you wouldn't notice."

She hadn't noticed. She'd just made that bit up. He stood aside to let her in. He took her coat and turned back for her hat, which he carefully placed on a radiator.

"Keep it nice and cosy. I like a warm bobble-hat to go out with."

She simply couldn't imagine him wearing anything with a bobble. He always wore a sort of trilby thing to church.

"They call them beanies nowadays."

"Oh. I wonder why?" He led her down the hall to the front room. "Please do take a seat, I'll go and make us something to drink."

The window looked back towards the village though all you could see was the roof line of the last house. It was not that far but it felt very lonely. At night she didn't expect you'd be able to see another light anywhere. She turned back to the room. Everything about the place was old fashioned and comfortable. The leather chairs had large silk cushions, a rather fetching dusky pink. Not Mr Wainwright's choice, of that Anna was sure. There was a small round table where a picture was propped, Mrs Wainwright Anna assumed. Still close. She looked nice. Anna wondered how long she'd been dead.

He brought in a tray. It had a coffee pot, cups with saucers, a milk jug, and a small bowl of sugar cubes.

"I haven't seen sugar like that for years. I used to love crunching them up when I was a girl."

He smiled. "Jean from the shop gets them in for me especially, I think. I should have given it up years ago but it seems a little churlish to take away such a regular order."

Anna picked up the photograph of Mrs Wainwright and then quickly put it down again. Perhaps he didn't like it touched.

"Is this your wife?"

"Moira. Been dead nearly ten years."

"That's a long time."

Anna felt a flare of jealousy. At least that's what she thought it might be. A churning down in her stomach that made her step back and search for somewhere else to sit.

"Do you have a favourite chair?"

"I suppose I do," and he vaguely waved towards the one closest to the photograph. Anna sat down opposite. She wondered how long it had been since anyone had been there. The leather was cold and slippery.

"Milk, sugar?"

It was strong coffee and probably good quality. She hadn't made the real stuff for years as most people seemed to prefer instant nowadays. Didn't they?

He was waiting for her to speak but she didn't know where to begin. Hadn't realised there was anything wrong with him, so how could she tell this tight, buttoned-up man who liked everything in its place, who seemed happy as long as everything was working, that she wasn't working, that she was broken? He'd been tireless in his efforts to keep

72

everything running since she had arrived. How could she spoil that?

"So how are you?" he asked. It was always his first question. To begin with she'd been touched, thought he was interested in her welfare, but then of course he was her churchwarden so it was his job. Everything is alright if your vicar is alright. Check.

She imagined telling him how she really felt, imagined watching the shock unfold. Except of course he'd been here when the last vicar... so perhaps he'd just think, oh, no, here we go again, and then when he recovered he might ask her to leave so that a proper incumbent could come or perhaps he'd give her options. This is what you can do. A: You need a retreat. B: You need some counselling. C: You need to leave and get a job more suited to your gifts.

He cleared his throat.

"I wish Moira were alive. She always knew what to say to people to put them at their ease, so they would feel able to talk. To really talk."

Anna's eyes widened in surprise.

"She was quite wonderful at that. I would listen with amazement at people unburdening their hearts. When she died I wondered how people would manage without her."

"What did folk do?" Anna asked.

"To start with they came to talk to me but it's not my thing." He shrugged. His mouth smiled but his eyes were impossibly sad and Anna felt a dull pain sinking down through her. It made her want to sit very still, to stop talking. "Before long they realised."

"Children? Grandchildren?" she managed to say, with hardly any catch in her voice.

"No, not for us."

"I'm sorry."

"It's quite hard sometimes, you know, high days and holidays when everyone else has a house full and well..." He stopped. "How do you manage? What do you do on those... you know, those difficult days?"

She thought he was being rhetorical, but after a while realised the silence was expectant and she was indignant that he thought she was like him, friendless and lonely. Only he was right. On the high days she had to be here and going home to her mum and the rest of her siblings was getting less and less convenient, less and less frequent. They didn't need her. They made space for her, pretended she was looked forward to but she'd stopped believing that was true a long time ago.

Was that what she really thought? That the joy with which she was received at home was fake?

"Look, Mr Wainwright..."

"Call me Archie. After all you've taken the trouble to visit."

So this was her reward for walking down the track, for braving the wind.

"Archie." She rolled his name around her tongue. "Archie, what did you do before? How did you end up here?"

He looked surprised, perhaps because she ought to have known that already.

"I was in the Navy, followed by a small engineering firm in Falmouth, then the Lizard because they needed a skipper for the lifeboat and it's where Moira's family came from."

"Lifeboat? How long?"

"Fifteen years before I had to retire, before they revamped it." And his face came alive with remembering. "There was still one man on the crew who'd actually launched off the Lizard. Billy Carter I think." He bit his lip and crinkled his eyes. "That must have been quite something. They often couldn't manage it of course, which must have been terrible. Knowing yours was the closest boat – that someone needed you – and all you could do was to stand to and hope the wind changed direction."

Anna felt there was more to his words, and ought to have probed deeper. That he'd just told her all about someone else's memories, as if his weren't good enough. Instead she asked, "How did Moira feel when you went out?"

He smiled. "She put me in God's hands and got on with it. At least that's what she told me."

"She sounds very strong."

Except of course Anna didn't believe a word of it. Could you have complete honesty in any relationship? She thought not. Surely no one would want to be party to everything that went on inside someone else's head. She absolutely didn't want anyone inside hers.

"She was strong, said I was the one needed looking after. It was a bit of a shock when she died. I think I got a bit lost for a while, like Derek."

From what she could see he hadn't got anywhere close to finding himself again. And the churning in her stomach, the sudden flash of irritation was definitely jealousy for what this man had had. She wondered why people called it the green-eyed monster when all she could see was red. She didn't want to be here any more. He was no use. She couldn't tell him her troubles, he had too many of his own ghosts.

"Well, I'd better be going."

"I'm sure you have plenty to be getting on with."

It was as if someone had pressed a button re-engaging his backbone. He straightened up and became all shiny so that she felt she couldn't see him any more. This was the person she knew at church, at their meetings. Actually this was the one she preferred. The other made her long for what she did not have. She didn't want to know all about him and his sorrows. Like Simeon she didn't want to be touched. Realising that allowed the loneliness to spread ahead, thick and firm and well able to muffle her tread.

***

"Terry, there goes Anna. Weight of the world on her shoulders as usual."

Terry turned and looked out the door. She shook her head. A little shake as if irritated. Any second now Jean would say something like, "Poor Anna, she just doesn't seem to be that happy, or manage, or understand."

"Poor Anna," Jean spoke on cue. "She always looks so burdened."

Terry pulled out the last of the tins from the bottom of the box, placed them carefully on the shelf and then stamped on the empty box, to squash it down.

"Careful Terry. I think that's flat enough."

Terry picked up the cardboard from the floor. She believed that if you were going to do something you ought to do it well, and there was always so much cardboard. Well this piece wouldn't take up too much room in the recycling bin.

"Now, how about putting on the kettle and we can discuss Easter. It's late this year so we'll have our choice of flowers."

Terry knew that Jean was having another dig about not ringing the nursery. It had only happened twice and she thought she'd managed quite well with what they had. She wished Jean would let it go. She always seemed to hold onto her grudges for such a long time. Let things build and mither until they became far more important than they really were. Terry wondered if Jean ever got angry enough to hurt someone.

She picked up two mugs and poured in a dash of milk. Jean could be quite fussy. Terry waited, leaning over the kettle. Jean was still talking, something about Ellie her daughter, Terry had heard most of it before and with the noise of the kettle she couldn't hear a thing.

Chapter 6

Archie filled the bowl with water, pulled on his washing-up gloves, and looked out across the garden. There was a slash of blue sky between dark grey clouds which was dramatic rather than reassuring. The wind was driving across the headland and he thanked God they had moved the lifeboat station. They wouldn't have been able to launch today from the old ramp under any circumstances. He sighed. He ought to have asked more questions of the vicar but he just wasn't any good with people. He'd ended up talking all about himself instead of finding out how she was. The water overflowed the bowl and he looked down with annoyance. He only had the two cups to wash and here he was sloshing water around willy-nilly. Rain began to spatter the window. Was she alright? He'd been oblivious to Revd Adams' problems. The whole incident had shocked him to his core, he simply couldn't let it happen again. And now that woman had died in the churchyard. Had been murdered in the churchyard! No, he wasn't having that. It was simply going to have to be an accident. Luckily the coroner's hands had been tied for lack of evidence, or it would have to have been unlawful killing.

Archie would simply have to try harder with Revd Maybury, he would be extra vigilant. He didn't want to cover up any other messes.

***

Simeon could see Harriet just inside the church. He thought perhaps she was praying but he didn't want to speak to her again quite so soon after his post-funeral encounter. He wanted to be sure that what he'd felt had well and truly ebbed away so that any new thoughts would be separate. He didn't know if this was how it was meant to work but it was how he would like it to be and as God had made him that way that was his problem.

Harriet was ages and Simeon was getting chilled to the bone before she came out, pulling the door behind her. He hated the cold because it made him feel as if he were turned inside out and it often took him hours to warm up. He hoped he wouldn't be too uncomfortable in the church. Today she wore some leather shoes he hadn't seen before. They were flat and shiny. He watched her lock up and place the key behind the stone. His stone. The one he thought best, not the one used by Anna. The others always put the key back where they had found it. The others were Archie Wainwright and the flower arrangers. He was glad no one else was allowed to let themselves in or he was sure they would have lost the key months ago and he wouldn't have liked that. He needed to be able to come and sit when it was right for him.

Simeon couldn't come to church on Sundays. He didn't like sharing things, and he didn't really understand why it was important but he referred God to his original premise which was that if it was that critical then it was God's problem to work out a solution. He was intrigued as to how God might make it possible, how he might enable him to come to church when the others were there.

He waited until Harriet had disappeared down the path. She paused at the grave where Fiona had hit her head. People often did even if they didn't realise it. Paying homage to the incident rather than the dead woman herself. Simeon had heard people refer to Fiona as that poor woman with the black dog. Not Harriet though, she'd known Fiona. She'd been very upset when she died. Simeon wondered how people would describe him if he were dead. He retrieved the key and went in. It was odd, it felt as though Harriet was still here. The place felt used and to begin with he couldn't settle. He wandered round and round, touching each of the pew-ends as he passed. Then after a while he realised he would have difficulty stopping, so he had to slow right down and walk for quite a while without touching anything. He stuffed his hands in his pockets though his fingers tingled and ached. When he did feel able to pause he wished he'd gone all the way round just one more time. He knew he had to be quite deliberate to break a pattern once he got started and he knew it would take ages before he was able to sit and think without the circular motion drawing him back. The door gave a squeal. Not as loud as usual, for Mr Wainwright knew just how far to push it.

"Hello, Simeon. Am I disturbing you?"

Simeon didn't mind him. Mr Wainwright never came too close. Simeon shook his head and returned to waiting.

After a while he thought, that maybe if God used people, he might be trying to use Mr Wainwright. Only Wainwright never talked to him unless invited to, so it seemed unlikely, but just in case Simeon turned around. He was re-arranging the noticeboard. Simeon was glad to see that he put all the spare drawing pins in a neat row along the bottom. He sat a while longer, only he couldn't help glancing back every now and again. In the end he gave in and went closer to examine a new leaflet. The diocese was running a series of talks in Helston, Truro, and Falmouth on community. He frowned. Perhaps this was God speaking to him? Except they were all scheduled for the evening. Simeon didn't drive, and there were no buses home at that time of night. He looked away as Mr Wainwright turned round.

"They look quite interesting, don't they? We've missed the first one as Anna didn't give me this until yesterday." Mr Wainwright was wearing stout leather brown shoes, which were well polished. Simeon liked Mr Wainwright's shoes; he took good care of them.

"No point. Can't get there or rather, can't get back."

"I guess we are a bit out of the way. Though I could take you if you like. I really want to go." Mr Wainwright paused.

Simeon froze. He hadn't sat in a car for a long time. Didn't like being that close to someone else, breathing the same air, or worse allowing them to be in control of where he was going. At least buses stopped at bus stops. If you wanted to get off you pressed the bell and that was that.

"I can't."

"Well if you change your mind, you know where I live. You can always come and knock on my door."

Simeon went back to his pew. He didn't notice when Mr Wainwright left, because he didn't say goodbye. He never did, never wanted to disturb. Simeon liked that.

There was a woman in the churchyard, down by the gap in the hedge at the bottom. She was one of the flower arrangers. She lived just across the road from the widower at the end of a short terrace and sometimes worked in the shop. Simeon didn't know her that well. He didn't want to turn his back on her to lock the door but he needn't have worried for she quickly disappeared into the lane. As he turned back he caught sight of the stone tomb and a wave of anxiety rolled over him. It made him feel tingly and sick. He hadn't felt this bad for a while but he supposed he had got a bit stuck in the church so he wasn't surprised. He still had to wait ten minutes to make sure that the woman had definitely gone and then he followed her out of the gap at the bottom so he wouldn't have to pass the spot. He jogged home, up the lane, past the church gate. He had to make himself go into the kitchen, to take the sandwich from the fridge, because it was time to eat. He knew he had to take care of himself or he might get sick. Then people would demand entry to his life and he definitely didn't want that. Simeon chewed to the last piece and then he went into the back room where he slept and curled up under the weighted blanket, allowed the dark heaviness to drape itself over him. He waited for his breathing to still and the feeling of disquiet to lift. It was a painful process for he had to allow it to expand and fill him before it could break through his skin and leave him calm again.

***

On his way back from Falmouth Derek drove past the end of a road that he recognised. It made him shudder a little. It had been one of his last site visits before Fiona's stroke, a moment when he had thought himself happy. Dolly whimpered. She was in the boot but he'd lost track of time so it had been a bit of a drive. He pulled over so she could have a sniff along the verge. When she was done she hopped back over the tailgate. He leaned in and scratched behind her ears. For an old dog she was alright, she just didn't have the stamina any more or the bladder.

He had worried about Dolly at first, worried that he wouldn't know what to do with her. That she wouldn't perhaps love him as she had Fiona. But it seemed that Dolly was pragmatic and as long as he fed her, stroked her soft ears, and let her wee when she needed to she didn't seem to be missing Fiona at all. He was pleased because he found that he was missing her enough for both of them. The hole she had left was profound. He simply hadn't realised that her absence would leave him feeling so shredded.

He pulled up at their house: their bungalow, a bungalow with a converted attic. Oh, God, he lived in a bungalow. It made him drop his face into his hands. Dolly stood up, gave herself a bit of a shake but Derek couldn't bring himself to go up the steps. The front door seemed huge, and the walls felt like they were rearing over him, almost toppling into the road. He decided to go to the pub. They often had pies at lunchtime and Phil was happy to run a tab so he didn't even have to worry about having any cash. Dolly didn't mind either, she liked the fire and sometimes Bowzer came out from behind the bar. They would lie together nose to nose, which always made the other punters smile, and helped Derek feel that there might one day be a place for him back in the world.

***

The bus was late and there was nowhere to stand out of the

81

wind. Harriet shivered, if it didn't come soon she would get wet. A dark squally wall of cloud was bubbling over the sea and she could see the rain falling under it as a line of blurred softness. She turned her back and pulled her scarf tighter. She hoped that Phil wouldn't ask her to take Bowzer out, not today. It would be horrible and she still hadn't been able to walk him anywhere near her favourite places, the places she'd been with Fiona. The first drops spattered across the road and before long she was dripping. A car would have been useful, but the last thing Fiona had said to her before the seizure was that if you accepted anything off Derek, thirty years would pass and you'd find that all your dreams had become impossible and all his were still to do. Derek had taken or ignored all the things that had been important to Fiona. First the archaeology, then the museum, and finally their lovely house north of Falmouth. The trouble was Derek didn't come across as an unkind man: with sandy hair that was thinning and a grey anorak with lots of pockets, shirts that were soft rather than stylish. Harriet was having trouble pinning him down. Fiona had never said he had a temper or mentioned a violent streak, only that he had this way of selectively ignoring the bits that weren't about him. There would be no shouting into the wind for him. On the other hand she could imagine him sitting across from Fiona, expecting her to wait on him, expecting her to be there, allowing her to become the sad and angry woman that Harriet had been drawn to. Wasn't it the quiet ones you had to beware of?

She left her coat dripping in the back porch and went through to Phil. He'd lit the fire and the pub was already reassuringly warm and dim. He was leaning against the bar chatting to a couple of tourists. It was always quiet in the week so there wasn't much to do but he liked to get his admin sorted while he was still morning cheerful and she was happy to get the extra pay for coming in early. At some point her landlord was bound to put some money into her place, then there'd be an increase in rent, and it would be advertised with the other holiday lets – comfortable studio flat with stunning sea views – so she didn't dare complain about anything, put up with a lot of niggles just in case he realised she was still there and not paying anywhere near the going rate. She wondered what Phil would do if she had to leave. Shrug and find someone else to man the bar, walk his dog, and wash the B&B sheets.

She heard the familiar whine, the clatter of Dolly's claws and for a second her heart expanded and filled her chest. Then she had to brace herself for the emptiness that followed. The feeling ebbed away quite quickly if she concentrated on her breathing. Derek sat down by the fire to read his newspaper. He'd ordered one of Phil's pies. Phil caught her eye and pointed at the cider pump. By the time she'd changed the barrel, sorted out the bottled beer, and swept around the doors where the leaves had blown in, Derek had gone, which Harriet thought was mean because she hadn't had a chance to say hello to Dolly.

Through the afternoon there was a trickle of customers. Bowzer didn't get a walk. The rain settled down to its usual blustery loveliness, and she was grateful to stay inside, did a bit of wiping around and polished some glasses. Phil joined her for the evening stint but they spent a lot of time simply leaning on the bar and chatting to the few regulars. At eleven thirty, after bolting the front door, he drove her home. Realistically, even if she had accepted Fiona's car she wouldn't have been able to afford the tax and insurance let alone the petrol and Phil always said he didn't mind running her back.

***

Anna waited in the porch for the last of the ladies to leave. They'd had a couple of visitors from Stafford this Sunday who'd sat enthusiastically near the front. They seemed pleasant, but she'd got her usual feeling that they thought they were doing her a favour, that by turning up and praying especially fervently she would feel encouraged.

Mr Wainwright, no, Archie, came out of the tower room carrying the register to sign and a small bag of money. She dutifully scribbled her signature to say that she'd been a good girl, that she had preached her sermon.

"So Vicar," he began (she was in church, she supposed 'Anna' was too much to ask), "that was a good morning this morning. It was nice to see a couple of new faces."

"From Staffordshire."

"On holiday I suppose."

"Yes."

They always had this conversation. Archie longed for people to move here, to be drawn to the church, to swell their meagre finances because each year he had to write a long and tedious letter to the diocese explaining why they were so woefully short of their quota, yet again. When Anna checked the accounts last year there had been several mysterious donations to the church. She was convinced that when things got particularly dire Archie topped them up from his own pocket to make it all look less pitiful. He was a man who truly seemed to care, which irritated her greatly.

"Don't lock up..." she hesitated for barely a second, "Archie, I'll stay on a bit longer."

"Right. See you on Tuesday for finance committee."

She smiled and blinked. It would be tedious in the extreme. Money always seemed to bring out the worst in people and as their deficit was growing steadily, as usual, it would all feel hopelessly inevitable. Once she'd made sure Archie had got to the end of the path she sighed. The sigh swelled and grew into a sort of screech though it was through gritted teeth, but she couldn't keep it in, not entirely, and it was loud enough to send some of the rooks nesting along the lane into the air, squawking in their turn.

"I know, I'm not supposed to give in like this," she cried to the woodwormed roof, to the uncomfortable wooden pews, to the unforgiving stones, "but I can't help it." She stared around her church with new eyes. It seemed that releasing the cry had made space for a thought, a clear single truth.

"Oh," she said and sat down on the back row. "Oh, God," she groaned again, and put her face in her hands. She rubbed the skin under her eyes as if she were trying to wake up. The problem was that it wouldn't have made any difference if the place had been full that morning, if her churchwarden was a man she knew how to talk to, if the only person she had meaningful interactions with wasn't Simeon, with his view of the world that was different and difficult to grasp at the best of times. It wouldn't have mattered if they'd had a music group and a bunch of teenagers sniggering through her sermon or even carpets or chairs – she would still have felt this yawning emptiness. Anna groaned again, "Oh, God, oh God."

***

Archie stood outside. He'd forgotten to put up the notice about offering lifts to the Lent talks, had forgotten to tell Anna that he'd decided to go. When Anna howled he thought she'd fallen and hurt herself, then he thought perhaps it was someone messing around. He was about to run back in, when something made him hesitate. The noise had felt visceral, deeply personal, and he didn't want to intrude. He waited. Now there was only silence.

Archie was filled with disquiet and then pity took himself across to Moira's grave. The raised stone was carved with the names of her family going back generations. Apologising to her many ancestors he sat down on it.

"Hello luv. Haven't been for a while. I've been trying to manage on my own." He patted the stone. "Can't seem to. Anna's in trouble. She's got a problem, perhaps depression.

Hopefully not like the last chap. Anyway I'm sure you'd have got to the bottom of it in an instant." He straightened up a little and then slumped again. With Moira he didn't have to cope. "I simply don't know how to help. Wish you could pop back just for a minute and tell me what to do."

Simeon had also heard Anna's cry. He'd crept away to sit behind his hiding tomb. It was a couple of metres long with a ledge running round the base which he could perch his bottom on. He could sit for quite a long time without getting damp. From there he couldn't be seen by anyone coming down the path. Anna's cry had made him tremble a little. It's why he didn't like to get too close to people because they always ended up doing something just like this, something he didn't expect, didn't like, and didn't understand. Then Mr Wainwright had started chatting to his wife. Simeon wanted to run away but couldn't do so without being seen.

"I know I need to let you go, isn't that what's said nowadays?" Archie continued. "That I need to move on, but I don't know what I should be moving onto." He sighed. "So unless you really mind I'd like to hang onto you for a bit longer."

There was a long silence, filled with the noise of the rooks squabbling at the top of the trees, amongst their fortresses of twigs.

"So God, what should I do?"

Simeon was close by, but he barely heard the words, Archie spoke so quietly.

"Do I have to?" Archie murmured a moment later. Then Simeon heard him walk away, crunching through the old leaves from the autumn before.

Anna was still sitting in the church where she'd sunk into a pew. She was stony-faced. She didn't need a mirror to know that she looked a mess, pale and lined and hard. For a blissful moment she thought she was about to encounter God, that he had crept in to comfort her but the hand laid on her shoulder was only Archie. She almost shrugged him off.

"Look, I don't know what to do," he whispered.

"Me neither," she replied.

"No, you misunderstand me."

"Yes, I do that a lot."

"I don't know what to do about you."

"Me?" Anna replied.

"Of course you. I'm not Moira, but there is something wrong and I want you to know that I know." Was he threatening her? "Tell me what I can do to help. I asked Moira, but I can't seem to hear her any more so I prayed and I think God said to come back in here. That you need me."

Anna turned to stare at him.

"How did he tell you that?"

"Just a feeling... a sort of thought in my head."

Anna turned away again.

"It's not fair, Archie. I'm the vicar, why can't he talk to me? He's supposed to talk to me."

"Perhaps you can't hear him because the pain is getting in the way."

"What pain?"

Archie shrugged.

"There's always pain, isn't there?" he said and patted her on the shoulder again.

And Anna wondered what would have happened if Archie had died and Moira had lived. Would she have been the someone who might have redeemed Anna from the disappointment? A useless train of thought. Another what if to add to the pile. For a brief moment, Anna thought how lucky Moira was to be gone, to have finally found out what was at the end of it all, then wondered if there was any point in living, but that took her straight back to Simeon and his new-found hope that because she cared, there was a God. She laughed. Archie looked uncomfortable, was standing awkwardly, one hand resting on the back of the pew, the other smoothing his hair.

"Come on Archie. I need a drink."

He looked startled but then nodded.

As they walked through the churchyard Anna saw a movement out of the corner of her eye, like a mouse scuttling across the grass.

"Simeon, I won't bother locking up. You can do that when you leave."

Archie looked around.

"Are you sure he's here?"

"Oh, yes. He likes to come in when everyone else has gone. I think it's a bit warmer or something."

"Is it just about being warm or could it be about God?" Archie asked.

Anna pursed her lips. "Up until a few weeks ago, it was just being somewhere familiar. He most definitely didn't believe in God, said he couldn't exist. Then apparently Harriet said something that got him thinking. So now he at least believes that God is... here."

"That's absolutely wonderful." Archie sounded so pleased. "I wonder how he is exploring this new-found knowledge."

"Don't know. Haven't spoken to Simeon for a while, not properly."

***

Harriet placed the drinks on the table, a half pint and a white wine. The wine didn't last long. And before Anna put the glass down Archie was up to get another. They drank in silence until Bowzer came across and snuffled round their feet. Archie tickled him behind the ears and Anna said, "Why don't you get a pet? It would be company."

"I'm allergic, and I wouldn't know how to look after one properly."

Harriet laughed; she was clearing the tables around them.

"Nothing to it Mr Wainwright. Look at Derek, Mr Harris

that is, he never did anything for Dolly before Fiona died and now he parades her round the village like they're best friends, like she's always been his dog."

Archie picked up his drink, peered down into the fire. He was patently embarrassed at Harriet's outburst. Anna swivelled around to face her.

"Derek's doing well. He's even thinking of going back to work."

It was strange standing up for Derek. But Anna felt that Harriet was making everything worse. Harriet kept making out that Derek was some sort of... Well that was the problem, she didn't know what Derek was. Harriet didn't like him, that was for sure, but Anna wasn't certain she particularly liked Harriet who was now sniffing, her eyes filling with the inevitable tears.

"I expect Fiona would have liked to go back to work," Harriet whispered. It was like something out of a film.

Archie was fiddling with a button on his coat. If he twisted it any more it would come off. Anna wanted to lean over and still his hand. Harriet needed to get a grip. Spreading such unkindness wasn't going to help anyone. She pulled a tissue from her pocket and handed it to Harriet.

"Would you like me to pop over and see you again?" Anna asked as Harriet dabbed her eyes. "I could come tomorrow morning after ten and then I could drive you to the pub, save you the bus trip."

Harriet nodded, as she backed away blinking.

"She seems terribly upset," Archie said. Harriet was now wiping around the pumps, and every so often made a bit of a show of wiping her eyes on the tissue.

"They were good friends. Took their dogs for a walk nearly every day. I guess that would leave a hole in anyone's life."

"I don't think I'll be leaving a hole anywhere," Archie replied, quietly.

Anna's eyes widened. Not now, she thought. I can hardly

cope with my own life and he's supposed to take care of me, that's what it says in the handbook. Oh God, it simply isn't fair. She took a big breath and said, "You'd leave a big hole in my life. I wouldn't know how to manage without you."

He looked embarrassed again, almost as much as when Harriet had been going on about Derek.

"Look," Anna said, "it's alright to be human, you know. Show a bit of emotion, it's what we do, how we get by."

Though she knew that what had happened back at the church had not been simply getting by. She hadn't been able to help herself. That groan had risen to the surface and made her feel as though she was falling, flailing through the air to the shiny waves below. Archie sat up.

"Navy and all that. You didn't show your feelings if you could help it and I suppose I wouldn't know how to do it now. But is there anything I can do? Do you need help with anything? Anything at all?"

She wondered if he asked lots of questions in the hope she would only answer one of them and forget the rest.

"I'm ok. I'll get through it. Don't worry."

She smiled and nodded reassuringly.

"I was quite worried. And it is good to have had a bit of a chat."

He stood up, hat in hand. She smiled but wanted to say except we haven't talked at all. She watched him through the window as he walked around the corner to his lane, clutching his hat to his head, leaning into the wind. A small man battling against the relentless weather.

"What now?" she muttered to the ceiling. She considered having a pie for lunch instead of the chicken salad sitting in the fridge but she'd been ballooning for years and if she wasn't careful she'd be going up a cassock size, which would be impressive in anyone's book. She got up to leave.

"I'll see you tomorrow, Harriet," she called.

Harriet nodded. Anna was pulling the door shut behind her

when she heard a shout, caught and thrown about by the wind.

"Vicar!"

Someone else who couldn't remember her name.

"Detective Inspector Edwards," he said, because for a moment she didn't look as though she remembered who he was. "Sorry to disturb you."

"It's been a while. What can I do for you?"

He looked pale. His dark hair had been cut recently. A practical shearing that didn't really suit him but she could hardly talk. Today her hair could do with a wash so she'd pulled it back into a tight ponytail. No part of her was softened or left to the imagination.

"Could we have a little chat?"

"At the vicarage, please. It's not very far away."

Chapter 7

Terry sat at her kitchen table and ate a sandwich made from a bit of ham that Jean was going to throw out because its sell-by date was coming up. Terry didn't believe in sell-by dates. A sop to the people in society who couldn't organise themselves was what Edgar had said, and she agreed with him. Later she'd eat the last of the casserole she'd made on Friday. She was saving the newspaper for the evening because Sunday night television had become vacuous in the extreme. She put the plate in the sink. She only washed up once a day. It saved on hot water and she didn't like to waste things. The kitchen looked out onto the back garden, a long narrow strip that ended in the side wall of one of the new houses – a cluster of homes from the nineties built along roads that wound tortuously around themselves, probably erected because the council thought the village could do with a bit of a boost population wise. It had meant her house hadn't been so expensive, had become more affordable so that when she had decided to buy she'd been able to get an extra bedroom for her money. The lawn ended in shrubs which she kept well pruned. She liked to be able to see the boundary of the garden, liked to keep it neat though it did mean she could see into next door's garden.

Church had been tedious that morning. Anna's sermon had started well and then had drained away into patronising drivel. "I'm sure, like me, you must... " As if by exposing her character flaws she could help them live better lives. Terry guessed the diocese must have been getting a bit desperate to have agreed to Anna taking over the parish, after the last chap. Jean said she tried, but was that good enough? Terry wasn't sure. The trouble with Anna was that over the four years she didn't seem to be getting any better at what she did.

Terry went out into the hall; her winter walking boots were on the mat ready. She often needed to scrape them clean after her daily constitutional but there was a tiny utility room out the back with a useful sink that made scrubbing mud off her things easy enough.

The sky was grey and low but it didn't look as if it would rain. She would walk around the point and come back up past Mr Wainwright's house. She had plenty of time before it got dark, though even the darkness didn't hold any fears for her. Edgar had once asked, "Does nothing ever scare you?" She'd said proudly, "No, I can't think of anything." Edgar had smiled, patted her arm, and said, "That's my girl."

As she rounded the corner of the lane just above the church she saw Simeon coming out of the porch. She hurried past the gate, when she looked back to check, he still hadn't come into the lane. She turned up to the gap in the hedge at the bottom of the churchyard. Peering through she could just make out Simeon locking up. Sometimes he got stuck on the path by the tomb they'd thought Fiona had hit her head on. Terry turned away and shivered.

She carried on down to the cove and up onto the southern path. It was muddy but she came this way every day and knew where to place her feet. Once past the lifeboat station she would be able to go a bit faster. Down at the point there was a large group of walkers milling around, about to head off to Kynance. There was a lot of laughing. Terry didn't want to get caught up with them, so she decided not to carry on to Mr Wainwright's house as planned, but to use the road instead. It wasn't such a good walk but you could get up a brisk pace because the path was stony and well maintained.

Lights were beginning to come on through the village and she was going to walk past the shop. It looked empty. She decided to pop in. As the bell on the door jangled Jean came through from the back.

"Oh, it's you. Do you fancy a cup of tea?"

"Would you like me to make it?" Jean never did anything herself if there was someone else to do it for her. Jean nodded and slipped up onto her stool behind the counter.

"That policeman is back to see Anna."

Terry watched them cross the green, then she slipped out the back. She leaned on the counter in the store room and allowed the steam to fill her head.

***

The vicarage felt cold, but then it always felt cold. Anna switched on the fire in the small back room but that wasn't where she would take the policeman. She always took her guests to the large lounge at the front. Only this time she hesitated because it was full of old sofas and dusty half-empty shelves. Undecided, she led him through to the kitchen. There was an oil-fired radiator in there that once it got going wasn't too bad. He began to unbutton his coat.

"I wouldn't do that if I were you."

He looked confused.

"It won't warm up for a bit. I'd leave your coat on until you feel more comfortable."

"Oh, the church can't afford central heating?"

"I've never asked. Perhaps I ought to. But I bet this place is a bugger to heat even in the summer and I simply can't afford it."

"Some parishes are selling off the big unwieldy vicarages and are finding houses more economical to run."

"Makes sense but I suppose they're worried that one day they'll get another family man back in."

"Or woman."

But Anna knew that no man would follow his wife down here unless he was ready to retire. Of that she had personal experience.

"You seem to know a lot about it," she said, putting on the kettle.

"My mum, back in Wiltshire. A churchgoer all her life."

"Not you?"

"High days and holidays. I suppose when the mood takes me, which is mostly when I'm off duty." He smiled but there was a grey puffiness around his eyes that made her wonder if he was ever off duty. He looked how she felt, weary, but then didn't everyone at this time of year?

"So what do you want to talk about?"

He sat forward. She pulled her coat tighter. She wasn't feeling any warmer.

"Fiona Harris. We had a call, a woman we think, said we should look into it again."

"Oh, for goodness sake."

"I know. And after all this time. I'm as annoyed as you are, but we have to take these things seriously." He looked down and picked at the fabric of his jumper as if he were slightly ashamed of being a policeman.

"It'll be Harriet. She's been mooning around the place, and crying a lot. She's really taken against Derek."

"The lady that works at the pub?"

"That's right. She and Fiona used to walk their dogs together. Dolly and Bowzer. Bowzer actually belongs to Phil, the landlord."

He laughed.

"Sounds like an opener to a rather seedy soap opera."

She didn't smile, was a trifle disconcerted at the use of the word 'seedy'. Did their lives look seedy to an outsider?

"Anyway," she continued, "Harriet keeps saying that Fiona was deeply unhappy about life, about Derek. She says he's not a nice man, but I'm fairly convinced that Derek didn't know that Fiona was that sad. He wanted to give Fiona's car to Harriet, only she refused it, rather publicly by all accounts."

Anna sighed. It felt good to talk about this stuff, even if it was just to the policeman.

"Could he have been trying to bribe her, to keep her quiet?"

"To keep quiet about what?" Anna's eyes widened. "You're

kidding? You've met Derek?"

"Ok, I admit it might seem to be a bit of a stretch, but we always look hard at those closest to the victim."

Anna simply couldn't believe that Derek had anything to do with Fiona's accident.

"You said victim. So you definitely think she didn't just fall?"

"An open verdict at an inquest means we didn't do our job well enough."

He looked down and began to pick at the thread of his jumper again.

"Look, I'm seeing Harriet tomorrow," Anna said. "I'll try my best to get to the bottom of this dislike, if there's any substance to it. I'll call you if I'm at all worried."

He sat back. The chair was an old one and wasn't that comfortable. She wasn't surprised when he sat forward again.

"Are you allowed to do that?" he asked, narrowing his eyes.

"I don't know. As long as I don't betray a confidence..."

"But surely that's exactly what you will be doing."

"Oh, OK. I won't call you." Anna was confused. She'd been trying to help him. Surely he didn't think she would cross the dog-collar line?

"Well, you should if anything seems off, but you shouldn't give up anything too personal if you don't think it's appropriate."

She stared. He was a very odd man and he was tying her in knots.

"I'm sorry, I haven't even made you a drink."

She began to get up.

"No, it's alright. I need to get on. I'll go and have a half at the pub."

"Won't that give the game away?"

"What game? Harriet will only know I've been to see you if you tell her."

Anna suddenly felt warm. She shrugged out of her coat as

he stood up.

"Give me a ring, tomorrow," he said and handed her a card with a mobile number neatly printed across the middle.

Tom Edwards. A friendly name. She wondered if he gave out cards to everyone.

***

The light was thin and dull, splashing across the pews, making Derek feel hollow. Just like he'd felt after the inquest. An open verdict was not what he had hoped. It meant that there was not enough evidence to say whether she had simply fallen or been clouted, because it had been the blow to the head that had killed her. So now everyone was asking who would have wanted to do that to her. He'd wanted someone to say that it was natural causes, and that all the policeman's questions would have been shown to be a waste of time. Though he had been reassured that no one was taking it further it hadn't felt remotely satisfying. He felt the village watching him. She should have been at peace now, laid to rest, and she wasn't.

Derek had only come into the church because it had started to rain. He'd thought he ought to visit Fiona, but there was just a pile of earth, with a mosaic of rabbit prints running across it. The stone wasn't due for ages. The undertaker said they would have to wait months for the ground to settle. Derek didn't like the thought of that, of the earth getting heavier above her, and suddenly he was afraid that they'd made a dreadful mistake, that she wasn't dead at all, that she might have woken up and couldn't get out.

"Stupid, stupid, stupid," he almost shouted out loud. There had been an autopsy, they would have checked. His breathing still took a while to slow. He'd got too much time on his hands, too much time to think but they'd told him not to come back to work yet. That there was no need. Of course they didn't want him to come back at all. They wanted to

98

ditch his clients, and his normal, honest-to-goodness architecture. He'd outgrown his usefulness and simply didn't fit their new shiny-tight image. Well he was a partner and he wasn't going to make it easy for them. In fact, he would go home right this minute and finish off a couple of projects. It would do him good to get going again. He would arrange a meeting back at the office to discuss his return. That would put the wind up them, good and proper. He really needed someone to talk to but the only person he could think of was Ned who had died the year before. He'd been a good man, he'd understood old school architecture, the sort that Derek loved. When Derek had first moved to Falmouth it had been Ned who'd introduced him around, had even if he remembered rightly put him in contact with his current firm, said they'd needed someone to keep them rooted in the here and now.

He continued sitting, staring at the shafts of light playing across the stones. Only white light, no coloured glass. It was a shame; it could be beautiful. Perhaps he could commission a window for Fiona, except she hadn't exactly been a churchgoer. To begin with Anna hadn't seemed to know her at all, even in this tiny community.

His feet started to tingle, so he stood up. Dolly shook herself and looked up at him with her large filmy eyes.

"You're a good dog," he said and pulled her ears gently. She didn't react, she was ready for home and simply continued to stare at the door.

On his way out he saw the man Simeon duck down behind one of the larger stones. Anna had explained that he wouldn't come in if anyone else was there. Derek waved but he'd already dropped out of sight. As Derek reached the gate he met Mr Wainwright coming down the path. The man always seemed to be doing something at the church.

"Hello, Mr Harris."

Derek nodded.

"Everything alright?" Archie spoke carefully.

"As well as can be expected," Derek found himself saying, and he wondered what that meant.

***

Simeon was getting cross. Was he never to have the church to himself? Lately it had been quite difficult to find a time when the place was empty. Perhaps this was God telling him something? He was too cold to wait any longer and it was only Mr Wainwright so he decided to brave it. When he peered in through the door Mr Wainwright was already dusting the pews. He watched him for a little while. The man had sensibly started on the far side so Simeon was able to go and sit in his usual spot.

"I went to that Lent talk."

Simeon turned to look at him. Mr Wainwright hadn't come any closer but had stopped dusting as he spoke.

"It was quite good. There weren't many of us and the room was nice and big, so I didn't have to sit near anyone. It took fifty-three minutes to get there and I was able to park right next to the hall. There were toilets, but no one used them."

Simeon turned back to the altar. He wasn't sure when Mr Wainwright left because as usual he didn't say goodbye.

***

From her living room, Terry watched Mr Wainwright head down to the church. He seemed to go most days for something or other though he didn't stay long. It was Jean's turn to do the flowers but since yesterday she was apparently developing a cold. Not a bad cold, only she always made a bit of a fuss. Terry was expecting her to ring at any moment to ask her to come and take over the shop, do the flowers for Sunday, or both. It irritated Terry immensely that Jean felt she could call at any time, without notice. That Terry would always be available to help. Jean didn't seem to appreciate that she liked to plan things well in advance. Liked to know what was coming next. Her Edgar had always said it was one of the things he most admired about her. So she kept a meticulous diary, even marking when all the bills were due, bin collection days, and telephone accounts.

She'd watched Derek take the dog out. He looked so downcast, so burdened, but unlike Anna he had every reason to be. He'd been gone quite a while, she hoped he wasn't over-exerting himself. The day before when Anna had passed by the shop with the policeman in tow she had looked serious, a little self-important. Terry was glad that the DI was back, still asking questions. He'd only been at Anna's for about forty-five minutes so Anna couldn't have had that much to say.

Terry checked her watch. Well if Jean didn't phone soon she'd just have to manage without her. It was time for a walk.

***

Anna settled back into the sofa. This time Harriet was seated on the upright chair from under the table. The cushions were straight, Harriet was dressed, her hair curled around a couple of tortoiseshell combs, and the bin was not overflowing with tissues

"This year I think I'm going to take up eating chocolate for Lent. How about you?"

"I normally give up caffeine," Harriet replied.

Anna was disappointed Harriet hadn't realised she was joking.

"Oh, that sounds a bit dramatic."

"Not really. I don't have much. I just think it's good to give the body a bit of a break now and again."

Anna looked down at her tummy. She hadn't ever worried about such things before but perhaps Harriet had a point. Not caffeine though, just food generally. The cassock joke was getting serious. Everything felt tighter, everything was becoming harder to get into.

"Really there's no excuse round here," Harriet continued,

as if she had read Anna's mind. "It's simply the perfect place for exercise. Wherever you go it's beautiful."

"Muddy and wet most of the year which can make running dangerous."

"You can walk, which is far better for you."

Anna was beginning to find Harriet irritating. She had an opinion on just about everything. It was getting tiresome.

"That DI came to see me Sunday. Said he'd had an anonymous tip off about Fiona."

"Oh, right," Harriet said, leaning forward to pour the coffee so that at the critical moment Anna couldn't see her face.

"You're not surprised." Anna spoke quietly, deliberately.

"No, I'm not."

Harriet was obviously not in a forthcoming mood.

"So do you think anything actually happened between Fiona and Derek?"

Harriet looked a little taken aback at such a direct question. Anna knew she had crossed a line but she thought surely this was all about getting Harriet to talk. It would be good for her, and then she would know that Anna was here for her.

"It's hard speaking about Fiona. I still get upset."

"I think it will be good for you and the more you do the easier it will become. All part of the grieving process."

That sounded quite plausible. Of course it wasn't always the case – it depended on the person. And that was as much as she knew from her not-so-long experience of being there for the bereaved. Or not being there for them. Which made her mouth twitch into a smile.

"Sorry, inappropriate thought warning," she said, which made Harriet frown. Of course it would. It's what they used to say at college when they couldn't quite keep up the facade, when what was asked of them was too absurd, too sensible, or too stupid even for trainee vicars. "Sorry Harriet, I'm afraid behind this dog collar is a rather ordinary person."

"Not that ordinary if you've been chosen by God."

Everything stopped right there. Anna blinked quite a few times, until she realised what she was doing. Was that right or had she missed her way entirely, because she'd never got over Peter's betrayal? Peter had left her, abandoned her, found someone else who was better. To begin with she thought the word 'betrayed' was a little dramatic but the more she said it inside her head the more it fitted.

Harriet nodded, as if she had decided something too.

She took a deep breath and said, "You're alright." She paused. Thought again. "Your heart is in the right place." Anna felt a little patronised. Harriet continued, "The thing is, Fiona said Derek didn't love her any more, that she was nothing more than his housekeeper. They hardly did anything together. He was at his desk all the time and she wasn't important enough for him to take the smallest breather."

"I thought he worked from home a couple of days a week."

"Only on a Friday but that day was worse than the others because he was there, but not there. He got up early, was at his board well before he should have been, and he often worked past five o'clock. She said he couldn't bear to be in the same room as her. She often welled up when she spoke about it." Harriet's eyes grew shiny. "It broke my heart."

They were walking the dogs out on the cliff path. Everyone's eyes filled with tears up there except on the balmiest days in high summer, Anna thought.

"She even said she thought there was another woman."

Derek with another woman? Anna tried hard to imagine it. She couldn't. It had probably just been a neglected wife's sop to her rather dull life. He can't just be fed up with me, there must be someone else.

"Do you really think there are grounds for getting the police to reinvestigate poor Fiona's death? Even if he was having an affair."

"You think I phoned the police?"

Why was she even denying it?

"I didn't say that." Though she patently had.

"But you do think it was me, don't you? Why does everyone think the worst of me?"

"I don't. Really I don't. It's just that they have to check again now and there really isn't any new information."

Harriet wasn't stupid.

"Is that why you agreed to see me today? Did that horrid policeman ask you to come?"

"Of course he didn't, Harriet. I saw him after I had agreed to see you. I came because I wanted to. I'm worried about you. You don't seem to be..." she hesitated because the cardinal rule was that people moved through grief at their own pace.

"Go on, say it now that you've started."

"You don't seem to be moving on that well."

"It's not been that long and I don't have to do what is convenient for everyone else."

"No you don't. Of course you don't, it's just that I'd like to help."

Harriet blew her nose and took a deep breath.

"I'm sorry, Anna," she said, dropping the tissue in the bin and reaching for another. "It's just she was so very kind to me, the first person to truly listen to what I had to say in such a long time." Anna took that on the chin. She deserved it. Harriet continued, "I'd not been able to speak of Ade to anyone. She was the only person who simply asked me what happened."

So Fiona was another Moira. Anna had suspected as much. People who left a swathe of kindness behind them, who were able to ask the right questions without putting others on the defensive, who felt they had every right to pry, who wouldn't have thought of it as prying at all. Anna wondered what sort of person she might have been if she'd had her own Fiona or Moira.

"And then she went and died on you. Left you," she said.

"I hadn't thought of it like that, but it does feel almost as bad as when Ade left. Like somehow I'm to blame. That I didn't listen to her enough." Harriet looked up, her face all squashed and trembling. "It's a bore, isn't it?" Her eyes filled with the inevitable tears. "Life seems to repeat itself. Here we go again. Don't you long for it to be a bit more fulfilling, to change its tune? For God's sake, I work in a pub where there are four regulars. I walk a fat old dog who doesn't belong to me and I'm still waiting for Ade to come back and tell me he was wrong to leave."

Anna wanted to cry out that she understood, that she truly understood. Instead she said, "What about Phil?"

"Me and Phil! Are you suggesting I need a man to be happy?"

Hadn't that been what Harriet had just said?

"Of course not." Back foot, back foot, back foot, a feeling Anna was well used to.

But Harriet only looked thoughtful, and then said brightly, "At least you have God. He must be a comfort."

"Yes, at least I have God." Now Anna wanted to cry.

***

The next morning on the way to check the post, Anna pulled the policeman's card out of her pocket. Was there any point ringing? Harriet hadn't really said anything worrying or sinister, and there was no big mystery about Derek and Fiona. He wasn't an evil man, just one who worked too hard. It probably wasn't his fault entirely; Fiona ought to have taken some of the blame for not shouting louder, for not demanding more, shouldn't she? Harriet had seemingly become dependent on the older woman so that her grief was intense and difficult. She was simply lashing out because an important prop had gone from her life.

Overall, Anna was pleased that she'd finally had a glimpse of the dead woman that hadn't come from Derek's head.

Except of course her glimpse of Fiona had been through Harriet's eyes and Harriet was clouded by grief, and her own needs. The word selfish sprang to mind. A word that Anna instantly swallowed back down, as the word unkind immediately rose up and plastered itself all over her.

Later that evening, as Anna walked up to the shop to get milk and a little more cheese, she saw Archie's car sail past. He waved but didn't slow. There was someone with him and she wondered where they were off to. Jean came out from the back.

"Hello Vicar." She sounded a bit bunged up and her nose was red.

"Call me Anna, won't you? I'm worried I'll forget my own name if people don't use it at least now and again."

Jean tipped her head to one side but didn't say anything. Anna felt there probably wasn't much to say.

"Just the milk and cheese then?"

She didn't want the shop to close, so she bought a packet of muffins and some more biscuits.

"Are your family coming down for Easter?" Anna asked.

"Yes, Terry is going to look after things for a few days so I can have a bit of a break."

"Oh, that's nice."

"Well I think Ellie's going to break up with her husband."

"Oh, I am sorry," Anna replied. So not that nice.

"It's been coming for a while. Sad of course and it means he won't be coming down to help with the children so we'll have our hands full."

"Oh, Jean, I really don't know what to say."

"It's what happens nowadays I suppose. And as long as he pays his way at least she'll be free to find someone who'll love her properly."

Anna wondered if that was what Jean really thought or whether she was just repeating what her daughter had told her.

"Well, give her my best."

Which was ridiculous because Anna had never met Ellie.

Anna walked down to the church. Today the vicarage was simply too big and cold to go back to. There were too many things piling up and for some reason Jean's news had left her feeling more than usually powerless. Whatever she did it wouldn't matter.

"It does matter though, doesn't it?" she muttered to the wind.

Terry was coming out of the church. She sort of bobbed in recognition of Anna and then hesitated. Anna nodded in return.

"I hear you're helping at the shop when Ellie comes down to stay."

Terry nodded. Anna found herself tangling up in the uncomfortable thought that Terry didn't think she was good enough, but then she felt that round most people. Terry was perhaps a little more honest about it. At least she looked at you, sometimes too piercingly, but she wasn't a Simeon which was a relief.

"Well Jean seems to be very grateful. She's getting over her cold."

"I would have helped out if she'd asked," Terry said, as if Anna was making a point.

"Oh, I'm sure she knows she only has to ask. What would we do without you lovely ladies to keep our precious shop running?" Terry was not lovely. Her face was too big, her shoulders too broad, though Anna had heard that in a previous life she had been married, but there wasn't anyone now. She was pretty sure of that. Terry sort of loomed and stared and her flower arranging was interesting and haphazard. Anna had even suggested an evening class but as far as she knew Terry had only been offended and had certainly never bothered. Anna gave her broadest smile and turned away. Instead of going into the church she continued down to the cove. None of the holiday cottages were let that week and she had the place to herself. She sat down on a bench overlooking the waves and ate the biscuits.

"I don't know how to make a difference," she said to God, or just the sea. "We are part of so much pain and that's without people dying suddenly, being mean or wilfully misunderstanding each other," she added, taking another biscuit. "Is it simply a matter of finding the right person to be with so it all makes sense?" Were Archie and Moira just lucky or had she secretly hated him too, had kept quiet, because that's what you did back then?

"How do I make a difference when I can't hear you any more? At least give me a small clue as to where to begin. I used to hear you, at least I used to think that I did. It was all so much easier back in college when hearing an answer to prayer was part of the everyday. Part of our culture." That's what they'd say now. It was all about making things part of your culture, like not smoking or shaving under your arms.

The waves were sweeping in and falling onto the slipway. She could see the sky through the smooth turning, the rising, rolling, overwhelming. And for a moment Anna wanted to walk into the water to burn and dissolve because there didn't seem to be anything else she could do. Only that wouldn't make a difference either except to Simeon, who would be incandescent that she had beaten him to it, or for poor Bishop Longbottom and Archie, who would have to find someone else to fill the gap. Find someone for a parish that drove its priests one after the other to suicide. She wondered if they would put central heating in for the next guy.

***

Anna was pulling her boots off, perched at the bottom of the stairs, when the phone rang.

"You were going to phone and let me know how you got on with Harriet."

108

"I was, Tom." When had he become Tom? It was definitely easier to remember than Detective Inspector Edwards. She still wanted to tell him she'd been too busy to call but had a feeling he'd know that wasn't true and then he might think she was trying to hide something. He made her feel slightly grubby, that she wasn't getting it right. Well patently she wasn't getting it right but she would like people to pretend that she was. To live in a nice successful bubble even if it was fantasy.

"Well, did you find out anything?"

Before she could stop herself she said, "He may have been having an affair."

"Really!" Tom sounded surprised, incredulous even.

"I know, I don't think it's true either. He simply doesn't look as though he has it in him."

The weight of her judgement made her sit back heavily onto the bottom stair.

"How do you do this?" she asked.

"Do what?" he replied.

"Constantly look for the grubby bits in people's lives and expose them."

There was silence for a moment and she wondered if he was cross.

"I don't think that is what I do." He didn't sound upset, perhaps a little weary. "I was told to check if the phone call had any merit."

"Alright, well let me know if there is anything else you'd like me to do."

Any more sneaking about, breaking of confidences or telling of tales!

"Thank you. You've been very... nice about it."

He put the receiver down. She listened to it burr until her handset began to beep to tell her that she still had it clamped to her ear.

Chapter 8

Easter Sunday dawned grey and cold. The sun came up but all Anna could detect was a lightening of the air. There were four of them standing on the point. Anna, Archie, Ellie, and Phil. Anna had been slightly taken aback. She wasn't used to doing this with anyone but Archie.

She spoke the liturgy into the dawn, Archie led the responses. They muttered hallelujah, a word that should not be used unless shouted or spoken by a hundred voices. Their thin reedy replies were caught by the wind and scattered over their shoulders before they'd left the warmth of their breathy mouths. They faced the sea and the growing light and spoke of resurrection and new birth. Ellie started crying and Phil offered her a handkerchief. It was freezing.

***

Anna thanked them all for coming and began to walk back to the lifeboat station where they had all met that morning. She wanted to go home for a cup of tea and to eat chocolate, as much as she could get in her mouth at once.

"Vicar," Phil called.

"Anna, please," she said, waiting for him to catch her up. She'd walked away quite rapidly, almost rudely she supposed.

"I've got bacon butties and coffee back at the pub. Harriet got it ready last night. It won't take me five minutes to fry it up. Come back and have some. You look like you could do with a bit of breakfast."

"Thank you. That would be lovely. Wonderful. So kind." And she choked and had to turn away. So desperate. She stopped when she got onto the tarmac, dropped back to walk with Ellie, allowed the men to stride ahead.

"Sorry about that, Vicar."

"Anna, please call me Anna."

"Anna. Sorry."

111

"About what?"

"The blubbing on the cliff. Sometimes I just can't keep it in any more."

"The divorce."

"Ah, Mum told you. She's being all practical but it's breaking her heart. She really liked him."

Anna marvelled at the ease with which Ellie spilled out the words, words that invited Anna, or more likely the dog collar, into her life. Wondered if like so many people she simply didn't have anyone else to talk to.

"It seems to be a part of our culture. To move on when things get difficult."

Oh God, that sounded so judgemental. Anna didn't know why they were splitting up but there were too many assumptions in that one sentence that she had no right to utter.

"I'm sorry," she continued quickly, "I was just finishing off a thought in my head. Something else entirely." She ended lamely.

"It's alright. You're right on one level. Three children and an extra stone, a part-time job, and clothes that don't fit any more. I haven't felt great for a long time so I suppose I stopped talking and then there was this pretty thing at work with all the time in the world to listen. And round we go." She hunched down in her coat, sniffing. "Only I miss him. I miss all we had planned to do together and I'm so desperately sorry for the kids because I'll be a rubbish single parent. I was tired before he said he was going to leave me."

"So he hasn't gone yet?" Anna knew she sounded hopeful.

"No, not yet. But me being here for a week gives him plenty of time for thinking and doing without us there to remind him to feel guilty."

"Have you told him how you feel?"

Ellie didn't reply. They entered the pub, out of the cold, the smell of bacon already beginning to fill the place. Anna muttered, "I'll pray, I'll pray with all my heart."

Ellie turned to her, shrugging out of her oversized coat.

"Would you? I would be so grateful to know that someone somewhere was fighting for us." Anna took a step back. Ellie really did sound grateful. "Perhaps God might help. Put a few obstacles in his way."

Phil came forward with two mugs of coffee, bitter and hot. Anna added half a spoonful of sugar as it was Easter morning and she hadn't had any chocolate yet.

"Thanks for this Phil."

"Oh, it's nothing. I used to do it for Doug every year."

"I didn't know." Anna had never heard Phil mention the previous incumbent.

"I supposed Archie might have mentioned it. We used to get quite a crowd."

Anna looked over to Archie, who was sitting beside Ellie. He was asking how the children were, discovering their ages, names, and whether they went to school or not. It was painful to watch but Ellie didn't seem to mind. Anna knew exactly why Archie hadn't said anything.

"So was this popular back... before I came?"

"It was always declining. Church is a bit of an option nowadays. You're up against too much other stuff but there's something about starting the year out on the cliff with the wind on your face."

"But I've been doing it with Archie since I came. Just him and me."

"I know. The first year my wife had just left. Up to the Midlands to start again where there was a bit of life. That Easter I was still trying to decide whether to go and join her."

"What made you stay?"

"Inertia, if truth be told. It took me a long time to stop thinking I still had a choice. She's been with someone else for nearly three years but up until last summer I thought I could arrive on her doorstep and she'd welcome me back with open arms. Idiot that I am."

Anna thought lucky was the word she would have used. To have at least known such hope.

"How long were you together?"

"Just on eleven years. Married for seven. Divorced properly not that long ago."

"I'm sorry Phil. You know that Ellie's going through something similar?"

"Yes. She told me out on the cliff. I remember her in pigtails going to school here in the village." He smiled. "She was such a sweet kid, then she went to secondary school and got a bit scary. I think the police had to go round a couple of times."

They looked across at Ellie. In her early thirties, dark hair cut short, rings under her eyes, wearing a black fleece and jeans. She looked so ordinary, so normal.

"Not scary now," Anna said, quietly.

"No, just sad."

**

Later that morning at the main Easter service, the church felt happier, filled with daffodils and silverware. None of those who'd been at the dawn service were there except for Archie of course and he did look tired. But it was nice to call out "Hello again" as she swept up the path. She'd even found her Easter stole which she'd never bothered with before. Today it didn't feel as though it would be over the top. She'd always liked the silver thread and green embroidery.

Derek came in and sat at the back, close to the door, as she began the opening sentences. Halfway through her sermon a movement caught her eye and she hesitated. Someone was standing in the tower room, the door ajar. For a second she lost her train of thought and had to reshuffle her notes to begin again. She knew no one would mind because they never expected much to begin with.

After the service she caught up with Archie, who was beginning to unpack the altar.

"Archie, I think there's someone in the tower."

"Yes, it's Simeon."

Words formed but nothing came out of her mouth.

"Why?" was all she could manage.

"He wanted to come but you know what he's like about people, sharing the same space and all that, so I set him up a chair in there. He came in early and he'll leave when everyone else is gone."

"Why did he want to come?"

"It's Easter. If you are going to try for the first time it's a good place to start. It was something one of the speakers at the Lent talks said."

"Who's been going to the Lent talks?" Her voice was thin and disappointed, like it had been out on the cliffs.

"Simeon and I. We had to have the window open and I had to drive a trifle carefully but he managed really well for someone who's only been in a car once or twice in the whole of his life."

"Why didn't you tell me you were going?"

Archie stopped folding up the altar cloth and stared at her.

"I put a notice on the board. It asked if anyone needed a lift. I'm sorry. Should I have asked you?"

"Well no. Yes. It would have been courteous."

She didn't mean that at all. She meant, why did you leave me out?

"I'm sorry."

She could see that he wasn't really. And he was right. He didn't have to tell her and she had seen the notice. A series of five talks on the 'Importance of Community Through Lent', as if Through Lent meant that suddenly everything made sense just because you gave up a bit of chocolate. She had thought about it too, a little, but the Importance of Community was something she had decided wouldn't be of any use to her congregation: her twelve regulars and her ten spurious others who tended to only come at Christmas and sometimes Easter. Anna turned away because Archie was waiting for her to say something and she couldn't think of a single thing. Jean popped up; she'd been sitting next to Terry towards the back. Anna assumed the shop had been shut for a few hours. Easter had to count for something. The two flower displays either side of the chancel were clearly Terry's handiwork. Too many twigs and not enough colour.

"I'm sorry about the flowers," Jean said, whispering, but so loudly that two of the regulars turned to listen. Anna backed down the aisle taking Jean with her. "She's been looking after the shop so I assumed I'd do the church but she'd already organised it. They are dreadful."

"Not that bad, Jean," Anna said, trying to speak quietly. "A little bit twiggy, that's all. The daffs look great."

"Well even Terry can put a few jam jars round the place without too much trouble."

"Well, I think it all looks very cheerful."

She hoped that was what Terry had heard as the woman stood up and strode from the church. Suddenly Anna longed to go home and find the chocolate egg she'd treated herself to.

***

Alice was back, but only for a couple of days. She was using the time to do a bit of cleaning because apparently he'd let things get into a bit of a state. Derek didn't like to watch as she sprayed and scrubbed, hoovering all the way into the corners, breathing hard and tutting a lot. The children, nice kids when they raised their heads, were on their phones, curled up on their beds. Alice made them switch off at meal times but apart from that they were lost to him in a world of social media and electronic entertainment, though now and again Nick did come out with him to walk Dolly. Nick wanted a dog but Alice had said no, there was too much going on already. Derek imagined that helping to walk Dolly was some sort of ploy to get her to change her mind.

Spending time with Nick wasn't easy. He didn't talk much and Derek often spent the night before thinking up things to ask him. Do you play sport? What's your favourite team? What's your favourite subject at school? Questions that weren't going to enthuse Nick beyond a quick smile or a shake of his head. Sometimes Derek thought he deliberately pretended not to hear him, though from a long way off and facing the other direction he always managed to hear, "Do you fancy a hot chocolate?" Luckily the café on the point was always open. They'd begun to look like regulars.

When Nick had first brought up the idea of having a dog, Derek had looked down at Dolly. He couldn't imagine anything being less trouble. Last week he'd had to wipe around her bowl where he'd kicked it, the water slopping and splattering everywhere, but there were plenty of spare cloths under the sink. Fiona looked as though she'd kept every tea towel and duster they'd ever had. He'd never forget that after Fiona, Dolly had been the only reason he'd got out of bed in the mornings. It had been her that had given his life some semblance of routine. The other things, the stuff he'd had to learn to do, had been nothing compared to finding a reason for the day. He'd wiped up crumbs, washed dirty cups, and worked out how to use the washing machine. He'd been quite proud of that and couldn't wait to tell Fiona all about it. She would have laughed.

That was the bit he hated most, the bit that stopped him in his tracks. The moment when he forgot and then had to remember again. He'd never get used to it. Wondered if that hollowed-out guilty swell would ever subside permanently. Still, he was back at work. Only mornings, and mostly from home, but now when he did have to go into Falmouth he took Dolly. It was nice sitting at his desk with his toes tucked under her and it made him get up and go out regularly so they both got some fresh air.

Until he'd discovered there was a partners' meeting coming up. They'd arranged it while he was off on compassionate leave. It didn't feel very compassionate to ban someone from work, so that all he had for company was his memories and a very old dog. When he was feeling particularly low he wondered if this was when they'd decided it was the optimal moment to put him under pressure to retire. Sometimes he wondered about starting up on his own, could he take some of the older clients with him? Most of them lived around Falmouth and Truro so he'd have to traipse backwards and forwards. He'd already decided he didn't want to move. When he'd mentioned all this to Alice, she'd said that if he was thinking of retiring, which he wasn't, perhaps it would be a good idea for him to come north to be nearer her and the children. That wasn't what he'd been suggesting at all though he understood why it would make her life a lot easier. The M5 was a nightmare, and beyond its end there was still a long way to go. After that little talk he knew he would have to try to get up to see her more often, in the hope that she'd feel less like relocating him.

There were so many things to think about, and he really didn't know where to begin. He was still struggling with what to eat, or worse Sunday lunch, which had been when Fiona had always cooked something nice and they'd sat at the table, used the mats and the good cutlery. He'd not been in the dining room for weeks. Alice was probably in there now, tutting and dusting and moving things to a better position. She was driving him nuts. All he wanted to do was to take her out for a drink and talk about Fiona but he hadn't been able to find the right moment to ask her if they could. She'd probably tell him to pull himself together. In that respect she'd always been more Fiona's daughter than his.

He felt a little sorry for himself. It was like someone had

placed a large hole in his life. He'd fallen into it and was waiting for someone to come by and let down a rope. Though if he was honest, he wasn't looking for the rope. He felt safe at the bottom of his pit. Nothing could get at him down here, he was sheltered from the wind, and as long as he had Dolly to rest her head on his knee everything seemed just about manageable.

He hadn't realised how cold it was but he still continued on down to the cove, out along to the hotel before cutting back up to the pub. Alice had been providing good wholesome meals, so he hadn't had one of Phil's pies for a couple of days. He wondered if he dare sneak one in on his way home.

"What do you think Dolly, shall we go and see Phil? You'd like to see Bowzer, wouldn't you?"

Dolly wagged her tail and trotted up the path. This was a good bit of the coast with only one very steep part right at the end. He'd never worried about it before, but it did occur to him that if he ever had a stroke out here, like Fiona, who would notice? Who would ring to see if he was back? That made him walk a bit faster at least until he could see the first of the houses along the lane.

Bowzer did manage to get up to greet Dolly but soon slumped down again. He seemed to be getting fatter. Derek supposed that now Fiona wasn't around, Harriet had stopped walking him. He'd also noticed that every time someone had a pie Bowzer got a little bit, which couldn't be good for him.

"Hey, Phil. I couldn't have a quick half and an even quicker pie?"

There were a couple of locals sitting at the bar and one couple in waterproofs, with rucksacks at their feet.

"I think I can manage that," Phil said, looking around and laughing.

"I'm a house cleaning refugee. Alice is home and giving the place a bit of a once over."

"Ahh," said Phil. There wasn't much else to say.

While he waited, Derek glanced through an old paper and was drawn to the small ads section.

"I was wondering if I ought to get a cleaning lady," he said to Phil, who was bringing in a clean plate for the pie. "Just to keep on top of things. Apparently I don't seem to notice what needs doing. Do you know of anyone who might be interested?"

"Well Harriet does all ours. It's part of her job." He glanced over his shoulder as if Harriet might be listening. "I'm not sure she'd be the right person to ask."

"She really doesn't seem to like me."

"Oh, now, don't let it worry you. She's always been a bit of an odd one."

"I didn't realise how close she was to Fiona." Derek wrinkled his nose and looked over his glasses, then continued, "I guess if Fiona was missing Alice, the mother daughter thing, then Harriet would have been the perfect fit."

Phil shrugged.

"The thing is, Phil, Fiona never mentioned her."

Fiona hadn't actually mentioned anyone much. She had occasionally passed on a bit of gossip from the local shop. He'd often shared news from the office, but that was because she knew most of them from the early years, when they'd had socials and parties and celebrated getting contracts. They hadn't bothered going to the latest knees-up. It had seemed too much bother and it was always organised for the Friday lunch time when he was working from home.

Derek got up and stretched. The pie had been lovely but he ought to get back and see how Alice was getting on. He also had to face Nick. Derek had sneaked out so he wouldn't have to share the walk with him. It really was quite exhausting trying to think of things to talk about.

***

"Is that you, Dad?"

"Yes. Sorry to have been so long."

Alice came through to the hall. She looked pleased with herself.

"I'm all done. The place is like a new pin."

"Look Alice, thank you. I'm sorry I'm not very good at cleaning. Do you think I ought to get someone in?"

"Mmm, that's quite a good idea. Then you could concentrate on learning how to cook."

Derek hung his coat on the rack which was reassuringly full of their coats and scarves. For a minute he stood and stared, there was something missing.

"I put them away with her clothes."

Fiona's gloves had been lying on the top of the radiator.

"When you're ready to take them to the charity shop, let me know and I'll come down and give you a hand."

"There's no need for that love, I can manage."

"I'd like to," she said, only her voice shook and she started to cry. "Oh Dad, I miss her so much." Derek had not expected this.

He put his arms around her. She was as skinny as a rake. He could feel her ribs through her jumper and he found it disquieting. Fiona had never been fat but you wouldn't have felt her bones like that. Alice didn't cry for long. She wasn't that sort of girl.

"I think you should eat more," he said. "Have you always been this thin?"

She shook her head.

"Dad, some people eat when they're stressed, some can't. I'm not always very good at food and Mum going so suddenly, well it's all been a bit of a..."

"How about we go to the pub and have one of Phil's pies? They're hot and warm and we could buy the children a glass of lemonade. Perhaps you and I could have something stronger," he asked, hopefully.

She hesitated.

"I was going to make some sandwiches. They'd be better for us, and I have a feeling you've been eating quite a lot of pies recently."

"Just this once Alice, let me treat you."

Phil didn't bat an eyelid when Derek returned with Dolly, Alice, Nick, and Sarah. He even went to a bit of trouble, bringing over knives and forks and serviettes. Alice's large glass of wine was generous and the children's drinks were in pint glasses which pleased them.

"You look like you come here a lot," she said.

Derek smiled. He did come to the pub quite a bit. He didn't seem to fit at home any more whereas here, tucked up by the fire with both dogs at his feet, he felt almost happy. That was important.

***

Derek strode up Cross Common Road. Alice had run out of milk. He had eagerly offered to get some from the shop. The two pies for lunch had left his stomach feeling stretched and a little uncomfortable. The walk would do him good.

"Hello," he called cheerfully. It was the other woman, Mrs Lovell, or Miss Lovell, who came from out the back. He thought she lived alone just across the road from him but didn't know much about her. She nodded and sort of stared.

"I need some milk," he said.

"I'll show you."

"There's no need. I know where it is."

But she was already squeezing past the end of the counter. She was quite a big woman and he had to squash back against the shelves so she could get past.

"Down here." She led him to the cold unit at the back. She bent in and handed him a four-pinter. He guessed she knew the family was down.

"Thanks, that's really good of you."

"Do you need anything else?" she asked, and blinked. She

had pale eyes with no eyelashes to speak of. She wasn't a handsome woman. He looked down. He didn't want her to think he was staring.

"That's all. Thank you very much."

He turned and led them back to the counter. She took the money. He was sure he ought to have had some change but she slammed the till shut with a finality that made him grab the milk and turn to leave.

"Bye Derek," she said.

"Bye," he replied, but wasn't sure enough to use her name with any confidence.

Chapter 9

The sun swirled pale colours across the stone flags, apart from three bright dots at the end of the shafts of dust-filled light, from the broken panes. Harriet wondered what the critical number was before Anna had to get them fixed. Outside it was unusually hot and dry for the latter days of spring. Inside the church was cool and her head felt less tight.

The door squeaked a little. She didn't bother turning around. It was either a visitor, in which case they'd soon disappear, or Simeon who would sit as far away from her as possible, so that he could do what she was doing, trying not to be disturbed.

She wasn't due at the pub until eleven, so had plenty of time. Phil liked to have her in at ten, but the day before they'd been really busy and he'd said she looked tired. She'd been grateful that he'd noticed. It had been airless behind the bar, there'd been a change of guests in all of the rooms upstairs and a double beer delivery. There was still just the one bus she could catch so it hadn't meant a lie-in, but it had meant there was time to come down to the church. She needed space because Phil wasn't quite as laid back as everyone thought. These days he expected a lot more from her. She used to get a break walking Bowzer but Derek had started taking him out now pretty much every day. The dog was looking better for it. Harriet wondered if Derek was doing it to spite her, that he knew how much that hour of fresh air had meant.

Harriet didn't like thinking about Derek. It made her angry. Thinking of Bowzer inevitably brought Derek to mind, so whether she liked it or not he was back in her thoughts, rattling about, and from there it inevitably led to Fiona. All the peacefulness fled out the top of her head like the rooks squawking from their nests. Fiona sneaking off for that last walk without her. Fiona being too tired to see her when she'd called round with flowers and a pile of books. Fiona lying in the rain, lifeless. There was no point staying now, so she nodded at the altar and began to make her way down the aisle. The man sitting in the back pew was familiar, she smiled at him, unsure who he was. He stood up and blocked her way.

"Hello Miss Green."

"Hello," she replied, searching her memory for a name.

"Detective Inspector Edwards," he said helpfully.

"Oh, yes." Now she could remember perfectly and he knew it. He didn't bother pulling out his warrant card.

"Would you mind if I asked you a few questions?"

"I've got to get to work."

"I could walk up with you." He stood aside to let her pass, a little reluctantly she thought.

"Are you still working on Fiona's death?" she asked. Her head had begun to feel tight again, a niggling pressure behind the eyes.

"Now, yes. Though it's dropped to the bottom of the pile but the powers that be aren't quite ready to put it to bed yet."

"It wasn't me that rang you," she said, before she could stop herself.

"Then who do you think it was?"

"I have no idea. Believe me, I've thought about it a lot because quite a few people have accused me of trying to make trouble."

"Who thought you were trying to do that?"

It had been Anna mostly in her slightly awkward way, but Phil had also muttered something about not putting off his regulars. Anna had said that unless Harriet had something specific to say she ought to shut up, that she ought to let things be, that she was causing unnecessary pain. "Who am I hurting?" Harriet had wanted to cry, but the inevitable answer was bloody Derek. Bloody, bloody Derek. In the pub there had even been moments when she was sure he was staring at her, wondering perhaps what Fiona had said. What she knew.

126

"Just people."

Tom kept right on looking at her.

She started to walk. Phil wouldn't mind if she was a few minutes late but she didn't want to have to explain why.

"But you were glad we got that tip, weren't you?"

"Yes, I was. Derek didn't know a thing about Fiona. Her hopes, how much she loved him, how angry she was when she thought there might be someone else."

Some days out on the cliffs Fiona had been tearful with frustration. Derek had refused to stop work even to have coffee with her. There was always a deadline. A client needing some alteration to their plans. Even a conspiracy of the partners to get rid of him. He apparently couldn't let up for a second. Fiona hadn't believed any of those things. She'd thought that everything should have been winding down, not ramping up. Harriet thought that all men were the same. They took what they wanted and walked away. Fiona would have been better off without him.

"It's just that who you describe isn't who we can see." Edwards sounded like one of her teachers when she'd been caught smoking behind the bike shed.

They'd reached the bend where it got quite steep and Harriet began to blow. The policeman, she was glad to see, had also started to go pink. She stepped just a little longer.

"We got on well, so she told me things she didn't tell anyone else, that's all." Harriet had to speak sparsely, between breaths. "Who else would there have been for her in a village this small?"

"She was old enough to be your mother."

"Sometimes age doesn't matter. We just seemed to click. I was comfortable with her from pretty much the first day we spoke." Harriet had wondered about the age difference, had wondered whether she was looking for a mother figure. Her own mother rang her weekly only there was never anything to tell her and their conversations had become strained. Harriet had decided she was probably disappointed in her educated daughter. Had hoped for more than just a barmaid after all the money that had been ploughed into her education.

"What else did you talk about?"

"I told her a lot about Ade."

"Who's Ade?"

"My ex."

"Where's he?"

Harriet wrinkled her nose. She hadn't seen him for a while. He'd not been back since the break-up.

"St Ives and London."

"What does he do?"

"He's a painter, a clever one. He knew exactly how to sell his canvases and who to sell them to. He's become quite the thing."

"So out of my price range then?" Edwards put his hands in his pockets. She was half expecting him to pull the linings out.

"Out of most people's."

"Was there anything else bothering Fiona?"

Fiona had begun to wonder if there was someone else. She'd joked about it at first but then it had somehow got fixed in her head. She'd brought it up more and more before the stroke.

"She told me how she felt about things, how she missed Alice, how she felt as though Alice didn't need her any more." They paused just outside the pub. Harriet was reluctant to take this inside. She turned her back to the door, looked down the way they had come. Terry was following them up the road. She stood on the edge of the pavement and looked both ways before she began to make her way across to the shop. Now the policeman's return and who he was talking to would be duly noted by all those who popped in to get a pint of milk. Edwards was silent, waiting. Harriet continued.

"She often said how Derek didn't seem to love her, no

matter what she did to please him." Harriet remembered the first time that Fiona had spoken about that. A glorious morning when they had stopped to catch their breath at the top of a climb out of one of the small inlets. They'd both been breathing hard, like now, and between gasps Fiona had muttered that nothing she'd ever done for him was good enough. Harriet thought she had probably replied something about those that we know best often not knowing us at all. It hadn't seemed anywhere near wise enough but Fiona had nodded, her eyes filling with tears. Harriet had wanted to wrap her arms around her, but had hesitated. Fiona wasn't the sort of woman who invited that kind of contact. Harriet regretted missing that moment. She wasn't normally that reticent, but from then on Fiona had begun to share her fears, the real ones, those she'd not voiced before. It was as though Harriet had passed some sort of test.

To begin with Fiona had simply thought it was work because Derek did love what he did. But then one Sunday he'd mentioned some client whom he'd spent the afternoon with, had said how much he'd enjoyed chatting with her. From that single sentence Fiona had started to worry that he was seeing the woman. A stupid niggle that grew roots. Harriet thought it was unlikely, but as Fiona began to voice it into the wind with tears and clenched fists she eventually began to accept it too, and now she told it to the policeman.

"I think it's quite possible that Derek was having an affair. He was very selfish and don't forget that four days a week he worked in Falmouth." Harriet twisted her hair around a finger. "A couple of times Fiona said she was going to go over, just to have lunch, and he put her off. Put her right off. She was very upset at that."

"Why didn't she talk to him about it or drop by to surprise him?"

"I'm not sure. I suppose she thought he was hardly likely to tell her the truth..." Harriet tailed off, felt uncomfortable.

She didn't know why Fiona had never confronted him. "These things are rarely straightforward."

"Why weren't you with her the day she had the stroke?"

"Because I couldn't make it."

She hadn't been there because Fiona hadn't asked her, because Fiona had gone off slightly earlier than usual. Harriet had waited, waited until it was almost too late to walk Bowzer at all. She'd been disappointed. Had always thought that perhaps they should swap numbers only Fiona could never remember hers and hardly seemed to carry her mobile with her at all.

"Do you think Derek had anything to do with Fiona's death?"

The question was sudden but not out of the blue. Harriet pretended to think about it. For some weeks it was all she had thought about and how she might answer it if asked.

"He had the most to gain," she replied confidently. Derek deserved to be investigated.

"What exactly was that, Harriet? What did he have to gain from his wife's death?"

Harriet thought the inspector was being naive. Sometimes it wasn't simply about money. It was often about control and fresh starts or even simplifying things. Ade had said something along those lines when he'd walked out.

When she'd contacted him to tell him to come get his stuff he'd said she could keep it, as if he were doing her a favour. She'd said that she didn't want it. He'd said, "Dump it. It's not my responsibility now" and put the phone down. She'd been speechless for quite a while, then she'd screamed, raged, and thrown his favourite mug at the wall.

***

Simeon watched Harriet and the policeman leave. He was concerned that the man was back, asking all his awkward questions. He had been relieved when they had seemingly

130

given up on Fiona, because it made it easier for him to forget. Discovering the actual truth of what had happened would complicate things. But even without that, Derek was becoming a challenge, for he had started coming to church, had started meeting Anna in the pub for a chat. He was about the place far more than he ever used to be. Simeon disliked seeing him, for when he saw Derek he saw Fiona. When he saw Fiona he inevitably replayed everything through to its conclusion.

He remembered the anger on the night she had died; how he had tried so hard to calm down, but his conversation with Anna had left him struggling. She had made him leave the church before he was ready to, it felt as if she was wilfully trying to misunderstand him, to control what he was thinking. And then the fast walk to the cove, the wind there blowing the rain into his face. It wasn't fair! Why couldn't he go and sit in the church? Why had Anna become so upset with him? Turning back up the lane, retracing his steps, he climbed into the churchyard through the gap in the bottom. It wasn't difficult, he knew it well. How pleased he had been to see that the church was in darkness, that Anna had gone so he would have it all to himself. He had made his way towards the door, keeping to the shadows, and then, just as he was about to cross in front of the porch to get the key, the movement along the path that had caught his eye. He had instinctively shrunk back as he saw a pale face peering down towards him. It was only for a second as he quickly looked away, pressing into the stones and shadows at his back, staring down at his feet wet with rain and held fast by the long grass. He held his breath and began to count. To begin with really fast because his heart was beating crazily. It wasn't that there was someone there, it was just that he hadn't expected to see anyone there, and in the darkness and the rain he didn't recognise them, it was definitely not Anna. He had got to nearly nine hundred, so it was a good ten minutes before daring to look again. The path was now empty. He was fairly sure there was no one there. But it was too wide, too open to simply walk along, so he scurried across the front of the porch and up to the hedge at the top of the churchyard. Once there, he was well hidden. He made his way along slowly, keeping close to the wet branches even though he knew he was getting very wet, and then just as he thought he'd got his anxiety under control it had happened. He wished it hadn't.

Of course in the end, despite the awful weather, he'd run down to the cove, jogged along the cliff path and from the coastguard station up the lane to his house. He'd had to use his torch in places. By the time he got back his legs had felt weak and trembly, his shoulders had ached with the tension of trying not to fall into the darkness to his left, and anxiety whirled about his head so that he couldn't concentrate on anything. It was days before he began to absorb the enormity of it all.

Simeon always wondered what he would say to the policeman if he ever came and asked about Fiona. His social worker had said he had to tell the truth but had also said that it would be better if he kept his head down. When Simeon had asked him what that meant, the man had said, "Don't ever volunteer anything and never be alone with one person."

Of course he had gone all the way to the Lent talks with Archie. Archie's low calm voice, making everything sound possible, ordinary, he always spoke to Simeon like he was normal. Lots of people had a special voice that they used just for him, even Anna had one.

To begin with he had dismissed going to the talks as impossible. They were something he wouldn't, couldn't even consider, but Archie had been gently persistent. Simeon explained the things he would find difficult. Archie thought about them and by the time Simeon saw him next he seemed to have worked out an answer for everything. They would sit at the back of the hall away from everyone and wouldn't even think of stopping for coffee afterwards. In fact, if Simeon was willing to give it a go, Archie said he would be happy to leave at a moment's notice. Simeon only had to nod and up they'd get. After the second week, Archie had offered him coffee and biscuits back at his house. He'd even started to quite enjoy the coffee though it was different to what he was used to.

Simeon slipped into church. He'd got into quite a routine. He liked routines, they made things easier, more ordered. He would unlock the church, walk all the way round, popping his head into the tower room just to make sure it was still tidy, then he'd sit for as long as necessary until a question popped into his head. He would try the question out on God, out loud if he was sure there was no one else about. Over the days or weeks afterwards he would look for an answer. After the first few replies he'd started writing them down. Archie thought that was a good idea. He had also suggested that Simeon should let Anna know what was going on as he thought that would be nice. But Simeon hadn't quite got around to speaking to her. He would, he had decided, when she asked the right question.

Earlier in the week Simeon had been trying to buy some bread. It was a damp day so there had been a mop leaning against the window and a red bucket full of water where Jean was trying to keep the worst of the muddy footprints from tracking into the shop. He had to lean away from it because the water was grey and scummy, but he couldn't move any nearer the counter because Phil was there buying matches and a pot of jam. Simeon began counting. He decided that if he got past fifty and Phil hadn't left then he would come back later. Jean was talking about Ellie, said there was something that she should have asked her husband but hadn't. Jean said that people never asked the right question because when they did they got the answer they needed, not the answer they thought they were looking for. Simeon had known straight away that that was from God, and that it was about Anna.

When Phil said thank you, nodded to him, and left, Simeon had only counted to thirty-three. That was a good morning.

Simeon was waiting for Anna to ask a question, and he'd know right away it was the one, then he could tell her about what God was doing, how easy it was to hear his voice. You just had to be alert.

Unusually the church wasn't cold, or even chilly, which was nice and made him think of Archie's front room. Whenever he went to the granite house Archie lit the fire, had even started having it laid ready just in case, simply because the first time Simeon had been there he'd said how he liked to be warm. Feeling cold, or worse still shivering, made him feel as though he couldn't think properly. Archie took notice of such things. Simeon appreciated that. Archie always let him sit down first, even asked where Simeon would like him to sit. Simeon had stopped going to visit Anna. He was scared she might cry out again. Like Fiona's dead face it was something he'd been trying to forget, though Archie said that if she had done any crying recently it was in the privacy of the vicarage.

Archie had told him that he was asking God whether to speak to the archdeacon about Anna. He didn't want to because it felt like going behind her back. On the other hand, he felt it was his duty to make sure she was alright and if she wouldn't talk to him perhaps she might talk to the archdeacon. Simeon had already decided that being a churchwarden was an awful job. It was fuzzy at the edges. Archie didn't seem to be able to work out where his responsibility began and ended.

Someone came in. Simeon assumed it was Harriet. She sometimes popped down in the afternoons if Phil could manage without her. She wasn't hard to walk past. But suddenly the church felt chilly and dark. Simeon thought a cloud must have moved across the sun, though he knew the temperature wouldn't have dropped that quickly, so it must have been one of those moments when your body reads the signals wrong. He shivered and stood up to leave. He would go and find Archie.

It wasn't Harriet sitting at the back but Terry Lovell. She was harder to walk past but not impossible. At least she wouldn't look at him, or try to engage him in conversation. She usually wore flat soled shoes, scuffed brown leather lace-ups. Her feet were tucked under the pew so he couldn't be sure what she was wearing today. It had always been how he decided how old someone was. Older women wore comfy shoes, younger women often wore things that were unsuitable. Not all young women of course because he had noticed that some of the school girls wore flat boots with laces that he imagined would be very comfortable once you'd walked them in. Harriet never wore heels, neither did Anna. It wasn't his best rule, there were too many exceptions.

Simeon walked past Miss Lovell out into the air. He felt fine until he reached Fiona's tomb. He stopped and laid his hand on the granite top, gritty with the fine mud brought in by the last storm. He couldn't help himself, which was upsetting because he hadn't had to do this for weeks. He was stuck, couldn't turn away. He caught the flash of her eyeballs and had to squeeze his own eyes tight shut, so tightly they began to hurt. He would never make it to Archie's. He had to go home. He wrenched his hand away and began to run, rubbing the palm up and down his coat to get rid of the grit sticking to his fingers.

He was glad in the end that that's what he decided to do for just as he reached the front door a shower came slanting in over the headland. The drops were needle sharp, he had to plunge his hands into his pockets and bow his head to protect his face. He could see the beginning and end of the cloud, a big fat cushion sitting over the village, getting heavier and lower, it made Simeon struggle to breathe, and though he was quite hungry, he didn't eat his tea-time sandwich but hid under his blanket until the next morning.

Archie sat and waited. He'd been sure that Simeon would pop in and for a moment he mulled over a gentle sensation of disappointment, which he hadn't expected. Simeon asked difficult questions, mostly about God, that Archie couldn't answer, had never thought of before. He had to write them down and then once Simeon had gone he would go and search for some form of answer. Together they drank coffee and ate biscuits, far more than was good for them, and he lit the fire even on warm days. Simeon made him feel as though he was doing something useful so he didn't give up waiting until the weather really closed in. Not until the village roofs disappeared under a blur of grey. Now and again there was a flash of light where a thin shaft of sunlight made it through, catching one of the roof tiles, shiny with rain, but it wasn't nearly enough to lift his spirits.

***

Derek had gone to bed feeling scratchy and cross, had woken with the same sense of powerlessness he'd felt just after Fiona had died, a little less acute to be sure but enough to make him feel very sorry for himself. He'd then spilt coffee over the counter top, missed a phone call from Alice, and taken an extra half hour to get into work, road works and cows in equal measure. He knew Alice worried if they didn't manage to speak every two or three days and he didn't want her to worry. It was the last thing she needed, with her busy schedule, the kids and their demands, and missing her mum so much. He'd also received an email from an impatient client. Veronica Lawrence, he thought, why can't you cut me a bit of slack like everyone else? She must not have realised how difficult life was for him at the moment. He couldn't place her. Thought that was probably the grief. He found so many things difficult to remember.

In this case there must have been a crossed wire because

she'd sent a new list of dates to his own personal email. Normally one of the girls in the office organised such things and they weren't supposed to give out this particular address. He wasn't sure how she'd managed to get past them. She seemed very keen to meet. It made him quite irritated, then angry for it crossed his mind that the front desk had been bypassed by one of the partners just to annoy him. He really shouldn't have to deal with such things, not so soon.

Usually he enjoyed meeting clients, working out what they really wanted, rather than what they thought they wanted. But he was beginning to realise that those nice chats with new people had been nice because Fiona had been waiting for him at home, because his whole life had been alright. Now his days were hard edged and difficult and he couldn't get away from the feeling that Fiona was watching him. It was as if the loss of her, the pain, had distilled down to the sensation of being brooded over.

Derek realised he'd been staring into space for some while.

"Dolly, how're you doing?" he whispered, bending down to pull one of her ears. She had curled up under his desk as usual. She lifted her head and looked up at him, but she knew it wasn't time to go home so she had a bit of a shuffle round and went back to sleep. He pulled out the brief for the Maslens. They wanted a conservatory that wouldn't get too hot in summer or too cold in winter, but gave them a view of the sea through a tiny gap between a row of houses built just below them. He wondered whether he ought to point out the horse chestnut sapling growing in the neighbours' garden, which would in a few years make the whole view thing academic, but somehow it felt like a deal breaker and he didn't want to give the company any excuse to question his usefulness.

The Maslens had been one of the last site visits he'd made before Fiona's stroke. Their home was like the rest of them in the road, grey concrete render with brown upvc windows, and

137

when he'd pulled into the drive he'd almost wanted to cry. It was a dull and practical house. There wasn't an unnecessary twiddle or clever design feature to be seen anywhere. The funny thing was that when he'd got back that evening his own bungalow had the same effect on him. It just wasn't the sort of house he'd imagined ending up in. For goodness sake he was an architect. Couldn't he do something, anything to make it a bit different, less functional?

About one o'clock Dolly began to whine. She was right, he'd been working long enough. He would take her for a good walk when he got back. More emails had come in. He didn't open them. They would have to wait.

Chapter 10

Anna was thinking of Ellie. The conversation they had had over a bacon butty at Easter had stayed with her as spring had given way to a rather pleasant summer, at least there were some quite lovely days here and there. Living on the peninsula you expected rain. When it didn't come sidling across the sea, it was disconcerting. She had noticed that most of the locals carried some form of mac with them at all times.

Anna decided to write to Ellie. Not an email but an actual letter. On the kitchen table was a biro and a pad which she'd bought from the shop. Of course she could have asked Jean how Ellie was getting on but that would have placed her between them and Anna didn't want that.

All through the Easter holiday she had bumped into Ellie, had noticed her standing in odd places watching the horizon, looking over her shoulder as if she were waiting for someone. With Ellie it was easy to see what was going on inside her head, and Anna hadn't felt at such a disadvantage as she did with the others. Ellie was someone who was easy to read, easy to talk to, and perhaps because she lived somewhere else the responsibility seemed less onerous. In the end Anna had invited her to lunch. Ellie had seemed surprised but had agreed. They'd met at the pub because Anna wanted to keep it low key, hadn't wanted it to be a big deal. It had worked too because Ellie had talked endlessly about why her husband had found someone else. Anna wondered if taking the blame so completely for the breakdown was entirely healthy but she wasn't sure how to put that without making it sound as though Ellie was slightly deranged. She was certainly worn down and a little dried out, but if she could only make a small effort, Anna thought she could be quite lovely. Worrying about the extra weight was nonsense – she looked wonderfully slim. In the end Anna suggested that perhaps

Ellie ought to go home and sort things out one way or the other, that staying with her mum was not doing her any good. She had been completely taken aback when Ellie had silently contemplated what she'd suggested and that it became a moment of decision for her, apparently the one she'd been looking for. Suddenly she was hardly able to contain herself, had rushed off to pack even though the kids had wailed and Jean had been a little bewildered. Anna was then worried that because Ellie had gone back so unexpectedly she might have found her husband at home with his girlfriend and made comparisons. As usual things in her head became a bit muddled and knotty. What if Jean blamed her for Ellie's swift departure? She decided that being there for someone sometimes meant not being there for someone else, which felt uncomfortable. Only that was a feeling she was used to, so didn't spend too long worrying about it.

The letter was grinding to a halt and she'd barely filled half a page. She could hardly just write a list of questions. She would have to intersperse them with bits of news, and that was proving difficult. Why would Ellie want to hear about the weather and how much of a struggle Anna was finding writing her sermons? She got up and had a hunt for some stamps. Couldn't find any and that felt like a good enough reason to get up and walk to the shop.

***

"I shouldn't have asked her to look after the shop for so long. She simply couldn't cope with it," Jean said, stacking shelves with some new biscuits that Anna thought she might try. "It's a good job Ellie went back earlier than planned. Do you know one day I found she'd given up on the till altogether and had simply started putting the money in a bowl under the counter." Anna assumed Jean was talking about Terry. "It meant I had no idea what had been sold and I had to do a mini stock-check. It took me ages."

140

"Have you heard from Ellie?"

"Yes," Jean said, straightening up from the box. "I wish she'd throw him out, so she could get on with her life. She's a very bright girl and could have had a proper career but now she's got three kids and will have to work part time in something horrible and convenient."

That didn't sound like getting on with life or making the most of her intelligence.

"Could she come back here so that she's nearer you?" Anna asked, while scanning the shelves for anything else that would be nice to try. She didn't normally have time for such a good look and it helped temper the feeling of emptiness brought on by the fact that no matter who she tried to help it didn't seem to make a bit of difference. Ellie and her husband were doomed and she'd been stupid to think there was hope of any kind.

"Do you think she might?" Jean answered, stopping again. It had obviously never occurred to her. "What job could she get round here? And how would I manage to run the shop? To make it pay we have to stay open such long hours."

"Oh and we wouldn't want to lose you. That would be a disaster," Anna added, quickly. "Don't worry, I'm sure Ellie won't do anything rash." Anna could imagine what a difficult position it would put Jean in, trying to juggle the children with the opening hours. There was always Terry to help out but Jean did the majority of the work. Anna watched confusion wrinkle Jean's forehead; it aged her so that it became hard to guess how old she really was. In her head Anna said calmly, 'I'll pray for you both', but she couldn't say it out loud.

"I know you're praying for Ellie. Thank you for that, Vicar," Jean said, her face smoothing out a little. "She's found it really comforting. She used to be very interested in religion at one point and the last vicar when he first came ran a sort of youth group. He had quite a few of the youngsters interested.

Of course when he went and... you know, that left them wondering what it was all about."

"He must have been so unhappy." Anna pictured the poor man sitting in one of the huge rooms back at the vicarage weeping and desperate. What made it worse was that in the kitchen there was a wife and on the school bus were a couple of kids who would never be the same again. Poor old Archie had been his churchwarden. Anna felt a wave of guilt at her cry of despair. She'd not thought about that at all, thought how difficult Archie would have found it, found her after last time.

"A little selfish not to see how it left everyone," Jean continued. "Can you imagine what his poor wife went through?"

"No I can't. Or your Ellie. I didn't know she'd been involved with him."

Anna decided she simply had to finish the letter. She couldn't let Ellie down too. She must go home and get it done. This was another layer to Ellie and her failing marriage and though Anna felt there wasn't anything she could do for her all the way up in Stockport, she knew she had to try.

When she got back Derek was coming down the drive with Dolly. She took him through to the kitchen.

"Tea?"

He only had coffee before midday.

"Yes, please. Not disturbing you, am I?"

"Not at all." Though the idea of the unfinished letter sat at the back of her mind, a pleasant feeling of something to do later, something that mattered. "How are you?"

"I'm still only doing mornings at work."

"That's good," she nodded encouragingly. She put the biscuits on a plate and found some nice mugs from the back of the cupboard.

"Do you have much on at the moment?" she asked.

"Yes. No, actually not a lot."

"Oh, ok." She was surprised by his honesty. Recently she hadn't been sure he was giving her anything more than what he thought she wanted to hear.

"I think it might be time to do something new but..." He picked up a biscuit.

"It needs to be your decision, not theirs."

"Yes," he said, and his head drooped a little. "You understand."

She didn't really but patted herself on the back anyway because she had seemingly managed to say something that had resonated with him.

"How is your decision making in general?"

"Better. I sometimes wake up and know what I want for breakfast. Though I still wish I were a dog. Fewer choices all round, you know."

"Look Derek, you're at a very early stage of bereavement. I'm not sure you're ready for any of the big life decisions yet, certainly not one as important as what you ought to be doing."

"But they're going to want me to come up with an answer to that in just about three weeks' time. In some respects I can see where they're coming from. I've only got one decent job on the go and I only have that because they thought it was a bit of a non-starter."

"Would you like me to speak to someone?" That shocked her. Who would be interested in her opinion? They were professional men and women!

"Would you? That would be wonderful. I really don't feel as though anyone is on my side at the moment and you understand about Fiona. What a shock it was, how much I miss her, how much it has stopped me from being myself."

Now she was in trouble. She had no idea what he'd been like before. She wasn't even sure that back when Fiona was alive, she would have been able to recognise him if he'd wished her good morning.

"Is there anyone in particular I ought to direct myself to?"

"Martin Hammond. He's the senior partner though he's still quite young." Derek wrinkled his nose in distaste, as if being young was akin to having some unpleasant disease. "He has a lot of clout with the others, brings in a lot of the high end projects."

"OK, I'll speak to him. Leave me a number. They can't force you to leave, not just like that."

She watched him sip his tea. There was something else, she was sure of it. She pushed the plate of biscuits towards him.

"I think I may have messed up. There's this woman, Veronica Lawrence..."

This was it, she thought, the moment when he was going to confess to the affair and she'd have to ring Tom Edwards and tell him. She felt a bit sick.

"There are certainly a lot of women about the place," she said, smiling a little manically she felt. He looked puzzled. Of course he looked puzzled. What an odd thing to have said.

"Well, there is one in particular."

"That's fine, isn't it?" What was she burbling about now? She needed to shut up and listen. Instead she said, "Did she ever meet Fiona?"

Oh God, Anna groaned deep within. Now she was feeling hot.

"No, I don't think so." He frowned. "Perhaps that is how she knows me. Perhaps she knew Fiona before she had the stroke, before she..."

"Died," Anna said helpfully, and then realised she was sounding strange. She needed to get a grip.

"Only recently she's started sending me emails."

"What about?"

"Dates, lots of dates. Normally I wouldn't worry except that she seems to have got hold of my private address. I thought one of our secretaries had made a mistake but they have all denied it. None of them can remember speaking to her." He took a biscuit, broke a bit off, and gave it to Dolly. "To begin with I simply didn't get round to replying, but the last couple have been a bit insistent. She keeps talking about when we meet for coffee, as if I have made some sort of promise about a job. I think I must have dropped the ball somewhere..."

"Oh, surely just tell her that you're still feeling the loss of your wife keenly and that one of your other colleagues would be happy to go and see her. Then if there has been some sort of misunderstanding she won't bother you again."

"Oh, that's good. That's very good. Would you mind if I wrote it down?"

"No, of course not."

He pulled out a well-used notebook.

"I seem to be forgetting things a lot so Alice suggested I carried this round with me. I must say it's been jolly useful."

Anna thought it had been her who had suggested the book. She said, "Perhaps I ought to get one."

"£1 at the shop. I'm sure Jean will be delighted to sell you one."

"How is Alice?"

"Not that great. Understandably she's missing Fiona a lot and I'm never quite sure what to say to her. Because I feel so vague about a lot of things I'm a bit worried about offering any advice."

"It certainly is difficult finding the right words. But I'm sure she'd appreciate you listening anyway." That made Anna think of Harriet who she hadn't seen for a while. She kept telling herself that it was because she knew this was the busy season, and that Harriet would be flat out at the pub. But that wasn't it at all. Anna had felt that her dealings with Harriet had got a little complicated and that she hadn't necessarily been as kind to her as she ought to have been.

In Anna's defence she hadn't seen that much of anyone

over the last couple of months. Simeon was nowhere to be found and even Archie hadn't popped in to church as much as usual. Jean and Terry were about the place but Terry wasn't exactly easy to talk to and whatever she talked to Jean about would be round the village in no time.

"I need to do some visiting."

Derek leapt to his feet.

"I knew I was keeping you."

"No, I didn't mean now."

"Well I'd best be off anyway. It's time to fetch Bowzer." Dolly got up and shook herself.

"She genuinely seems to know what we're talking about," Anna remarked, in wonder.

"I expect she just needs a wee," Derek replied, laughing.

For a moment she got a glimpse of a quietly handsome man, with dark eyes and a nice smile.

***

After another cup of tea Anna decided to lie in wait at church for Simeon. But first she had to go and find Archie. It felt a bit like a chore, like cleaning the loo, a job she often put off for as long as possible only to feel really virtuous once it was done.

His house sat heavily and as sharp edged as ever even though the lawn was surrounded with pretty shrubs and velvet roses. There were even a couple of pots filled with geraniums either side of the front door. They looked cheerful but were not dramatic enough to compete with the austerity of the house. She pressed the bell. She couldn't hear it ring, and pressed it again. She imagined poor Archie sitting in his lounge hungry for visitors while streams of them stalked off in disappointment because he'd not noticed the bell was broken.

"Vicar, how nice to see you. Do come in."

"Call me Anna. Am I disturbing you?"

"Not at all. There's only me and Simeon."

He had turned away and was walking back to the lounge so Anna was left standing motionless, half in, half out of her coat. Simeon was here! She thought Simeon only ever came to see her. Yet why shouldn't he be at Archie's? They'd gone off to the Lent course together, and Archie had managed to get him to come to church most Sundays since. They must have become quite good friends. Except that Simeon didn't have friends. Did he? There it was, that nasty scratchy feeling of the little girl not asked to the party. The one left out, unthought-of, neglected. She hurried after him, shaking her head to clear away the nonsense. She needed to be a grown-up.

Simeon nodded but didn't get up, in fact he hardly acknowledged her at all. The fire was smouldering in the grate and the room was desperately stuffy. She undid her cardigan.

"Can I get you a drink... um Anna?" Archie asked.

"She will have a cup of tea, a dash of milk, and no sugar," Simeon said.

He spoke matter of factly. Anna wanted there to be an element of smugness about the way he'd said it. Looked for a sense of it amongst his words even though she knew it was unfair to judge him so.

"Do you happen to have something cold? It's a bit warm in here," she replied, sweetly.

"I'll get you a squash," Archie answered.

Anna couldn't decide which chair to sit in. In the end Simeon pointed at one and said, "Archie is sitting on that one so you may choose any of those that are left."

"Thank you Simeon, how kind of you." She hoped he didn't detect the sarcasm in her voice.

"I'm sorry I haven't spoken to you for a while," Simeon said, while staring at his shoes. "I've been waiting for you to ask the right question. But Archie pointed out that you couldn't ask me the right question unless I was with you."

So he had been avoiding her. She wasn't even of use to Simeon any more. She drew in a deep breath and told herself to stop being childish.

"Oh. Does Archie know what the right question is?"

She hoped not, with all her heart. She couldn't bear to be replaced so completely by Archie.

"No. Of course not. I'm not even sure I will know straight away."

She was relieved.

"So how are you finding church?"

Not just words, a question she genuinely wanted an answer to. Except what if he hated it?

"I don't sing because it's too echoey in the tower room, so I just read the words. Archie said I could take a hymn book home to give it a proper clean so that I'm comfortable using it. I've hidden it so that no one else will be able to use it." He glanced up briefly. "Your sermons always end on a question that you never expect people to answer because you never give us enough time to think about what you've said before we have to start doing the next bit."

She blinked slowly. So much information.

"I'm sure I don't always end on a question."

"You do," he said, flatly.

"Well, I've never pretended to be much of a preacher so I don't suppose I expect people to want to think about what I've said." Anna knew she sounded peevish, but she couldn't help it.

Simeon risked another quick look at her.

"You're not going to howl, are you?"

"I didn't realise you'd heard that."

"Yes. It made me feel very uncomfortable."

"I'm afraid I wasn't thinking about you at the time."

"What were you thinking about?"

The futility of my life, she thought.

"Oh Simeon, sometimes I can't put it into words."

"Is that why you sounded like an animal?"

Well surely that was just downright rude. She turned to look out the window. Staring at the top of his head in the hope that he would look up was a waste of time.

"I don't know."

"That's the first time you have ever said that to me." He made it sound like a good thing.

Archie appeared with a tray, another plate of biscuits and a tall frosted glass. The squash had been poured over ice but was still squash and despite the temperature she would have loved a cup of tea.

"Simeon says I hurry the services too much. There's not enough space between things."

"He could be right," Archie said, carefully. "But Simeon, not everyone is as good as you at mulling things over. Not straight away anyway."

"Then what's the point?"

"Well, sometimes the things that Anna says come back to me later on in the week. Often when I'm washing up, as it happens. I think about them then."

Anna smiled at him, gratefully.

"Because we're all different, so that what suits me wouldn't suit you or Jean or Mr Harris?" Simeon said.

"Precisely."

Anna sat back. This was exhausting.

"We've been trying to get to grips with the word community," Archie said, turning to her. "We tend to try and talk about it once or twice a week."

"We often end on a question that we don't know the answer to and then we go away to think about it," Simeon continued.

So why were they allowed to end on a question and she wasn't?

"Or look it up on the internet," Archie said, smiling. Anna hadn't thought that Archie would even know what the

149

internet was. "There are some very interesting sites and it's made me get the old Bible out again."

"Well that's wonderful," Anna replied, because she thought that's what she ought to say, that she ought to be pleased with such a positive sign of life within her church. Simeon flashed her a look. He was frowning.

"Reading your Bible is a good thing," Anna continued. Simeon still frowned. "At college we were expected to pick it up every day and of course we always said the morning service together."

"How wonderful to say it daily." Archie actually sighed.

"It wasn't that wonderful," Anna said, remembering. "We used to have to get up ridiculously early and often spent most of the time trying not to fall asleep."

"Why are you a vicar?" Simeon asked.

"Simeon, I think that might be a bit too personal," Archie said, quickly glancing at Anna. She was staring at her hands, noticing that her nails were grubby and there was a dry patch on the edge of her thumb that was starting to itch a little.

"No, I can answer that," she replied, lifting her head to look at them both in turn. She even noticed the fine lines around Archie's eyes and that Simeon could do with a shave. "First of all, do you have to gain pleasure from something for it to be of worth? And secondly, I was called. It's the only thing I'm certain of."

"God is a kind God," Simeon persisted. "The bishop who led the Lent course said that a lot. And if he's kind, why would working for him make you howl?"

She wondered if he would understand the depth of sadness, uselessness that she had felt. The yawning hole she was leaning into.

"Let it go, Simeon. I was particularly sad that day, but if I'd known you were outside then I wouldn't have made such a noise." Archie shook his head, just a tiny bit. He was right. She wasn't sure she could have stopped that awful welling-up.

Simeon continued, "It's just that sometimes I can't help remembering seeing Fiona lying there and with your horrible screeching it's spoilt a place I've always felt safe in."

Anna looked at him, surprised. "I didn't know you'd seen Fiona. I thought you had left before... When did you see her?"

Simeon became very still.

Archie came to his aid. "It wasn't a great day for any of us. Poor woman lying there in the dark and Derek nearly tripping over her body."

Simeon shuddered.

"Don't worry," Archie continued quickly, "we won't talk about it any more."

Anna thought they should but then Archie might be right, he usually was. She needed time to think. The clock on the mantelpiece chimed. She should go. Archie placed his cup carefully down beside Moira and followed her to the front door.

"Archie, I didn't know that Simeon had seen Fiona, I thought he'd gone straight home. We need to find out when, because Derek didn't leave her side once he got to the churchyard. Simeon must have been there before that. He might have seen something."

He might have done something, she thought.

"The police thought the timeline was really important," she ended lamely, as she remembered that of course she must have walked past Fiona when she'd gone back to check the church, too caught up in her own misery to notice the woman lying there.

"Oh you know Simeon, he probably peeped into the tent when the forensic people were on a break or something."

Anna didn't think it was the sort of thing that Simeon would do. He was much more likely to sit behind his tomb and listen.

"I don't know," she replied, suddenly very tired. "But you ought to try and find out what he meant."

Archie frowned at that but as she walked away he called after her, "Come back again, it was good having you here. We can get off track sometimes and you are very adept at seeing through to the important bits." He spoke brightly, cheerfully, and Anna thought irritably that he had no intention of asking Simeon anything.

"Archie," she said, swinging back to face him, "I'm not very good at seeing through to the important bits. Really I'm not."

She was about to turn away when he replied, rather fiercely, "So you're basically saying I don't know what I'm talking about. But actually, in this case I think I do. So please try to be a little kinder to yourself and to us."

He closed the door, gently, but he might as well have slammed it. It was too much for Anna. Archie had always been so kind, but even he was turning on her now. It was only just three o'clock but she would go to the pub. Phil wouldn't be unkind, and surely it wasn't too early to have a small glass of wine. Why not?

Chapter 11

Anna sat up at the bar and waited patiently until Phil noticed her. He was reassuringly normal and poured a large glass, though she'd only asked for a small one. When she took a long swig, he said, "You look like you've had a tough day."

"Nothing worse than normal," she replied. "Only I think I'm losing perspective a bit."

"I'm not surprised. You're all on your own. Who do you bounce things off? Who do you go to when someone's asked you a really difficult question?"

She was a little bewildered.

"But you don't have anyone either."

"Actually I talk to Harriet. She's surprisingly useful at the end of a hard shift, though sometimes," he chuckled, "I think she listens because she's too tired to answer back." He wiped around her glass. "I also ring my brother when I need some serious perspective, if I'm really not sure what to do."

Anna thought of her family, her mum, her sister, her two nieces, and her newly born nephew. She'd rushed up to see them just after the latest birth, bought bunches of flowers for everyone, had even bounced a bemused toddler on her knee while her sister fed the baby, and then had driven back down the M5 feeling that she'd done something important, something she could tick off her list.

"I'm not sure I have anyone, Phil."

"Precisely."

"Perhaps I need a support group," she said, half laughing.

He smiled and nodded. It made her want to run home. Do a Simeon. When he was hiding, it didn't matter who came to the door. He stayed under his blanket until they went away again. It suddenly seemed a sound principle and very inviting.

"Hello, Vicar."

"Anna," she said, swinging round. "Why can't people call me Anna?"

"Because I don't know you that well," Tom Edwards replied, quietly.

"I'm so sorry," she said, picking up her drink and taking another large gulp.

"What can I get you? Tom isn't it?" Phil asked, in cheerful landlord mode.

"A half please." He hopped up next to her.

She hadn't realised how useful it was sitting on a bar stool. You didn't have to look at the person beside you unless you wanted to. She didn't want to catch anyone's eye just now.

"How are you?" he asked.

"I'm fine."

"You look cross."

"It's just that I've tried and tried to get people to call me Anna only no one seems to want to."

"May I call you Anna?"

"Yes, that would be humanising."

She wasn't sure she cared whether Tom called her Anna or not. It was Archie, Phil and Harriet, Derek, Simeon, even Jean and Terry. They were the ones that mattered. Why couldn't they simply remember her name? Perhaps she'd start calling them parishioner one, parishioner two. See how they liked it.

"Well, Anna, why are you so cross?"

She thought she'd just told him.

"Because I'm not very good at my job."

"Ahh," he said quietly, "I don't expect you're the worst vicar there ever was."

"Very reassuring." Particularly as he wouldn't really know what she was like.

"I really don't know you well enough to comment," he said, taking a sip of his beer.

"Then why did you ask?"

"Because that's my job, remember?"

"So you weren't asking me how I was, not really. It was a question relating to the job."

"Well actually, it's my day off, so I was asking you how you are."

Anna shook her head.

"I am very confused," she said.

"Let me get you another."

Drinking away the afternoon was the sort of thing other people did. Still, what the hell? She wanted to be normal for a change. The pub was quite busy, and Phil was at the other end of the bar so she was quite impressed when another large white wine appeared before she'd satisfactorily argued herself out of it.

"Go on," Phil said, so quietly that she thought Tom couldn't possibly have heard, "let your hair down for a change."

So she had a mouthful.

"I've got a couple more questions for you," Tom began.

"I thought it was your day off."

"It is, but I wanted to follow up on something." He took another drink. "Has Derek ever mentioned another woman?"

"Possibly, though it sounded like a bit of a misunderstanding. Derek came to chat to me earlier about how to handle someone called Veronica, I think."

"So what have you discovered?" He sounded interested. She glanced across at him. He was looking round at her, and smiled, encouragingly she thought. She turned back to her drink.

"Derek said she'd emailed a few times with dates. Like she expected them to meet. He can't remember her; thinks perhaps she might have been friends with Fiona."

"Do you believe him?"

"Yes." Anna turned to look at him properly. His dark hair was swept off his forehead, but only because it was probably the easiest way to deal with it. In fact he needed a haircut. He had a small mouth that he often squashed together as if he were trying to hold everything in, a thin face with dark eyes that widened when he didn't believe you, and his shirt could do with a bit of an iron. There was nothing polished about DI Edwards. Anna had answered him quickly only she wasn't really sure whether she believed Derek or not. About what precisely? That he didn't know this woman or that he thought she might have known Fiona?

When Derek had talked about the emails, he had looked thoroughly miserable, confused even. But she could imagine someone getting the wrong end of the stick. He could be quite vague sometimes, leaving you wondering where his conversation was leading. He had this way of talking that willed you to be on his side. He might easily have said something that had mislead the woman, drawn her in without realising it. Anna began to feel a little sorry for her, sitting alone somewhere waiting for Derek to set a date for a promised coffee.

"Do you think Derek could have been having an affair?" Tom asked.

Anna made the jump in her mind.

"I don't know. Are you thinking that some girlfriend might have…" Anna simply couldn't bring herself to say it.

"Well, we're still not sure." He turned to look at her. She just knew he was studying her profile. She dragged her fingers through her hair. "As long as you don't think there is anything else to add," he said, as if she were the pin around which everything hinged. Anna bit her lip.

"I don't think Derek knows what's going on half the time. He still isn't in a great place. He's missing Fiona a lot, and this Veronica woman is probably just a needy client wanting someone to talk to. Add to that the fact that his colleagues seem to be trying to get rid of him and I think we could use the word vulnerable about him without being too dramatic."

"Not such a bad vicar then?"

"I don't know what that's got to do with anything," she said. "But Fiona's death hasn't really gone away. It's still

156

affecting some of us quite badly."

"Who else is still upset by it?" he asked.

"Well, Harriet for one and, of course, Derek, Simeon."

"Who's Simeon?"

Anna stopped. Would Tom understand Simeon?

"Just one of the congregation. But he's special."

She couldn't believe she'd just said that.

"I'm sorry Tom, too much wine. I must go. I've got loads to do."

She slipped rather inelegantly off the stool. Bowzer yelped when she trod on his paw and backed away when she bent down to apologise to him.

She almost jogged home. Two glasses of wine on an empty stomach had been a bad idea. She wanted to sleep, to hide under the duvet. She was drowsy and muddled, but knew she still couldn't give herself permission to go and do that so early in the day, was worried someone might come to the door needing her, so she curled up on one of the chairs in the back room, where she kept a useful throw for the chillier evenings.

***

"Look Terry, that policeman is back and he's going into the pub. Didn't the vicar go in a little while ago?"

Terry was checking milk supplies in the fridge at the back. She thought it was ridiculous doing it every day but Jean kept meticulous records. Jean said that a shop could get a terrible reputation if it ran out of staples. Terry was a little annoyed because she'd only popped in to get some tea bags. Jean had this way of taking advantage so while Terry was doing her job for her, Jean was staring through the door with nothing better to do than gawp. By the time Terry had made her way past the shelves the policeman had disappeared inside.

"I wonder why he's back this time?" Jean asked, though Terry didn't bother to reply. Jean tended to answer her own questions. "Perhaps they've found some more evidence. I wish

157

they would. Every so often I think there's still a murderer out there!"

Terry would have been surprised if they had found anything new. They didn't seem to have done a particularly thorough job considering it was such a serious crime. For a start no one had interviewed her or Jean. A young constable had knocked on her door the evening of the incident and had asked if she had seen anyone or anything out of the ordinary. She hadn't of course. But she had seen the comings and goings of various people which she would have been happy to have shared but the police didn't seemed particularly interested.

Terry had been looking after the shop for Jean for well over an hour that afternoon. Of course Anna had been about the place and Mr Wainwright went down to the church every day to check on things. Terry had seen the barmaid walking the fat dog from the pub down to the cove, along to the lifeboat station and up. Terry often saw her mincing along, dragging the poor dog behind her. Now that Derek had taken over the walking, the dog was looking trimmer. Derek was a good man.

"I wonder if he's taken a shine to our vicar? She could do with a bit of love in her life."

Terry almost laughed out loud and said quietly under her breath, "She's got God. That should be enough love for anyone."

"What was that?" As per usual Jean didn't wait for an answer but turned back to the door. "She could do with making a bit more of herself."

***

Anna woke to the doorbell and dragged herself upright. She didn't remember falling asleep and it was gone seven. She was also very thirsty. The hall was dim and whoever was waiting had been content to ring only the once. She knew immediately who it was and hesitated, wondering whether he

158

could see her, a small patch of dark in the dimness. But it was no good. Whatever happened she couldn't hide. She pulled open the door. His hood covered his face, his hands were in his pockets, and she knew they were clenched into tight fists.

"Simeon," she said brightly. "Come in. You haven't been round for ages."

"I'll come into the hall. I don't want a cup of anything so I don't want to go through to the kitchen."

"Ok. What can I do for you?" She forced herself to sound cheerful.

"You broke a confidence. I can't trust you any more."

She'd thought he'd stopped trusting her after the howling incident.

"How exactly did I do that?"

"You told the policeman I was in the churchyard when Fiona died."

"I did not."

She felt guilty. She remembered feeling as though she had given something away. She had thought it was more that she had called him special, or even that she'd mentioned him at all. She'd only known what he'd let slip at Archie's – that he had seen the body. Oh, God, she muttered, this was serious.

"Then why did he come to my house asking me what I know?"

"All I did was mention your name and that you were still upset by Fiona's death." Except suddenly she couldn't be sure that that was all she'd said. It had only been the two glasses of wine but it felt like more.

"He came and banged on my door, showed his warrant card. Said I would have to talk to him or he'd take me to the station for questioning."

"He can't do that, Simeon, not without cause."

"I don't think people like me always get treated like people like you."

People like you! Anna didn't want to think about what sort

of person she was right now. Certainly she wouldn't use the word integrity. She was running behind events, certainly not shaping them or better still standing aloof from them.

"My social worker always said to keep my head down because I might get blamed for things I didn't do."

"Simeon – that was an awful thing to say. It simply isn't true."

"You're not me, and that is how people treat me, all the time."

"Is that why you didn't say anything?" He nodded.

"What did he do?" she asked, desperately.

"He asked me what I knew about Fiona's death. He asked me why I hadn't come forward. He said he had better things to do with his time than follow up old leads."

"So what did you say to him?"

"Only that I'd seen someone else leaving the churchyard and that I'd had to walk home along the cliff."

"Is that all?" Which sounded as if she thought he had more to say. She quickly added, "Why did you take such a crazy route home? It was an awful night." But the word she instantly regretted was 'crazy'. Simeon straightened and took his fists out of his pockets.

"I'm not crazy. I was just upset. I'm going home now."

"Simeon, I'm so sorry," she called to his retreating back, but he was already turning up the drive and hurrying away, head down, shoulders hunched. He looked hunted. She shut the door and leaned back against it. She was almost sure she hadn't told the policeman anything important but it wouldn't have taken more than a couple of conversations in the pub to find out who Simeon was and where he lived. Barging into Simeon's home would have shaken him to the core. She wasn't angry now, she was ashamed. She bolted the front door and switched off the lights. She made hot chocolate from a packet and took herself to bed. She'd been right. She should never have gone to see who was ringing the bell.

It was still bright outside but she pulled the curtains, carefully overlapping them. She lay on the bed fully clothed until it got dark and then she slipped into a nightie. She ought to have changed the sheets, they smelt musty, but it was all too much effort. She stayed there for hours, heavy and still, but didn't close her eyes until a grey-grubby light began to filter into the room.

**

Harriet watched the rain dribbling in through one of the broken panes. It trickled down the inside of the window leaving a dirty track down the plaster. It was a shame they didn't work harder at keeping the church clean. As far as she could see, all it needed was a bucket of soapy water and a scrubbing brush. She rubbed her eyes. Lately if she stopped still for even half a minute she felt the achy tiredness of not enough sleep. She was so tired of being tired, had even considered visiting the doctor for something, because no matter how hard she worked through the day, two thirty in the morning she would wake. She would lie there tossing and turning, ending up staring at the ceiling trying hard not to think of Fiona. Sometimes it was that last walk, just before her stroke. When she had left early, leaving Harriet waiting, waiting, waiting. And sometimes she was in the churchyard standing over her. At that time of night her thoughts were unruly, so that she often didn't get back to sleep.

She breathed deeply. Sitting in church was good but she needed to get a grip as she only had half an hour left for herself.

Someone came in. Harriet didn't move. There was absolute silence which was a bit disconcerting, as if whoever it was was simply standing there. So not someone she knew. She turned slowly. They must have noticed the movement for by the time Harriet had twisted enough to see who had come in they had gone, leaving nothing more than a sense of their presence.

After that Harriet didn't feel comfortable with her back to the door so she moved across to Simeon's seat. She slid right to the wall and sat against it, her legs stretched along the pew. Now she could see the door without being seen and just hoped that Simeon didn't turn up. This was his space and he wouldn't understand sharing it. She rubbed her eyes again. She was weary. The summer was warm but it was happening too quickly. The thought of winter weighed her down. The darkness that began and ended the day, her skin tightening and drying. She hated all that. Her mother always said she just had poor circulation but Harriet knew it was those dark months dragging at her soul. She examined her long slender fingers. Artists hands Ade had said, only she hadn't been able to draw for toffee. Her fingers were bare, Phil didn't like her wearing her rings at work. So she'd got used to their absence and hardly bothered with them any more. Great big chunky things that Ade had liked, that had caught on her clothes but sparkled in the light. There was the sound of footsteps. Only Harriet didn't tense like last time because she knew who it was. Anna bustled in.

"Hello," she called to her around the pillar.

"Harriet, you look cold."

"I am a bit. And tired."

"It's that time of year," Anna said.

Harriet wondered what Anna meant. It was lovely outside. Warm and balmy. She supposed she'd sat too long.

"To be honest, Vicar, I'm feeling a bit down."

"Still missing Fiona?" Anna asked.

"Of course." Why did everyone expect her not to miss Fiona any more. Like recovering from a cold. Are you all better now? Derek was allowed to wallow, and look miserable. Why wasn't she?

"Sorry," Anna said coming to perch on the end of the pew. "You can miss her as long as you want to."

"Thanks." Harriet didn't bother to hide the tinge of

sarcasm.

Anna smoothed her coat over her knees. It was her usual one, her only one, and Harriet thought she could do with something less grubby and functional.

"You ought to buy a new coat. That one's looking a little tired."

"I like it. It's cosy, though you're right, nowadays it doesn't always keep out the rain."

"We could take a trip to Helston. There's quite a good outdoor shop on the high street."

Anna looked surprised.

"I'd like that," she said.

"I'd just like to do something that wasn't the pub. It's been a miserable few months, and I need a change."

Anna picked at her fingernails.

"Say it, Anna. There is obviously something you'd like to get off your chest."

"There's nothing in particular. Really, there's not."

Harriet waited. She knew that in a moment or two Anna would blurt out whatever it was that was simmering.

"It's just that Derek is..."

"Ah, Derek! Your number one parishioner."

"I just wish you would talk to him. I listen to both of you, and you both loved Fiona. It's sad that you can't be a bit kinder to each other."

Harriet's eyes filled with tears, at last not because of the absence of her but because finally someone got it. Harriet's reaction to her death had been harsh, deep pitted, surprising. So yes, she had loved Fiona, and been disappointed in her, and angry with her, and so many other things. Anna passed across the pack of tissues she always kept in her pocket but didn't say anything more for a while. She must have realised that this was an important moment for Harriet.

"What would I say to him?"

"I don't know." Anna sat straighter, stretched her back, and then leaned forward. "Forgiveness might be a good thing to explore."

"You want me to say I'm sorry."

"No, I'm not sure that I do. But allow him to have loved his wife in his own way, to have loved her with all his flaws and blindness." As per usual Anna was close, but not spot on.

"He can love her any way he wants. I would just like the right to have loved her too. In my own way." That was it. Just there. That was what she'd been trying to say for weeks.

Harriet was already late getting back to the pub. Phil wasn't cutting her half so much slack as he had to begin with, and Tuesday was one of their busier days. She squeezed past Anna, patting her on the shoulder as she passed.

"I'm sorry Anna, it's not as simple as you'd like it to be."

Harriet left her hunched in the pew. She knew it was unkind of her to leave her so, for Anna was the most tangled of them all, always having to weave carefully between her muddled parishioners and her own deep pain that no one was allowed to touch. Still having the last word was sometimes the only thing Harriet felt she had left.

***

Derek was relieved that he'd made it through to Friday. He pulled on his coat and picked up the lead. Dolly was sitting at his feet. Though it was chilly outside after a couple of days of rain, it wasn't unpleasant. He needed to think about work. He'd needed to get out of the house, to get away from the empty desk. The guys at the office were putting together an agenda for the partners' meeting and had asked him what he wanted to add. Anna had said she would talk to them but he didn't think she had yet. He'd also sent an email to the client about not having coffee with her, using Anna's wording almost exactly. He hadn't heard anything back and each day that had gone by had left him feeling more and more relieved. He'd been quite surprised at what a burden she'd become. A splatter of raindrops fell around him. He turned into the church. He decided to wait out the shower inside, it wouldn't be long. He could already see blue sky out in the west. He walked halfway down and sat.

Someone came in behind him. He didn't bother to turn round until they came and stood at the end of his pew.

"Harriet!"

"Hello Derek." Dolly was already up and tugging to get close to her. He let the lead go. Harriet knelt down and wrapped her arms around the dog.

"Hello old girl. Have you missed me?"

Dolly's tail said she had. She even reached up and licked Harriet's face. Derek looked away. There was a flare of jealousy at Dolly's enthusiasm. The only other person she had done that to had been Fiona. He could do without this, he really needed to think about the practice, but he couldn't get past her, not without climbing over the back of a pew.

"She has missed you, by the look of it." His voice came out high pitched and whiny. He cleared his throat. "You could always have come out from behind the bar to see her, any time." That was true. It wasn't like they didn't go to the pub almost daily.

"I wanted to, but I thought you could probably do without me crying all over her."

"Oh." What was he supposed to say to that? Dolly was now sitting next to Harriet, leaning on her. Harriet remained on her knees, her arms tightly around Dolly. He hoped her pale trousers would be covered in dog hair.

Harriet began to blink tears and said quickly, "Anna has had another go at me, says I'm being unreasonable."

Derek didn't reply but looked towards the door. It was suddenly outlined in sunlight, and looked very inviting.

"It's just that," Harriet continued, her voice getting smaller and smaller, "Fiona and I talked a lot, about life, about all sorts of stuff. She was quite unhappy."

Fiona hadn't mentioned anything to him about being unhappy. But then he didn't remember them talking much beyond Alice, the grandchildren, and sometimes the weather. Certainly there hadn't been much about... life and stuff.

"She never said anything to me."

His voice like hers had shrunk away to nothing, as if the walls of the church had squashed them both down to Lilliputian size. Tiny people in an enormous moment. He began to cry. He hadn't wept for Fiona for quite a while. Of course he still experienced the sudden crushing sadness that often came out of nowhere but there had been no actual tears. He wasn't sure he was crying for her now. In fact he was pretty sure he was crying for himself. Fiona was alright wherever she was, but she'd left him alone, had left him to manage without her. It wasn't fair. All the things he thought they'd do together once he'd retired he would now have to do alone and he didn't feel up to any of them, couldn't imagine a time when he would. Surely if she'd been that unhappy she would have said something? Should have said something? But she hadn't, not as far as he could remember. The stroke had been a different matter. She had kicked and struggled against that relentlessly, angry about what she could no longer do. When she had first come home she'd been so emotional, so desperate. Not something he was used to. Fiona had had a temper but she'd never been vulnerable, frightened. He'd even taken to sneaking Dolly out for her walk when he thought Fiona was asleep, always a little anxious that when he returned she'd be awake, ready to grill him accusingly on where they had been, how long Dolly had been off the lead, how she had behaved, etc. It was exhausting and he wasn't sure how he would cope if she didn't come to terms with her new limitations.

Harriet leaned across and offered him a tissue. He hesitated before snatching it, the anger burning in his face.

"You're not kind," he shouted.

"You don't get to shout at me like that." Her voice was shrill.

Pulling a very reluctant Dolly, he managed to get past Harriet kneeling in a shaft of cold sunlight. She looked like some kind of stone saint.

**

Simeon ducked down behind a gravestone. He'd heard the raised voices, and had to sit down and breathe slowly, to quell the rising panic.

"Hello, Simeon," Derek called loudly, "I can see you. I don't know why you bother hiding."

Simeon couldn't wait any longer. He had to get home. He left by the gap in the hedge at the bottom of the churchyard so he wouldn't have to pass the tomb. He was far too upset to do that and it was also the afternoon that the flower ladies tended to come down to make their arrangements. Facing an upset Harriet was bad enough, bumping into anyone else would be beyond his control. He didn't see Jean disappearing into the churchyard, and, if he had, he would have known that she had overheard everything.

**

That night Simeon was unable to sleep and it made him feel achy and disconcerted. He supposed he might be going down with something for not even lying motionless and monitoring his pulse helped. It was something he particularly worried about, getting sick, because that gave people permission to interfere. He hoped his insomnia was because he was still upset with Anna and now Derek, who really had no reason to get cross with him. Anna ought to have played by the rules and Derek had always seemed so gentle before. Speaking like that to Harriet was out of character and Simeon liked people to behave within their boundaries. He knew he needed to talk to God. Archie had said he could pray anywhere but he wanted to go in to church. It was where he was used to going and he needed to feel comfortable until these horrible feelings went away. Trying to pray somewhere different was too much like trying something new and he wasn't ready for that.

***

When Harriet finally fell asleep she had nightmares. She was climbing through a rubbish dump, sliding backwards, her shoes filling with squashy, smelly things. She knew that if she could just get a little higher she would find Fiona. But then she didn't want to climb too high in case she did find Fiona. When she woke late she made strong coffee and opened the windows. There was a slightly peculiar smell in the flat. Probably her drains, which she daren't complain to the landlord about. She still didn't want to give him any excuse to update the place and increase her rent. She ran lots of water into the sink and splashed some bleach around. As she left for work she noticed a rather foul rag lying on the door mat. Honestly the place was getting disgusting. She'd probably walked it in on the bottom of her shoe the night before. She carefully picked it up and dropped it into the wheelie bin on her way to the bus.

Chapter 12

Simeon walked up the path to the church. The grass needed cutting, was spilling onto the path. He preferred it when the gardeners had been, with their strimmers and shears, imposing some sense of neatness. The door was already open. If it was Archie or Anna he would be alright but anyone else and he'd need to back out quickly to go and wait in the graveyard. Jean and Terry arranging the flowers was the worst. He didn't like the chaos, the dead flowers in a heap. The bunches of new blooms unevenly poked into the stands. A long time back he'd got trapped because Terry had spread her debris across the main door. He'd had to listen to the snip of her scissors and the crunching, grating sound of stems being forced into the soggy green oasis. In the end he'd pulled his hood tight and made a run for it. That day she'd worn walking boots with lime green socks poking out the top.

He also hoped it wasn't Derek as he peered round the door. He wasn't ready for another telling-off quite so soon. The church was empty, which was odd. They weren't supposed to leave it open unless someone was there. He would have to tell Anna when next he saw her. He took himself across to his pew. His heart began to slow almost immediately.

"Thank you," he murmured. "But I couldn't sleep last night as you know and this is the first time I've felt calm since the policeman came to see me, even though someone has left the church unattended which isn't allowed." He sighed. It felt good to get a good lungful of air right down into his ribs. "I guess I'm what people call uptight, or stressed." That made sense. "Ok, God, I am uptight. There are lots of causes. That policeman coming into my cottage, Anna letting me down, not protecting me, and of course Fiona." She would never go away. "Please stop me seeing it."

Anna had let him down badly. His social worker had warned him not to be too trusting, that people might let him down. Unfortunately, he hadn't said what to do about it. Worst of all Simeon hadn't expected it of Anna though logically he should have. It was inevitable.

Archie came in at the back. The door squealed just a little. Archie had put lots of oil on it once Simeon had mentioned it to him. Simeon listened to the quiet rumpling of paper as he sorted out the noticeboard. Any old leaflets and posters went into his pocket to be taken home and recycled. Then there was the familiar quiet rhythm of him running his fingers along the hymn books, straightening them up, making sure they were all there. He guessed that at some point Archie would let him down too, but he hadn't done so yet. Simeon decided to ask him what he thought he should do about the things that were upsetting him. "Archie," he said, without turning. "I'm stressed about what happened with the policeman and I couldn't sleep so now I'm tired. In a minute I'll go home and rest but before that I want to ask your advice."

Archie came and stood at the end of his pew.

"I'm not very good at advice, but ask away. I'll do my best."

Archie folded his arms across his chest and then put his hands in his pockets as if he had forgotten himself. Then just as Simeon was about to begin he folded his arms across his chest once more. Simeon waited a few seconds for him to settle.

"It's Anna. I thought she was my friend but she sent the policeman to see me and she must have known how hard I would find that."

"Did the policeman tell you exactly what Anna said?"

"No."

"What did Anna say she'd said?"

"She said she'd mentioned my name. Nothing more."

"Well Simeon, we live in a very small village. Do you know everyone in the village?"

"I don't know all their names."

"That's not what I asked. The people that you see about the village, including the ones you don't know what they are called, do you know where most of them live?"

"Yes. Of course I do. I have also worked out that forty-seven per cent of the houses are holiday homes."

"So if the policeman thought, I've not heard of Simeon before, I wonder what he's like or where he lives, do you think that a lot of the people around here would be able to tell him at least a little about you?"

Simeon sat very still.

"But why would she have mentioned me at all?"

"Well perhaps we were on her mind because she was upset when she left us."

Simeon was used to taking the blame for things. There had been a miserable few years before his mum died when they'd taken him out of his usual school and sent him to the local comprehensive. He'd seen his social worker a lot during those months and the headmaster. His mother was having her treatment so she couldn't come and be with him. He remembered that feeling of growing incomprehension, as he was blamed for something he truly didn't understand.

"I think Anna is struggling and what I said to her couldn't have helped," Archie continued. He was blinking a lot and his hands were now clenched into fists. "I basically told her she was too hard on us, and on herself. That must have left her feeling... well I don't know."

Simeon shrugged.

"Perhaps feeling left out," Archie said. "You didn't tell her that we were going on the Lent course and neither did I. We didn't think she'd be interested. But when she found out she was disconcerted. Then you didn't tell her about your notebook of questions, so she didn't know how helpful she'd been. We didn't invite her to our talks. She just walked in on us. You know what that's like."

Simeon was still trying to work out why Archie seemed to

be making excuses for her.

"How did you feel when you thought that Anna had let you down," Archie continued, "when you realised she had given your name to the policeman?"

"I couldn't sleep. It kept going round and round my head."

"You said that you felt stressed, didn't you?"

"Yes," said Simeon. So had they caused Anna to feel stressed but over a number of weeks? Had she also experienced that awful disconcerting scratchiness that he felt, as though his insides were on the outside? "What do we do about it?"

"First of all, I think, you have to forgive her."

Simeon frowned. So to help Anna he had to forgive her?

"I've been reading some of Moira's books and though it is a bit simplistic I've learned that forgiveness isn't necessarily about allowing the other person to understand what they've done to you, or even that they need to be sorry. It is more about you letting the sense of injustice go. After all Moira isn't around to apologise to me." Archie swallowed and looked away.

"How do you do that, Archie?" Simeon asked.

Archie snapped back to the present. It took him a few seconds to remember where they had got to. He thought he could just about answer that.

"Well, I tell God what the person did and how I feel about it. Then I ask God how he feels about the person I'm cross with and then I tell him I forgive them for whatever they've done."

Simeon tipped his head to one side.

"Who do you have to forgive?"

"I... Moira... One day, Simeon, one day."

Archie's back began to twinge, so he slid into the pew opposite.

"It can't be as simple as that though, Archie?"

"No, I think if you've been hurt very badly it can take a

172

long time. That you keep on having to say I forgive you until it becomes real."

"Like me with Anna?"

Archie dropped his voice.

"No, I was thinking more of murder or rape."

"So like Derek and Harriet."

Archie hadn't wanted Fiona to have been murdered, but he'd found that he wasn't one bit surprised at the open verdict. There simply wasn't enough evidence but surely the police should have made some progress by now? Was it always going to be unsolved, leaving the community watching and waiting for someone else to die? Who on earth phoned the police to get them to look at it again? It made Archie worry that someone knew something important but was holding it over them all. Simeon was waiting to say something. Archie looked at him and nodded.

"Harriet is still upset about Fiona. She comes into church a lot and she has been very angry with Derek. Perhaps she believes he is to blame. Archie, you should talk to her about forgiveness, it would help her feel better."

Harriet had been the obvious candidate for the phone call but Anna said she absolutely denied that it had been her. Archie didn't think that was something she would have lied about.

"Simeon, do you think Harriet really believes Derek hurt Fiona?"

He could see that Simeon didn't know where to begin to answer that question. After a while he said, "Would you like to read the book about forgiveness?"

"Yes. I would."

"It will certainly be a lot more eloquent than me," Archie continued.

"But what shall we do about Anna?"

Archie folded his arms.

"I'm not sure. Perhaps we ought to go and see her?"

Simeon didn't like that idea. Anna could be quite unpredictable when she was upset.

"Together?"

Archie had another think.

"Ok, let's say sorry separately and see where that gets us. But wait until Monday – tomorrow is a busy day for her."

That made Simeon feel lighter. Archie could go first and tell him what happened.

"Only I thought you said forgiveness, why have we got to say sorry?"

They were in church another half hour unravelling that one.

***

"Derek," Anna said, "come in."

The knocker had been used rather heavily, making her think she should take her Mondays off. She'd thought it might be Simeon or someone with a package. He looked... uptight, she decided.

"You look... upset." She decided that telling someone they looked uptight might not be helpful.

"I'm angry, I hope you don't mind."

"With me? I'm quite used to people being angry with me." She turned away and began to walk down the hallway.

"With you?" Derek followed her. He couldn't imagine Anna doing anything that would make people rage, rage and spit, which is how he felt. "No, it's not you. You've been..."

Derek paused. She had stopped to peer back at him. Anna hadn't made the best of herself that morning. Her hair was pulled tight in a ponytail but it looked greasy and her skin looked dry. She was pale and there were dark rings under her eyes, fine lines around her mouth.

"Have you been crying?" He surprised himself. It was quite a personal question to ask.

"No, just not sleeping that well. I'm going to make coffee."

"Yes, please. And I'm not really angry, just ashamed, and I suppose a bit hurt."

Anna nodded. He slid onto his normal chair. The table could have done with a bit of a wipe and he noticed the floor was grubby too.

"We both need a cleaner," he said. "I'm sorry, that wasn't meant to sound..."

Anna looked around. She supposed it was a bit unkempt but because the lino was brown and swirly she hadn't really noticed. Come to think of it she couldn't remember the last time she'd moved any of the things crowding the work surface to wipe underneath them.

"I think I need a new kitchen."

"A bit drastic, but yes, I think you could do with something a little more practical. Can't the diocese do something? It's a bit sad and it can't be nice coming home to a great big barn of a place when you're on your..."

"Perhaps I should take in a lodger," she said quickly. She couldn't bear the thought that even Derek was pitying her now.

"Perhaps. Though I bet Archie could get them to organise something more manageable, something with central heating. There are enough houses for sale round here and if they didn't want to sell this place surely they could rent it out, particularly if they spent a bit of money on it." He looked round and sighed. "It could be lovely."

Anna couldn't see it. She couldn't see anything. She was tired and Derek was right, the place was awful.

"I don't know if I can keep this up much longer."

"What? The vicarage?"

"Being a vicar."

Derek laughed. Anna thought he was probably wondering how hard the job could be. She wanted to remind him of the awful days just after Fiona died. That sometimes it had its moments. She shook her head and sighed too.

"I suppose I can keep going just for now so you can tell me why you're so upset."

Derek told her about Harriet.

"She actually came and spoke to you?" Anna said in surprise.

"Yes, but it does feel particularly mean because there isn't anything I can do about what she said, except wonder why Fiona felt so unhappy and ask myself why she didn't talk to me. I've spent the whole weekend trying to work it all out."

"Did you talk much?"

"Yes," he said, firmly, remembering their Sunday lunches. They had chatted quite happily about all sorts of things across the dining table. What colour they wanted to paint the garden fence or whether they ought to get a new bed for the spare room. They'd had quite a few conversations about whether to take Dolly to the vet because she was so stiff in the mornings and whether to take out that blasted hedge. Maybe, with hindsight, none of those conversations had been particularly deep and meaningful, they hadn't been about life and stuff.

"She did tell me how much she missed Alice and we even talked about moving to be near her, but we both love living here. Loved living here, and it felt as though we hadn't given it a fair chance."

He did remember there had been the odd conversation about going to the pub for lunch on a Friday, and she had mentioned walking Dolly together more often. He'd always hoped there would be a time when that would be possible, when work was less intense. He'd said as much and she'd seemed satisfied.

"Was she jealous of anyone?"

Derek stared.

"I don't understand."

"Was there anyone at work you mentioned that she might have thought that you..."

"Why would mentioning work upset Fiona? I really don't get what you're trying to say."

"It's ok, just something Harriet said." Anna looked down at her hands, then began to pick at the crumbs.

"What did Harriet say?"

"Oh, you know how Harriet's been." Anna wouldn't look at him, and it was quite difficult to hear what she was saying. "I think she misses Fiona terribly and is trying to find someone to blame for her loss."

Derek wanted to cry out, what about my loss?

"Did she make Fiona think that I liked someone else? How could she know anything about me, except what Fiona told her?" And he pushed his chair back, his face crumpling, his eyes blinking tears. Dolly, who'd been lying at his feet, stretched and stood up expectantly. "That's awful. Fiona must have thought there was someone else. She may even have died thinking I was having an..."

"No, Derek, I'm sure that's not the case."

"That policeman asked me the very same question. I just assumed it was routine but what if other people thought I was having an..." He couldn't say it out loud. "Fiona wasn't always easy to live with but I would never..." He started to sob, slumping into his chair and dropping his head onto his arms. Anna grabbed the kitchen roll and pressed some into his hand. Dolly was sitting with her head on his knee. Anna came and stood behind him, and patted his shoulder. Then she made coffee and found some biscuits.

"Sugar in some form seems to help," she said.

When there were just long juddering sighs, Anna pushed a cup towards him. For a split second she was jealous of his grief, purely because it was rooted in their marriage, their love. Only then she remembered the moment in church when her despair had surged into her throat. How dreadful it had been, how out of control she'd felt.

She wanted to say how awful it was of Harriet, only that

was far too simplistic and though Harriet had implied all of those things about Derek at one time or another she hadn't recently. That wasn't what was really bugging Anna. What was upsetting her was that she should never have told Derek that Harriet had said those things in the first place. Her conscience was twisting and turning, she was unable to see where her perfidy, her meanness, began or ended.

She pushed the coffee a little closer and the biscuits. He picked up the cup and sipped it.

"Do you think the whole village thought I was unfaithful?"

"No, absolutely not. I don't think they thought about you and Fiona at all." Which seemed a little harsh even though Anna believed it was true. "It doesn't matter what anyone thinks. It's what you know that is the point."

For the briefest moment Anna wondered whether there was more to Derek's account of the death of his wife.

"That's not the case though is it, because I have to go on living here. And Harriet may have said things."

Anna desperately wanted to make things right. She wasn't handling this well and Harriet was getting unnecessarily blamed.

"Have you experienced anything other than kindness from anyone except Harriet?" She thought of those Derek would have the most dealings with. "Phil?"

"No, he's been great."

"So Phil's alright," Anna persevered. "What about Jean?"

"Jean and her boxes of slightly odd makes of biscuits. She's started stocking my favourite crisps and once she told one of her customers that she didn't have any coffee because she was saving the last one for me."

That was just like Jean. She was very protective of the locals and their needs.

"So Jean is ok. Who else?"

"Archie. Archie was great about the funeral and always has time for a chat whenever I come to church. I know he doesn't find it easy but he's a good bloke."

"Yes, he is... a good bloke." Not words that Anna would have naturally used, but they did describe Archie well. She began to think that perhaps she had been a bit hard on him, only he had been quite harsh on her when they'd last spoken. That door shutting in her face had been difficult.

"Even that woman from across the road has been kind. She always asks me how I am."

"Terry? Goodness, I can't get her to talk to me at all."

"Perhaps she would if she thought you needed it."

Anna didn't think that sounded like Terry.

"Some people are just kind," he said.

"I suppose we're not that great at cutting each other slack." She obviously hadn't meant him too but he was nodding.

He said, "You don't when you're grieving. It's hard to think of anyone but yourself, much too hard."

"But I'm not grieving, I've not lost anyone."

Only she had. She'd lost Peter to Frances and God hadn't been there for her of late. Only God didn't usually turn his back on you, so perhaps she'd deliberately shut him out to wallow. That was more like it. At least that's what she would have said to one of her parishioners.

"Derek, you need to hold on to what you know is the truth about you and Fiona, to grieve your loss of her. There will be things you regret not having said or not realised, in which case if I were you I'd go and tell God about them, see what he thinks. And I'm here whenever you need me. The next few months, years even, may not be easy because you were together a long time." She sighed. "You're not going to get over this just like that."

When he'd gone Anna began to walk about the house. She couldn't settle. During that conversation something had happened. Something had changed though she couldn't work out what. And she'd forgotten to tell Derek that the day before she'd had a chat with his boss about how vulnerable he was. She was glad she'd plucked up the courage because the last hour had most definitely proved her right. It made her step towards the phone again. There was something else she'd been putting off.

"Hello, it's Anna Maybury."

"Hello," the archdeacon said carefully. "What can I do for you?"

Anna heaved another sigh.

"I need to reconnect with my spiritual director, but it's been a long time. I'm not sure I'd be able to find the number and I'm not convinced they were the right person for me."

"Oh, well that's easy. I have someone you could talk to that I think would be a perfect fit." There was a pause. "I actually went through three before I found the person I wanted to see."

"Three. I thought you got what you were given."

"Well, we don't want you to swap about without some consideration but I don't think you'd do that. You're far too..." She held her breath while the man searched for the right word. "Far too sensible to change something that important without being sure."

Ok, sensible wasn't terribly exciting but surely he'd implied that she was a sticker and not simply a failure. Anna wrote the number down carefully.

***

Harriet was elbow-deep in washing up. The dishwasher was on the blink again but she enjoyed the simplicity of turning the boozy debris into racks of sparkling glass. They had been rushed off their feet over lunch time, which felt good. Phil now had her making sandwiches rather than just heating pies and they were proving popular, though they did tend to leave the kitchen in chaos. Most of the fillings ended up scattered round the work surface as if she had deliberately thrown them about no matter how careful she tried to be.

"Harriet, can you make me a list for the cash and carry? Those sandwiches were great."

"Thanks. Though I think we need a better system," she said staring about her. "It's hard keeping up with the orders, and managing the drinks."

"Perhaps now and again we could get an extra pair of hands in. It's just difficult knowing when we're going to be that busy." He wiped along the edge of the draining board with a bar towel. "But I think we manage quite well, we're a good team."

She followed him back through to the bar. She'd never thought of them as a team.

"So are you ok?" Phil asked, "You came back from church last week looking a little upset."

"Oh, I'm fine. I'd just bumped into Derek and tried to talk to him about Fiona only he got really upset. He said I was mean and I've got to thinking he might have a point." Phil wiped the already spotless bar with his towel but didn't move away so she continued. "I liked Fiona, we talked a lot. I talked a lot. I miss her. There's Derek getting all the sympathy. Yet I don't understand why Fiona didn't talk to him about her worries. Why didn't she tell him how sad she was?"

"He doesn't strike me as the sort of man you'd have difficulty sharing stuff with," Phil said slowly. "Of course, he's not himself at the moment, and I didn't know him before."

"His Fiona is so very different from my Fiona. He seemed bewildered when I said how unhappy she'd been."

"Oh." Phil began to polish the beer taps as if his life depended on it. Harriet slumped.

"I know. Cruel or what?"

"A wee bit harsh, Harriet. After all he can hardly go and sort it out with her, can he?"

"I know," she sighed. "And I don't know how to take back what I've said to him. I feel dreadful."

"Give him a couple of weeks to calm down and then tell

him how awful you feel. That you realise you made a mistake."

"But that was probably the last straw. If I were him I wouldn't want to come anywhere near me ever again. In fact I expect your profits will dip alarmingly."

Phil laughed, as the door opened.

"Pint and a pie, Derek? Or would you like to try one of our sandwiches? Hey, Bowzer, your girl's here."

Harriet flushed pink and fled to the kitchen.

Chapter 13

Anna's heart sank. The woman was tiny, looked about eighty, and for a moment Anna wondered if she'd come to the wrong address. She stepped back smiling, to check she'd got the right house number. The woman looked up into her face and nodded, turned away without a word. Anna followed her in.

"You can call me Irene. A drink?"

"Yes please."

"Tea or coffee?"

"Tea, please."

Irene brought through mugs of tea, and home-made biscuits on a yellow-rimmed plate. There was more silence. They sat back in their chairs and stared, Anna over Irene's left shoulder, Irene straight into Anna's eyes. Anna felt as though she was in some old western. How could this lady with her grey velour cushions and her uncluttered, dust-free house help her?

Leaning forward to pick up her tea, Irene asked, "So what do you want from me, Anna?"

Anna didn't know what to say to that. She studied the whorls on the carpet for a moment. Irene continued not interrupting her.

"I honestly don't know. I just don't want to feel like this any more."

Irene nodded.

"So let's start with where you're at. I'm only willing to see you if you're willing to dig deep, to tell the truth. Otherwise we may as well talk about the weather and I'm not the person to do that with."

She didn't sound eighty at all. She sounded like Anna's old headmistress.

"Shouldn't you be gently gaining my trust and..."

"Is that what you want?"

"No. I don't suppose it is. You won't tell the bishop how I

feel though will you?"

Anna had meant it as a joke, to lighten the intensity of the room. Irene seemed to take her seriously.

"I promise not to blab to the bishop unless you are being abused of course."

Anna smiled. You weren't allowed to promise true confidentiality to anyone nowadays. Child protection, vulnerable adults, elderly parishioners, there was training for all of them.

"Where would you like me to start?" Anna asked, because she didn't have the first clue where to begin.

"Wherever you think you'd like to, then go back a little further. Set the scene for me."

So Anna started just before her calling, when she'd been a middling English and Philosophy student with a rather clever boyfriend. Irene listened. She had to, there was no space for questions as it all came pouring out. There was Peter and his marriage to the perfect Frances, her own mum and sister becoming a chore on the list, the fact that even Simeon and Archie didn't need her any more, Ellie and her marriage and Anna's sense of powerlessness, her inability to reach Harriet even though they were both so lonely, and Terry who left her feeling so inadequate. It was all there, piled up behind her eyes, a dam that was starting to crack, a dam that was beginning to leak and tumble.

Irene finally went to make more tea, and came back with the tray and a fresh box of tissues.

"Do you want some homework?"

Anna blinked in surprise.

"I don't know. Are you supposed to give me homework?"

"I can do whatever I want. I'm your spiritual director, not your boss."

Irene picked up the biscuits and waved them under her nose.

"Have a couple, you look like you need them."

So Anna did and through the crumbs she managed to say, "Ok, so what homework?"

***

Archie waved to Jean in the shop. She was standing by the door as he crossed the green. He'd have to pop in on his way back and pick up some more coffee. Perhaps it was time to tell her he'd given up sugar. He bought it because she stocked it especially for him, but most of it went to the food bank in Helston. They never lacked for sugar lumps in their boxes.

It was a dry morning but dull. He always tried to appreciate the small things around him but this morning nothing caught his eye. Puddles were just puddles, and there hadn't been a single bright dandelion growing out of the kerb. The shops were shutting down for the winter, the only brightness were the vans coming to do the seasonal maintenance. A couple of ladies from the bungalows were shuffling around the triangle. He didn't stop to chat as he'd only seen them the day before, so had already caught up with their news, the antics of grandchildren with names he ought to be better at remembering. They called good morning, and he nodded back. Today he was heading down to the church to sit. Archie wanted to pray for Anna. It felt important, something he could do.

The church was locked up tight, which was good. He studied the roof and the guttering. Made sure there was nothing blocked or spilling over. It was just as well to nip such things in the bud. Later he must ring the gardeners so they would come one last time to mow the grass between the graves. They didn't really like to beyond the end of September but it was what they were paid to do and Archie didn't like it when the grass got too straggly. The key was under its rock and the door only squealed a little. There was a limit to what he could do about that because it was the bottom of the door that scraped over the flagstones and it wasn't the sort of door

185

you could simply take off its hinges. It was the sort of door you bolted shut, where the key was too big for your pocket, so no one ever took it home by accident, like a castle. He closed it behind him, dropped the catch, and walked to the old tenor bell at the back. He ran his gloved fingers over the metal and then walked to the front. It's what he did whenever he came in. Facing the altar he waited. It was freezing but that made it feel right. If something was worth working for, suffering for, then it was worth doing. When he was really uncomfortable he began to ask God to be with Anna. To help her get over whatever it was that was gnawing away at her soul. Then he prayed for Simeon, because his life would never be straightforward. And of course he prayed for Derek, that he would find some measure of peace again. By now his back was twinging. He asked God to forgive him and to help him once again forgive Moira.

He'd been quite nonplussed to realise that he'd been holding on to some quite complex feelings about his long-dead wife. One day after putting away a couple of biscuits left from a Simeon visit he was suddenly reminded of the number of times he'd come back from a walk to find crumbs all over the work surface. He'd teased her about it, though he had also been a little annoyed she hadn't bothered wiping them away. But over the years that annoyance had blossomed into something far larger, something that had begun to eat away at him. She should have taken better care of herself. She didn't like going to the doctor and had wrapped that up in not wanting to bother them. But what if she'd had pains and simply ignored them? He was sure he'd caught her rubbing her arm now and again. When he'd mentioned it she'd said something about a strained muscle. Her heart attack had come out of the blue, but perhaps it needn't have. Wasn't that selfish? Had she thought of him at all? Her death had meant leaving him all alone for a very long time.

These were the thoughts that woke him in the night, that

were there lurking at the edge of his shaving mirror in the morning. To begin with he'd not even felt able to whisper them to God, only they wouldn't go away. Then he'd noticed that the Psalms were full of that sort of stuff, only much bigger, larger, more important hurt than his. So he knew God probably wouldn't mind hearing his smaller concerns. It had still been difficult, but he found that if he whispered the pain and the what-ifs it helped. It was a forgiveness of sorts.

A pain shot down his leg. He needed to move. He'd be alright once he got going. Everyone was alright once they got going.

**

When Anna got back she walked down to the church. Irene had told her to sit there an hour a day. She had also had to promise Irene she would make it as comfortable as possible so she'd brought a cushion and a blanket from the vicarage and made herself a cup of tea. She wasn't allowed to read her Bible or write anything down, which Anna thought was strange and very un-church-like. Also, annoyingly, Irene wouldn't tell her what she expected. She just said to do it and see what happened.

So far nothing had happened. She idly planned putting in a loo but there wasn't an obvious place anywhere, not without negotiating three steep little steps. She thought about whether she might speak to Archie about selling off the vicarage. His face would be a picture. Then she wondered, at great length, what she thought might happen in this hour of nothingness. Wasn't this simply what she had tried to do before, pray in church? Though she supposed technically it wasn't praying, as she was just sitting. Irene had made that quite plain. She heard familiar steps.

"Simeon."

"Am I disturbing you?"

"No... yes. It doesn't matter. I haven't seen you for ages.

I'm so sorry I gave your name to the policeman, DI Edwards."

"Thank you. I have forgiven you. Archie said I had to and he showed me how to do it."

"Did he? I must ask him about that." Anna shook her head, frowning a little. "It's obviously worked whatever it is he told you to do."

"Not the first time. In fact I have tried to come in to talk to you seven times. This is my eighth. I kept telling God I had forgiven you but whenever I tried to walk through the door I couldn't because I was still very angry and hurt, so I went home again. Today when I tried I realised I could see you and you look very sad."

"So forgiveness is about seeing someone?" That felt deeply profound.

"It might not be the same for everyone. Archie says we're all different."

"Archie's become a good friend of yours."

"Archie hasn't let me down."

Anna felt the blade slide between her ribs and begin to turn. The rational part of herself said not to take it personally but it was difficult.

"That's a very high standard. In fact, Simeon, I think it's an impossible definition of friendship." Her voice was weary and sad. "Archie will let you down at some point but friendship is about accepting the whole person, warts and all." At least she hoped that's what it was all about.

"But that doesn't mean you find everything about them easy," Simeon replied. "Sometimes they will do things that make you uncomfortable. For instance when you howled I thought I would never be able to talk to you again. But now I'm only a little worried you'll do it again."

Anna felt her stomach turn over. It always did whenever she remembered that moment.

"I don't particularly feel like crying, but if I do I'll let you know so you can get away from me."

"Thank you."

She began to feel strangely dislocated from the conversation.

"So how are you, Simeon?" That was a nice normal question.

"I'm well. I am having some very interesting conversations with God."

"Really! With God?" Why hadn't he told her that before?

Dislocated wasn't the word. She felt like she was floating above them.

"Yes. Archie said I should tell you but I've been waiting for you to ask the right question."

"What is the right question?" she said, beginning to feel once again the usual exasperation associated with talking to Simeon. They'd had a similar conversation not that long ago.

"Well, I think it's not about the right question any more, it's about how you ask it."

"I haven't changed, Simeon, not since the last time we spoke. I'm just the same flawed person I was. Nothing is different."

"And yet everything feels different," he said. Anna felt that the sentence warranted a sonorous clanging of a large bell. She shrugged. Perhaps he was right.

"Has the policeman come back?" she asked.

"No. He said he would as a kind of threat, but he hasn't yet."

"If he does, will you ring me or Archie immediately so that we can come and be with you?"

"Yes. My social worker said I should never be on my own with anyone."

"You're on your own with me. You are often on your own with Archie."

"You don't count."

Anna was comforted by that.

***

The following week Harriet was surprised to find Anna sitting in the church wrapped in a blanket, sipping tea.

"Hello, Harriet. Would you like a cuppa?"

"I guess. Don't suppose you have another blanket? It's quite chilly in here."

"No, but if you put your feet on a kneeler it helps."

Harriet sat down. Anna pulled a kneeler out from under the pew in front. It had a rather fetching Blue Peter ship picked out in white wool. Somebody a long time ago had lavished a lot of love and many hours on the kneelers, they were dotted about the church, spots of vibrant colour that made praying on your knees an actual possibility. Of course nowadays people sat to pray. She shrugged off her throw and got up to boil the kettle. She'd been adding mugs and biscuits and had even put up a little sign, "Help Yourself". It wasn't much but she felt as though it made the church feel more used. She hoped it was what Irene had meant by making it as comfortable as possible.

"It really does seem to help," she continued, as the steam of the kettle curled up the wall. Harriet would wonder what she was talking about.

Anna couldn't help laughing when she handed over a mug covered in holly and reindeer. Harriet now looked bemused.

"Another invaluable Christmas present," she said. She had lots of mugs like that, even one that said The World's Greatest Vicar. It had been given to her at a particularly difficult time in her curacy and was now gathering dust at the back of the cupboard. She never dared use it but couldn't bring herself to throw it away either.

Harriet sipped her tea. Anna had brought down some Earl Grey just in case.

"It feels like autumn," Harriet said, while Anna wrapped herself back up in her blanket.

"It does. I'm not looking forward to winter. I shall have to invest in some seriously woolly socks."

"My flat gets ridiculously cold and I'm wondering when my landlord is going to decide to do it up and chuck me out. No, he'll chuck me out and then do it up." She nodded, and made a face. "Much more convenient. He may have started his campaign. I think he deliberately left some rubbish on my steps. Of course I trailed through it in the dark and a particularly disgusting rag came in with me. I didn't notice until the next morning. I thought the drains had given up."

"Can he do that?"

"The loo is getting dodgy and I can't always get hot water. All he's got to do is not fix anything and I'm up a gum tree."

"That doesn't sound very nice."

"I'm not paying that much rent. He could make loads more if he turned it into a little holiday let. Truth be told I've been waiting for him to get on with it for months. I'm surprised I've lasted as long as I have."

"Well, I've plenty of room at the vicarage, only I can't always guarantee hot water and my loos don't flush properly either."

They laughed.

"I wonder if I could talk to you about Derek," Harriet asked, shivering a little. Anna unwrapped the blanket and handed it over. Harriet was so skinny, she'd be frozen in no time. She watched the steam from the mug curl up around Harriet's thin face. She did look as if she'd had all the stuffing knocked out of her.

"Of course you can talk about him but you know I can't break any confidences."

As she said it Anna felt the guilt soar. She was always breaking that rule, and she remembered her last conversation with Tom. No, not Tom on that occasion, DI Edwards. So she waited for Harriet to explode with laughter at her hypocrisy. Harriet didn't because she patently had other things on her mind. Anna watched her straighten up, look across to the altar, she even put the mug down beside her. She began to speak and though she began well it was as if the weight of her words dragged her eyes back to the flagstones.

"I want Derek to know that I feel dreadful about what I said to him," Harriet spoke quickly, if she hesitated she might stop and not have the courage to go on. "And though it was the truth, it was my truth, not his. I'm sorry I've added to his grief."

"Why can't you say that to him? It's quite eloquent."

"Because if I were him I would run a mile before I got anywhere close and that would make things worse than ever."

Anna had to agree. Derek was a little scared of Harriet and what she might say next.

"True, but I think you've got to try. Simeon has been telling me all about forgiveness, how it's not about what the other person has done to you, it's more about seeing them."

"I don't understand that," Harriet said, looking suitably confused. "But do you think Derek might ever come to understand why I said what I said?"

"I don't know, but only you can explain it to him."

"You talk to him all the time. He's not afraid of you."

Anna could see where that was heading.

"He's not afraid of you either. Not really." Anna knew she was painting the picture too rosily but she ploughed on anyway. "He's angry with Fiona for leaving him and he's only just working out that he didn't know her as well as he thought he did. I think you simply got caught in the middle." She thought that was probably close to the truth.

"How do you do it?"

"Do what?"

"Be a vicar. Be everyone's confidante and no one's friend."

Anna sighed and muttered, "Ouch, that's harsh." She sipped her tea trying not to dwell on the fact that Harriet thought she had no friends.

"Sorry. But isn't that how you see it?"

"The bit about being friendless? I suppose so. The dog

collar does make it difficult. They warned us about it at college but I hadn't thought it would be impossible. It feels like people can't see past it." She sighed. "If truth be told sometimes I can't see past it."

"Oh, bugger. I didn't mean that you didn't have any friends. We get on alright." Harriet laughed. "After all you and Phil are the only ones with the guts to tell me when I've crossed the line. That's friendship, isn't it?"

Anna was more than happy to accept the small peace offering and ignored the obvious backtracking, otherwise she would have to acknowledge her usual default position niggling away at the back of her mind... that she was the girl at the end of the line, the one picked last and then only because she had to be on someone's team.

Harriet left not long after. Even with the blanket she couldn't stop shivering. Anna was just wrapping herself back up again when Archie came in. The thing she loved about Archie was that he hardly ever looked surprised, like he'd known all along that she would be sitting here cocooned in a tartan throw, sipping tea and, well, just sitting.

"Am I disturbing you?" he asked, hovering at the back.

"No, I'm just about finished. But I'm glad to see you."

She wanted to catch him up with what had been happening. He came a little closer and smiled tentatively.

"How are you?"

"Better, thank you Archie. Nothing's really changed but I don't feel quite so panicky."

"Oh that's excellent." He nodded and she didn't immediately think that he was simply ticking his to-do list. "And I must apologise for being a bit sharp with you. When you last came to the house. When I said you could be easier on yourself, and on us." As if she might not remember the occasion. "I could have spoken more gently."

So he wasn't taking back what he'd said, just the way he'd said it. Anna felt her hands scrunch into fists under the blanket.

"I rang the archdeacon," she said, thinking there was no time like the present. "And he has given me a new spiritual director." She sat a little taller. "Whom I have already been to see."

"Good. Er, what's a spiritual director?"

Anna laughed. She supposed normal people didn't have them.

"Someone who sits and listens to you. You tell them all the stuff that is going on. They in turn help you keep your spiritual life on track, or in my case get my spiritual life back on track."

"I'd like one of those. It would be fascinating to have someone help me get my spiritual life together." He placed his palms as if he were praying.

"Really? I'll ask the archdeacon if he knows of anyone." She had to swallow another mouthful of hurt, though she wasn't one bit surprised that he didn't see her in that role.

"I wouldn't want to take up anyone's time." Now that was the Archie she knew. "But you see I've started reading some of Moira's old books, mostly you know because Simeon keeps asking me these complicated questions. Luckily he's quite patient so I have time to research the answers."

"Well if you get stuck you can always come and talk to me. I've still got most of my essays from college to remind me what I'm supposed to believe." He winced at that and she was sorry. "I've actually got a couple of bookcases full of good, sound books if you'd ever like to borrow one, not that Moira's aren't good of course."

He brightened up at that.

"You see," he said, his eyes creasing into half-moons, "I like mulling things over and books don't stand there impatiently waiting for a reply."

"Right," said Anna. She'd never thought of them like that. Her theology tomes were gathering dust because she really didn't want anyone telling her what she ought to believe. That made her blink. She hadn't known that's what she actually thought. So that was something else she would have to raise with Irene next time she saw her.

"By the way I've told Simeon that if Tom Edwards, the detective inspector, comes back he's to call one of us so that we can go and be with him." She patted her jeans pocket. "From now on I'm going to keep my mobile on, just in case."

"I'll do the same then."

That was a surprise. Archie knew what the internet was and had a mobile.

"I think we ought to treat Simeon as a vulnerable adult," she continued firmly. She'd been on two courses all about them. A custard-cream and ginger-cake jolly if ever there was one.

"I can't imagine he'll like that. I can't imagine he'll like that at all." Archie folded his arms across his chest. Anna knew he was right.

"No, I don't suppose he will. But I can imagine him being misunderstood and I'm absolutely not going to let that happen."

"Then let's go and be with him because he's a friend, not because he's vulnerable."

That word 'friend' again. Well, just so long as one of them was there, she thought. But after her conversation with Harriet she did wonder whether the true nature of friendship was something that would always elude her.

They sat a bit longer and she realised she'd been in church well past her hour. Archie had shut his eyes so she supposed he was praying and she wanted to pray for him praying only Irene had said she wasn't supposed to. But then Irene wasn't the vicar; Irene wasn't responsible for their souls.

***

The following week as Anna walked down to the church,

carrying more milk and some extra throws, she bumped into Terry coming out of the churchyard. She wondered what monstrosity of a flower arrangement awaited her inside and then told herself to stop being so mean.

"Hello, how are you?" she called before they were even close.

"I'm well." Terry stopped and waited for Anna to come down to her.

"Good. Derek said you have been very kind to him." Terry's eyes widened at that and Anna wondered if she'd broken a confidence. Still she ploughed on. "Well, he needs his friends at the moment." Terry seemed to stand a little straighter at that and nodded. Anna was encouraged. "So is it your turn to do the flowers?"

"No. I've been for a walk."

"Well, it's a lovely day for it." It wasn't a particularly nice day but Anna was as usual beginning to struggle and words tumbled out of her mouth uncontrollably. She wondered why she found Terry so difficult. Wondered if it was because she felt she ought to feel sorry for her but instead it was she who seemed to pity Anna. That wasn't the right way round at all. "So keep up the good work. And if you ever need to talk..."

Anna turned away. If Terry ever did turn up at the vicarage wanting to talk she'd have to pretend she wasn't in. She'd do a Simeon and hide in one of the back rooms. Anna mused on what Terry might want to open her heart about, but she couldn't imagine she and Terry would struggle with the same things. She shuddered. She wasn't like Terry, not at all. The hart's-tongue ferns around the gate caught her eye and she allowed her hand to skim the top of them. There were still a few beads of dew at their centres. Small sparkles of life. She wondered which of her parishioners would visit today and was a little relieved that Terry was heading the other way.

It had become apparent that whenever she came down to do her homework, Harriet, Simeon, or Archie would turn up and sit with her. Sometimes they chatted, sometimes they didn't. Even Derek had been down to talk about work and of course Terry had walked in and out again. She didn't mind even though it meant she wasn't able to get much thinking done in her own right. She was due to see Irene at the end of October, which was fast approaching. As far as she could see there'd been no deep and meaningful revelations, no steps forward, and she still didn't want to get out of bed in the morning, still didn't feel any closer to being worthy of her calling.

The church was open but empty. Now that wasn't right. She would need to have a word with them about making sure they locked up after themselves.

"What do you think, God?" she asked, as she had a quick look in the tower room. And then remembered she wasn't allowed to pray. But it was ridiculous. She had to be able to whenever she felt like it, and when she didn't feel like it. But then Irene would probably say that she had the other twenty-three hours to do her praying in. Anna decided to stick to the rules for now.

"Of course it depends how you view prayer," Anna continued out loud as she made her way to the front pew and wrapped herself up in her blanket of choice.

"How do you view it?" a voice echoed from the back.

Just for a second the thought flitted through her mind that finally she would have something amazing to tell Irene. Only it wasn't God who'd turned up, but Tom.

"Oh, hello, Detective Inspector. Would you like a cup of tea?"

"Yes I would. But please call me Tom." He raised an eyebrow. Anna had to smile.

"Touché," she said, remembering her opening words in the pub the last time they had spoken, "You can have a rug too," she said, when she came back and handed him a mug. This one had a dog on and said inevitably, 'Top Dog'. She hoped she had remembered right that he liked a half teaspoon of sugar.

"No, I'm thermally lined already. Part of our training is to grow a layer of blubber to keep ourselves warm when standing at football matches, parades, important court cases..."

"I bet you haven't had to do that kind of duty for years."

"No, but I still have the blubber."

Not as much as me, she thought sadly.

"I'm glad you're here," she added, "I need to talk to you about Simeon."

"Ah. I did wonder if I'd been a bit heavy-handed. Though he said he did see someone leaving the churchyard."

"If he said he did, he did. Simeon wouldn't lie. Can't lie."

"Ok but he doesn't always tell the whole truth, does he. He should have come forward."

"What did he see? He obviously didn't recognise them and if it was a stranger he would have gone out of his way to avoid them."

"All of the above. He says he saw Fiona on the ground, didn't touch anything. But I think sometimes what Simeon doesn't say is more important than what he does." Anna frowned. Tom continued, "He said he knew she was dead. He should have raised the alarm. That doesn't leave a great taste in the mouth when it comes to innocence."

"He's got these rules taught to him by his social worker."

"He has a social worker?"

Tom's eyes widened. Anna watched a little flush creep across his neck and tried not to enjoy his discomfort too much. Interviewing someone without due care and attention and all that could be big trouble. She took pity on him.

"No, you're alright. He hasn't had one for ages. But he did growing up and Simeon has built his life round the things the chap used to say. Like 'never be on your own with someone', 'expect to get the blame', 'don't expect to know what's going on', 'never volunteer information'."

"Not exactly how we'd handle it today, but, if you think about it, that's how an awful lot of people live their lives. Keep your head down, don't get involved. Except you, of course," he said, turning to look at her.

"That's not quite true," Anna replied, sucking hard at her bottom lip. Though she often did wish she could keep her head down, walk by on the other side, not have to give advice.

"By the way, how's Harriet getting on? Any more accusations?" Tom asked.

"No, actually she and Derek have tried to talk. It didn't go well, but it is a start. They both need to budge a little." She laughed, a tight high sound that she realised was how she felt when Tom was around.

"Could be the beginning of a long and beautiful friendship?"

"Oh, my goodness, no."

And she thought how shallow of him to think that it was all Harriet and Derek needed – to hook up – to have someone in their life to make it better.

"Sorry," he said, "I guess I touched a nerve."

Her voice had betrayed her.

"No, it's just that sometimes finding someone isn't the answer."

"Unless it's finding God, and then surely it must always be the answer."

"Is that what you believe?" she asked, wondering if he was teasing her or pandering to the dog collar. He straightened up.

"I don't know what I believe. Anyway, I just wanted to ask you if you'd seen anyone else about. You must know pretty much everyone round here."

Of course she had been keeping her eyes open, most of them had.

"I can't say that I have seen any strangers and neither has Archie. He gets quite excited by new people. Thinks they're going to move here and join us."

She paused, "Tom, do you really think someone clouted Fiona, on purpose?"

"The forensics aren't cut and dried but they do lean towards someone taking a chunk of old gravestone to the side of her head but unless I can come up with something new the boss said we have to put it to bed." Anna peered round at him. So this might be his last visit.

"You could ask Simeon if he has seen anyone about. But please if you're going to speak to him then you need to have either Archie or myself with him."

"You know I don't have to do that," Tom said, quietly.

Anna felt a wave of anger.

"I'm not talking letter of the law, I'm talking common human decency, and you'll get a damn sight more from him if one of us is there."

"Alright Anna, there's no need to get upset."

But she was upset. He could have met her halfway any number of times, but he never did.

"So if it wasn't an accident, whoever did it is still at large. And when I came back to check the church, they could still have been there. Who are we talking about here? Some random madman?" She took a breath. "And if you do put it to bed we could still be in danger." The last bit had sounded less like an accusation and more like a cry for help.

"The trouble is, Anna, I haven't been able to find out anything about the someone Simeon saw, who, let's face it, may have arrived after Fiona died so they might not have seen her anyway – might not have had anything to do with it."

"And Simeon is absolutely positive it wasn't me he saw?"

"It can't have been, you would have been coming back at about half past four. Simeon is very sure that he was only down at the cove for ten minutes. So he saw the person leaving at about four ten. And even in that dark drizzly rain I think he would have known it was you."

"Perhaps," and Anna had to squash her lips together quite tightly, to stop everything from spilling out. "It was all so upsetting. If only I'd stayed with her, walked back up the road with her. But Simeon had been so difficult, had said some really hard things."

"What had Simeon said that was so upsetting?"

"I can't say. I'm sorry."

"Anna, please."

"He talked of committing suicide." Tom scribbled something into his notebook.

"You don't have to give me details, but you're sure he was calm when he left you?"

"Yes, definitely," she replied.

"So tell me about Derek?"

Anna knew what he was doing, why he had jumped to Derek, but she went along with it anyway, Surely Derek was in the clear by now.

"Well, he's not actually going to retire. When it came down to it, his partners didn't want to lose him, offered to buy him out but to keep him on as a consultant." By the end of that sentence her voice was sounding almost normal.

"There are some things that he's really good at and I suppose the firm simply didn't want to lose his expertise." Which had surprised Derek. They had genuinely seemed worried about him leaving and had offered him a very generous consultancy rate. A figure that Anna sadly noted was beyond a vicar's stipend by a couple of multiples.

"So when does that kick in?"

"Pretty much straight away, though they'll have to get some paperwork organised."

"It's all working out for Derek. Is he going to stay round here?"

"I think so, though he's a bit fed up with the bungalow." Anna wondered if that was simply because Fiona was no longer there to fill up the space. "I'd swap with him if I could.

Central heating. A small garden, magnolia on the walls. Perfect."

Tom folded away his notebook.

"But you have to have extra rooms for a study, and visitors. It wouldn't be big enough for you and you can only get up to it by those really steep steps"

"You really do know a lot about being a vicar."

"Well, as I said before, my mum's life is the church. She's been a churchwarden, has run afternoon groups, prayer meetings, and we always had a home group at the house."

"Wow! So you're an expert then."

He didn't laugh, he looked disconcerted.

"Actually Mum has been somewhat neglected over the years. My wife didn't like her and it was easy to make excuses about not inviting her down quite as much as we ought to have done. I'm beginning to feel a little guilty about her."

"I bet she still prays for you though."

"I'm sure she does."

Tom stood up. He didn't smile either.

"Well, thank you," he said. "I may need to bring something for you to sign. Just be careful. In most murder cases it isn't usually a stranger."

Chapter 14

Phil was trying to decide whether to get his accounts from out the back. The year before he'd got into a terrible mess, and it had cost him a fortune to get them sorted so he was determined to keep on top of them. Harriet was out walking Bowzer because Derek was off on a job, so he still had to man the bar but there were only a couple of lads sitting by the fire. They were talking pigs and had apparently spent the morning inoculating a local herd against something horrible that Phil didn't want to think about. It seemed as good a time as any to sort through the week's till receipts. The door jangled as someone pulled when it clearly said push. The woman from the shop came in. Terry Lovell.

"Hello. We don't often see you in here." Never to his knowledge. "How can I help you?" She looked as though she wasn't quite sure what to do. "Can I get you something? A coffee, red wine, orange juice?"

She looked relieved and said, "An orange juice please."

"Ice and lemon?"

"No thank you."

"It's suddenly got a lot colder."

She nodded, gave him a tenner, waited for her change, and then took her drink over to the fire. For a moment Phil wondered if Derek would get back early enough to find her there. They looked about the same age. But last time he'd mentioned something like that Harriet had given him a hard time about women not needing men to be happy. Funnily enough a bit later on so had Anna.

He slipped out to get the books. Despite the changeable weather over the last few months they hadn't done that badly. Perhaps because of the weather people had decided a pie and a pint were preferable to walking down to the lighthouse, even though there was a handy little coffee shop overlooking the old lifeboat station and the glorious seas. Sometimes he slipped down there himself. They did an amazing crab sandwich. He got himself organised. Terry was still sitting there sipping her orange juice. She had her dark hair tied back in a ponytail, and a pale green wool jumper. It was an unusual colour and made him think of jumble sales and charity shops. He supposed she might be waiting for someone.

"Hey Phil," Harriet called from the kitchen. "This old dog is getting fitter and fitter. On the way back he pulled me up the last bit of the lane."

Bowzer did look slightly less round. His walks with Derek were doing him the world of good.

"You look all pink."

"Me or the dog?" Harriet replied, smiling. "It's windy out but not too cold, not for October anyway."

Terry was getting up. She buttoned her coat and glanced over to the bar. Harriet turned to watch her leave.

"What on earth was she doing in here?"

Phil shook his head. "I have no idea."

"I guess I'll sort out the sheets," Harriet said, putting her coat on the hook and dragging the reservation book towards her. "Unless there's anything else you'd like me to do."

"I wondered if we ought to update the crockery. There are quite a few chipped bowls and we could do with some more knives and forks. Have a look, will you, and then perhaps we could pop to Truro tomorrow. We'd have to open a bit later to give us enough time, but I don't think anyone's going to mind."

"We don't have any guests in?"

"No. Just a couple of enquiries that didn't come to anything. How about if I buy you breakfast?"

Harriet went back to the kitchen. She got quite engrossed in her inventory and in the end Phil had to call her to come and give him a hand. The teachers from the local primary had popped in. Harriet handed over her list before she turned to the pumps. It was long and detailed. She'd even suggested some white table cloths, which she thought would lift the place. Make it look more cheerful.

He liked that. He knew they'd never make their fortune doing B&B, but he thought they could be doing better than they were and Harriet could make the place look classy on a shoestring. It would be nice to be able to afford a winter break now and again, or even upgrade the van. Tomorrow morning perhaps he'd see whether she had any other ideas.

The teachers were celebrating, because for the first time in years the children's numbers were up. The headmistress, not much older than Harriet, had blurted that out before she'd even taken off her coat. There would be cuts but not so much as previously, and it meant a little more hope that the school wouldn't get the chop. They were supposed to be having a staff meeting but she'd decided the pub was a better idea. There was a lot of laughter.

Archie arrived in the middle of it. He went over to say hello before coming up to the bar. He ordered a rum even though it was a little early for him. He used to take his drink to the fire place, but since the coffee on Easter morning he often clambered onto a stool and, if it wasn't too busy, he and Phil had a bit of a chat. Archie was a nice man to talk to even if he kept trying to get him to come back to church. Phil had patiently explained that Sunday mornings were out of the question.

A little later, after Phil had dealt with another round for the teachers, he wandered back to Archie, surprised he was still there. Phil wondered if there was something else he wanted to discuss.

"I'm trying to persuade Simeon to come and have a drink with me," Archie remarked. Phil began wiping nozzles and stacking the dirty glasses. There was still a possibility the bridge club might pop in or a couple of the younger WI members before their meeting. Tuesday evening was a busy night for clubs. "I think it would do him good and would help the other villagers get to know him."

"He can come across as a little... standoffish," Phil agreed. He'd decided the word 'odd' would offend Archie.

"Until you get used to him," Archie added. That didn't sound right. Phil could see that Archie wasn't happy with that statement either. He was such an honourable man he'd be in knots in a moment.

"The policeman, Tom Edwards, was back again yesterday," Phil said quickly. He thought it was kind of Archie but Simeon was never going to come into the pub.

"Oh surely he can't still be investigating Mrs Harris's death? Honestly I think if he carries on Derek ought to make a complaint or something."

"I'm not sure he's here officially any more. He can't be." Phil wiped the bar with his towel. "I expect he just likes the place."

Archie nodded. He wasn't sure about DI Edwards.

"Well, I suppose," Archie replied. "We are within commuting distance of Falmouth if he wanted to move."

"How do you think the villagers would feel?" Phil asked. "Safer or spied on?"

"Interesting question." Archie frowned in thought. Phil waited. "It's just that the open verdict was... distressing. If she'd simply fallen it would have been sad, but the coroner obviously thought there was something suspicious only there simply wasn't the evidence to support it."

The implication being, Phil thought, that the policeman hadn't quite been up to the job though of course Archie would never dream of saying such a thing. Phil turned to get the rum bottle down. Archie pushed his glass over.

"And then that stupid anonymous call, it's made it all feel a bit sinister."

Phil nodded. But they'd been over this ground before, quite a few times, and it didn't get them anywhere. Archie didn't seem able to let it go.

"How's Anna? She's seemed a bit more cheerful recently," Phil asked, pouring a double.

Archie scrunched up his eyes and pursed his lips, obviously deciding how much he could say. Phil almost laughed. The man was full of secrets that weren't really secrets. He was so careful about what he talked about, though Phil decided that if he did want to share a confidence Archie would be the first person he'd go to.

"She's been seeing someone called a spiritual director and I think it's doing her the world of good," Archie said carefully, weighing each word.

"I'm assuming that's not anything like a funeral director..."

"No, more about your inner soul than your outer body."

Phil laughed.

"Well I'm pleased for her. I think she has a tough time."

Archie nodded vigorously in reply, took another drink, and then said casually, "So how's yours?"

"I'm assuming you mean my inner soul as you can quite clearly see my outer body is beyond redemption." Phil knew this was the prelude to another talk about coming back to church. He didn't mind. Archie meant well.

"Nothing a little exercise wouldn't cure. You ought to walk that dog of yours yourself." Phil quickly chuckled so that Archie wouldn't have time to worry about whether he'd been rude or not. Then Archie's phone buzzed. He wouldn't like checking it while talking to someone, because that was rude, so Phil turned away to move some glasses around. Out of the corner of his eye he watched Archie take the phone from his jacket pocket.

He was heading out the door before Phil even had time to wish him goodbye. He wondered what was going on now.

***

Archie had promised Anna he'd be available in case Simeon needed him.

When Phil turned away Archie had a quick look at the message. It was from Anna and all in capitals. He hoped it wasn't for effect and that she just hadn't managed to switch them off.

"JUST HAD A MESSAGE FROM TOM TO SAY THAT HE'S COMING BACK TO TALK TO SIMEON, OFFICIALLY. SOME WOMAN HAS MADE A COMPLAINT AGAINST HIM. THAT HE FOLLOWED HER INTO THE CHURCH AND WOULDN'T LET HER OUT AGAIN. GOING OVER THERE NOW. CAN YOU COME TOO? IT SOUNDS SERIOUS."

It didn't take Archie long to get to Simeon's cottage. It backed onto the lane that led down to Bass Point and the coastal path. There was only the one door round the back. You had to walk down the side of the house and through the garden, a wilderness of shrubs that had been allowed to grow large and straggly, grass like a meadow, with the odd splash of orange from some hardy crocosmia growing in what might have been a border. The path alone was kept tidy, raked and weed-free. Clear white gravel, enabling thoughtless easy steps to the door. As usual all the curtains were drawn, not a gap anywhere, shut up tight, just as Simeon liked it. His fortress, his safe space. No one was allowed in as far as Archie knew. Anna was there already. She swung round, relieved to see him.

"I've knocked. I've called through the letterbox too. I'm not sure he's in there."

Archie stood for a minute and then said, "He's in there."

"How on earth can you tell?"

"If he's had an altercation with a woman at the church," Archie said, "this is the nearest of his safe spaces. He's bound to have come here."

"He might have gone to yours."

"No. I think despite how regularly we meet he sometimes finds it quite difficult crossing the village. Often he can't even bear to glance out the window. When it's very bright I draw the curtains a little."

"Should you make it so easy for him?"

He had often thought about that.

"I'm never quite sure what's best for Simeon. Normally I ask him, but in my defence I never shut out the light completely."

Archie looked back up the path, checking for headlights. Tom would have to walk down the last bit or risk blocking the lane completely. Anna turned to stare at the door. She didn't look as though she agreed with him.. The house did feel empty.

"If Tom comes now what will happen? He's hardly likely to want to batter his way in."

Archie shrugged and replied, "I suppose it depends on what happened. Do you know who complained? Or why?"

"No, and would he really have threatened someone? Not allowed them to leave?"

"No, I would have thought the exact opposite." Archie just couldn't imagine Simeon squaring up to anyone. Anna nodded. He continued, "He probably wouldn't have gone into the church if they were in there already."

"So, they must have arrived after him. Oh, Archie, I wonder what could have happened?"

"Let me give it a try."

Archie knocked softly, so softly that Anna wondered if anyone would possibly hear it even standing with their ear pressed to the door.

"Simeon," he whispered, "it's only Archie and Anna. We'd very much like to talk to you. I know you're probably quite upset but remember we're your friends and want to help."

For a long time, there was nothing. Anna was about to speak again but Archie put a finger to his lips. He held his breath and then heard the chain slide. Simeon was putting it on, not taking it off. The door opened four inches.

***

Simeon had recently had a haircut. Anna hated how vulnerable he looked with his ears sticking out and a straight dark fringe sitting high on his forehead. He stood back from the door so they could talk to him through the tiny gap. The light from the hall made a sharp wedge across the garden.

"What happened at the church, Simeon?" Archie asked.

"I was talking to God. The flower lady came in."

"And what did she do?" Archie asked.

"Normally I hide and slip out as soon as I can."

Archie and Anna shared a look.

"Only she came down the aisle as if she were looking for me. I tried to stand very still in the shadows but there weren't enough of them. She saw me almost immediately." Simeon's voice was flat and factual and Anna noticed that Archie had folded his arms tightly across his chest. This was upsetting them both.

"What did she do when she saw you?" Archie asked.

"She pulled off her hood and kept coming. She said she just wanted a word. I didn't want to speak to her. I really don't like her. I tried to climb over the pews to the back but she said loudly, Oh, no you don't."

"Why would Jean do that?" Archie said. "That doesn't sound like her at all."

"You mean Terry, don't you Simeon," Anna said, realising in a rush who they were talking about.

"She got very close. I knew I wasn't allowed to push past so I screamed very loudly and pretended to jump at her, just like my social worker said I should if I was ever cornered. She did step back and I managed to get over the last pew. I don't think I touched her but I did have to go very close to get by. I was worried that she wouldn't leave me alone so I ran home." He stopped and then said, "I need to lie down again until my heart beat gets back to normal."

"Tom is coming," Anna said, "Terry has made a complaint. He needs to talk to you."

"Is he coming now? It's late."

"We think so," Archie said. "But why don't you go and try to calm down and we'll wait for him out in the lane. Try and forestall him a bit."

Simeon closed the door.

"Archie, why on earth would she have called the police?"

"I guess if he screamed and lunged at her. He knew he wasn't going to touch or hurt her, but she wouldn't have known that. She might have been really scared."

"But everyone knows not to get too close to Simeon."

"Well I'm not sure they do. We've got to know him really well over the last few months, but to the rest of the village he's still a bit of an enigma."

"Ok, but what do you think she wanted to talk to him about?"

"I don't know."

"I'll go and see her. Find out. I'm sure it's some terrible misunderstanding."

"Hopefully DI Edwards will be able to tell us something."

But Anna didn't think he would.

"Look, if you've got things to do I don't mind waiting," Archie said. "If he's coming from Falmouth, he could be quite a while."

"You can't just hang about all evening either. I'll ring him and find out how long he's going to be."

Despite everything she was still a little disappointed that Tom hadn't left her a message regarding the incident. He didn't answer his phone either, so in the end they decided to go and stand at the end of Simeon's track.

"I hope he comes soon," she said, thinking longingly of the throws and kettle just a short distance away.

"I'm sorry to say that I think the longer he is the better."

Once again Anna felt she'd missed the mark. Archie was such a good man, but his standards always seemed impossibly high.

After half an hour she was ready to go and make them a mug of tea whatever the circumstances, her back was aching quite badly from all the standing about, and her eyes were tired from peering up the lane. There wasn't much of a moon so it was hard to see anything clearly. Luckily only a few seconds later Tom's old green Audi came nosing round the corner, headlights blazing in the early evening darkness. He saw them while reversing into the hedge to park, would have had difficulty not seeing them as Anna was waving and calling out like a mad woman. He wound down the window.

"Don't worry Revd Maybury. I'm not going anywhere without the two of you."

Revd Maybury, Anna noted! This was official business. Archie didn't smile and stayed close until Tom had got out, then he turned to lead them down the track, a guard of honour. She began to see that though Tom was authority, Archie didn't trust him much.

"Before we go in do you want to hear what he told us?" Anna said, feeling out of breath even though she'd only walked a couple of yards.

"Were you there?"

"No," said Archie.

"Then I'm afraid not. I'll need to ask him my questions first."

"But it's so unfair," Anna burst out. "Terry trapped him. He tried his absolute best not to touch her. She won't have realised how distressing it was for him."

"Anna, this is police business and there's no real reason why I should have you with me. He's not on any register, and I've been on that many training courses, I know how careful I have to be." Anna frowned in frustration.

Archie then said, "Well the first thing we have to do is get him to open the door. You'd best leave that to me."

But when the three of them walked up the path the door was already ajar. Neither Archie nor Anna had been in before, but Tom had so he led the way.

"Mr Tyler, DI Edwards, where are you?" he called.

"In here."

Simeon still sounded flat, emotionless, as if he had shut down and yet the first thing Anna noticed was that his fingers were opening and closing, squeezing into fists, then stretching as if they were stiff. It was the only movement in the dimly lit room, so gloomy that Anna's eyes took ages to adjust after the brightness of the hall. There were three chairs in a row facing the front window. But there was no danger of her bumping into anything. Apart from the seats the room was empty.

"Don't you have a television, Simeon?" she asked in wonder.

"No, I listen to the radio. I listen to the news and the weather but I don't want to talk about that right now."

"Of course not." She felt a little foolish, it was just that the room seemed alien, unused, and she was sure it wouldn't make a good impression on someone who didn't know Simeon.

Tom pulled out his notebook.

"Do you know why we're here?" he asked.

"Mrs Lovell in the church."

"Yes, that's right Mr Tyler. She has made a complaint."

Simeon looked down at the floor and repeated what he had told Anna and Archie pretty much word for word. Tom wrote a few notes but they didn't seem to be that comprehensive. Anna wished she'd bought a pen and paper. She wasn't sure she'd recall everything exactly and didn't know how important it might be. Tom folded his notebook away.

"Is there anything else you'd like to add, Mr Tyler?"

"No," replied Simeon.

"Have you ever encountered Mrs Lovell before?"

"Yes," said Simeon.

"What is the nature of your relationship?"

Simeon stopped and though he was staring at the floor she could see that his eyes had widened. He hadn't expected such a question.

"What do you mean?"

"What is the nature of your relationship with Mrs Lovell?"

"I don't have a relationship with her. I see her about the village. Sometimes I see her in the shop. I don't like to go in there when she is serving."

"Why is that?"

"Some people make me uncomfortable."

"Do you have any idea why she might have made a complaint?"

There was a long stretch of silence. Anna felt an acute need to fill it with words. She had never heard Simeon hesitate before. It was disconcerting.

Eventually he said, "People don't understand me. She kept coming closer and closer and I needed to get away. I pretended to lunge at her so that she would step back as I knew I mustn't touch her."

Anna and Archie exchanged a glance.

"Right," said Tom. "Did you feel threatened?"

"I don't know."

"Scared?"

"I don't know."

"Then why did you have to run away?"

"Because she made me feel uncomfortable."

Would Tom understand the distinction? Did Simeon? Tom flipped the notebook out and scribbled something else. Simeon was motionless. His hands had stopped moving, were now simply clenched into tight fists.

"Well, that will be all for now."

Tom stood up. Archie caught Anna's eye and nodded towards the door.

"Archie, I'll see you later. Perhaps at the pub?" she called, following Tom out.

Tom strode away, but once he was halfway to the road he swung back.

"I can't talk about what's been said, Anna." He spoke quickly, while she was still trying to decide what to say.

"But you could ask us for a character witness or something. I'd like to say that I've never heard Simeon speak anything but the truth."

"But have you ever seen him misinterpret something? Like if you got too close, or not shut up when he wanted you to?"

Well of course she had, when she was getting to know him, when she had tried to treat him as normal, whatever that meant. So yes, there had been lots of moments. Tom read her mind.

"Right," said Tom. "So you can see my difficulty."

"Will you interview Terry properly? Ask her why she cornered him like that?"

"Anna, I can't discuss this with you."

"Now you're a proper policeman! That's not fair, Tom. All this time you've been coming to the village getting us to feel at ease around you and suddenly you've put your professional skin back on."

Tom looked taken aback.

"I'm sorry if I've ever been anything less than professional."

Anna clenched her own fists. She felt let down, even a little angry though she wasn't sure what she'd expected, not really. But here was something about Tom she didn't get and it disconcerted her.

"I'm sorry, but I'd best be off," he said climbing into his car.

She stood and watched him reverse, then followed him up the lane to Cross Common Road where Terry lived just across from Derek. Tom's car was now parked outside Terry's house. Anna would have to return to the vicarage and wait. When she got there she made a cup of tea, but couldn't settle, was heartily relieved when she got a text from Archie saying If convenient, can we meet? Archie's texting used full sentences and punctuation, which always made her smile. She texted back that she'd meet him at the top of the vicarage drive and they could walk up to the pub. It was a good idea too; she could do with a drink and it would be useful to know what Archie thought and whether he had found out anything more from Simeon.

"Are you alright, Archie?" she asked.

"Bit shaken. Poor Simeon." Archie was walking quite fast. Anna had to work really hard to keep up with him. "All the things that have happened to him in the past, all the things he's been slowly sloughing off over the months have just gone and tipped all over him again. Has left him covered in..." Anna patted his arm. She knew what he wanted to say, wish he'd said it, thought perhaps it had been a common word in his Navy days. "Anyway, poor Simeon is reverting to some very deeply ingrained behaviour."

"What can we do?"

"Give him time. But he won't be coming out for a while."

They both clambered onto bar stools. He ordered himself a coffee and Anna decided she needed a wine. Phil took himself off to the other end of the bar.

"Should I offer to get him some shopping?" she asked.

"He's already given me a list. Has told me to leave it outside his front door tomorrow morning at eleven."

"That's very precise."

"It means he's only got to look out for me for a few minutes. I can see the logic of it."

Anna took a sip of wine. She twisted the glass slowly round and round.

"Should we be... going along with this?"

"For a couple of days let him hide under his blankets, let the adrenaline subside, and then hopefully we can persuade him out."

"I could kill Terry. I'll definitely go and see her to find out what she was playing at."

Phil had come a little closer, was hovering near. Archie looked as if he could do with something stronger than coffee.

"Are you talking about Mrs Lovell?" he asked. "She came into the pub the other day for an orange juice. Didn't stay long, left when Harriet got back. I thought she might be waiting for someone."

"Has she ever been in before?" Anna asked.

"No, never."

"Perhaps she's lonely," Archie said, quietly. "And Simeon can come across as very odd. Never looks you in the eye, only recognises people by their shoes."

Anna patted his arm. Archie could be right. That Terry was simply another Simeon who needed people to take a little time to give them a chance. She suddenly felt the guilt soar around her ears at the number of times she'd cut short their conversations because she was feeling uncomfortable.

"I wonder what on earth she wanted with Simeon?" Phil asked.

Archie shrugged. And Anna was once again impressed at how quickly Phil got up to speed. How did he find out what was going on?

"Could you ask her?" Phil said, looking at Anna.

"Ask her what?" Derek chimed, dropping Dolly's lead so she could sniff along the bar to Bowzer.

"Terry Lovell went too close to Simeon in the church and really freaked him out," Archie said.

"Oh, poor Simeon. He won't have liked that," Derek replied.

Anna added, "No, and to make matters worse she made a complaint, so DI Edwards has been to see him."

"A misunderstanding I expect," Derek said, carefully putting his coat over a nearby chair before clambering onto a stool.

217

"Well, I'm not sure..." Anna replied.

"We're just worried that it will make Simeon a bit reclusive again," Archie said, quickly, as if to stop Anna saying something she shouldn't have.

"He'll come out when he gets hungry," Derek said, and smiled. Anna didn't think it was that simple. Archie began to clamber down.

"Well, I'm off. Keep in touch Anna, and I'll let you know if there are any other developments."

"Join me in a pie, Anna, won't you?" Derek said. "I've had another email from that woman."

Anna watched Archie leave. She would have talked some more, felt there were still things he was thinking that she would have liked to discuss, and wondered whether it might be worth ringing him later. But she was hungry. Derek was wittering on about a new client the firm had sent his way. They seemed to want to build a huge extension, to make the most of a stunning view down a long narrow valley. Derek sounded a little envious. After a while she lost track of what he was going on about. She kept wondering about Terry and Simeon.

She didn't know how long Derek had been silent. Phil appeared with their pies.

"Penny for them?" Phil asked.

"Which of us do you mean?" Derek asked.

"Sorry, Derek," Anna said. "This thing with Simeon was quite upsetting."

"I was wondering if this is what I used to do to Fiona. Tell her all about my day and not notice when she stopped listening."

"I'm really sorry."

"No, I'm just kind of pleased and a bit worried I noticed."

"Worried?"

"This must have been what I did to her. May have been why she was so unhappy."

"We don't know how unhappy she was. All you know is what Harriet says about it."

"But I ought to have a better idea. All my memories, the ones that come back to me are from a long time ago, from when we were younger. I can't remember any particular shared moment from the last year. Even from the last five years."

"It's still early days."

"You keep saying that but what if I was a first-class, selfish..."

Shit, Anna said in her head. Surprised that the word had popped up so large and satisfying. She decided they were all sitting waist-deep in it, so some of it was bound to stick and wondered if she could use the word in front of Irene, whether any of her other priests said such crude things. Still it was obvious that Derek needed someone to talk to, she would have to try and concentrate.

"What was your very last memory of Fiona, before being... dead?" she asked.

Derek had obviously thought about that, a lot.

"Getting up from the kitchen table. She was frustrated because just a month earlier she'd have jumped up and walked out. I could see that her head had done just that, but her body was still trying to unfold itself, and her feet got tangled in the table legs. I pulled her walker over to her and said I'd see her for a cup of tea later, I had some work to do. I didn't think she would go much further than the top of the steps."

Anna suddenly frowned.

"How did she get down the steps?"

"I helped her. She was quite cross. Said she needed a proper walk."

"How was she going to get back up them?"

"She was going to ring me. She could be very determined," he said, quietly. "It was the first time she'd left the house, but she insisted on going alone. I thought she might go to the shop."

"But you went back upstairs to work."

"She was going to phone me." He was beginning to sound quite agitated. Phil came over. "I wish she'd just died in her sleep." He spoke so quietly that Anna took a few seconds to work out what he'd actually said. "All this murder in a churchyard is too dramatic for people like us."

Was he the only one still clinging to the idea that Fiona's death was an accident?

"She would have been absolutely exhausted by the time she got to the church," Anna said, her throat constricting around the words. "Completely and utterly spent. And I accused her of treating the church like a bus shelter."

"You said what?"

Well she had said it now, and she didn't feel any better for it being out in the open.

"Didn't I tell you?"

"I knew you'd seen her, but a bus shelter? You must have been the last person to see her alive."

"I don't think I was." Anna knew she sounded defensive. And couldn't understand how she had managed to tell Derek of all people what her last words to Fiona had been. Then wondered whether this was the moment to say that Simeon had also been in the churchyard.

"Then who?" Derek began to sound angry. He pushed his half-eaten pie across the bar.

"Derek, I didn't know it was her. Didn't know that she was the lady who'd had the stroke."

"She had her walker with her, didn't she?" He spoke accusingly, as if Anna should have known.

Derek started to blink back tears and Anna wished with all her heart she could dissolve too. She'd not been able to have a good cry since... seeing Irene of course. A couple of hours when she'd barely been able to stop crying. Derek clambered

220

off his stool and stalked out, his legs stiff. Dolly stood up and followed him, trailing her lead.

"Phil, put the drinks and food on my tab, would you?" Anna whispered, before he could offer sympathy or judgement or whatever it was he thought most appropriate.

At the crossroads she watched Derek unlock his front door. He'd at least got hold of Dolly. She looked over at Terry's house. She didn't know if she had the heart for a talk right now and it was getting really late but then what if Terry were sitting in there frightened and lonely.

***

Terry was expecting the knock. Had watched Derek come back in the light of the streetlamp, his face fixed and suffering. Anna had appeared soon after, looking as downcast as ever. She was such a terrible advert for God, so miserable all the time. Her shoulders rounded, constantly weighed down by her weakness. Terry assumed she would pass on by, heading back to the vicarage. Hadn't expected her to straighten and walk up the garden path. Terry moved to the back of the lounge, out of sight for a couple of moments while deciding whether she would answer the door or not. It was, after all, gone nine. In the end she decided it would be best for Anna to hear what really happened.

"Come in, Vicar."

"Thank you. I've just come from Simeon's house." Via the pub she should have said. Terry nearly corrected her. "So, are you alright, Terry?"

"Yes, I am now."

"It's just that Simeon hates being cornered. And he would never have meant to hurt you."

"He screamed at me, spat in my face. Pushed me out of the way."

"Oh, Terry, he wouldn't have done it on purpose. I promise."

221

"How can you promise that?" Terry was angry. Why shouldn't she be? Why was Anna taking the boy's side? The policeman had done that too, had asked all the wrong questions. It wasn't fair. He had even implied it was a simple misunderstanding. That Simeon, Mr Tyler, had not meant to hurt her. That he had been more frightened of her than she of him. How did any one of them know how frightened she'd been?

All she'd wanted to do was to ask Simeon what he knew about Mrs Harris's death. Everyone else talked about it all the time. Jean, her main source of information, simply repeated the same thing over and over again, who could it be? Who would have wanted to kill such a nice woman? It was deeply frustrating. When Terry had walked up to Simeon, just to talk to him, he'd crouched like an animal, screamed spittle at her before jumping over the back of the pew. He would have shoved her hard if she hadn't stepped back in time. There had been no need for such horrible behaviour. She'd just wanted to know what they all knew already. They were all so cliquey, huddled up together all the time. Like no one else counted. Afterwards, Terry began to think Simeon must have something to hide, that perhaps he had even been there that night. She shivered.

"I'm sorry, Terry. Were you badly scared?"

She hadn't been scared so much as startled. Then angry, that he'd not behaved with any respect. She missed Edgar. He'd been the only person who'd valued her, treated her properly, only of course when the wife wasn't breathing down his neck, telling him what he could and couldn't do.

"He was very aggressive. He shouldn't have behaved like that."

"No, he shouldn't have. It's just that Simeon is... finds life difficult. But couldn't you have come and spoken to me rather than phoning the police."

"I was in danger. He's a menace. I wanted something

done."

"I think they've got their hands full at the moment."

"Why? Because they aren't doing their job properly. Poor Derek needs them to find the person who killed Fiona. They need reminding of their priorities." She looked at Anna, looked into her eyes, and found nothing there to help her, nothing at all.

Anna left not long after, moving as if she were walking into a head wind. Terry watched her go. As a vicar she was simply not fit for purpose and she wondered if she ought to have a word with someone. Anna never saw what was really going on, was never there when she was needed. Poor Derek could do with somebody to help him, someone who really understood loss. Anna had too many of her own problems to be able to see anyone properly.

Chapter 15

Derek was concentrating, chopping onions very small. Fiona had always cut them too large though he had forgotten how painful the eye streaming was. Still it was for a good cause. He was going to make a casserole; how hard could it be? Fiona had made them all the time and they were one of his favourite things. There hadn't been anything that looked right in her recipes, the five or six dog-eared, fat-splattered books sitting on the shelf above the fridge. Eventually he'd resorted to the internet, and had quickly found one he liked the look of. He was very carefully following the instructions. Dolly who'd been watching hopefully, particularly when the beef appeared, had given up and gone back to bed. He'd bought far more than he needed but he would put some in the freezer. Which was another thing that had raised a whole pile of issues. Fiona had been in charge of that and it was filled with packages covered in her neat, boxy handwriting. Each one had a date and how many portions were included but didn't say what they were. The night before he'd defrosted a couple of likely looking bags and had ended up with stewed apple and uncooked rhubarb. The defrosting fruit had made him angry with Fiona for being so... he wasn't sure what word quite fitted. In the end he'd had to slip out to the shop to get what he needed. He couldn't face the pub in case Anna or Harriet or in fact any of them were there. By now they'd know that he had helped Fiona down the steps, gone back to work, and forgotten all about her. He felt the tears begin to prickle and his stomach to hollow. None of them would understand the pile of work he'd had to catch up on. That Fiona's stroke had set him back weeks.

He had another go at the onions. He couldn't really see them properly through the blurring and stinging and cut neatly along his thumb. He dripped blood over the sink. Of course just because he'd forgotten Fiona didn't excuse Anna.

That the last words Fiona had ever heard had been unkind, unfair, and had been uttered by a woman who ought to have known better. He wrapped kitchen roll around his hand, turned on the radio because he couldn't bear the silence any more and the frying pan, which always took a while to get going. He pulled open the drawers to find the plasters. Dolly whined.

"Do you need a wee, girl?" he asked, tipping the onions into the pan, only then the bell rang, chiming through the overloud radio. He yanked open the front door still clutching the kitchen roll around the cut. Harriet was standing there biting her lip. He shook his head.

"This is absolutely not convenient." He began to turn his back on her.

"Please Derek, don't do that. I promise I'm not going to say anything unkind." He was still shaking his head as he turned back, as if once started he couldn't stop. "Anna told me to come, that you might listen."

"Oh, Anna!"

"You sound upset."

Damned right he was upset. Poor Fiona, neglected and forgotten by... well, Anna had been terribly unkind, hadn't she?

"Anna... well she's not always as nice as she ought to be," he said, the words spitting out before he could help himself.

Harriet looked relieved.

"Well I know that. But she tries very hard for all of us."

Derek shook his head angrily.

"It was what she said to her. Such a heartless thing to say."

"What did she say?"

"That Fiona was treating the church like a bus shelter."

Harriet seemed a little taken aback at that. She probably couldn't imagine Anna saying any such thing.

"I thought she'd offered to open the church back up for her. That's what Phil told me." Harriet did look as if she didn't believe him. "Anna can miss the point sometimes but she wouldn't deliberately leave a parishioner in distress."

"Well it's what she told me," he said, triumphantly. The truth had had the last word. Only Derek was on his own slippery slope when it came to the truth, feeling a deep gnawing need to tell her how he had forgotten that Fiona was out. She was bound to have noticed the tall steep steps just behind her and how impossible it would have been for Fiona to have got back up them by herself. He decided to skip that part.

"Fiona just needed somewhere to rest and Anna didn't have time for her." He squashed his lips together but she could see it was a precursor to tears. He swallowed, and stumbled on. "She turned her back on her."

"Oh, Derek. That's awful. Poor Fiona. And poor Anna. She must feel dreadful."

"Oh Fiona," he whispered, his voice cracking. Tears were spilling over. Large satisfying drops of remorse.

"Look, I simply came to say that my truth is not your truth."

"Oh, very philosophical."

"I mean what I knew of her isn't what you necessarily saw or knew. And of course I didn't know her like you did." Derek looked up in surprise, it must have cost her to say that. "But I did like her very much and I think I've spoilt your memory of her, which I shouldn't have done."

"No, you shouldn't have. It was cruel."

That sounded a little harsh, he wondered if he ought to cut her some slack. She took a deep breath and continued.

"It was. Lots of excuses but none of them important. I'm sorry. I won't disturb you again."

Just then the smoke alarm began to screech and flash. Dolly sat down and howled. Derek left Harriet standing at the front door with her hands over her ears. The kitchen was full of smoke, the onions scorched mounds in the frying pan. He turned off the stove and opened the back door to hurl the pan onto the grass. Dolly tried to follow it out but he was worried she'd burn herself so he hauled her back in. Harriet peered in from the hall. Derek sat down with a thump and put his head in his hands. He dripped blood across his cheek and onto the table.

"Here," she said, taking charge, "let me." Harriet opened both the windows, turned off the radio, put on the kettle, walked back to the front door which she wedged open with one of his trainers. The alarm faltered. She came back and began to make tea.

"You're not having a great day, are you?" She picked up the packet of plasters next to the onion skins.

"No. I used to love Fiona's casseroles but it's all such a faff."

"Would you like me to finish it off?"

"No, it's alright. But..." And he groaned, "I miss her so much."

"Me too."

They both took a sip of tea and he said quietly, "Tell me what you miss about her."

"Do you really want me to?"

"Yes. Actually you're one of the few people in the village who spent any time with her. It's not really about what you remember specifically, it's just nice to hear her name and not have to explain all about it. My wife was called Fiona, she had a stroke, and now I am a widower."

"I'm not sure how to do this."

"Well, start at the beginning. Can you remember the first time you met?"

Harriet took a deep breath.

"Not really, I think we'd smiled and said good morning for months before we actually spoke. It was probably Dolly."

Dolly was sitting with her head on Harriet's lap. Harriet stroked her ears. For a second Derek was jealous, Dolly did

228

seem to have a bit of a thing for Harriet. He supposed it was because she associated her with walks, which were still her favourite thing. The doorbell rang again. He and Harriet jumped. Dolly got up and wagged her tail.

"Is it always like this?"

"Never," Derek replied. Apart from Anna no one ever visited. "I'll just go and see who it is. I won't be long."

"Ok."

***

Harriet waited. Dolly had gone with Derek. Harriet looked around, the place needed a good clean, nothing major, just a hot soapy cloth right into the corners. She finished her tea. There was still no sign of him. She really did have to get back to the pub. She went into the hall. The front door was open and Dolly was sitting on the top step. She turned to look at Harriet but stayed where she was.

"Hello, girl. Where's that master of yours?"

She squeezed past Dolly, who immediately got up and tried to follow her down into the road.

"Sit, stay," Harriet said firmly. Dolly was a good dog and her bottom dropped but Harriet could see she wasn't happy. "You tell Derek I had to go." She wondered where he'd got to. She began to head up to the pub and immediately saw him, still in his slippers, talking to the flower lady who lived across the road. The one who'd caused all the trouble for Simeon. She was standing on her front path, the gate between them.

"Bye, Derek," Harriet called as she walked past him. She didn't bother saying anything to Terry. She knew Terry didn't like her so there wasn't any point. Derek nodded, as if he wasn't sure what was required of him.

***

Archie was sweeping out the fire, just in case Simeon came to visit, though he knew it wasn't likely. The day before he'd taken the shopping down as requested, had left it outside on the step, on the dot of eleven. He'd put a note amongst the potatoes to say that he'd get one more load of groceries but after that Simeon must try and go shopping himself. Hiding wasn't the answer. The phone rang and Archie gratefully got up off his knees.

"Hello, Phil. What can I do for you?"

Phil explained that Anna had been a bit upset when she'd left the pub the day before. That he hadn't rung because he thought Archie might pop in for a drink. Archie smiled at that, who'd have thought he'd have been to the pub so often recently he'd become a regular. He didn't ask for details as that would have been prying but thanked Phil for letting him know. Anna was his responsibility though it felt like everything was happening at once. He'd have to go and see her, after he'd checked his phone to make sure that Simeon hadn't left a message. He wasn't expecting one, Simeon never contacted him except face to face. Even through the latest crisis he hadn't rung for help. Archie thought it was because Simeon preferred to see the person he was talking to, so that he had a chance of working out what was going on. Talking on the phone wouldn't give him enough clues. Which made Archie smile again. They all had rules that made sense to them on one level but that you wouldn't want to roll out to their logical conclusion. Anna's problem was that she kept trying to live up to what she thought others expected of her when most of the time it was actually what she expected of herself. He pulled on his overcoat. Late October and already the winds were coming in from the north-west, big clouds bowling across the sky, rising over the cliffs to dump their sucked-up melted icebergs all over them. He turned into the lane, pulled his hat down (his beanie as he now called it), and stopped. Anna was coming towards him, shoulders hunched, her coat darkened with rain splotches. He waited for her to reach him.

"Oh, Archie, are you on your way out?"

"Only to see you. Come on in and I'll light the fire. It's cold."

"Too cold, too soon," she said. "It's going to be an awful winter."

"Yes, probably not the mildest."

He made coffee and found some of the nice biscuits he kept at the back of the cupboard especially for her. When he took the tray through he realised how dark the room was. Her face was turned to the window, away from the glow of the fire. She looked pale, cold, and he wasn't sure that any of his logs would be sufficient to warm her through.

"Anna, what's happened?"

She peered up at him, like a small child, and he drew a sharp breath down into his ribcage.

"I really do have to move on, Archie. I can't hack it here. I'm a hypocrite and a liar."

Archie started to pray. He was going to need all the help he could get with this. He couldn't face another crisis, let alone another interregnum, but more to the point she needed help to see herself a little less harshly.

He poured the coffee and handed her the plate of biscuits. She took it, put it beside her on the little table, just in front of the photograph of Moira. That was just what Moira used to do. She always took the whole plate and he'd let her. But he mustn't get sidetracked by those thoughts. Anna was here and needed him.

"Tell me what happened," he asked again, gently.

"Simeon came to see me and told me he'd tried to jump again."

"Oh, no. He's not talked like that for months."

"Sorry," Anna interrupted. "I was talking about the day it happened. The day Fiona came to the churchyard. The day she was... you know." Archie swallowed and nodded. "Simeon had just told me about jumping again."

"Of course, he only ever talked about it."

"But that's my problem. You knew he only talked about it, I didn't. I don't have your history. I only had to go on what I saw. So every time he came to speak to me I had to face the possibility that he was serious. It was terrifying."

"I can see that," Archie said, wondering why she hadn't come to him for advice.

Startlingly, as if she had read his mind, she said, "It was different back then. I didn't know you as well."

He sat up a little straighter. She was right. Things were different now. Better.

"So when I saw Fiona I was still really upset. She'd never been to church. I didn't know she was the one who'd had the stroke. I thought it was one of the old ladies we often see about the place. She wanted to go and sit inside but I was so uptight after Simeon talking again about... I was so very angry."

Archie hadn't realised how often Simeon must have told Anna about wanting to die. Most people had seen him out on the cliff at some time or other. Most people had asked him if he was alright. They were then secretly relieved to see him in the shop the following day or getting on a bus to Helston. After a while people stopped worrying about him standing so close to the edge because he never actually jumped.

"I'm sorry Anna. I hadn't realised that you didn't know about Simeon."

"Even so Archie, I shouldn't have taken my anger out on Fiona. She was exhausted. Why couldn't I see that? She was wet and cold. I should have noticed." Anna picked up her coffee, then put it down again without taking a sip. "But I was selfishly indulging my own misery. I muttered something about the church not being a bus shelter. I swear she didn't hear me. But there's that bloody verse about getting angry with someone being just as bad as murdering them. Only," and here she turned her pale, frightened face to him and whispered, "only Archie, what if it was my fault? What if I'd

232

simply walked with her to the church and phoned Derek to come and fetch her? Maybe she'd still be alive?"

Unless it was Derek himself, Archie thought, and then dismissed that as nonsense.

"If he'd come to find her earlier, Anna, then things might have been different too. He left it an awfully long time before he phoned the police. Why didn't he simply go and look for her?"

"He says he got engrossed in his work, then panicked because she'd been gone a while, so felt he ought to do something decisive, but he was also worried he'd miss her call if he was out looking. You know how patchy the signal is round the village."

"Well, whatever he did or didn't do, I don't think we can possibly live our lives based on what-ifs or should-haves. Isn't that the whole point of our faith? We get to confess, we get forgiven. No one else gets that deal, no one else gets to start again with a clean slate."

"I know," she said angrily, "I know we get all of that, but there are consequences to what we do. It doesn't all go away."

"Of course it doesn't. God never promised us it would. Paul wrote some of his best letters from prison! All we can hope for is to muddle through. There's no golden path. He knows we wouldn't manage to stick to it for half a second, but I think he redeems the path we're on. Helps us to do the best we can with what we have."

She stared at him.

"Bloody hell Archie, that's awesome."

Archie blinked. Bloody hell, it was. But was it the truth? He wasn't sure.

"I don't know if it is or not," he said, sounding like his old self, which felt better, more familiar, though Anna still seemed knocked out.

"You're amazing," she whispered. "Why can't I be like you, forgiving and gracious and seeing?"

"You're not supposed to be like me. You're supposed to be like you."

"Ha, ha!" she said, picking up another biscuit. "But I am supposed to be like you. I am supposed to see people as they really are, I am supposed to have time to stop and talk to them even if I am scared and angry. I am supposed to be able to forgive them. Even bloody Simeon and all his talk of jumping." Now she would have to add Terry to that list, who she was pretty sure had a very low opinion of her. That visit had gone spectacularly badly. Anna glared at Archie. "I know I'm supposed to be able to forgive myself."

"Yes, yes, and yes, but Anna, you don't know what's going on in my head. You only see what I am able to do, sometimes. You don't see all the times I don't walk into church when Simeon is there because I don't think I have the strength to deal with him that day, how angry I am at Moira because she indulged her sweet tooth and died far too young of a heart attack, which I can't help thinking she could have done something about. I've been reading everything I can lay my hands on to find answers to the questions that Simeon asks because I don't want him to think I don't know. And yes, I tell everyone I'm not that knowledgeable but inside I want you to believe that I am."

Anna took another biscuit, looked at his face, and put it back.

"It's trite to say," he continued, "but I suppose it's true, that what other people think of us is none of our business. Only sometimes it does matter."

She pulled a tissue from her pocket and blew her nose.

"We expend so much energy worrying about it," she said, "instead of going to the one person who really does know what we're like. But I still don't feel able to forgive myself for what I did to Fiona. That's the place I always come back to."

"Actually, I don't think it is. You were very sad and angry before Fiona."

Anna didn't want to do this. She knew where she'd end up if she was really honest about everything. She tried to get a grip. It almost worked only her next words were swallowed and gulped and could only surface as a breathless whisper. "So what do I do?"

He looked startled. His eyes widened and his hand involuntarily rubbed his chin.

"Well, you have someone to talk to now, and she gave you homework. I think your homework is genius."

"You do?"

"Yes," he said. "She's sent you, a struggling vicar, into your own church for an hour a day and you're not allowed to pray."

"I know," Anna said. "It's bizarre. I don't know what to do half the time."

"Anna, what is prayer and how do you do it?"

"Oh, God," she groaned. "Of course I'm praying. But I'm having to go cold turkey on all my usual expectations and methods."

"Sometimes it's hard to see the wood for the trees."

"But why couldn't I see that? Why do I have to be so resentful all the time? And why are you making so much sense all of a sudden?" she asked, squinting at him through swallowed tears.

"Because I'm not walking in the woods, but I can see that you are. And it's easy when it's not you. Everyone sees us so much better than we see ourselves."

"But you said we shouldn't try and guess what people think of us."

"I think the key word there is guess."

"You don't need a spiritual director, you are one," she said, under her breath.

Archie laughed.

"No, I'm just as flawed as you are but that's what we take to God. That's what he forgives and that's what he redeems, saves us from, however you want to call it."

Anna knew it made sense but she still didn't want to give in.

"Yes, I suppose so." Now Anna sounded like a reluctant teenager who'd been told to go and apologise. "But the honest truth is I don't want to think about this stuff. I want to sneak away somewhere by myself to cry, and eat chocolate. For no matter what you say Archie, I don't think I'll ever be able to face Derek again. But thanks. I will go and do my homework. Then I suppose I ought to go and find Derek."

"Hang on, don't jump ahead of yourself. By all means go and sit in church and then see what happens."

***

Anna sat in church. No thoughts, nobody, nothing.

"Come on, show up. Like you did before. Send Harriet, or Phil, or even Derek. I know what you're up to now."

She made another cup of tea and then needed the loo. But she still had forty minutes to go. She wondered if anyone would notice if she nipped into the churchyard. She stood up. No, she couldn't wait.

She unhooked the key for the north door and squeezed through the vestry. The grass was long and wet, but still the glorious emerald green left over from the warm, damp summer. The graves mottled orange and mauve with lichen caught a brief ray of sun and glowed. Just for a second she forgot what she was doing and simply stared.

"Very lovely, but it will look even nicer when I've had my wee," she said quietly and pulled the door shut. There was a large chest tomb under the hedge. She got covered with drips of water from the wet branches but was out of sight and just hoped that Simeon didn't turn up.

Once she had re-adjusted her clothing she decided she didn't want to re-enter the church by the rarely used north door. That somehow screamed of what she had just done. Instead she trailed round to the south porch. Was the door more ajar than she had left it? The back of her neck prickled. She hesitated. She shouldn't be afraid, but she was suddenly, inexplicably.

"I'm not having this," she said out loud and pushed inside.

"Tom." She couldn't help the relief.

He was sitting about halfway up, and twisted round to smile at her.

"Do you normally leave the church open when there's no one around?"

"I was around. But no, not normally."

"You come in here pretty much every day."

"Yes..." She wondered what he wanted. Perhaps to ask her more questions about the bloody timeline.

"You ought to lock yourself in."

"I can't do that. I simply can't. It's a church and we don't leave it open anywhere near enough as it is."

He went to the back and put on the kettle. A bubble of resentment expanded in her stomach at his ease within her space, her domain. But it quickly popped as she realised how glad she was that he was here. She wondered if it was an official visit only that might remind him to become DI Edwards. And she much preferred Tom. He was bound to make the transition to policeman at some point, which she was sure she would deeply resent. He handed her a cup of tea.

"I've had another chat with forensics. They are pretty sure that the rock embedded in Fiona's skull is slightly different from the stone she was sitting on. Though it's not much of a difference. As was said at the inquest."

"So, she was probably hit with a chunk from another gravestone. There are bits about the place, they sometimes sheer off after a nasty frost."

"There are a number of stones that would fit, and some of them do look as though they have bits missing. Of course once the deed was done the murder weapon could have been carried to the nearest cliff and simply chucked over. It certainly wasn't left lying around in the churchyard." He took a sip of tea.

"But we're back to who would have done such a thing."

"Well, we did have that tip off about looking into it again. We traced it back to a phone box in Falmouth. So there's nothing more we can do with that."

"None of us have alibis." Anna laughed. Tom didn't. A little more seriously she asked, "What about the woman who emailed Derek?" Tom shrugged. She continued, "Though he still can't remember who she is."

"Well, I could speak to him about it."

"So is this an official visit?" She bit her lip and looked down at the floor. She had told herself she wasn't going to ask him that. "A top up?" she asked, quickly. He nodded, which was a relief.

As she stood up he said, "It's probably my last time here. There are no new leads." He sort of slumped.

"You sound... defeated."

"I'm just tired and I... this mustn't go any further."

"Are you asking me to put my vicar hat on?"

"Yes, I suppose I am."

"Alright," she said, very slowly, "I will put it on and what you say will be confidential unless of course it involves some form of abuse and then I will have to pass it on to the relevant authorities."

He nodded and she thought there was the hint of a smile. She handed him a biscuit. The biscuits in the tin were soft, another sure sign that Simeon was still holed up at his cottage. She felt a flash of anger and swallowed it, like she should have done on the night Fiona died. It was his fault that Simeon was still holed up; that she had felt scared to enter her own church. Still, she needed to listen to this man, not as DI Edwards but as Tom and not with resentment but with a gentle heart, because she was a vicar.

"The thing is, Anna," and the use of her name settled her,

"I've never been able to shake the feeling that I've missed something, something important about Fiona's death. But there simply aren't the resources to keep the investigation active."

They sat and drank their tea, Anna twisting a little so the door was in sight. Then she was able to unhunch her shoulders. She wondered if it was because she was facing the slither of light or because Tom was with her.

"So the long and the short of it," Anna said, "is that Simeon probably saw Fiona's killer but he recognises people by their feet, so the best you'd get from him is a fleeting description of a shape in the rain."

"Not even that as he looked away so quickly. Unless," Tom said, looking at her sideways, "he accidentally scared Fiona and she slipped and fell. Then he removed the offending rock she hit her head on and made up the story of the figure to throw us off the scent."

Anna laughed.

Tom continued. "Of course none of that will stand up in court, m'Lud." Finally he smiled at her. His eyes and nose wrinkling, the lines deepening. But he was right, it was all speculation, nothing more than vague scrabbling around.

"There is always the mystery woman who emails Derek coffee with menaces," she added.

"Hardly a motive for murder."

"I simply can't imagine Derek is the sort of man you'd kill for."

"That's presupposing they are even the same person, Derek's lady and the person seen leaving the churchyard," Tom said, sipping his tea.

"Surely that's a simple matter of tracing her."

"Sadly not going to happen. I cite once again the lack of resources. And she's only been a little insistent. So we've nothing to go on."

He sounded really sad.

"I see, even though she's somehow managed to get his personal email."

"That's not such a big deal, I bet I could find it within a few minutes on the internet. For example which one does he use for the RIBA?"

"I don't know," she said. "I don't suppose I can help at all?"

"No, absolutely not."

"That's always what the policeman says, too."

"I'm serious, Anna. Whoever clubbed Fiona to death might still be about the place."

Yet they were not putting any more resources in. There it was, the switch from Tom to DI Edwards. She sat back.

"What's the matter, Anna?"

But this time the use of her name jarred.

"Well, I will still keep my eyes and ears open for anything pertinent," she said stubbornly, and stared at the altar. She knew he'd be looking exasperated at her.

There was a pause.

"Look, would you like a drink?"

He'd got to his feet and was looking down at her. She took the dangling cup out of his hand.

"No thanks. I need to be here a bit longer."

"I know you won't, but couldn't you lock yourself in?"

She shrugged.

"You can't have it both ways," she muttered to his retreating back.

Chapter 16

The following morning Anna was eating toast in her kitchen, and not praying.

"I just don't know what to make of Tom," she said to God, then laughed. If anyone else spoke to an invisible being they'd be carted off to the funny farm. Mind you, she supposed it might be a great deal worse if she confessed to hearing a reply. Where did the medical world draw the line? The still small voice in the head, the thoughts that were so definite you changed direction, the words that jumped from the Bible and stopped you in your tracks? At what point did you become a danger to society? She was a vicar, so it was what she did. "What do you make of him?" she asked.

The doorbell rang. It had started cutting out and she knew one of the wires needed replacing. Something else she probably wouldn't get round to. Her parishioners would soon learn to hammer on the door.

"Harriet!"

"Hi Anna," Harriet replied, exuding misery.

"Come in. I can do toast and honey."

Harriet looked as if she needed feeding, something Anna knew she could do without screwing up.

"Yes, please."

Once they were seated at the kitchen table, a pile of toast between them, Anna nodded at Harriet.

"Well?"

"It's happened. It came yesterday, when I was at work."

"Your eviction notice."

Harriet winced.

"He didn't call it an eviction notice. He just said that some of the more pressing problems needed sorting and he'd like me to move out while he put them right."

"Well, that doesn't sound like he's asking you to leave."

Harriet snorted.

"That's exactly what he's asking me to do. He's making it impossible to stay and then when the work is done he won't let me know that I can move back in and if I ask him he'll mention a not unreasonable hike in rent commensurate with a new boiler and bathroom."

"Ok. Well, I meant what I said. You can move into the vicarage, at least until you find somewhere else."

"I love the fact that you believe that would be alright, but I'm never going to find anything around here that I can afford." Harriet had cried a lot when Anna had first got to know her but these tears were different. She didn't sob. She simply sat there, water spilling from her eyes, her nose running. Anna gave her some kitchen roll while she went through to the lounge to get the proper tissues.

"The thing is, it means I'll have to leave. I'll have to try and find another job in a place more affordable and it's bound to be somewhere horrible."

"Have you told Phil? Perhaps he can up your wages or something."

Harriet laughed.

"He does alright with the pub but only because it's just him and Bowzer. He'd never be able to keep a family on what he earns. I get a bit more than minimum wage. He tops it up whenever he can, except when he does there's always the worry he won't have enough for the electric or the next council tax bill."

"I didn't realise. He's always so cheerful."

"Well, I don't think he's unhappy it's just if he did meet someone and they wanted children it might be a different matter."

Anna thought they were looking a little far ahead.

"Isn't he a bit old to start a family?"

"It's different for them than for us," Harriet said, blinking away the tears. Anna thought how attractive she was, even soggy. Whenever Anna cried she bloated up like a... she

242

simply couldn't think of a word that wasn't gross.

"You've got to tell him though. And please move in here for a bit. Give yourself some breathing space."

"Are you allowed to sublet?"

Anna wasn't sure she knew what that was.

"Pay towards the electric and the food. Stay as a friend. As you know I have few of them so it would be nice, good to have someone else about the place."

The thought popped into her head that one of the silver linings might be that it would curtail the evening biscuit binges.

"Well alright, it would give me some thinking time. There is plenty of room." Harriet tucked a strand of hair behind her ear. She pursed her lips.

"Have you made up with Derek?" Harriet asked, her head tipped to one side. Anna didn't want Harriet knowing how unkind she'd been, how in all probability it had been her fault that Fiona had died, that she had had it in her power to help her. But perhaps it was time to come clean, to be truly honest for a change.

"He was justifiably upset because probably the last words Fiona ever heard were My church is not a bus shelter," she continued.

Harriet nodded. "He said."

Anna went through Fiona's last moments. Relived the dimness of that dull winter evening, the rain on her face, her chilled fingers, and the anger. That Simeon had used her so readily and didn't seem to care that what he said ground away at the very fabric of her soul, had made her feel powerless and overwhelmed. Made her feel as though God didn't exist... She finished the silence with "Only he does."

"Sorry, who does what?"

"God does exist." She was sure of it, just for a moment.

"I'm glad because otherwise I wouldn't be the only one looking for a job."

Harriet smiled but Anna didn't want to get sidetracked.

"I'm not sure I was simply angry with Simeon, I think I might have been angry with God too. I felt so lonely, so overwhelmed." It was good to let that spill out. To finally say it. She felt as though it had been growing and stretching inside her skin for quite a while.

"I know how that feels," Harriet murmured.

"You do, don't you? When Ade left you."

"In a way, but sometimes even now." Harriet took a sip of tea, then said, "I don't think what I feel has anything to do with him any more."

Anna pushed the plate of toast towards her. If Harriet didn't have another piece, she'd feel obliged to eat the rest herself.

"The truth is I hardly ever think of him now and when I do I feel sort of neutral."

"So what are you going to do with your life?" Anna asked. "In ten years what would you like to be doing, where would you like to be?"

Harriet stared at her.

"What sort of question is that?"

"One that needs answering, I think."

"No one knows what's going to happen to them that far ahead."

"I'm not asking you to gaze into a crystal ball, but do you really want to be behind the bar? Simply subsisting?" Anna turned away from Harriet's look of surprise. "It's true though isn't it? Just staying somewhere because it's beautiful or because it's where you ended up is not really good enough."

"Well, Miss Smarty Pants Vicar, when you can answer those questions yourself then let's talk again."

Harriet got up and walked to the kitchen door, but when she got there she turned back and smiled. Anna heaved a sigh of relief. She'd thought she'd managed to alienate someone else. She thought that Harriet wasn't being entirely fair turning the ten-year question round. For Anna it wasn't about where she wanted to be, but where God wanted her to be. Which was entirely different. She got up to follow Harriet out.

As Harriet pulled on her coat she added, "By the way, I popped in to see Derek, like you said I should."

Anna was sure she hadn't said any such thing, but Harriet's voice didn't carry a portent of doom.

"So how did it go?"

"We had a nearly civilised conversation and a cup of tea, but then Terry, the flower lady – the one who upset Simeon – came to call and Derek left me to drink it alone. I really did have to get back to the pub."

It didn't sound all that promising.

"Not a total disaster?" Anna asked hopefully.

"I guess not. Though he ought to have told her he already had a visitor, and that it wasn't convenient to chat."

"It's odd," Anna frowned, "I just can't imagine Terry chatting to anyone. Certainly not to me anyway."

"No, she doesn't like me either but then we are not eligible bachelors."

Anna was a little shocked. "But he's only just lost Fiona. He's still grieving."

"Oh, Anna," Harriet said, laughing. "That is precisely the moment to go in for the kill. He's at his most attractive and most vulnerable."

Anna just couldn't imagine Terry being so calculating. Granted she was difficult to read, aloof even, and always left Anna feeling intensely inadequate but the one thing she had learned over the last few months was that snap judgements were more often than not wrong. That everyone had a back story that needed taking into consideration.

***

Simeon sat in shadow, feeling the heaviness of the absence of light. He could see the corners of the room but they seemed fuzzy and far away. He rested his hands on his stomach. He curled them into fists, squeezed them as tight as he could, until the ligaments along his thumbs began to ache. Then he relaxed, only that made it difficult to lift his head, to fix himself back on the bed. Nothing felt right. Finally it began to dawn on him that what was holding him down was disappointment.

He was disappointed with Archie who had brought the wrong sort of milk even though Simeon had clearly specified it had to be full fat. He had also said he would only do one more trip to the shop which Simeon thought unkind. It didn't give him enough time to recover. He was disappointed with Anna. She should have at least tried to come and visit him. It was what vicars were supposed to do. He was disappointed with the policeman, who seemed to be singularly stupid. Terry must have had some motive for cornering him and that was what ought to be under investigation. Instead it was being treated as a simple misunderstanding. Lastly, Simeon was disappointed with himself. It had taken him nearly two days to stop shaking, which meant it had taken him two days to be able to think again. He hated the surge of adrenalin that caused such breathless panic. It was one of the worst episodes he'd had for a long time.

He wondered what he could do. He didn't feel safe venturing out just in case Terry was there. He certainly couldn't go to the church because he might get cornered again. He couldn't go to the shop in case Archie saw him and refused to help him even that one last time. He couldn't go to visit Archie at home because that meant crossing the village where everyone would see him. Anna said that people didn't think about him as much as he thought they did, but she had never been him. He tried to lift his chin just a little so he could locate the corners of the room again, but his head felt too heavy. He twisted it to one side, that meant he could only see one side of the room and he needed to be able to view all four of the walls holding up the ceiling. At least his heart rate was steady. He slept. When he woke he got up to make a cup of tea. The offending milk was sitting on the side. It may even have separated a little. Simeon could barely look at it, let alone touch it so it had to remain on the draining board. It wouldn't be long before he'd be unable to come into the kitchen, before the cardboard stretched and bulged from the bacteria multiplying inside. By then he hoped that Archie would have come round to deal with it.

He put on his parka, the outsized one that used to belong to his mother, one of the few things his social worker had suggested he keep, one of the few things of hers he'd been able to touch. For a long time he'd left it in the spare room draped across the bed until he'd had to get a new shirt. There was a pile of the ones he liked in the wardrobe. Plain navy, soft cotton. He'd never looked at the coat before but for some reason it had caught his eye. He'd been surprised at how much he'd wanted to run his fingers over the furry edging, how good it felt to wrap himself up in it. It had taken him a while to get used to the fur around his face but it still had a faint smell of the woman who had stood in front of him through his childhood, protecting him. Luckily they'd been short of money back then so she'd bought an outsized coat because it had been a bargain. It fitted him with ease. It was the only coat he wore. The hood flopped over his face enough to shut out his peripheral vision, it was heavy enough for the worst winds to drive him along but not to get in at him, and nearly waterproof as long as he didn't get drenched. He zipped it up. Usually it made him feel warm and safe, but today he couldn't shake the acid churning. He wanted to see Archie. He needed to see Archie.

For a long time he stood in the hallway peering through the narrow slit of the door pulled ajar, a patch of life starting with pale blue sky, then red and yellow from the last of the leaves on the hedge, down to the green and brown of the grass. He went close to the gap but he couldn't see far enough. She could be waiting for him just around the corner.

He had spent a lot of time wondering why she had tried to corner him in the church, that like most other people she didn't understand how he worked. Only it still didn't make sense. Sometimes he wished he'd had the courage to ask her what she wanted, or that Archie had been there to stand beside him, even Anna would have done. Anna had said it was because she simply wanted someone to talk to about Fiona's death. That she'd heard that Simeon had been questioned by the police. That she like Simeon didn't understand how to open up a subject, how to chat. But Simeon didn't think that was what had happened. That didn't feel how it had been at all.

In the end he slipped out onto the lane, turned right, and quickly hurried down onto the coast path. It was the long way round but a walk he knew well, one that held no surprises. If he moved quickly once past the point, he could be at Archie's front door within a few minutes. He moved as fast as he was able when so much of the path was sticky with mud. It always fascinated him how through the winter the land soaked up the rain, spilling over into streams and deep puddles, yet how quickly in summer it dried out, how quickly everything hardened and cracked.

Soon it would be the anniversary of Fiona's death. He thought it would be interesting to review the year because things did feel different. There were more people in his life and he hadn't been out to the cliff edge for quite a while. Anna had been right about exploring the existence of God, it seemed to have changed everything. He came to a particularly tricky bit of the path where it narrowed and the mud deepened into a long slick puddle. He had to walk wide legged; it pulled his thigh muscles for even though the cliff was a good eight feet away, he had to lean away from it. He gave himself a rest at the far end and looked back along the way he had come. At Bass Point was a figure standing just under the coastguard station. Though they were too far away to see properly it didn't matter, his heart began to hammer against his ribs, and a line of sweat gathered under his hair. He began to jog. The café was less than a quarter of a mile away and he wanted to get there before the person behind him saw which way he went. Just further on round was the path that went straight up to Archie's house. The only part where he might be seen was at the Lizard itself but he would pull his hood down and run that bit. If it was Terry he was fairly sure he was far enough ahead to make it without the danger of being cornered again.

By the time he got to Archie's house he was gasping and was very glad that Archie opened the door quickly and without fuss.

"Welcome, Simeon. How very good to see you."

Simeon concentrated on his breathing. It was far too fast. He needed to slow it down.

"Catch your breath and I'll go and light the fire."

Archie knew better than to take Simeon's coat until the room was warm and settled.

"Please pull the curtains," Simeon said, as calmly as he could. Archie remembered his conversation with Anna.

"I'll draw them a little but not all the way."

"Please Archie."

He'd never heard Simeon plead before.

"I suppose it is the first time you've been out since it happened."

He closed them. Simeon's breathing began to slow.

"I need some milk but I couldn't go in the shop."

"Have you come round on the coast path?"

"Yes."

"Why couldn't you come up the lane?"

"I was afraid she'd be waiting for me."

"You told Tom she hadn't frightened you."

249

"I don't always know what the word ought to be," Simeon said, beginning to clench his fingers. Tighten and release, tighten and release.

"Well you sound scared to me. But Simeon, the policeman's been to see Terry and Anna. I'm sure Terry has got better things to do than to wait around in the lane for you."

"I'm being irrational?"

"A little. I thought I got you milk."

Simeon sat himself down in his usual chair, then he said, "Just because I'm made differently from the rest of you doesn't mean that what I do is right all the time. And the milk you got me was wrong."

Archie almost laughed. Simeon had just acknowledged his humanity while criticising Archie's own.

"I don't think you are that much different from the rest of us. And," Archie continued thoughtfully, "I think sometimes you highlight the way we truly are, that's all."

Simeon didn't reply, so he either didn't know or didn't have an opinion one way or another.

"They didn't have full fat milk at the shop. Sorry. I thought some milk was better than no milk. I'll go and make coffee." Archie closed the door carefully behind him. He left Simeon sitting there staring at the fire, a single flame trying to wrap itself round a large log. It began to falter even as Archie pulled the door to. To his surprise, Simeon followed him. He didn't want to be on his own. Simeon hadn't ever gone beyond the lounge, but from the hall there was only one door lined with light. Archie was laying out a tray when he came through.

"Oh, it's you. You made me jump."

"I don't like being on my own."

"That woman has really spooked you. I'm so sorry, Simeon."

"I don't know if I can walk home." Simeon peered out of

the window in the back door.

"Don't worry, I'll come along. I need some fresh air. I won't leave until you're as snug as a bug in a rug." Something that Moira used to say.

"My mother used to say that. I really want to go home, Archie."

"But you've only just arrived."

Simeon pulled his hood up over his head and shivered. Then he pulled the hood back down.

"I will try and stay for at least one cup of coffee."

Archie patted his arm even though he knew it would make him jump.

"Thank you Simeon, I appreciate that."

**

Archie had to stay a couple of hours with Simeon, and when he left, it was quite dark. He'd removed the offending carton, and picked up a couple of pints that Jean had set aside, while Simeon waited across the road. He had smiled when Simeon gave him the exact money – he had half expected to have to pay for it himself.

Leaves were clogging the ditches either side of the road and the temperature was dipping with every gust. There was rain forecast, wave after wave of dark blue-grey fronts, rolling in to enclose the point in winter misery. He knew Anna hated this time of year, and now Derek did too. The anniversary was never far from any of their thoughts. He hesitated at the end of the drive leading down to the vicarage, wondering whether to go and visit unannounced. Wondered what Moira would do. Decided that she would at least try.

When Anna opened the door, he barely recognised her. Her clothes were stretched around her as if she'd been pumped full of water. She looked most peculiar. On closer inspection he realised it was because she had on so many layers. He narrowed his eyes and wrinkled his nose. It felt colder inside than out.

"This is ridiculous. Can't you put on the central heating or something, just for once?"

"It hasn't had a service for two or three years and you hear such awful stories of carbon monoxide poisoning."

"I think there are so many draughts, cracks, and holes in this house you'd be perfectly safe. Let me come and have a look."

She led him down into the cellar. Two large rooms full of junk. Not hers, he decided. There were a couple of pink bikes and what looked like a mouldy Tracy Island. There were bags of logs and cans of paint. The boiler was sitting at the back. He couldn't decide its age, but she'd been right, it would need a proper service before they could fire it up. He took off the front. There didn't seem to be anything obvious he could press or clean though he blew away a lot of fluff from around the wires.

"Look, let's have a standing committee meeting. We haven't met for ages."

"We can't have one just like that. We haven't circulated an agenda or anything."

Archie shook his head, and then narrowed his eyes.

"May I have a cup of coffee? If you've got time, of course." He looked and sounded quite serious, almost formal apart from a tiny twitch at the corner of his mouth.

"Yes, I've plenty of time. Do you mind coming into the kitchen? It's the warmest room."

"I don't mind at all. Do you have a piece of paper?"

She clattered about. It felt good to make a noise, felt good to get the electric heater going, to shrug out of the top layer of clothes. She wondered what Archie was up to. When she finally sat down he pushed the piece of paper across to her.

The meeting was dated for that day and time, the minutes were recorded as having been signed. There was nothing on the agenda apart from AOB: sorting out the vicarage.

She laughed.

"Archie, you can't do this."

"Yes, I can and I'm absolutely positive the others on the committee will be happy to take forward our initial proposals and to sign the actual minutes when we produce them."

"We don't have any proposals."

"Right, so where shall we start?"

She looked down at the paper again. Sort out the vicarage. It seemed such a tiny sentence, but the implications were too big for her to manage in one bite.

"What about selling and buying somewhere smaller?" she asked, warily.

"Definitely a possibility, only they have very strict criteria for new vicarages and the only houses that would be suitable are the new ones up on the main road."

Anna thought of Tom. He'd known all about that, because of his mum.

"Far too pretentious."

"More than here, Anna? A late seventeenth century gentleman's house?" Archie began to laugh.

"He wasn't a gentleman," Anna replied.

"We have no way of knowing that. I think selling and buying one of those 'executive' properties would be perfect. So option one is that. Option two is sorting this place out."

She looked around. She'd already thought about it quite a lot during her homework in the church and, apparently, so had Archie.

"There would be re-wiring, and probably re-plumbing, and that's only after we've worked out what we might use it for. It would have to be a good proposal."

"That's true," she replied

They discussed talking to Derek. But Anna still hadn't spoken to him so Archie said he would approach him, in an unofficial capacity. He wanted to keep everything as informal as possible until they had to start filling in forms. The diocese red tape was legendary, complex and tangled. They wondered if it was viable to use the house for the parish, but make her living quarters smaller. Even if she moved downstairs, there would still be plenty of room left for a proper office and accommodation for people who came to stay, preach, or whatever it was that Archie had in mind.

"But we don't do anything like that."

"No, not at the moment but what if we thought about the future, what it might look like?"

"I can't, Archie, I can't see past..."

"Derek, Fiona, Simeon, Harriet..."

"Don't forget Ellie, Jean, Terry, and..."

"And everyone else you carry round with you."

"It's my job."

"No, it's not. It's absolutely not your job. Bring us to God by all means, but that's where your responsibility begins and ends."

"Not true. I've been put here to take care of you. The cure of souls and all that."

"You're not God, you're just the vicar."

She was beginning to uncurl. Her face pink, not pinched, and the coffee was nice, which he hadn't expected. It was the same brand he bought from the village shop.

"When are you next off to see your spiritual adviser?" he asked, wondering if he could ask for another cup.

"Wednesday as it happens."

"What are you going to tell her about your homework?"

Anna sat back a couple of inches as if suddenly he was sitting too close.

"I hadn't thought. I don't often prepare ahead of time. Usually I just turn up and talk."

"Except when you preach, of course."

She raised an eyebrow, opened her mouth as if she were going to reply, but hesitated.

"I don't often put that much time into my sermons, not as

much as I ought to."

Archie didn't say anything, and for a moment he reminded her of Irene, simply waiting for what was coming next. "I suppose I could tell her that praying isn't quite as overt as I thought it was. I always thought if you didn't set aside time for it... it wasn't proper."

"Me neither," Archie said, quietly. "It had to be perfect or it wasn't good enough and it was never perfect."

"Do you think God minds that I normally end up writing a shopping list or, worse still, a list of things I need to get done?"

"No, lists aren't necessarily a bad thing. In one of Moira's books it said that you could try asking God what he thinks of each item."

"I should ask his opinion on whether I ought to get chocolate or plain biscuits? Do you do that?"

"I do now, though perhaps not about the actual biscuits."

Except he had asked God all about the biscuits because they'd been the thing that Moira had eaten the most of, and he'd wondered whether he ought to stop eating them altogether because it always reminded him of her, and not in a good way. When he was last in the shop there had been some new varieties, all dried fruit and nuts, and he knew that Moira wouldn't have liked them at all. He thought he might give them a try. On his way home he'd had a bit of a chuckle because it looked like God did have an opinion on biscuits after all.

"Does it help?"

"Yes. It feels like then it's not all my responsibility."

"And we're back to where we started." She shook her head.

"That's because where we start is the place that's most important to us. Everything's bound to track back to it sooner or later."

Anna began to feel as if she was standing in Church Cove and the sea were dragging at her ankles, pulling her further

255

in, trying to get her out of her depth.

"Perhaps I shouldn't be speaking to you at all. Perhaps I should be saving this all up for Irene. She has the ear of the bishop, you know."

"Pearly Longbottom! Having his ear is no big deal."

Anna giggled.

"Pearly Longbottom! Why?"

"Because he has very large white front teeth."

"School or Navy?"

"Navy! He went through the ranks like he'd got wings and when he came out, a couple of years ahead of me, he went straight into the church. I wasn't one bit surprised he flew to the top of that tree too. A very bright man."

Anna couldn't help but smile and Archie was relieved. He had sensed her irritation building.

"So do you call him Pearly Longbottom now?"

"No. I very carefully call him Your Grace."

"Oh, Archie. You've cheered me up no end."

"Because you've discovered the man in charge is human."

"That's it exactly."

Chapter 17

Derek couldn't sit still. To begin with Dolly had got up and stretched every time he'd launched himself out of his chair, but eventually she'd given up and was now simply following him around the room with her eyes. She reminded him of Alice, a little disapproving with a huge dollop of love that she didn't quite know what to do with. He settled back only it wasn't long before he found himself standing by the window again, staring at the hedge opposite. He had been trying to fuel his anger with Anna, reminding himself of how selfish and unkind she'd been, but it couldn't mask his own sense of discomfort. A feeling that was writhing away in the background, always there, always ready to rise up and make its presence felt. The long and the short of it was that he'd been to blame that day, because he had forgotten Fiona. At the very least allowing her to go on her own had been negligent. It was her first walk out. For goodness sake, he'd had to virtually carry her down the steps. But she'd been so angry, so adamant that she wanted to be by herself that he'd backed off like he always did when she got like that. He wondered if her belligerence was because she thought he was cheating on her. He still couldn't imagine how that had become a reality. Not for someone like him, not for someone who'd never even been half-tempted. It made him think Fiona couldn't have known him at all. It wasn't fair. She should at least have given him the chance to tell her his side of the story.

What worried him was that already others were jumping to the conclusion that he and Fiona hadn't been happy. That he might even become a target for all the strange lonely women of the village and with perhaps more questions from the police. He didn't want to be misunderstood but no one seemed to hear what he was actually saying. When Terry had knocked on his door the afternoon Harriet had come round to apologise he'd thought he'd made it quite clear that he was busy, but somehow he'd found himself across the road listening to her wittering on about her husband, who'd also been an architect. Apparently he'd died quite recently too but then Derek had become confused because Terry had mentioned his wife, who was apparently a very difficult woman. He simply couldn't imagine Terry having an affair but Terry and the man, whoever he was, had been having lunch when he'd had a heart attack. It had sounded awful. Then Harriet had walked past with a face like thunder and barely a wave. She must have thought him so rude to have left her drinking tea alone in his kitchen, filled with the smell of burned onions and uncooked meat. To cap it all Jean had said that morning that she was pleased that he was beginning to get his life together. How did she know that and who was she trying to kid?

All this upset and who was the common denominator? He was. He thought one thing and everyone else thought the opposite. He thought he'd told Terry he didn't want to talk but had ended up across the road seemingly chatting over the garden gate. So Fiona thinking he'd been having an affair wasn't too big a jump to make. That day she had left the house incandescent with rage. He'd thought she was angry at the stroke but she was probably angry with him. Perhaps he needed to accept that he was difficult, that how he viewed the world wasn't how everyone else viewed it. That he had been the problem all along.

He'd only disentangled himself from Terry when her phone rang. He was just halfway back across the road when she had called out that she would pop over later in the week to make sure he was going on alright. He'd felt the imposition of that. He knew it was the sort of thing Simeon would understand – how annoying it was when people turned up without an invitation, trying to make you feel obliged. He was uncomfortable about Terry coming into the house. He really

258

didn't want her sitting on chairs that Fiona had sat on. Didn't think Fiona would like that at all. It had been so awkward, standing there, feeling his slippers soaking up the rain, with Harriet waiting in the kitchen.

Fiona had never turned up uninvited. He'd always been the one to go and find her, to go and dig her out of the archaeological section of the uni library. She had loved grubbing among the bones and artefacts. She had made him work hard, refused to commit to him for nearly a year, though he'd tried to pin her down a couple of times, wanting her to commit. His course was pretty full-on so nothing between them was ever going to proceed quickly, and they simply weren't the sort of people to make rash decisions. Except that since then his life seemed to have roared away with him. Alice was married with teenage children and Fiona was dead. He was looking at old age, old age with a dollop of raw loneliness. It wasn't meant to be like this. How could it have happened?

He watched the hands of the clock tick round, watched them moving, jumping whole minutes at a time. When the doorbell rang the lounge was surprisingly dark. He didn't put the hall light on so he could clearly see the shape of whoever it was in the frosted glass, backlit by the streetlamp. He was suddenly worried it might be Terry. Then he felt ridiculous, to be afraid of the woman who lived across the road. He took a deep breath, and opened the door.

"DI Edwards."

"Call me Tom. Can I have a word?"

Derek didn't think policemen needed to ask permission.

"Of course."

Derek turned back to the kitchen, only he couldn't face the dim rooms. Putting on a light wasn't going to make a difference.

"Why don't we go to the pub? I don't really want to be here at the minute." Dolly was already staring expectantly at her lead dangling over the bannister. Tom nodded.

They settled down at a small table around the corner of the bar, out of sight of Phil and Harriet. Tom didn't seem to have an issue with drinking on duty, mind you it was cracking on five pm so perhaps he considered himself done for the day.

"So what do you want?" Derek asked, absent-mindedly rubbing the top of Dolly's head with the tips of his fingers. Tom took a sip of his pint.

"We're closing down the investigation, keeping it open of course, but the powers that be think we've done all we can. As a courtesy I want to clarify what we know, see if there is anything else you'd like to add."

Derek thought that was an odd way to phrase it. As if it were Tom that was keeping all his options open.

"As long as you don't think I had anything to do with her death."

"You said you were at home at the time of the incident."

"She wasn't an incident, she was my..." He wanted to say beloved, but Fiona wasn't his beloved, she had been sensible, efficient, and... took care of him. Anyway it wasn't how you defined love; it was its absence that was easy to describe. An appalling emptiness, darkness you could touch.

"Sorry Derek. It's hard switching off the policeman part of me."

"Right, so tell me what you want to tell me." Derek lifted his pint and swallowed as if he were thirsty. Big gulps that hurt the back of his throat. Tom settled back on his chair.

"This is the sequence of events as we know it: Fiona was leaning on the tomb when Anna came out of the church. They had words and Anna left."

"Unkind words," Derek said and his lip quivered. He took another drink. Tom nodded and continued.

"Simeon had left earlier, had headed down to the cove. Anna went back to the vicarage. In the meantime Simeon had decided to go back to the church. He went in at the gap in the bottom of the hedge, walked along to the porch which was when he noticed someone at the end of the path. A white face, nothing more. No idea of height, size, or even sex. Not helpful but it did scare him. And he began to count. So he reckons he stayed in the shadow of the porch for ten minutes.

"Then seeing that the path was empty he went across to the hedge at the top, because he didn't want to walk along the path. He knows the place like the back of his hand so he didn't bother with a light. He made his way along the hedge towards the gate, very slowly. At the end he came down through the graves which is where he says he almost fell over Fiona. He only put his mobile on for a second to see what was lying there. He had also said that he definitely didn't touch her.

"He says he found her dead. Says it was obvious that she was not breathing. He was spooked and went home along the coast path."

"That's mad," Derek retorted. "His house is literally just across the road from the church. Going round by the coast path would be like three sides of a triangle. And the weather that night was terrible."

Tom frowned. "It was. But more to the point he didn't go for help either."

"Well he probably thought he'd get the blame."

Tom stared a little hard at him and Derek wondered if he'd said the wrong thing.

"If Simeon's account is true then apart from the person whom he thinks he saw then Anna may have been the last person to talk to Fiona. But we can't discount the possibility that Fiona had already gone down by the time the unknown person entered the churchyard." Derek winced. In his mind he imagined Fiona falling gracefully to the floor, but this Fiona was young and unencumbered by a walking frame. The reality was that she'd have dropped like a sack of potatoes. When he'd found her she'd been lying twisted, as if she'd fallen while trying to see who had hit her. He shivered. He could see that Tom was trying to be fair, dispassionate, but to Derek it was obvious that he believed someone had murdered Fiona. Derek swallowed hard, and breathed a couple of deep breaths. He unclenched his fists and nodded for Tom to continue. "The unknown person might not have seen her as she was off the path, behind the tomb. They might have walked to the porch, found it locked, and gone away again. But there are too many questions. Like why would anyone go to the church after dark and expect it to be open? If it had been any of the regulars, wouldn't they have found the key and gone in as usual?"

"Doesn't Simeon have any idea who he saw?"

"Sadly not, because as we know he won't make eye contact, he always looks at people's shoes to identify them. It was dark, pouring with rain, and he was seriously freaked out."

"Did he hear anything either?"

Tom shook his head. Then Derek plucked up the courage to ask the question that he desperately wanted an answer to.

"How can you be sure it wasn't me?" For a minute he thought Simeon might have a point. He simply couldn't look Tom in the eye.

"We can't."

"But I was working."

"Your computer clearly showed you sending emails up until three pm. But after that, nothing. You had plenty of time to get down there and back up again. We have no way of knowing that your coat wasn't drenched through because you'd been out in it more than once."

Derek thought he might be sick. Tom stood up, went to the bar, and was quickly back with a whiskey. Derek sipped it. The burning squashed the nausea. He'd have liked another only then he wouldn't have been able to keep his wits about him.

"So who else have you considered?" he asked. His voice squeaking.

"Harriet."

"Harriet?"

"Why not?" Tom said. "She really liked Fiona. Fiona apparently listened to her, made her feel special. And the boyfriend had left her so perhaps she was trying to get Fiona to leave you, to balance things up a bit, only Fiona wouldn't." Derek didn't think that made sense. Tom continued, "I've been there mate, through divorce. I put up, shut up, and to this day I regret being such a push-over. I even let her take my dog. I shouldn't have let her take Milo." And he took a long drink from his near empty glass. "But the whole thing can leave you feeling raw for a long time." Tom was getting off track. Derek cleared his throat. Tom started and took another sip of his pint. Derek would need to get him another one. The policeman straightened up and continued, "Harriet took Bowzer out for his walk. Later than usual and got back when it was dark. Phil didn't think it was particularly strange." Tom hesitated, he seemed to be considering what to say next. "But I think that if it had been anyone that local, Simeon might have recognised her shape."

Derek noticed it immediately.

"Her? You said her!"

"What about your lady friend?"

"I don't have a lady friend," Derek said, angrily. "I don't know how else to say it so that you will believe me."

"But what about this woman who emails you. Anna says she's been in contact again."

"I don't know who she is. I can't remember her, I think she's got me muddled up with someone else. We have no records of a job done for a Veronica anything. I even had one of the girls go down into the basement to check on the old plans. The paper ones. She couldn't find anything either. And I ignored the first email, only then she sent me another one. It was a bit pointed, so Anna told me what to say. I can show you if you like. I think we made it quite plain that I didn't want to meet. We really did. Let me show you."

Tom shook his head.

"There's no need. But I'll have a chat with the boss and see if we can't get the tech guys to take a look. Forward her email to me." Derek didn't think that sounded like they were closing the case.

"So why don't I just agree to meet her and you could lie in wait or something?"

"Let's do the research first. I don't expect it's anything sinister."

Derek didn't find that at all helpful. Tom's pint was empty.

"Another?" Derek asked, but Tom was already rising to his feet.

"No, thanks. I'll be on my way. It's quite a trek back and I've already had a long day."

Derek suddenly felt cast adrift. Surely the woman was just a client who'd got the wrong end of the stick, and Fiona had simply slipped and fallen? That's what had happened, that's what he was going to stick to. It was so much easier to think that. He took a deep breath, he needed to follow Tom out, stride home as if he had lots of things to do. Instead he went and leaned on the bar until Phil had finished serving down at the other end. He ordered another pint and settled in for the night.

***

Harriet carried the last of her boxes up to her new room. It was virtually the size of the whole of her old flat and just as cold so she felt right at home. She found one of her many oversized woolly jumpers and pulled it on. It was disconcerting to see herself in the old-fashioned dressing table. She'd become rather wan over the last few months.

Phil had loaned her the van for the afternoon. It had only taken the one load. She wondered if he'd mind if she nipped into Helston to do a bit of shopping. It seemed a waste to take it back so soon.

She had felt a little sad looking round the old place for the last time. How tiny and shabby it had looked, her temporary resting place. She hadn't filled it with nice things, and had made do, but without the mug tree and the throw over the couch it looked positively spartan. She'd always thought of it as only a place to lay her head and now she was going to just a room, though Anna had said she should treat the vicarage as her home. They had even discussed housework and how they would split the jobs, which seemed a little academic as Anna didn't seem to do much of anything. Harriet wondered if she would end up doing most of the chores out of sheer gratitude. Anna had also warned her of the cold, that she couldn't afford to get the boiler serviced, so hadn't switched the central heating on for a couple of years. For hot water she used the immersion heater and there was a thin electric shower over the bath. The bath was magnificent – it had claw feet and a stain under the taps like a blood spill, rusty brown with frilly copper green edges. The first thing Harriet would have to do was hoover the spiders out from underneath. It all felt a bit studenty, but with some effort she thought she could make it quite nice. Harriet pushed into the kitchen.

"Tea, Harriet?"

"Yes, please."

Anna had the bags in the cups just sitting there.

"I can see you have a lot to learn about tea."

Anna looked round. She was washing up from the night before.

"I'm sorry. It's just ordinary. I don't have any more Earl Grey."

"Don't worry, I don't mind normal tea and I've got supplies in one of the boxes. Where...?"

Anna swung open a cupboard. It was empty, with sticky patches and crumbs in the corners.

"Will this do? I've cleared a shelf in the fridge, too."

"Perfect." Though Harriet decided she wouldn't unpack until she'd had a bit of a wipe round.

"I have to go out tonight. We have a standing committee at Archie's."

"What's a standing committee?"

"Oh, buildings, maintenance."

"Well I guess you need to keep on top of it all."

Anna laughed.

"Actually Archie's really got the bit between his teeth about sorting this out." She waved vaguely around.

"Excellent. It could do with a bit of love. Does he know I've come to live here for a bit?"

"Yes. He said it was a good idea. That you'd be company."

"He's a nice man, Mr Wainwright."

Anna found it odd hearing Archie referred to as Mr Wainwright. She'd been calling him Archie for so long now she realised that the formality didn't fit any more.

"I wasn't sure what you'd like for lunch so I've got some bread and cheese. We probably ought to discuss how we're going to organise eating."

"Oh, you needn't worry about me. I often get my meals at the pub, so carry on as usual."

Harriet knew she'd said the wrong thing. Anna looked deflated. "But of course we can sometimes eat together," she added quickly.

"Yes, that would be great." Anna had to clear her throat, her voice had become hoarse and squeaky. "It would be a good way of making sure we were, it was...working."

Harriet replied, "We could take it in turns if you like." She decided that it was best to remain practical, but she was definitely going to cook first so that Anna would know how high to set the bar otherwise Harriet imagined it would be frozen macaroni cheese and cold ham.

After Anna had left for her meeting, Harriet decided to finish unpacking the last of her boxes. Just as she had begun the front door bell stuttered to life, then there was a tentative knock. Harriet wondered if it was a parishioner. She flicked on the landing lights though couldn't find a switch for the downstairs until she was down there, which she thought was a little impractical. The hall was gloomy with shadows and cobwebs. She hauled open the front door which stuck rather inconveniently on the tiles after about six inches.

"Sorry, I can't get it any further. Oh, Derek!"

"Hello Harriet. Shall I give it a shove from my side?"

"If you want to come in then yes, if you just want to speak to Anna then..." She was going to say no, but it sounded a little unkind.

"I actually came round to see you."

"Then put your shoulder to the door." Harriet hesitated. "So would you like tea?"

"Yes, please."

The door squealed and opened enough for Dolly to push in. Harriet dropped down to give her a hug. It was dark outside, the path from the drive pale and narrow. She would have to start remembering a torch.

"I wonder if there's an outside light. Anna ought to be able to see who is calling, don't you think?" she said.

"I could bring a plane down, take off a couple of millimetres from the bottom where it's catching. She wouldn't mind would she?"

"I should think she'd be delighted."

"I'm sorry about last time you came over."

"What did Terry want?" Harriet couldn't help her voice sounding a little peevish. She turned away and headed for the kitchen. She'd had a bit of a tidy up and a wipe round but it still wasn't a particularly welcoming space. In fact harsh and unhomely were the words that sprung to mind. Derek didn't seem bothered. He shrugged out of his coat, draped it across the back of a chair, and sat at the kitchen table. Harriet wondered how many times he'd done that before.

Derek wasn't sure what Terry had wanted.

"I don't know. She went on and on about her husband. I

didn't really get a word in edgeways."

"I didn't know she was married."

Derek shrugged. He didn't look as though he wanted to talk about Terry. He said, "I hope I don't become fair game for all the lonely spinsters in the parish." Harriet was about to retort in kind only she quickly realised he hadn't meant her. She smiled. He opened his arms and said, "So what do you think of the place?"

"It could be gorgeous but it's so big I think Anna is overwhelmed by it. She sort of lives in the kitchen and a box room at the back."

"Well hopefully we'll be able to do something about that. If she opened up just one of the chimneys she could have a fire in either of the front rooms."

"Now that would be lovely. The whole place needs warming through."

"Don't worry, Archie's on the case. He wants to make it more than bearable for her otherwise I think he's afraid she might move on."

Harriet stared at him, her eyes narrowing just a little.

"Oh I do hope not. Now how about that cup of tea Derek?"

***

"Hello, Archie. Any news of Simeon after his first venture out?" Anna handed him her coat. She had come early for the meeting, simply because she knew he'd have a good fire going and would make her a fresh cup of coffee. She had felt a little guilty at leaving Harriet all alone on her first night, and hoped she'd manage to work out how to use the TV.

"I popped in yesterday and we walked up to church together. I think you'd just finished your homework, the kettle felt warm."

"Oh, that's odd. I didn't go down yesterday. It was my day to see Irene."

"How did that go? Was she pleased with you?"

268

Anna followed him into the kitchen.

"She didn't really say much. Truth be told, I was a bit disappointed. All she said was that she thought another couple of months of the same would be good, even though when it came down to it, I think quite a lot has happened."

Archie looked disappointed too.

"I'm not sure what I expected." Anna leaned back against the counter, so he could reach the mugs. "I guess a bit of encouragement wouldn't have gone amiss. You know, Well done Anna, you're on the right track." She pursed her lips and tucked her hair behind her ear. "But simply keep going seems a bit of an anti-climax."

"Well at least she didn't tell you that you were doing it all wrong."

"I guess."

"How's Harriet?"

"Good, I suppose. She doesn't own much. It didn't take long to unload her life." That had made Anna feel a little sad. "Perhaps it's how she likes to be. Not weighed down by a lot of stuff. Only now everything feels worse than ever, shabby and cold and big."

Archie smiled.

"Don't worry, Vicar. That's what we're here for."

***

The others on the committee were a bit shocked that she'd been managing without proper heating for over two years. Anna had assumed it was her responsibility, but Archie explained that because they thought it would cost thousands to put right it ought to be a church matter, hand in hand with the diocese of course. In the end everyone agreed to at least see how much a replacement boiler would cost. Archie also wanted to see some of the older bills. Anna was sure she'd seen a box full of them down in the cellar.

"It's not all about capital; some of this will be about

ongoing expenditure and long-term planning. I think I may have an idea for a long-term solution." He really did sound as if he were enjoying himself. The phone rang and Archie disappeared to answer it. He was back almost immediately.

"That was Phil. He says there's a fire at the vicarage!"

Chapter 18

"A fire?" Anna wondered if Harriet had tried to light one in the many grates dotted about the house. Then she remembered, "Harriet is there alone. Is she alright?"

"He doesn't know. He's shutting the pub and will see us across there."

"Has he phoned the fire brigade?"

"They're on their way."

Anna started to run. She supposed Archie was coming behind her. As she crossed the village she heard the siren from along the main road, a wail that stripped away her skin and left her heart beating through her ears. She'd listened to a thousand sirens, but this one was for her and it seemed to push her along ahead of it. When she finally got to the top of the drive, her breath was scraping in and out of her lungs. It really hurt and she had to bend double. There was already a line of people standing at the front of the house. Derek, Harriet, Simeon, and Phil. Harriet! Thank goodness.

"Are you alright?" Anna had to shout above the noise of the engine.

"Yes, I'm fine. Luckily Derek left his gloves behind. When he got to the front door he smelled the smoke. He came round the back to get me."

Anna turned to Derek. He was standing with his hand held protectively across his chest.

"He says he's alright but it looks quite bad to me," Phil said quietly. "He won't let me look at it properly."

The fire engine reversed across the grass, leaving a deep gash. Behind it was Archie. He didn't look quite so out of breath.

"So where's the fire?" a man shouted as he swung down from the cab.

Anna turned to Harriet. Harriet was trying to get Derek to show her his hand. She turned back to them.

"I was in the kitchen at the back. Derek said the front door was hot, that the hall was alight. He's burned his hand on the handle. I didn't go through to check. I was worried about the smoke." At that moment the light changed, as the windows above went dark.

"The electrics have just gone," Phil added, rather redundantly Anna thought.

"The fuse box is down in the cellar. Is that bad?" Anna asked, her face pale and a little shadowed. She felt a pang of loss. It wasn't much of a house, it was far too big and draughty, with lumpy ugly furniture, but it had been her home for over four years. She felt as though she might even be crying except that the smoke was streaming out from under the door and it could have been that that was irritating her eyes. A young fireman moved them further back.

***

Simeon was standing in the shadows watching. Derek and Phil were either side of Anna so he didn't feel he could go and speak to her, but he could see that Derek was standing awkwardly, that he kept dancing from foot to foot. Simeon wondered what was wrong. Dolly was there, of course, and she too kept looking up at her master. As the smoke began to fill the space between them, Derek suddenly dropped to his knees and began to moan.

"I'm sorry, it's quite painful," he mumbled.

"I think we need to get him to hospital." Anna knelt down beside him.

"I'll take him," said Archie. "I'll get the car, it's at the top of the drive. I won't be a moment."

"But what about Dolly?" Derek sort of whined. He'd actually gone a little grey.

"I'll take her," Simeon found himself saying. He stepped forward. Everyone turned to look at him. He concentrated on the puddle of foam forming at the end of a dripping nozzle.

"Here's my key," Derek said. "Everything's in the kitchen."

"I'll come and help you find what you need," Phil added, and then more quietly he said, "You can ask me any questions you have about looking after her."

Simeon tried to speak but it was too hard for the moment. Anna and Harriet began to walk Derek slowly up the drive. Phil already had hold of Dolly's lead.

"Come on Simeon, there isn't much we can do here."

***

Dolly came along quite happily. Every so often Simeon stopped and patted her head just for reassurance. Phil had been very clear about what was needed. Simeon should try and feed her each day at a regular time and he mustn't give her too many titbits. Dolly was slow and gentle because she was old, which he found reassuring. Simeon had thought he would be upset because the vicarage was burning down but he didn't have time for that right now because he had to look after her.

That night Simeon lay awake. He could hear Dolly breathing; he wasn't used to sleeping with someone else in the house. Last thing he'd taken her out on her lead to have a wee in the back garden.

Eventually he must have fallen asleep for he woke at his usual time. It was hard getting up knowing that he couldn't follow the normal routine because he had to let Dolly out first. She sniffed hopefully at her food bowl, but he'd decided that she should be fed at eight o'clock in the morning and six o'clock that evening. Later, after his breakfast, he took her for a walk along the cliff. They walked along the path for quite a way. When he got too far ahead, she trotted to keep up and when she went too far ahead, she sat and waited for him. It was nice. It was so nice he decided to walk her all the way round to Archie's house. He hoped he wouldn't mind Dolly visiting, it also meant he could find out how Derek was.

"Come in," said Archie. "You too Dolly. How nice to see you both."

"It's quite early, is that alright? She has muddy paws. I didn't bring a cloth to wipe her with."

"Not a problem. I have some old towels. She seems very settled with you."

"I didn't sleep because she breathes very loudly and I didn't want to close the door in case she needed anything."

Archie turned away so that he could smile. He didn't want Simeon asking him why.

"Well the fire is lit and I'll go and make us a drink."

Dolly walked into the middle of the front room and waited for Simeon to sit down. When she seemed satisfied that he was comfortable, she laid down by the fire and went to sleep. Simeon was glad that Archie's coffee was strong because he felt like dropping off too. For the first time in ages the anxiety that had been gnawing in his stomach was hardly apparent at all.

"How's Derek?" he asked as soon as Archie sat down too.

"They kept him in. He's going to phone me once they discharge him. It was quite a bad burn, right across the palm where there isn't that much skin."

Simeon felt a little hot and hoped that Archie wouldn't say anything more about it.

"Anyway, he was in a lot of pain but was pleased that you had Dolly. He knew you'd take good care of her."

"Where did Anna and Harriet sleep last night?"

"Up at the pub. We're meeting a fireman down at the vicarage later to talk about the damage."

"Do they know how it started?" Simeon asked.

"Oh, probably electrics. It hasn't been rewired since the sixties and I expect Harriet plugged in a hair dryer when Anna was cooking or something."

"I thought Anna was with you when it started."

"Well, yes she was. We were having an emergency standing

274

committee to talk about the vicarage, which is ironic." He leaned over to pour the coffee. "Perhaps Harriet plugged lots of things in to charge and then tried to cook something."

Simeon thought about that.

"Most modern electrical devices don't draw that much current and Harriet only had a few suitcases and boxes."

"Well, the fireman will surely be able to solve the mystery and then we'll get the repairs sorted. Can Dolly have a biscuit? They're the right sort."

"Yes, but only one and I'd like to give it to her."

Dolly snatched a little but afterwards she gently nuzzled his hand as if to say sorry, though he knew she was really checking there wasn't any more. He patted her head and shook his own so she'd know there was only the one on offer.

When he looked up, Archie was smiling broadly. Simeon didn't understand why he was so happy. After all, the vicarage had nearly burnt down, and as Anna's churchwarden, it was probably Archie's responsibility to get it re-built, re-decorated, or whatever else was needed.

***

Anna was looking crumpled. She and Harriet had slept at the pub and hadn't been allowed to get anything from their rooms back at the house. She'd combed her hair with her fingers and washed her face, which felt dry and tight because she hadn't any face cream. She was hoping the meeting wouldn't take too long because Archie had just phoned to say that Derek was ready to be picked up and she knew how sad it could be waiting around in hospital, getting in the way and not being allowed to do anything.

Anna noticed that Harriet was looking tired, but definitely not 'crumpled'. She had also refused Phil's cooked breakfast.

"I'll just manage with a bowl of cereal," Harriet had said virtuously.

Anna wasn't going to refuse such a treat even though

sitting beside Harriet made her feel like a pig, and later she knew she'd suffer the niggling discomfort of indigestion. Walking down to the vicarage she did feel uncomfortably full.

"Revd Maybury?"

Anna smiled. The man looked tired and the returned smile was mechanical.

"Have you been here all night?" she asked.

"No, only since about six. I get called in if there are any issues."

"Are there issues?"

"Do you mind if we wait just another couple of minutes? They're sending over a policeman and it will save time if I speak to everyone together."

Anna felt disconcerted. 'Issues' didn't sound like a good thing at all. They both nodded to Archie as he came striding up the drive. He shook the man's hand.

"Hello, William."

"Archie, I thought I might be seeing you," the man replied.

Anna wondered where they knew each other from. The way the man was now standing made her think Navy.

"So is there much damage?" Archie asked. Anna was annoyed that the fireman addressed the rest of his replies to him and now didn't seem worried about waiting around for a policeman.

"Not structurally, so you'll be able to get back in whenever you like but I must warn you downstairs is a terrible mess, and of course the place will need to be rewired. I'm afraid a couple of the sofas have gone as well."

"What about the kitchen?" Anna asked, trying not to sound too upset. Worldly goods and all that.

"Mostly smoke damage, so a bit of elbow grease will soon set it right."

It sounded awful, and yet whatever else happened all she wanted to do was get up to the bathroom to retrieve her toothbrush, face cream, and deodorant. It was a bit of a moment realising that these were the things she was worried about, even though they were easily replaceable. She hadn't once thought about the photographs of her family ranged across the mantelpiece or her record collection, the one she'd fallen out with her sister over.

Tom hurried down the drive looking official and serious. They all nodded to him and he flashed his warrant card at the fireman. Anna's heart was sinking lower and lower.

"William Roberts," Archie said.

"Tom Edwards." One side of Tom's collar was tucked in his jumper, one side was out, and as per usual his hair was sticking out at slightly odd angles. He'd had it cut recently, a little short in Anna's opinion, certainly not long enough to do anything with. Strangely, it reassured her.

William led them across to what remained of the front door. Only the top panel was left, the door knob that had so badly burned Derek was lying on the front step.

"This is actually the seat of the fire. The rest of the damage was mostly caused by smoke and the hoses. The smell will be pretty awful. I expect your insurers will have emergency numbers to ring for getting everything safe. If not, we have some that might prove useful."

Archie nodded.

"I rang this morning and they'll send someone over first thing tomorrow morning," he said, patting Anna's arm.

Anna smiled at him, but with thin lips and a hammering heart. She turned to the fireman.

"So what do you think happened?" she asked.

"I think there's a high possibility it was arson. Something pushed through the letterbox." He pointed to the remains of the letterbox lying next to the door knob.

Tom blinked. Very slowly he swivelled round to look at Anna. She stared back, quite speechless, her head empty of anything useful to say. Archie stepped a little nearer to her.

"Show me, will you," Tom said. The fireman took him onto

the front step where they peered into the hallway. Quite quickly, he came back and said to Anna, "Has anything like this happened before?"

She shook her head.

"I don't mean a fire. Perhaps someone has threatened you because of the dog collar?"

"No. I can't think of a single person who'd want to hurt me, not like this. Shout at me perhaps," she said, laughing shakily.

"Who's wanted to shout at you recently?"

Anna's shoulders drooped a little. Derek, Harriet, Simeon. Mostly anyone she'd tried to help.

"Don't worry for now. I'll come and get a proper statement later on. What about Harriet? Who knew she'd moved in?"

"Everyone, I think. We didn't keep it a secret."

"So that's not going to narrow it down at all. Where's Simeon?"

"Walking Dolly," Archie said. Anna raised an eyebrow, because Archie had smiled, just a little. "They're getting on very well," he added.

"Ok. I'll go and see him later," Tom continued. "You can be there Anna, if you like. It's only to check if he has seen anyone about. He's very observant."

"What about that woman, the one that Derek's got tangled up with?" Anna said.

Archie swung round to stare at them.

"Derek is tangled up with a woman?" He looked surprised.

"No, not really. It's just some client who got a bit friendly after Fiona died," Anna continued, carefully. "There really isn't anything in it."

Tom's face remained impassive.

"So are you sure you haven't seen anyone around?" Tom asked again, looking at each of them in turn.

"There really hasn't been a single stranger who hasn't turned out to be a proper holiday maker, who stayed a week and then went home."

Archie was frowning. "It's not as if we haven't been super vigilant."

Anna had to fight back a picture of Archie in a cape and tights.

"I'll have to call in forensics though I expect the fire itself will have destroyed anything useful." The fireman nodded in agreement.

"What about my meeting with the diocesan insurers?" Archie asked.

"As long as you don't go past the tape. I suppose you could go in through the back without disturbing anything."

"Can Harriet and I get some things?" Anna asked a little desperately. They probably thought she was talking about her Bible and precious family mementos. They didn't need to know it was all about her toothbrush, deodorant, and comb.

"Once the tape is up, and we know the area we're dealing with. Someone will have to escort you," Tom said.

Not you, Anna hoped, thinking about her knicker drawer, faded pyjamas, and her current bedtime reading.

"Oh, this is awful. Where are we going to stay? We can't keep living at the pub."

"Come and stay with me," Archie said. "I've at least three spare rooms I don't use. They'll need warming up, airing a little, but it won't take me long to get that organised."

Anna had a thought. "What if it wasn't me but Harriet who was the target? After all she was on her own here for the first time. It was only by luck that Derek came back in time."

She could see by Tom's face, which became still when he didn't want to comment on something, that he'd already thought of that.

He said quietly, "I don't think you want Harriet freaking out about something that might not be true."

"But what if it is? She could be in danger. We ought to warn her."

"No, not yet," Tom replied, sharply. "Just let me know when you get back from picking up Derek. I'll come and get that statement, and if you see Harriet, tell her I'll want one from her too."

"What about the press?" Archie asked. "There may be some interest. There was after Fiona."

"Well if you could avoid talking to them that would be helpful." And Tom smiled at Anna. She stared at him in disbelief. Who cares about the press, she thought? She couldn't understand how he could be so calm. Someone had tried to burn down the vicarage.

***

"Hello Terry," Archie called, as they walked up the lane to get the car.

"Hello Mr Wainwright, hello Vicar. Is the vicarage badly damaged?"

"It's hard to be sure, they won't let us in to see. Not yet anyway," Anna replied. "Of course poor old Derek seems to have been the only casualty."

"I saw him go off in the ambulance. Is he alright?" For a second Anna thought she saw a twinge of anxiety in Terry's impassive face. Perhaps just the tiniest frown.

"Yes, it was lucky he forgot his gloves and went back for them," Archie added. "But then unlucky he tried to get in by the front door. We're going to Falmouth to fetch him now."

"Well as soon as he's home I'll pop across and make sure he's got everything he needs."

"You are good," Archie said. "He'll be reassured to know his neighbours are looking out for him."

Anna wasn't sure that was how Derek would see it at all. She hoped he was feeling stronger because Terry might be a little difficult to repel. She smiled brightly. She really had to try harder to be a better vicar, had to be kinder. Terry was lonely like the rest of them and if she had a bit of a thing for

Derek so what.

"Will you be helping up at the shop at all this week?" she asked.

"No, I'm going to be too busy."

"Well, we won't keep you then," Archie said, and tipped his hat to her.

***

Anna settled into the car. Archie always had the heater on far too high and she was already feeling drowsy. There was far too much excitement going on at the moment for her to have slept well. How on earth was she going to sort out the vicarage on top of everything else?

They drove out past the pub. As Archie turned onto the main road she spotted Simeon sitting on the bench right in the middle of the green.

"Archie, what's he doing? I've never seen him sit there before. It's very... public."

"I think he's letting Dolly see people. He was round first thing this morning, and said that he was worried she would get too sad down in his house all day, so he has planned a series of walks and outings to cheer her up."

"Oh my."

"I think once all this is sorted out, we ought to take Simeon to the dog pound. I bet you anything there will be some old dog there desperate for a home."

"It can't be as simple as that, can it?"

"Someone else to think about. He mentioned that his anxiety has been a lot less since he's been looking after her. I guess that he thinks that if Dolly hears anything, she'll bark so he feels safer too."

"Dolly is an old dog. I bet she's as deaf as a post."

"We don't have to tell him that, do we?" Archie said. "It's her company that seems to be doing the trick."

"But could she become a substitute for human contact?"

"He was sitting on the green! Plus we'll keep an eye out for him."

Trust Archie to have the right answers.

"Who do you think tried to set fire to the vicarage?" The only person she could think of was Derek's mysterious woman. But that was ridiculous. "Kids being stupid?" she said, a little desperately.

"You must know most of them round here. Do you think any of them are capable of doing such a thing? The fire could have seriously hurt someone."

"They might have started it when they were drunk?"

"But surely if it was drunken lads someone would have seen them or at least heard them. Particularly Derek or Harriet. You know how loud you are when you are trying to be quiet."

Anna raised an eyebrow. One of these days she was going to have to ask Archie what he'd got up to in the Navy. Archie annoyingly didn't add anything more.

***

Terry walked across to the bungalow. It was bin day and she thought she'd put Derek's dustbin out. She was glad that Simeon had the dog, and that she hadn't had to offer. Dolly had barked at Terry a couple of times making her jump and once Terry had got something nasty all over her shoes. She didn't like dogs. She hoped Derek wasn't in too much pain. Thinking about it, she ought to have offered to go and fetch him, save Mr Wainwright a job. He'd have more than enough to do sorting out the fire.

Terry hurried down to the shop. Jean was standing at the door.

"Hello Terry, any more news on Derek?" Jean asked. Terry knew better than to attempt a reply. Before she could draw breath Jean was off again. "Poor man, first his wife and now this. I don't suppose he realised Anna would be at Archie's house for our meeting. Do you know Anna hasn't been able to afford to have any heating on since she came here? Isn't that dreadful?" Terry wasn't surprised Anna wasn't managing her finances any better than the parish doings. "Still apparently Derek has said he'd help her get one of the chimneys uncapped so she can have some open fires. Though I hear he's not going to be able to use his hand for quite a while."

"They've only kept him in overnight. I expect it's more of a precaution."

"Can you help me unload this box?" Jean asked, turning into the store room. "My back is quite sore today. I'm hoping the physio tomorrow will help."

Terry went into the back to see what needed doing. Jean remained standing in the doorway.

"Did you know that Harriet had moved into the vicarage?" she said.

"Yes. Another one who can't manage her finances properly. I'm not sure the vicar is allowed to sublet." Terry began to lift teabags onto the floor.

"I'd heard her landlord chucked her out. Trust good old Anna to offer her somewhere to stay. What a shame they'll both be homeless now."

Terry straightened up. Derek had a couple of extra rooms, she hoped they wouldn't impose on him for accommodation.

"What about the pub?" she said.

"That's Phil's livelihood. I don't expect he can offer to do more than he's done already."

"Mr Wainwright then? His house is huge. He must have tons of room," Terry continued. She thought that was a very sensible idea. Harriet and Anna could stay with Mr Wainwright. They were all very chummy at the moment, so it made sense. She took a pile of teabags through to Jean. Jean took them off her and began to fill the gaps.

"I saw Simeon this morning with Dolly," Jean said, over her shoulder. "They did look sweet together." She came back to get some more teabags from Terry who was now having to reach into the bottom to get out the last few. These she left in the store room. "Have you bumped into him since..." Jean asked. Terry shook her head. Truth be told she'd been avoiding him and didn't like talking about it. No one else seemed to have taken the attack seriously at all, though she was sure that eventually they would see Simeon for what he was. Even Derek had been less than sympathetic. Of course his reasoning was still clouded with grief, she understood that, but he was definitely getting his life more together. He was a strong man. A kind man.

"Jean, I don't think I can come into the shop tomorrow. Something has come up."

"Oh, Terry, why not? I can't rearrange my physio at this short notice." She frowned at Terry, who simply looked away. "I'll either have to close up for the afternoon or cancel the appointment. But I've waited so long already and I'm not getting any better." Terry turned her back. Jean would go on about it for a bit but she'd stop when she realised how much she needed Terry. If Derek needed anything Terry wanted to be available. She was certainly willing to give up an afternoon's money, though it would have come in handy.

***

Anna and Archie were stuck in traffic. Archie was whistling something under his breath and Anna had probably been dozing, though she wasn't absolutely sure.

"It must have been lads being stupid," she said.

Archie turned to look at her. He looked thoughtful for a second then said, "I'm sure someone would have seen them or heard them, but what if someone came up the lane, not down. Say from the coastal path? You could easily park a car down at the lighthouse among all the other tourists and walk back, or even park up on the main road and cut across the fields."

"I suppose," Anna replied. "Though it still brings us back to why."

"We're assuming everything is linked. That Fiona was hit and it wasn't just a bungled forensics report, and whoever did that then set fire to the vicarage." The cars ahead inched forward. It was always slow on this bit. Archie pulled on the handbrake and took the car out of gear. "I suppose the attack happened at the church, and you are the vicar. Could it be some stranger who is holding a grudge against..."

"The church in general or me as its representative?" Anna said, laughing. "It's been nearly a year between incidents so it could be months before anything else happens." She shivered as she realised she was expecting something else to occur. She didn't think she could stand another week let alone months of keeping her wits about her, watching her back, feeling spied upon.

"Don't worry Anna, at least you'll be safe and sound at my place."

"Thanks Archie. That does feel better." He nosed into a very small space in the car park.

***

Derek was waiting in the hospital lobby, nursing a very large cup of coffee. He was pleased to see them and apparently wasn't in any pain because he had been prescribed some pretty hefty pain killers. Anna thought he looked as high as a kite. Despite the coffee he fell asleep in the back of the car and was still quite drowsy when they got home. Archie persuaded him to go for a lie down.

"I think perhaps Simeon ought to hang onto Dolly a little longer," Anna said quietly. Derek hadn't mentioned her at all. Archie nodded.

"Good idea. I think he'll sleep through now. Apparently he didn't get much rest last night as it took them a while to get the pain medication right."

"I think they might have got it a bit too right," she replied, laughing. "He did sound a little sparkly."

"Should we leave him on his own?" Archie said.

"I think he'll be fine. It's not like he's hit his head or anything," Anna replied. "I expect the pain will wake him tomorrow or Terry checking he's ok."

Archie smiled.

"Right, Anna. Let's go home. I'm exhausted."

For the first time in ages Anna had a good look at her churchwarden. He wasn't a young man, and though she would mostly describe him as calm, even stalwart, lately he'd been knocked about quite a bit. She'd noticed him brace himself when Simeon was upset, and she didn't think that was just about coping with the vagaries of Simeon any more. They had become good friends. She wondered if you noticed the moment you crossed that particular line, when being with someone was no longer a chore or a duty. Archie was worried for Simeon simply because he was. She wasn't entirely convinced there weren't other things bubbling away under his calm exterior, that Archie might not be over the death of his wife. Did you ever get over such a loss? It had been ten years and he still went to sit on her grave to talk to her. Anna needed to keep more of an eye on him, take him less for granted. She patted his arm as she climbed into the car.

The spare room was perfect. Overly warm and the bed wonderfully soft. She didn't think it would do her back any good long term but for now it was exactly what she needed and Harriet had fetched her some clean clothes, all her toiletries, and a hairbrush.

***

Tom and Harriet were sitting in the pub, round in the quiet corner. The pub was empty. They both nursed coffees. Harriet looked pale, her eyes large and a little red.

"Are you alright?" Tom asked.

"Just tired. I'd forgotten how uncomfortable Phil's box

room can be."

"I'm sure Archie would be delighted to put you up with Anna."

"He is being wonderful. I don't know what Anna would do without him."

Tom stirred his coffee.

"She'd manage. She's tougher than she looks."

Harriet was surprised, she'd never heard Anna described as tough. Tom pulled out his notebook, his small mouth a firm line. This was his policeman face, which Harriet found reassuring though Anna was right, he did need sprucing up a little.

"I know you've been through this before, but I want to hear it again."

Harriet repeated what had happened. Derek had come for a chat, Derek had left, and then he'd reappeared at the back door shouting for her to get out. He was clutching his hand to his chest. She realised he was hurt but he'd said he was alright. She hadn't gone into the hall but had phoned the fire brigade and then Phil, because she thought he had Archie's home number and she knew Anna's mobile would be on silent as she was at a meeting. No, she hadn't seen anything or anyone.

"Is there anyone who might want to hurt you?"

Harriet considered the question. A few months ago she'd have said Derek, definitely Derek, but not now. A few weeks ago she'd have said her landlord because he really did want her gone so he could redevelop the flat. Only that was all resolved too.

"What is it, Harriet? You look thoughtful."

"Not long back, at the end of the summer, I got home from work and there was a most peculiar smell in the flat. I thought the drains were acting up but I was knackered, it was late so I went to bed. I think I might have even opened a window." She frowned. Her hair was tied back but bits were coming loose.

They were annoying her. She pulled the scrunchie out and slipped it on her wrist. "The next morning I found a smelly rag on my door mat. I assumed I'd walked it in in the dark or that my landlord had pushed it through the letterbox because he wanted me gone."

"That's an offence. You could have reported him."

"But I wasn't sure. I could have easily walked it in myself. I put it in the dustbin." She blinked. "But thinking about it now it's possible it could have smelt of petrol rather than of drains."

Tom had been scribbling in his notebook. He looked up.

"You're right, it's probably nothing," he said, "But I will go and have a word with your landlord."

"He'll deny it. What's he got to gain by admitting something like that?"

Tom nodded. "Nothing I suppose. But if we keep it off the record at least we could discount that incident as connected with the fire at the vicarage. It's worth a try."

Harriet gave a long outward breath.

"I'm quite scared."

"Don't worry, but I wouldn't wander about after dark on your own just for now."

Chapter 19

"Golly this place is quiet." Anna whispered, looking around the pub. She felt as if she was back in the old college library. A place that had been archetypal despite the attempts of the young librarian to make it less stuffy. The pub wasn't usually this empty but she was glad they had it all to themselves. The three of them were sitting in a line at the bar. It had been a month since the fire but they were still feeling subdued and careworn. At least, she was still feeling subdued.

Harriet shook her head from behind the bar and said, at normal volume, "It wasn't quiet earlier. Phil and I were run off our feet. The bridge club and the teachers were in. Unusual for them so late on in the term."

"They looked glum," Derek added. "I hope it's not numbers again. I do worry we're going to lose the school."

Anna wondered why it would bother him.

"Do you want another?" he asked.

Anna immediately felt guilty. She hadn't been at the pub as long as the others, but they were still nursing their drinks. Her large white wine was mysteriously down to a few drops in the bottom.

"Yes, that would be nice." She promised herself that she would make the next one last. "So how are bookings after your mini makeover?" she asked Harriet, once she'd returned from the fridge.

"Too early to say, though there have been some nice comments on the web. We'll have to wait and see whether they work through to actual reservations." Harriet looked at the wine bottle, tipped the last centimetre into Anna's glass, and lobbed it into the recycling bin. "November is always popular with older couples, lucky so-and-sos."

"Why are they lucky?" Derek asked.

"Because most of the cottages are dirt cheap at this time of year, most have central heating, and the weather can be spectacular."

"Not today though." Archie shook his head. "It has been foul."

"It was so wet I didn't even get down to do my homework."

"I thought we'd agreed you wouldn't go there on your own." A frown wrinkled Archie's forehead.

"Oh, Archie, I'm not going to be scared out of my own church."

But she was. The rain had been a good excuse not to go. A few days before she'd walked down, opened up, and barely made it to twenty minutes before she'd given up and gone back to Archie's.

"That bloody woman." Anna spoke between pursed lips as she tried to visualise Derek's emailer. She couldn't think beyond that.

"I'm sorry," Derek said, looking glumly into his beer. "This is all my fault."

"It's not your fault," Harriet jumped in, rather fiercely. "It's Tom's really, for not being able to find her. How hard can it be to locate a woman from her email address?"

"Tom said the email was from a company from years ago. It ceased trading back in the seventies and the building it used to be in was knocked down for a new trading estate. He's put a trace request in, but these things take time, and resources," Anna said, a little defensively.

Archie shrugged. "We don't even know if she's got anything to do with any of this. She hasn't emailed Derek since last time."

Derek shook his head. "Tom said not to do anything, but couldn't I agree to meet her, then at least we'd find out one way or another."

"It might be dangerous, Derek. Tom's right," Harriet said, folding her arms across her chest.

"Look," Archie said, it sounded a little desperately to Anna. "We really don't know that Derek's lady has anything to do with Fiona or the church." Derek winced at the mention of Fiona. "All we do know is that he or she has made us jumpy." Archie was angry. "Since the fire there hasn't been anything unusual. I think we ought to try to get back to normal."

Anna wasn't sure what normal was. She was still living at Archie's and Harriet was camping in a box room upstairs at the pub. It wasn't all gloom and doom because Archie had used the damage to the vicarage as an opportunity to get some of the internal alterations done. Derek had drawn some quick plans and had come up with a simple solution that Anna had to admit was quite clever.

She was going to have some private rooms at the back of the house, small and manageable, easy to heat. They would paint over the smoke stains with a nice bright white emulsion and put a new shower over the bath, something to do with the electrics frying the old one. They were even going to tart up the kitchen. Anna hadn't known where to begin with that, but Harriet had some very good ideas about what needed doing. Anna was surprised at how quickly it had all been sorted. Apparently the bishop had put in a good word. There was even the possibility they might move back in just before Lent if all went well.

Anna had watched Archie get quite firm and fierce with anyone who wasn't getting their act together. She was seeing a whole new side to him, as if his Navy days were reasserting themselves. She wondered what else he could do if she pointed him in the right direction. Despite being a very dark and wet November, there was an energy developing about the place. Even Derek had caught a whiff of it and was beginning to think about what to do next.

He'd announced the week before that he was going to put the bungalow on the market. He'd got his eye on a holiday cottage just past the church, on the way down to the cove. It needed serious renovation but was exactly what he wanted, a fresh start with a large project attached. Back at the bungalow he still couldn't get over the feeling that Fiona was around every corner, commenting on everything he did. He'd checked it out with Alice, who was quite supportive, especially when he'd said there would be space for at least three spare bedrooms. In the bungalow the kids had to share and it always caused arguments.

"So are you busy?" Derek asked Harriet, when she leant forward to top up his beer.

"Yes, a bit. Why do you ask?"

The others turned to look at him.

"Because I wondered if you could find time to do a bit of cleaning for me." He twirled a beer mat round and round. "Just a couple of hours a week."

Anna had hoped he'd get round to asking Harriet. It would be extra pennies for her and Alice would feel her dad was being looked after. Harriet nodded and leaned back against the sink, crossing her arms once more over her chest.

"Let's talk about it tomorrow when we walk the dogs," she replied. "It would have to fit in around the job here, but I could do with the money. Though if you're moving..."

"There will always be cleaning, even at the new place."

Anna thought that was a little optimistic. She'd seen the plans and it looked as though it would be little more than a building site for quite a few months. Perhaps Derek would have to move into the vicarage too.

Archie tipped his glass to Harriet and she got him another. It was his third. Not that Anna was counting, but it was unusual. He suddenly straightened up; it almost made her jump.

"What do you think of taking Simeon to the dog pound?" Archie said.

"I don't think they'd take him. He's not house-trained," Derek replied, quickly.

They all laughed, a burst of sound that surprised Anna. Where had it come from? She took a sidelong glance along the row of them. Harriet was leaning on the bar as Phil idly wiped the beer pulls. What an odd bunch they were.

"Seriously though. I gave the pound a ring and they've a number of older, quieter dogs that they'd be delighted to re-home. Don't you think it would do Simeon the world of good? He blossomed when he had to look after Dolly."

Derek stretched out his hand. The palm was still a little pink and tender.

Archie continued, "We all bumped into him at some point as he was taking her to visit someone so that she wouldn't get too lonely, didn't we?"

Derek nodded and smiled as he reached down to pat Dolly's head. She was lying nose to tail with Bowzer and ignored him.

"Have you asked him what he thinks of the idea?" Anna asked.

"I've tried to a couple of times but it's never quite come out right."

"Have you checked with God?" Phil asked. Anna wondered if Phil was teasing Archie. It was an odd thing to say but the others seemed unfazed, in fact they were all looking as if they were waiting for a reply. She wondered when God had become so normal for them.

"I have tried running it past the main man, but I haven't had much back."

"Does it matter?" Phil continued. "I always know when I've made the wrong decision. But to get that feeling you have to make a decision in the first place."

"Yes, I see that," Archie replied carefully. "Makes sense. It's just that I can't imagine Simeon standing outside the cages trying to decide. The smells, the noise, their waggy tails, all those eyes begging you to take them home."

"Hang on a minute," said Anna. "It sounds to me that it's you that might be in trouble here. Have you ever been there before?" Archie shook his head and took another sip of his rum. "I had to once," Anna continued. "Do you remember Mrs Frobisher's dog?"

"Oh, yes," said Harriet. She wrinkled her nose, almost closing her eyes. "That horrid black poodle that was always trying to nip you."

Anna too had been snapped at, a couple of times.

"Understandably," she said, "the family didn't want the snappy little bugger so I took him over to that place just outside Helston. It wasn't brilliant having to leave him, but I didn't feel the need to bring the rest back with me. Though a couple were quite cute."

"Well, regardless," Archie said, and he hiccupped, which made Harriet and Derek raise their eyebrows, "I'll go and see if Simeon would like to come with me."

"I'd like to be in on that venture," Derek said quickly. "I've not got any impending consultancy at the minute. I think it's a great idea."

Recently he and Simeon had started going for walks together. Or rather Simeon came to visit Dolly and then they'd all head out around the coastal path. Derek found Simeon refreshingly easy to be with, and they talked about a lot of things he wasn't sure anyone else would be interested in – buildings, bricks, and architecture generally. It was nice. It had been Simeon who'd pointed out that the holiday cottage was coming up for sale and who he ought to speak to, to show an interest.

Anna was also pleased with the plan, for it meant that for some part of a morning she would have Archie's house to herself. She missed being alone, not all the time of course, just now and again. She'd realised that going down to the church had sometimes been about solitude and head space. The realisation made her thoughtful. She never minded when one of the others inevitably turned up, but when she had the church to herself it was like a jewelled moment. Just her and God and the place he'd given her to look after. Though of course that brought her inevitably back to the fire and Fiona. Would she ever be able to go into the church and turn her back to the door again?

***

Terry had followed Derek and Dolly up to the pub. One day she'd pluck up the courage to go and join them. Instead she pushed open the door to the shop. Jean came through from the back where she'd just put the kettle on. At least there hadn't been a delivery that day. Jean definitely saved those up for Terry. Her back never seemed to get any better and was always a convenient excuse for Terry to do most of the heavy work. Jean was now talking about Christmas. Terry knew she was angling for some time off around the holidays but she hadn't actually said anything specific yet. Terry would wait to be asked but she hoped she might have plans of her own this year. Jean wouldn't understand but she really shouldn't take Terry for granted.

"Ellie and the family are coming down and I want to make it special," Jean said, her head on one side, the cloth in her hand hovering over the counter.

There was a momentary pause in the stream of words that Jean could keep up almost indefinitely. It didn't last long.

"Mr Wainwright, Archie, popped in on his way to the pub, to pick up his sugar though I haven't seen anyone else about." She must have missed Derek and Dolly walking past earlier. "I'm surprised he still takes sugar. So many people don't nowadays, and how he manages to stay so trim. Still I suppose he does get out for a walk most days."

"Like Derek."

"Well that's good old Dolly. She's such a grand dog."

Terry wasn't so sure. The dog had left more poo on the verge when the girl from the pub had bought the bulldog for its walk. Dolly had been dancing round Harriet making her laugh so she supposed Derek had forgotten to clear it up.

They'd set off to Church Cove together. It was very inconsiderate of them; anyone could have stepped in it. It was quite disgusting. She thought she would have a word when next she went across to see how he was getting on.

***

A couple of days later Anna was mooching about. It was a good word to describe how she felt. Not quite attached to the world, unable to focus on anything in particular. She'd put on some washing, and then written a paragraph of her sermon, checked her phone a dozen times, and drunk a lot of tea. Archie was off on the dog trip and was then going to pop down to the vicarage, so he wouldn't be home for ages. Peace and solitude was what she wanted, what she'd asked God for, but something wasn't quite right. She decided to take herself down to the church. God would have to come with her and make it right somehow.

It was a bright sunny morning, the last weather front having passed through before the dawn. There was a gentle winter sparkle to the hedgerows and she felt there ought to be a spring in her step, but something was niggling at her and she couldn't shake it off. She wanted to go and thrash it out with God, and she needed a cold hard pew under her bum to focus. Of course it wasn't praying as such just in case Irene asked. It was thinking out loud and waiting to see what God had to say about it. Perhaps she'd even lock herself in so Archie wouldn't get too cross with her.

Simeon had moved the key again and it took her a little while to find it. She shivered away her annoyance, set the kettle boiling, and went to find a couple of blankets from the tower room. She decided that on her way home she would go and see the progress at the vicarage too, and show an interest. The rural dean would want to know how it was going and she had an appointment with him in a few days to discuss... well she wasn't sure what he wanted to discuss. He was going to come to Archie's and Archie had promised to make himself scarce.

Rural deans visited as a matter of course. It was all part of their job but she never felt able to take such meetings in her stride. She always assumed that she was failing somewhere and that those in authority had noticed. She stiffened. There was the crunch of gravel as someone came up the path. It shouldn't be like this, she told herself, it's not fair to be scared in my own church.

"Oh, Harriet, you made me jump."

"I'm sorry, Anna. I saw you coming down from the pub. I hope you don't mind only I hate being in here on my own now and I didn't want to miss an opportunity."

"Do you want a cup of tea? I have plenty of Earl Grey."

"I know you do, because you are a kind and thoughtful woman."

Anna laughed, and then became serious.

"Do you think we'll ever feel at peace here again?"

"Of course. How big is God if we don't believe he can protect us in his own house?"

"I don't think it works like that," Anna said, thoughtfully. "He didn't promise to stop bad things happening, just that he'd be with us through them. The valley of the shadow of death and all that."

"Don't you believe in miracles then?" Harriet asked, her eyes sparkling in that annoying way she had when she knew she had a point.

"Yes, and no."

"Ok, Vicar, explain yourself."

"I believe in a God who is big enough to do miracles. It's just that I haven't seen any lately." She brought the mugs over. Harriet's Earl Grey looked dis-satisfyingly insipid.

"I suppose I haven't either. Nothing big anyway."

Anna thought that was cheating.

"Of course little things are happening most of the time,"

she said grudgingly. "The sunrise, creation. I appreciate them, when we can see them through the murk and we do live in an exceptionally beautiful place." She sipped her tea. Harriet looked thoughtful too, a line deepening between her eyes.

She said, "Actually, when I said nothing big I was discounting all the big stuff that has happened, you know, to us. For example, Simeon. Simeon is so much better than he used to be. Derek told me that they go for walks now. He visits Archie to talk theology and he sits in the tower room through most of the services."

"Derek and you talk quite a lot too."

"Yes, we do. The real miracle is that I like him. He's rather kind when he looks up and manages to take an interest."

"Right," Anna said, hesitantly, "I would agree that Simeon and Derek have improved somewhat."

She wouldn't ever dream of saying anything, of course, but there was the tiniest flush to Harriet's cheeks when she spoke of Derek.

"Perhaps they haven't changed. Perhaps it's us," Harriet mused.

"You are claiming that as some sort of miracle?"

"Yes, I think I am."

Anna had to contemplate that thought.

"Well even so," she said, "it still means we have to deal with sadness, alcoholism, cancer, and death."

Harriet laughed.

"You're such a ray of sunshine. Talking of which, have you heard from Ellie at all?" Harriet had noticed one of Anna's letters to her sitting on the bar on its way to the post.

"Not for a couple of weeks. They are trying hard to make a go of it. She still loves him desperately, but he seems to be struggling with depression and his job isn't going well."

"How do you pray for that?"

"Well to be honest I don't. But I've started doing something Archie suggested. I simply imagine Ellie, Greg, and the children standing next to Jesus and I let him give them whatever it is he thinks they need."

"That sounds lovely but a bit too easy."

"It is and it isn't. Sometimes it means I don't know when a prayer has been answered."

Harriet glossed over that and asked, "What does Jesus look like?"

"Mostly the white robe and a beard. I don't get up too close, though I think he did once seem to be wearing jeans."

"I like the sound of that," Harriet said. Her eyes widened into the smile that made Anna think that she could have any man for the asking, which made her feel a little sad for herself.

"So have we changed, Anna?"

"I'm not sure."

Harriet sipped at her tea and then said, "A year ago I wouldn't have looked forward to coming down to church for a mug of tea with you, even knowing it might mean digging deep into my soul." She sighed, but not unhappily. "I like trying to work out how to do life with you."

It was a big sentence. Anna found herself blinking, a lot. Harriet must have realised how stuck Anna had become for she added, "I think you've changed quite a bit."

"I don't think so." The old protestation was out before she could stop it, partly because it was the only thing she could think of to say.

"You have too." Harriet leaned over to pull her hair, smiling and laughing.

"Perhaps I have a little but not all for the good. The sense of disquiet sitting here makes me so very angry. That bloody woman."

"I bet she's off somewhere laughing at us." Harriet looked back over her shoulder.

"I wonder," Anna replied. "I do wonder if we haven't made it all real just by going along with it. That Fiona fell over, that the stone she hit her head on simply got kicked under a bush or something."

"I suppose you could be right."

Anna felt relieved, it seemed a small moment of sense.

"How often do you think she actually came and spied on us all?" Harriet asked. Then said quietly, "There were a few times the kettle was warm. I always assumed it was you, only then you'd arrive later and it made me think that perhaps it had been her."

"Yes, that's happened to me too," Anna replied, and shivered. "But it could have been Simeon or Archie. Even Jean or Terry when they were doing the flowers." That's what she'd always told herself.

"But why did she ring the police to ask them to keep looking?" Harriet asked.

"Perhaps it had simply gone too quiet, that for whoever they are it's about keeping the incident alive. Keeping us all jumpy."

"But how could she know we're all in such a lather about her?"

"I think we should try and do as Archie suggested, stop worrying and get on with life," Anna replied. "Nothing's happened for weeks. Let's think about something else... what about Christmas?"

"Christmas?" Harriet shook her head in bewilderment.

"I've been wondering if I should do the same old same old at church. I think we're ready to change things a little. Not too much," she added quickly.

"You'll come up with something suitable," Harriet said and patted Anna on the arm.

The hour was up and Harriet needed to get back to the pub. Anna decided she would go back to Archie's and write a bit more of her sermon. She locked up and put the key under a rock that was closer to the path but not too obvious. As they walked past the shop Archie was pulling up outside the pub.

He waved.

"Come and help us celebrate," he called. "Simeon has got a dog. He won't pick her up until next week," he continued, coming over to meet them. "There will have to be a home visit, but we're going to get everything ready, aren't we Simeon?"

Simeon nodded as he climbed out of the car with Derek.

"The woman in charge has given me a leaflet and Derek is going to be there when she comes," he added. Derek nodded too and looked important. That made Anna tip her head to one side.

"So Simeon, what is she like?" Anna asked.

"She's like Dolly, only white, and she's nearly nine."

"I expect the lady was delighted you were happy to take an older pooch," she said, unable to stop the grin from widening her mouth and scrunching up her eyes.

"She was," said Archie, "And we didn't have to go and look in all the cages. She brought likely candidates into the waiting room."

He held the door open and they all trooped into the pub. Simeon too, Anna noticed.

"You old softie, Archie. I reckon if you'd had to look around the cages, you'd have come home with one as well."

"They look at you so imploringly," he said, quite seriously.

"So a white lab then. What's her name?" Harriet asked, slipping behind the bar.

"Her name is Belle," Simeon replied, and nodded, satisfied.

"Oh, that's lovely." Harriet clapped her hands. Phil came down to join them.

"My round, guys," Derek said, "I'll have a pint, please Harriet, but do mine last, I want to go and get Dolly. She's been on her own for a couple of hours now and I'm sure she'll want Simeon to tell her all about Belle." He threw a twenty pound note on the bar.

Simeon nodded slowly, but looked confused. Archie came

to his rescue.

"Derek wasn't serious, Simeon. He'll not expect you to talk to Dolly."

"He promised to wink if he was teasing me."

"He did," Harriet said, sounding a little disappointed. "He clearly winked. He hasn't forgotten the rules." Anna wondered if Harriet had thought the wink had been for her.

"What have you got to do so that the house is right for Belle?" she asked.

"Make sure the garden is secure. Derek said he could help me put a fence across the side. Find a draught-free spot for her basket and store her food where it will not get eaten by vermin."

"That seems straightforward. It will be nice to meet her," Phil said, putting Derek's change on the back shelf.

"You'll need to buy quite a lot of things," Anna said carefully, not knowing how else to ask him if he could manage financially.

"I have lots of savings. I don't spend much money except on food and utility bills."

She wondered if Archie knew where the funds came from, whether she could ask him without seeming nosey.

Chapter 20

The front door banged open. Everyone swivelled round. Derek stumbled in. He was white faced and out of breath.

"What is it?" Phil asked. Harriet was already rushing round from the bar. Anna got down from her stool.

"Dolly. She's gone. The back door was open. She's been taken."

"Have you been burgled and she's got out?" Archie asked.

"No, her lead is missing. It's the first thing I looked for when I went in. I always leave it draped over the bannister. Always."

"Is everything else still there? Food, bedding, her bowls?" Phil asked.

"What about the spare key under the plant pot?" Harriet added.

"I don't know. I just couldn't find her lead."

Phil took charge.

"Right, Anna, you call Tom. Archie, you go back to the bungalow with Derek and see what you can find."

Anna could tell that Archie was torn, so she said, "Archie, why don't you take Simeon back to his house and Harriet can go back with Derek just until I've got hold of Tom. Then I'll join Derek so Harriet can come back to work."

"Oh, don't worry about that," Phil said immediately. "I'll manage. You guys do whatever needs to be done."

"Thanks Phil," Harriet said. Grabbing her coat she propelled Derek towards the door.

Anna went and stood outside the pub to ring Tom. The first time it went through to voicemail and she left a rambling message about dogs and break-ins. Then she thought about how often she didn't quite get to her phone in time, so she rang him again. He picked up immediately.

"Are you alright?" he almost shouted.

"Yes, but please can you come. As quickly as possible."

Apparently he was already heading out to his car.

"Where are you going to be?" he asked. She heard the engine start.

"I'm going down to check on Simeon and Archie and then I'll head back up to Derek's."

Tom swore.

"What's wrong with that?" she asked, her hackles rising.

"I wasn't swearing at you. I nearly knocked a woman over on the crossing."

"For goodness sake Tom, you're a policeman. You can't drive and use your phone. I'll see you when you get here." She cut him off. Silly man. That would be his career down the tubes. She shook her head. Then she realised he'd have a hands-free set anyway and felt a bit foolish for cutting him off. She checked the time and reckoned that even driving with his blue light on it would take him over forty minutes to get there, so she had plenty of time to go check on the others.

***

Simeon was distraught, unable to sit still, or to speak. Archie was making coffee. He didn't seem to know what else to do.

"He's terribly worried about what might happen to Dolly. Nothing I say seems to get through," Archie said, handing her a mug that looked a little strong.

"I think you just need to be here," she replied, patting him on the arm. He nodded.

She stayed a little while but quickly realised she wasn't able to do anything. None of them knew what was going on. She made sure that Archie didn't give Simeon any of the coffee, and suggested he made himself some tea, he looked so pale. "Phone me at any time but I ought to get back to Derek and Harriet, to see what the police have decided to do."

He nodded. "Of course."

She left him standing at the back door.

As she passed the top of the vicarage drive she could

already see blue lights flashing off the windows of the bungalows. Tom must have driven like the clappers. At the front door she recognised the constable and for a second it all felt too familiar. Here we go again, she thought, and had to swallow the anxiety creeping up her throat.

"Hello, Sandra."

"Hello Vicar. Go on through, the boss told me to look out for you." She smiled as if they were old friends.

"Thanks," Anna replied, feeling a little less panicky. Tom was here and would sort it all out. She hoped it would be a straightforward burglary and that Dolly would be found sitting outside the pub. She bit her bottom lip because somehow she knew that wasn't going to happen. A large white van pulled up outside. Tom had called in forensics already.

"I'm glad to see you," Tom said, coming out of the kitchen, carefully closing the door behind him. She had glimpsed Derek leaning against the sink, staring out into the garden. Tom smiled but it couldn't quite erase the lines between his eyes, the worry flattening his cheeks. Her panic went up a notch. He reached out and touched her arm as if he were seeking reassurance from her and not the other way around. Her heart rate went up again. She had to get a grip. "Anna, I think we ought to ask a doctor to look at Derek."

"He'll be in shock," she replied. "Dolly was his lifeline, his link to Fiona. If someone has taken her, then finally we have our answer. Fiona, the fire, must all be about Derek."

Tom raised an eyebrow. He took Anna by the elbow and guided her into the front room. "Look, I am taking this seriously. I've called in forensics though I'll never hear the last of it but it does feel like everything is linked. And there may have been another arson attempt earlier, though I'm still trying to work out how that fits in."

"Where was that?"

He hesitated, but only for a microsecond.

"Harriet's old flat."

"So it's Harriet, not Derek. Unless Harriet was a threat because she was Derek's enemy, and now she's a threat because they are friends. The fire at the vicarage may have been because she'd just moved in, or more significantly it may have been because Derek had just been to see her there."

Tom nodded slowly. "It's a possibility, Anna. Well at least that would knock one person off my list of suspects. But we mustn't lose sight of Fiona. Dog napping is hardly the crime of the century."

"Setting fire to a house when someone is inside is attempted murder."

Tom didn't seem to hear her, he was thinking. His eyes narrowed, his brow wrinkled up into his hair.

"The boss will have to agree to a few more men so we can do a proper search."

"It all feels so sinister," Anna added. "Yet I suppose from your boss's point of view it's still just a stolen dog." She smiled though her bottom lip felt tight where she'd bitten it. He continued to frown. She left a space for him to say something reassuring. He remained silent. "And they do seem to have an incredible capacity for hitting us when we are at our most vulnerable."

"Go on," said Tom.

"Someone knew that Dolly was in the bungalow alone. Derek hardly ever leaves her by herself. In fact only when he comes to church. I think they must have known that taking her would really hurt him."

He nodded.

"You're ok, though?"

She wondered why he had suddenly asked her that. Wondered what he might want from her "No, I'm not. I haven't been for weeks. When I go into my own church I can't turn my back to the door. None of us are comfortable sitting in there alone. Whoever is behind this has hurt us all and instead of feeling compassion for a very damaged soul, I'm angry."

"Stay angry and for goodness sake keep your eyes open."

Anna was really scared. Tom seemed to think that anger made you strong, but she was sure it was a terrible weakness. It meant feeling powerless, it meant reacting to a moment. She knew there was no wisdom in that.

"If it is that woman then we've never seen her coming through the village, so she must have a route in and out that none of us frequent that much," she said. Talking was better than thinking.

"Around by the next bay?"

"Too far probably, the path has some really long stretches of deep mud. Archie and I wondered if she parks at the lighthouse, walks from there along the coastal path, and cuts up to Derek's in any number of places."

"So she'd have to use a car."

"Everyone round here uses a car."

"You've not thought about this at all!" He smiled. She was so relieved that for a moment he looked less worried, she smiled back. "Right, then that's where we'll start," he added, as if what she'd said was important.

Harriet had called the doctor and was now fluttering around, organising tea and biscuits, but Derek wasn't really there, wasn't taking notice of anything. Over and over again he muttered, "Please find her." He hadn't been that upset about his wife.

"I think it's probably just shock, but we ought to get him checked out." Harriet was whispering though Anna didn't think Derek was in any danger of hearing them. "In the meantime I'll make sure he stays warm and drinks plenty."

Tom was muttering to one of the forensic guys.

"Harriet, Anna, will you stay with him?" Tom asked. "I'll leave a PC, but I think you two would be better."

"Of course we'll stay," Harriet said. "But Anna, could you

pop back to the vicarage and get my spare phone charger? It's in the box on the bed with some other leads and stuff. The battery didn't charge overnight. It's been doing it on and off for a couple of weeks. Wish I'd sorted it sooner."

"Of course," Anna replied. She was grateful for something to do. Harriet was more than capable of dealing with Derek. "It won't take me a moment."

Anna did up her coat and wrapped her scarf a little more tightly. When all this was over, she was going to buy herself a new scarf. Something less scratchy and a colour she actually liked. More importantly, a scarf that hadn't been bought for her by Peter. What strange things bubbled up in moments of stress, she thought.

It was later than she'd realised, turning into a gloomy afternoon. The heavy clouds formed a low dark ceiling. There was a slight metallic tang to the air, almost as if there might be snow. Despite her gloves her fingers were already tingling, even curled inside her pockets. It started to rain as she passed the end of Simeon's track and she wondered how Archie was getting on settling him down. Once she'd found Harriet's charger she'd pop back to see them. Make sure they were alright. Archie had looked so lost and she didn't want him to feel he was on his own.

**

"Simeon, lock yourself in as soon as I've gone," Archie said as calmly as he could, hoping it wouldn't set Simeon's panic off again. Simeon nodded. "And promise me you'll ring me if you need anything. It doesn't matter what the time is."

"Please call the lady at the dog pound," Simeon said, quietly, just as Archie was turning away. "Tell her I won't be taking Belle after all."

"Why would I do that?" Archie spun back straight into Simeon's personal space. They both jerked backwards.

"Because it's not safe."

Archie didn't have time to think about this.

"I'm not going to do anything just now. Tom will find whoever is doing this and we'll get back to normal."

"But they've only taken a dog. They will say that they need psychiatric help but they won't send them away. What have they done that would merit a sentence?"

"They set fire to the vicarage."

"Prove it. There were no fingerprints and the cloth was a duster you could have bought anywhere."

"Perhaps they'll confess."

"No one ever confesses."

Archie supposed that was true. Most people saw the world from their own perspective, were rarely able to walk in other people's shoes, to see the real damage done by their actions. Still he wasn't willing to give up. He added firmly, "I'm not calling the dog lady yet."

"Alright. But I don't want to wait too long. I don't like having everything hanging over me. It makes the inside of my head feel scratchy."

Archie patted Simeon's arm, though it made him jump again.

"Now lock up," because, he thought, I have a feeling she knows where we all live.

***

Anna was pleased to see lights on all through the vicarage. There were a couple of vans parked outside, an electrician and a decorator. She went in through the front, it didn't feel right using the back when she wasn't living there.

She stood for a second listening to the men upstairs, a scratchy radio, the clouting of a hammer, and some terribly off-key singing. It made her smile but just as she put her foot on the first tread of the stairs she heard another sound. She almost ignored it over the squealing of the electric drill, except it was just like claws clacking across a vinyl floor.

The kitchen door was ajar, the room beyond in darkness. Anna listened again, there was nothing, but she knew she would have to check. She crept down the hall though there were still all sorts of noises coming from upstairs which would mask any sound she made. She pushed into the kitchen. She quickly saw that the back door was wide open, a grey rectangle of lighter air, so that she dropped her hand away from the light switch. She supposed that just now the vicarage would be the perfect place to hide out if you didn't want to be caught wandering around the village. All the doors were open, workmen coming and going. If you were spotted you only had to say you'd come to speak to the vicar.

Anna stared across the back lawn. The shrubs, tall and straggly, had muddled together, yew and laurel with privet bullying them between. She had always thought the bigger they were the less grass there would be to mow only she hadn't bargained on them blotting out so much sky, creating dark places where someone could stand unseen. She wondered about getting one of the workmen from upstairs, only it would take too long to explain. Whoever had Dolly could disappear, never to be seen again, she thought dramatically. Anna shook her head. It was getting out of hand and the bubble of anxiety in the pit of her stomach was threatening to send her scurrying back to Derek's. She wondered what whoever it was had in mind, what they intended to do with the dog. That took her to places she didn't want to go. She must get a grip, would have to hurry if she was going to see which way they went, up or down the lane. Up the lane led to sanity and civilisation. It was filled with police. Down led to the coastal path and any number of routes out.

She wanted to be able to tell Tom something of use, which was all that propelled her around the corner of the house where the wind caught the rain hanging in the air and flung it in her face so she could only peer into the dimness through narrowed eyes. Why couldn't the rain simply fall down, vertically, like it did in other parts of the country? On the Lizard it either drove you along or stung your cheeks. Such wildness was glorious from inside the café on the point, or from Archie's front room, but out here in this narrow funnel of a valley it made her tuck her chin down, and hold her hood tightly with already frozen fingers. She really wanted to be able to see clearly, a long way ahead. For in Anna's mind there was the vicarage fire, Harriet's smelly rag, but worse still Fiona lying in the churchyard. The side of her head smashed in. If they had used a rock or a bit of stone frost had sheared off a grave that made it unpremeditated, which she found unnerving. It meant that Fiona had been killed by a person who was suddenly overwhelmed, had lost control, and was unpredictable. Anna's steps slowed. It was ridiculous chasing after someone who'd stolen a dog. Only then she remembered Derek's face as he'd crashed back into the pub.

She'd twisted round on her stool. He was hardly recognisable. It was as if the dog had given him form and purpose and now that she was gone he had deflated, his face sagging and pale. Standing at the top of the drive Anna felt she didn't have much of a choice. She took a deep breath and walked purposefully out onto the lane. She prayed that God would at least go with her, which was easy while the workmen's lamps were shining brightly through the vicarage windows, patchworking the ground with comforting squares of light. Once she was heading down towards the sea, another choice she'd made in a heartbeat, it was another matter and again her steps began to falter. Her courage always lagged behind even though she knew that while she was faffing about Dolly was being dragged further and further towards whatever the woman had in mind. No, not being dragged, Dolly would be happily lolloping along beside her. After all, a walk was a walk.

Anna tried to hurry but the lane got very steep at the end,

twisting and turning about, no longer tarmac but ridged concrete. The cottages either side were in darkness. She tried her phone, there was no signal. She wondered whether she should call out. Perhaps if Veronica knew someone had seen her she might come to her senses.

The coastal path veered up from the road, a narrow muddy ribbon leading south to the lifeboat station, and beyond that to the Lizard point itself. In daylight, when it was dry, it took about ten minutes to get to Beacon Point, the place where they had celebrated the dawn service. Back when relinquishing the call God had on her life, even letting go of God himself, had seemed a real option. Quite a lot had changed since standing in that cold drizzle whispering a shameful hallelujah. Stepping away from God, not doing the thing he was asking of her wasn't really a possibility any more. Harriet was right. She had changed.

"So you'd better come with me," she whispered. The path going northwards to Cadgwith ran up behind the three holiday cottages clustered around the cove. It quickly widened out to become shoe-sucking mud for a long stretch beyond. It was hard squinting through the rain, but Anna thought she should have been able to see if anyone was making their way along there. Surely they wouldn't go that way? To get back onto the main road they would have to trail across the fields, looking for handy gaps in the tall thick walls. It would be an exhausting route and perhaps nearly impossible in the dark, so Anna walked down the last few metres until she was level with the southern path.

None of this made any sense. Veronica didn't make any sense. Going south to the Lizard put Veronica back in the village with all the police but if it was where she'd left her car then what choice did she have? Anna checked her phone again. She usually didn't get a signal until she was a lot higher up but it was worth a try. Emergency calls only. It was an emergency but the person she needed to speak to wouldn't be on the end of 999.

Chapter 21

Now there was darkness, early because of the rain and the low hung cloud. There had been no moment of gentle twilight; one minute visibility was reasonable and then it wasn't, apart from when the sea surged into the cove. Then she could make out the pale lacy surf gleaming around the edges of the waves, and feel the white noise thundering under her feet. She turned her back on it and began to climb. She used her phone to light the path ahead. It was easier but the cone of brightness flattened everything so that depth became difficult to judge. Flat shapes masked patches of deep mud that sent her slithering all over the place. She kept telling herself it was simply the absence of light that made it so scary. Even on the worst grey winter's day this part of the coast stopped you in your tracks with the wonder of it. Steep cliffs, unending views, a sense of being at the very edge of the world. Now all she felt was the sense of being too close to the long drop, which was not awe inspiring at all.

At the top, breathing heavily, Anna stopped to listen. She could hear the water sucking and sliding over the rocks below, the wind hammering in from the west. Sometimes on a sparkling blue day you couldn't hear the sea but most of the time it was there, a background noise that filled your head with the enormity of everything around you. Then came a flash that dazzled as the lighthouse turned its lens towards her. Standing motionless, expecting nothing she heard a voice, carried across from beyond the lifeboat station, a tiny thread of sound that if she had even half turned away she would have missed.

"Come on, Dolly." It must be Veronica.

Her voice sounded cross, so perhaps the dog wasn't cooperating. Perhaps Dolly instinctively knew that something was wrong. Anna was relieved that more by luck than by judgement she had made the right decisions: up or down the lane, south or north along the coastal path. She hurried forward, slipped sideways, and landed in the thorn bushes growing along the seaward side. She felt she was hanging over nothing, but didn't have enough breath to scream as she scrabbled away from the drop. She calmed down when she realised this stretch of path had a bit more edge to play with. She rolled onto her knees and wrenched herself clear, feeling the brambles twist and tear at her coat. Well, she needed a new one anyway. Once she was upright her feet began to slide out from underneath her again. There was no edge to the path here, too many brambles and mud like glass. She had to be confident. She took four quick steps before she slipped again. How had Veronica managed it, she wondered.

Finally at the end of the wind-turned bushes she recognised the top of the lifeboat station. A large white shed sitting seemingly across the path. It housed the winding gear for the cage that took the crew and equipment up and down the ramp. The roof far below was a hoop of iron, a wave-shaped arc protecting the lifeboat from the waves themselves. Surely there would be a signal here and she could give Tom an idea as to what she was doing, somewhere to aim for. She needed him to come and find her. She couldn't do this on her own. She peered up towards the road, which was just a strip of tarmac running through the fields. It ended in a small car park. There could have been half a dozen vehicles there but from where she was standing she would need to be ten feet tall to see them. Behind her the steps to the boat house dropped vertiginously into the darkness. She'd been down quite a few times for various events, they'd even asked her to come and perform a short service of blessing, though only the once. It made her smile that they thought such things lasted indefinitely. She knew more than anyone that nothing lasted forever. There was though a single bar on her phone. Tom answered quickly and began shouting.

"Where are you? Harriet's worried sick."

She hissed at him, "Tom, do shut up for a minute." He did. She told him where she was, what she was doing.

"Stay there," he shouted back.

"No, I can't do that," she whispered, though whispering was ludicrous. The wind was all around her, sound wouldn't carry more than a few yards. Tom was shouting again. She spoke over his voice, now fading in and out. "She's heading on to Beacon and then Bass Point. We don't know what she intends to do with Dolly. Just come and find us as quickly as you can." The phone sighed, and she knew she'd lost the signal. She laughed; it was just like any film she'd ever watched except that round here it was normal. You got a signal when you got a signal. Her phone worked well upstairs in the vicarage, up near the shop, and always once she'd driven past the Welcome to the Lizard sign on the way to Helston.

She negotiated the short flight of concrete steps, reassuringly straight and solid, back onto the path. She hoped Tom would have enough sense to drive to the hotel and walk back from there. If he hadn't been shouting she probably would have had time to say so. She had expected him to be cross with her for following Dolly and the woman, but grudging admiration for her courage wouldn't have gone amiss. She was not built for courage. This was hard for her. She'd have hoped he'd have realised that. Then she wondered why she cared so much about what he thought.

The path rose twenty or thirty feet, thorns shielding her from the drop below. Beyond that it curved inland a short way. Back behind her was one of the most beautiful views in the world, where the cliffs ran north and then east. From any spot beyond here she could lose herself for hours, just sitting. To be fair she only came when the weather was gentle and the sea kind but she couldn't imagine anyone not being changed by it. Tonight the weather was not gentle, nor the sea kind.

Up ahead for the briefest moment, she saw movement. A

shadow, no more, making its way through another line of thorn bushes leading onto the next promontory. This point of land was bare, short grass, a good place to sit. A large rock looked as though it was falling onto the path, rearing out of the ground, tipping over. Though it was locked in place, rooted deep, Anna could never bring herself to stand under its shadow for long. She watched the patch of darkness step forward, stop, then press forward again. It looked as though Veronica was having to haul Dolly along. She had had a good head start, but Anna was gaining on her. She thought there might be no more than a hundred yards between them.

The rain had stopped. The weather was clearing, everything was coming into focus. She peered ahead, but the woman too had halted right at the top, a small figure, dark against the deep navy blue sky. She was looking back down the path. She must have spotted Anna almost immediately. Before she could stop herself, Anna lifted a hand to wave, as if they were both out for a walk and it wasn't a ridiculous clifftop chase on a dark night because Veronica had stolen a dog.

Except... Anna paused mid-step, astonished, and then things that hadn't made sense began to fall into place. There, standing beside Dolly, wasn't a faceless, unknown stranger, but Terry Lovell. Terry's rounded shoulders, her long purple coat all too familiar. Everyone had been looking for a stranger, no one had considered Terry, not even after her encounter with Simeon. Of course Terry had had a life in Falmouth before she'd come here. There had been a husband who had died recently. Hadn't Derek mentioned something? How Anna wished she'd taken more notice and the trouble to listen to her. Grief was such a strong emotion to deal with, Derek and Harriet were proof of that. So in her own grief Terry might easily have become fixated on him. Anna had seen a frail, lost quality in Derek that seemed to appeal. Terry's house was just opposite his bungalow so she would have had no problem monitoring his comings and goings. Anna had been pleased to encourage the friendship, the neighbourliness, while laughing a little at Terry's obvious regard.

Perhaps knowing that Harriet was angry with Derek had caused the rag through Harriet's letterbox and then Harriet trying to make things better between them had caused the fire at the vicarage. Terry's confrontation with Simeon was simply to find out what he'd actually seen the night Fiona had died, whether there was anything she should be worried about.

Anna had to take a big leap from thinking that Terry was simply falling for Derek, to believing the woman was disturbed enough to take a rock to his wife's head, but leap Anna did.

There was no doubt Terry had recognised Anna, for Terry grabbed Dolly by the scruff of the neck and disappeared over the top of the ridge.

"Terry, it's me. Anna, Anna Maybury. The Reverend Maybury," Anna shouted. She wanted Terry to stop and say, "Oh, it's you. I'm sorry I hadn't realised," but instead Anna had to start up the next incline. At least here the path was wide and stony. At the top where the rock loomed over her Anna could see across to Beacon Point, the promontory where they had held the dawn service. Terry scrambled off towards its edge. Anna thought it odd for if she'd stuck to the main path she'd have got to the lane leading down to the coastguard station and from there she could easily have got back into the village, up past Simeon's cottage. When Anna had gone a little further she saw the headlights of a car, slowly making its way down between the hedges and wondered if Terry had seen it too.

From where she was standing the ground dropped away until it flattened out at the cliff edge, a fat fist reaching into the sea, rimmed with a rocky frill. The path continued on, following the line of the next bay. In daylight it was simply beautiful, giving views north and south along the cliffs. A place of short green grass dotted with sea pinks and yellow vetch, from where Anna had seen seals, dolphins, and once a basking shark. Below the rocks were often blotched bright yellow with lichen that glowed in the sun and matched the patches of dense gorse growing up the slopes. Now as she looked out she could only see sky and the odd white crest of a wave falling, breaking, and fading.

The wind gusted, dropped, and then leant against her, pushing her off the path. Up here there was nothing between her and the horizon, nothing to shelter her, to protect her. She could just see Terry hauling Dolly across the last few feet. Anna checked her phone again. There were five missed calls. It would be Tom telling her to stay where she was, to leave it to the police. Only the police weren't here, she was. And there was a dog's life at stake, perhaps even a woman's. What if she had to choose? Would God ask her to decide between Dolly and Terry? Some sort of test of her fitness to serve him? Anna worried she'd make the wrong call. As if to emphasise his point the lighthouse swung its beam around and blinded her.

She started to pick her way across to Terry, who had finally stopped moving. She was standing right at the edge, her shape once more outlined by sky. Anna knew it wasn't sheer into the sea just there but it was still a nasty drop onto rocks and if you rolled just a little you'd fall again. Terry was staring at Anna in the disconcerting way she had. Anna continued towards her because she didn't know what else to do. Finally, Terry called out, "What do you want?"

"Just to talk to you."

"Now you want to talk to me!"

"We've spoken, lots of times."

"Is that what you really think?" Terry snorted, her eyes narrowed and tiny. "Only ever because you needed something or simply because I was there. Never for my own sake."

Anna thought that was probably true, but recently she'd

hoped that Terry was being listened to by others, by Jean, even Derek, she realised a little shamefacedly.

Terry pulled Dolly in close to her side.

"You never once asked me about me, about my life, about Edgar."

Anna hadn't asked her anything meaningful because she'd found her so difficult to talk to, and hadn't known there was an Edgar to ask about. It seemed unfair, Terry had never offered her the smallest way in, the smallest encouragement, as if she had been setting her a test which of course Anna had failed, time and time again. Like it had been at the start with Simeon, except Simeon had softened, had eventually met her halfway, and had perhaps never expected that much from her in the first place. Anna felt sick. In all likelihood she was standing near to the woman who had taken a rock to Fiona, in her grief perhaps, in her longing, but if Anna got this next bit wrong it could be fatal. She was completely out of her depth.

"Oh, God, I can't do this," she muttered. "So what happened to Edgar? How long has it been?" she asked.

Terry blinked and her face crumpled.

"Nearly a year. Just like poor Derek." She paused, her eyes losing focus. "We were having lunch as usual. He liked to make sure I was alright, that I had enough money. We were talking about what I should do with our old house in Falmouth. He gave it to me so there wouldn't be too much upheaval when he left. He was thoughtful like that." Terry straightened up and let the lead hang a little looser.

He had allowed her to stay in their house while he went off to make a new life with another woman. Anna thought Terry was focusing on the wrong issue here. But that was surely the point. Terry was shaping reality to fit her own view of things, in whatever way she could.

"Oh, Terry, what happened then?"

"He went a bit pale. Said I should phone his wife. But I was right there." She narrowed her eyes. "I gave them my address, which was all they asked for, but apparently that makes me deranged."

Only deranged if Terry had given the police the impression that she was his current wife. Derek had been confused when Terry had told him about Edgar, but Anna was beginning to understand. Terry was the ex. There was a whole new family who'd been waiting for Edgar to come home that day. They must have had to report him missing, must have been going mad with worry, and then they would have had to reconcile the fact that he had been with Terry when he'd died. Grief was a strong emotion, jealousy was terrible.

"I couldn't go to the funeral," Terry said bitterly. "She wouldn't let me. Said I had no rights. She took out a restraining order, because apparently I upset the grandchildren."

There were grandchildren! How long had this been going on?

"Terry, I'm so sorry."

"The problem was that she was his age, and I was so much younger, so people didn't understand. It was like it was my fault, that somehow I had upset the natural order of things. Do you see?"

Anna nodded.

"I thought perhaps he'd realise I needed him more than she did, that eventually he would come home. He said he couldn't but that he would always find time to make sure I was alright."

Anna frowned.

"How long has this been going on?" she finally had the courage to ask.

"They've been married twenty-seven years."

Anna gasped.

"How often did you meet?"

"When he could get away, when she was off doing something with the children so she wouldn't notice. She hated him spending time with me. She hated the fact that I had the house. Was furious when I bought the one here too." Terry smiled.

Anna was appalled. No wonder Terry was muddled, damaged. She had been strung along by a man who had left her for an older woman. A psychologist would have a field day. For a moment Anna was distracted by a flash of light, too low and gentle to be the lighthouse. Then she heard her name, tinny and distant, from where the path merged with the lane leading up to the coastguard station. He must have seen them. She felt a flood of relief. He really had got to know the Lizard well for if he'd come down by the hotel as she had thought, he would still be walking round. He called her name again. She hoped he'd be careful, perhaps from where he'd got to he couldn't see how close to the edge Terry was. Anna was sure there was very little rock before she must fall back into wind and air.

Just off to their right was where Simeon used to come and stand to contemplate death, or was that life? On past the coastguard station on the next promontory was the hotel where Fiona had walked Dolly, where she'd had her stroke. Here on Beacon Point was where they had stood for the dawn service.

Anna finally asked the question that she had not dared ask before.

"Why Fiona?"

"Fiona was always shouting at him you know. They weren't at all happy. Then there she was, with that stupid dog growling at me." Terry jerked the lead so that Dolly's head snapped up. "I thought it was justice. God's justice. Something you ought to know all about." Terry's face became still and fixed. "We were going to retire here. It's why I bought the house. He said he loved the Lizard."

Anna realised that there were two threads, Edgar and his new life and Derek and Fiona. Terry blinked at Anna for a long moment so that when she shouted it made Anna jump. "She should have died out on the cliff path. She should never have come home."

The blurring of stories did not surprise her. She remembered how desperate she had been when Peter had married Frances so soon after they had broken up. That pain had tainted everything for years. When it was new and fresh the roaring of that hurt could make her do and think terrible things, had made her doubt herself to the core. At the time it had felt as if he'd been waiting for her to end it, to come to her senses and realise that she was only ever going to be a stop-gap. That it had dragged on so long was her fault. How quickly and completely she had taken the blame. But right now she needed to concentrate.

"Why did you phone the police, Veronica?"

"Don't you call me that. Don't you dare call me that!" She reared over Anna, her eyes dark and angry. "Only Edgar ever called me Veronica. It's my middle name." She said it proudly, confidently. "I couldn't let anyone else use it, spoil what we had. So when I came here I used my proper name, Terena, and my maiden name."

"So to us you are Terry Lovell. But why the police?" For a second Terry looked confused. "You rang them and said they should look at Fiona's death again."

"Because they needed reminding of their obligations. Poor Derek needed to know who killed Fiona so he could move on and they were giving up. I couldn't have that." She smiled again. "At the end of our road in Falmouth there's a phone box. They often talk about anonymous tips, I thought I would give them one."

"But Terry, didn't you kill her?"

Terry tipped her head on one side as if Anna were particularly stupid.

"Derek needed someone who understood him. Fiona was a very selfish woman." Terry folded her arms across her chest.

"We were going to meet for coffee you know. Once he'd got a bit more sorted. I found his email address in Edgar's old address book. He still carried it round with him though he'd been retired for ages. I thought if I used that, he'd know I wasn't a stranger."

"And you used Edgar's old work email making it difficult for the police to trace you." Terry frowned. Anna realised that perhaps Terry hadn't realised how effective that would be.

"Are you alright?" Anna asked gently, wanting Terry to know that she understood about wasted years, about wanting what you couldn't have, even if the object of your affection was a total shit. Terry looked confused.

"Yes... no. Why shouldn't I be?"

Well you killed a woman and are out on the cliffs with a stolen dog in the dark, Anna thought.

"Because you're grieving and hurting."

Terry shook her head, and stood taller.

"You don't know anything about me. You never did and you never bothered trying to find out." Now there was something else in her eyes that Anna thought looked horribly like pity. The lighthouse flashed its beam of eye-scraping brightness around them. Anna's eyes watered. She was tired. She wanted to tell Terry to come away from the edge, to stop being so melodramatic, only of course that was what Terry wanted, needed. She had been playing second fiddle to a whole other life. No wonder finding Fiona alone in the churchyard, vulnerable and exhausted, had seemed like the ideal opportunity – it probably had made perfect sense to her.

Destroying Fiona was a shortcut to the life she longed for. Though Terry's words had been muddled Anna knew she must have seen Fiona out on the path when she collapsed from her stroke, and had probably hoped she would die there, leaving Derek for Terry, or Veronica as she was in Falmouth.

The fire at the vicarage and Harriet's flat were to protect Derek from those that were seemingly causing him harm.

Was it all simply about creating a new starting place that would turn everything around? A snapshot arranged by Terry, which would put her at the centre, where she longed to be, so that she could start again. Anna understood that longing.

"So why take Dolly?"

"I thought I could bring him to his senses. That I could find her for him so that he would see me. Only suddenly there were police everywhere and I was worried they'd find us at home, so I went and hid down in the vicarage because I knew no one would look for us there."

"Weren't you worried about the workmen?"

"They've been upstairs for weeks and I thought that if I heard one of them coming I could slip into the back garden. Only instead of one of them, it was you!"

"Look, Terry, at least come away from the edge. It's terribly steep just there."

"I know that." Terry sounded like a sullen child.

"Anna, come away now. Leave it to us," Tom called, a lot nearer. For a second Anna almost did. Almost turned round and walked away. What a relief it would be to clamber back onto the path, to clump up past his car with her mud-clodded feet. To leave it all to Tom. "There's nothing you can do now," he added, but that was caught by the wind and she barely heard it. He was still thirty yards back. Close but not close enough. She couldn't turn away for though Terry was terrifying she was still one of hers. She had to try and make this right. Please God, she mumbled, hoping that God would do his thing.

She said, "Come on Terry. Come with me. It'll be easier walking back together. You've made your point. Derek will understand. And I will try harder."

Terry looked from Anna to Tom, then back over her shoulder. Over and down to the waves below. Surely she wasn't really considering it? Dolly was pulling away, trying to get to Anna. Her tail wagging vigorously. Terry yanked Dolly back and Anna knew for sure now that this was why they were here.

"Oh, Terry. Please think of Derek." Anna's voice came out thin and pitiful, which mattered because it only reinforced what Terry must think of her. Terry smiled.

"But it is Derek I'm thinking of. It's just that the dog gets in the way. She was always her dog. Never his. It stops him from moving on, from forgetting." And she nodded, because Anna could see that she really believed she was right. "Don't come any closer."

Or the dog will get it, Anna finished in her head. It made her want to laugh.

"I'm just doing him a favour," Terry continued.

"Oh, no, Terry. Derek loves Dolly. She's all that he has left."

She knew she'd said the wrong thing. Terry's eyes narrowed and she clutched the lead to her chest.

"He has me," she cried. Terry dropped down beside Dolly, unclipped the lead, and grasped her collar. Dolly looked up at her. It wouldn't take Terry a second to pull her to the edge and push her over. Anna stepped forward. Out of the corner of her eye she saw Tom drop down too and then he whistled.

"Come on girl. Dolly, come!"

She did. Dolly bounded over to him taking Anna and Terry completely by surprise. Terry had simply let go. When Dolly got to Tom she licked his face. He grasped her collar and stood up. Anna wondered if she dropped to her knees and whistled whether Terry would come to her, fling herself into Anna's arms, and weep for her second-hand life. Terry was staring at Tom and then turned slowly back to Anna. She was shaking with anger, her face white and pinched as if she were frozen.

"Now, Terry, please come away from the edge. Look, Dolly is safe. Everything is going to be alright."

Terry's chin was vibrating with unshed tears, her lips squashed tightly together as she tried to keep it all in.

"You're a liar. You don't know anything. Now I can't help him." Her voice dropped away to a whisper and tears spilled down her cheeks. "Stupid dog. Stupid, stupid man. If she wasn't here Derek could stop being sad. Don't you see that?" Terry looked so angry, her eyes tiny pinpoints in her large white face, that Anna leaned away from her. She didn't want to step back as that would have been too obvious and drawn attention to the fact that she was standing so very close now. "I knew it was you following me right back at the vicarage," Terry suddenly spat. "I thought someone was bound to see me. I'm glad it was you. Poor sad Anna. I've watched you when you thought no one else was looking. You can't keep it up, pretending to know what you're doing." Anna winced. "From the first day you arrived, with your shiny cassock and bright white dog collar, you smiled a smile that I knew wasn't right, and I couldn't trust." Terry stepped back. Anna could imagine the air opening out behind her. "Perhaps I can still help Derek."

"Anna!" Tom called. What frightened her more than anything was that Tom sounded really scared. Now he wasn't shouting, or in control. He let go of Dolly and began to run.

Anna was glad he was here, that he'd know the truth about what happened next. Terry grabbed her arm. Anna instinctively pulled away, then changed her mind. Instead she lunged forward and grabbed Terry's coat, so that they were standing nose to nose. Then Anna yanked Terry sideways. It felt satisfying to do something positive at last, and terrifying too as she was sure she was about to plummet onto the rocks. Terry, surprise opening her eyes wide, staggered, her right leg dangling in the air. Anna leant back and hauled again as Terry began to slip over the edge dragging Anna with her. In that moment Anna didn't have to cry out to God, she knew he was with her. She held on, both fists tightly grasping Terry's coat and she would not let it go. She was pulled down until she lay face to face with Terry dangling over the edge and their eyes locked. Anna's arms began to twist and scream with agony so anything deep and meaningful was lost as they began to slide over. At last Tom was there lying next to her, taking the weight, holding Terry, hauling her up, Terry's legs wildly scrabbling for purchase. She hadn't wanted to die, not in the last instant.

Chapter 22

"You just couldn't leave well alone could you?" Tom said over his shoulder as he pulled Terry to her feet. She didn't struggle, all the fight had gone into the last few moments, and there wouldn't be anything left, not for a while. Anna lay still, not quite sure for a minute which way to roll so that she wouldn't fall over the edge. "Don't move. Don't move an inch. I'll be right back for you," he said, using his in charge, don't you dare disobey me voice.

She heard him; she just wasn't sure she understood. She knew she should do everything very carefully, very slowly, and that she had to breathe, and breathe again. She became aware of the wet grass soaking into her jeans. There were patches of stars between moon-edged clouds. She was very tired and didn't want to get up. Just wanted to lie there. She was cold and her arms ached but the sky was so beautiful. It felt as though it was one of those moments you should savour, her God moment, except she couldn't completely forget the policeman on the path waiting for her. He wouldn't appreciate God trying to get in on the act which made her feel terribly sad. When she clambered to her feet she allowed herself one tiny glance at the drop, just inches from her toes. She was far too close. She stepped back, three large steps, keeping her eyes on the edge until she felt safe enough to turn away but she couldn't stop her breath coming in quick shallow gasps. Then she became aware that there was quite a group of policemen gathered at the point where the lane became the coastal path. She made her way back towards them.

"Wait there Anna, I'll come and give you a hand."

She wondered why he didn't send one of his minions. The lighthouse beam skidded round, squashing the blue lights of the cars to nothing, causing her to blink. She watched it sweeping across the wrinkly sea. When he got to her, he took her arm. She found that she was trembling. She guessed it must be shock.

"I'm really sorry, and I'm so muddy," she rambled, apologetically, as he led her to the car.

"Do you want to go in the boot with the dog?"

"No, I'll sit up front with you but please can you get the heater on, I'm frozen."

Tom laughed and she realised he'd been making a joke but she was too exhausted to react. He started the engine. He looked round at her, his lips pursed, his forehead creased up into his fringe.

"You should never have gone after her," he said. "But you never switch off the vicar part, do you?"

"That's rich coming from you. I prefer to think of it as the God part of me, which ought not to have an on-off button, don't you think?"

He shook his head, a tiny movement that dismissed her profound thoughts. Though she was still trembling she giggled.

"I knew I'd made a mistake, but I kept making choices which kept getting further and further away from good sense. When it got dark, really dark, I knew it was mad." She shivered involuntarily and realised she could do with a wee. "It was only when I saw who it was I realised I had to keep going. That I understood what was happening."

Tom put the car in reverse and began to head back up the lane. Then he slammed on the brakes and said angrily, "But Anna, she tried to pull you over. I saw the look on her face. It may have been Derek she loved but she hated you. Why couldn't you just wait, like I begged you to?"

She didn't remember him begging her. She really couldn't. She supposed because she was tired and cold she found herself saying, "If I had waited, Dolly would be dead and we still might not know what had really happened. We'd all still be living in fear and just once, oh God, just once it would be nice for someone to say well done. How brave of you, how clever of you to have worked it all out." Which she spoiled by crying, wishing she had crept into the boot where he thought she belonged.

He put the car into gear and they bumped their way up the track. At the end of the lane, just past Simeon's cottage, he stopped again. "I'm sorry Anna. I shouldn't have shouted at you. You've been through more than enough. It was brave, brave and stupid, and I shall need you to explain what you think went on tonight, because I haven't a clue. I just thought she was going to pull you over." She turned to look at him but he kept staring forward over the steering wheel. She could just see the tomb through the church gate, picked out by the edge of his headlights. She might have worked out what was going on with Terry but she didn't understand what was happening now, she needed more clues from him, time to think. And a wee would help immensely.

"I'm sorry for shouting at you too. I don't think I've ever shouted at a policeman before. It feels like I've picked a fight with the bishop."

But she hadn't been shouting at a policeman, she'd been shouting at Tom. Dolly whined, so he put the car back in gear and they moved off. Anna began to shiver again. Despite the warmth blasting from the heater she was cold and she wanted to get Dolly to Derek, which was all that mattered really.

Anna waited in the car while Tom took Dolly in. She was too muddy and cold to uncurl from her seat. Didn't really want to move at all until she had to. Tom wasn't long.

"I've been thinking and it's worrying me," she said, as Tom slid behind the wheel. "There's no real evidence for any of this."

"I know what I saw, what I heard," he replied. "So try not to worry about it just this minute Anna, you've done your bit for tonight."

He swung the car into Archie's drive. The house was a

blaze of light.

"Anyway, Tom, how were they?" she asked.

"Derek cried. Harriet poured a huge bowl of food and Dolly wagged her tail. She's a nice dog. Harriet's going to stay over and will make sure everything is secure."

"I wonder if I've lost my lodger?" Anna said.

Archie opened the front door. The hall light spilled into the garden and Anna could have cried with relief. Tom came round to help her out of the car. She was in quite a state.

"Archie, I'm covered in mud. I'm so sorry."

"Slip your shoes off on the step and get yourself upstairs. There's plenty of hot water and I'll bring you up something warming. Have a bath – you look absolutely frozen. Tom, do you want anything?"

"No, I'll get on my way. I've still got stuff to do."

***

"Simeon, it's Archie."

The door opened and Simeon stepped back to let him in.

"I can make you a cup of tea or coffee."

"Coffee would be nice. Thank you."

Archie waited until Simeon had produced a mug.

"You're not having one?"

"I had one earlier."

"So how are you, Simeon?"

"I didn't sleep well."

"I don't think any of us did. It was all a bit of a shock."

Simeon led Archie through to the lounge. The garden chairs were now placed in front of the electric fire.

"Please sit down."

"Thank you. Have you thought any more about Belle?"

"Yes."

Archie waited a little longer and then said, "So what did you decide?"

"I want Belle to come and stay."

"Oh, Simeon, I'm so pleased." He was, so much so that his eyes began to prickle and he had to swallow away a large lump in his throat.

Archie didn't know why he'd been so upset that Simeon had decided to leave Belle at the pound. His reaction had felt visceral, stomach wrenching, and so he was only a little surprised he now felt he could dance around the room.

"I need to go to church," Archie said.

"I'll come with you, but I need to eat something first."

"Thank you, Simeon. I'm so glad that it's all over, though it's really sad that it was poor Terry all along."

"It's not all over," said Simeon, standing up. "She stole a dog."

"She set fire to the vicarage and... Fiona."

"There's no evidence."

Simeon was right but Archie wasn't going to let it worry him. For now it was over. Terry was in custody, Anna was alright, and Dolly was back. He sighed. Somehow they would have to learn to trust themselves again, live without keeping one eye on the door.

***

Anna had expected Tom to call her the following morning. She waited around until it was gone nine. Archie had left much earlier, before she'd even come down, but there was porridge and toast ready in the kitchen. He'd written her a note telling her as expected he'd popped over to check on Simeon. She decided to go and see Harriet and Derek.

The village centre was its usual winter empty, the only movement a plastic bag twirling in the wind. Anna looked in at the shop. Jean was sitting at the counter reading the newspaper. The bell made her jump.

"Hello, Jean. Everything alright?"

She looked as if she'd been crying.

"I'm fine, really, Anna, but I should have realised. I always thought she was a bit odd. She had such definite views on things, on people, but surely she didn't actually..." Jean caught her breath. Anna wondered what she was going to say, wondered if she ought to fill her in on what had happened the night before, then decided that the gossip would get round soon enough. "Fancy stealing Dolly. What a dreadful thing to do." Anna almost laughed out loud. Crashing a rock onto an exhausted woman's head or trying to push the vicar over a cliff was nothing compared to stealing a grieving man's dog.

"She was very troubled. Psychologically her ex-husband has a lot to answer for," Anna said firmly.

Jean's eyes gleamed and then she frowned.

"You're too forgiving. Far too nice."

"Oh, Jean, I'm quite the opposite. I'm all the usual mixtures of meanness and... selfishness."

Jean tipped her head a little to one side. That was a mother's I don't believe you face, if ever Anna saw one. A police car slid by. It made her jump as she caught sight of it out of the corner of her eye, the bright orange band slicing through the dull day.

"I'm off to check on Derek." Anna didn't mention Harriet. That would certainly set the tongues wagging.

"Oh, take him his usual coffee, will you. I think he's alright for tea, though he may need some Earl Grey."

"That's thoughtful." With her hand on the door she turned back and asked, "Any news from Ellie?"

"Yes, actually there is. They're coming for Christmas."

"Oh, that's nice."

"They're all coming for Christmas." Jean grinned, crinkling her eyes to sparkly half-moons. "Of course it's early days but they are trying to make a go of it. He's even looking for a new job. They want to be a bit closer." Anna could see that that bit alone was good enough for Jean. To be a little nearer her daughter, to be able to help out now and again, to be needed. Anna turned away, her heart beating a little more quickly. For there had been a tiny intake of breath, and now there was a smile that wouldn't stay down, a lightness in her step. Despite everything that had happened, this was a nugget of joy.

***

"Who is it?" Derek shouted through the front door, quite fiercely, Anna thought. She hadn't realised he'd got it in him.

"It's me, Anna."

"Oh, sorry. Come on in, you." He opened the door and enveloped her in a hug.

"What was that for?" she said, stepping away from him to undo her coat. She'd had to borrow it from Archie as her old one was only fit for the bin.

"You saved Dolly."

"No, I didn't."

"Yes, you did. Tom told us you followed that woman to Beacon Point, that you prevented her from chucking Dolly over. Archie said you were in quite a state when you got back, that there was mud everywhere."

Anna had been worried about that, but he must have cleaned up most of it when she was in the bath. Harriet was hovering, waiting for Derek to move out of the way. In the end she squeezed past and hugged Anna too. She whispered in her ear, "You are quite wonderful."

Anna thought they were all making a bit of a fuss. She'd got muddy and cold, a bit scared, but this morning it wasn't such a big deal.

"So where is she?"

"In her basket in the lounge."

Anna went through and Dolly got up stiffly, her tail wagging. She allowed Anna to pat her head and then nosed through to the kitchen.

"I'll go and watch her in the garden," Derek said.

"I'll make coffee," Harriet said. Anna remembered the packet in her pocket.

"Good old Jean." Harriet nodded. She and Anna followed Derek out into the kitchen. He was standing on the back lawn watching Dolly mooching about.

"How is Derek?" Anna asked.

"He's fine. As soon as Dolly got back and he'd had a bit of a cry, it was like a light bulb came back on. He gets very angry when he thinks of Terry but that's understandable." Harriet filled up the kettle and started finding cups. "Do you think she has any idea how she's affected us?" she said, turning back to Anna.

"I think it was all about Derek, who she muddled up with her ex-husband. He left her a long time ago, but didn't let her go. I think we just got in the way."

Harriet said, "So do you think it all started when she hit Fiona? That Terry simply wanted to get rid of her so that she could have Derek?"

Anna shrugged.

"More like the culmination of lots of things."

They took their coffee back to the lounge. Derek appeared, bringing in the cold and a few dead leaves. He looked pink and smooth cheeked. Dolly came over and snuffled each of them. Anna patted Dolly before the dog went and settled between Harriet and Derek.

The doorbell rang. Everyone jumped. Derek returned with Tom, who was looking very satisfied with himself.

"She's safely locked up, so now we'll get some answers."

"What will you charge her with?" Anna asked.

"Breaking and entering the bungalow for sure. Trying to kill you." Derek and Harriet gasped rather satisfyingly. Anna tried very hard not to look smug. "And she may confess to some of the other stuff. I need Anna's statement to fill in the blanks."

"Soon before I get muddled. She'll need some help too, Tom," Anna said. "She's had an awful life and that ex-husband of hers sounds dreadful."

Harriet's eyebrows were through the roof but Derek simply nodded and said, "From the first moment I met her I haven't been easy in my mind. She's always given me the creeps."

Anna wasn't sure if that was entirely true, or just hindsight.

***

After Tom had taken her statement Anna saw Harriet at the pub. Harriet quizzed her unrepentantly because she wanted to hear Anna's story. Afterwards Derek turned up and she left them chatting with Phil. Outside, Anna hesitated, unsure what to do next. In the end she decided to head down to the church. The door was ajar and for a minute her heart hammered. Only then she reminded herself that for now she didn't need to be afraid.

Archie was sitting on the front pew, Simeon was tucked away on the other side of the aisle. They were praying. She pushed the door a little wider so it would squeal just a bit, to let them know she was there. They both looked round in alarm. It was going to take a while for everything to get back to normal.

"Well, this simply has to stop," she said, striding in. "I can't have praying in my church, what is the world coming to!"

Archie grinned; Simeon looked annoyed.

"Simeon has decided to go ahead with Belle," Archie said, jumping to his feet. The words had burst out as if he couldn't contain them. Anna looked at Simeon who simply nodded his head.

"Oh, that is good news. Terry is in the right place to get some proper help so everything can go back to normal." Simeon's eyebrows nearly disappeared into his short fringe.

"How's Derek?" Archie asked.

"Fine. Though for now he's not letting Dolly out of his sight."

Simeon asked, "What will they charge her with?"

"I think they're sending her for a psych evaluation first."

Simeon folded his arms and said, "It's not enough. She'll get treatment. They'll let her go and then she'll come back here."

"Simeon, we don't know that," Anna replied, beginning to feel the start of an acid bubble forming in her stomach.

"But it's a possibility."

"Yes, but you are crossing bridges way before we have to," she replied.

Archie was walking to the back to put the kettle on. He turned and said, "I guess we have to trust God for the next bit, that eventually we'll all stop being jumpy and frightened."

Anna wished she'd said that because Archie was right. There was no human way this was going to be resolved all nice and neatly, so it was up to God to do his thing.

"Tea and prayer. Quite right, Archie, that's exactly what we need to do."

"You're not allowed to pray." Simeon spoke quietly. "Your spiritual director said you couldn't."

Anna waited for the bubble of annoyance to float up but it didn't. Instead she smiled at Simeon.

"Well, I'm the vicar and I'm telling us that it's time to pray. Ask God what he thinks we should do."

"Ask God to help us forgive Terry," Simeon said firmly.

Anna was surprised and then wished she'd said that too.

Instead she said, "Let's take it a day at a time."

THE END